MW01052949

SYNTHS

ALSO BY JAMES C. GLASS

Eagle Squad
Imaginings of a Dark Mind: Science Fiction Stories
Sedona Conspiracy
Toth
Touches of Wonder and Terror
Visions
Voyages in Mind and Space: Stories of Mystery and Fantasy

SYNTHS

JAMES C. GLASS

For Manny,
Hope you like this one,
James C. Glass

WILDSIDE PRESS

For all my loyal readers who have followed my imaginings over the years, this one is for you. Special thanks go to M.J. Engh and Steve Perry for their useful comments and suggestions during the rewrite of this book.

Copyright © 2018 by James C. Glass
Published by Wildside Press LLC.
wildsidepress.com

AUTHOR'S NOTE

Melody Lane and Carl Hobbs first appeared in "Reinventing Carl Hobbs", published in the April, 2005 issue of ANALOG magazine.

PART ONE: BEGINNINGS

CHAPTER I

Melody awoke suddenly, as if an internal switch had been thrown. One instant she was dreaming, the next she was totally awake and squinting in the bright lights from the ceiling panels above her. She was lying on her back and the mattress felt hard; there was some pain in her shoulder blades and hips, and she stretched her legs carefully when one of them threatened to cramp. It seemed she had been lying there in the same position for a long time. Something was making her eyes sting, and she blinked hard to clear them.

At the foot of her bed was a row of racks housing instrument panels glowing with data streams in green and red, but she didn't seem to be hooked up to anything. She was covered with a thin blanket up to her breasts. A cool breeze from the ceiling washed over her face and made her feel comfortable.

The sweet odors of polymer solvents were strangely familiar to her, and filled the room. She looked left and saw two other beds with single instrument racks on wheels at their heads. One bed was empty. On the other lay a human sized lump covered with a white sheet. The following morning the lump wasn't there, and she never thought to ask about it. Beyond that was a wall with a long counter top and a sink beneath an opaque window and next to it a door which suddenly opened. A young man in a white lab coat stepped inside, took one look at her and smiled.

"Well, hi there. You're finally awake," he said, and stepped up to the side of her bed. "Can I get you anything, some water or juice?"

"I'm not thirsty," said Melody. "Who are you? I don't remember you."

"Of course not. I'm the new guy here, helping your dad." He held out his hand, Melody pulled the blanket aside, shook his hand, and saw him wince.

"I'm Darin Post. That's quite a grip you have there." He smiled again.

"Are you a doctor?"

"Engineer. Just got my Ph.D in Mechanical at M.I.T, class of 2310. Your dad hired several people from my class. We all feel privileged to be working with him. I'll tell him you're awake. He's in the next room working on a little floor polishing robot that blew a chip yesterday. You sure you don't want something?"

"No thanks. I just want to see my father."

"I'll get him. Nice to meet you, Melody."

"Nice to meet you too. You have a nice smile."

"Why thank you," said Darin. He walked past the foot of her bed and her eyes followed him across the room to another door which was partially open. He opened the door wider and said, "Doctor Lane, Melody is awake now. She'd like to see you."

"Good, good," said a deep, familiar voice. "I'll be right there. I think my little helper is working again. These old chips just don't last."

Melody worked her jaws to make a smile for him when Donovan Lane came through the door. The lab coat hid his lanky frame, but not his long, chiseled features and prominent nose, and his eyes twinkled when he saw her. "How is my darlin' today?"

"Hi, Daddy," she said. "I don't remember coming here. Did I have another episode?"

Donovan Lane took her hand in his, reached down and brushed some hair from her forehead. "Well, it's more like you sort of went to sleep on me again, right in the middle of a conversation. What do you remember?"

Melody thought, and memories came flooding back to her. "We were having breakfast. The holo was on. There was some kind of explosion on the moon, and a cult was being blamed. The next thing I knew I was here. What happened?"

"You took a bite of cereal, leaned back in your chair and went to sleep. Your circadian rhythm was messed up, and your sugar level was low. It's all fixed, now. I have a good physician on my staff. You were asleep for two days, and I admit I was worried. You're okay now, sweetie. Don't worry about it."

"Just before I woke up I was dreaming about Mom again," said Melody. She saw the twinkle disappear from her father's eyes, and squeezed his hand gently.

"I'm sorry," she said. "I forgot."

Donovan put his other hand on top of hers. "That's okay, hon. I'm gradually dealing with it, but there's not a single day I don't remember how much I loved that woman, and still do. I see her in you, Melody. I hear her in you. You are all I have left."

His voice cracked, and tears filled his eyes. He leaned down and hugged her. The gesture seemed strange to her, and she didn't know how to respond to it. Her father seemed so emotional, an attribute she didn't share with him. She didn't remember her mother as a stoic person, but rather quiet and reserved.

"I wish I could remember more, but what usually comes in my dreams is that last day, that last horrible moment with the truck coming straight at us and mom trying to swerve the car while she held me with her other hand, and then—nothing. No new memories for so very long, all that time lost.

What's wrong with me? Why do I keep blacking out? I've had twelve years to heal. I want to be with people again, like I remember. When, Daddy?"

Her father hugged her hard, and she patted his back lightly with one hand. She felt the wetness and salt of his tears on her neck as he spoke close to her ear.

"Soon, sweetie, soon. This last episode has isolated the problem, and I think we've fixed it. Another month should verify that. I have to be sure before I let my little girl go. You are still my little girl, you know. If something happened while you were outside these walls I might not get to you in time. I couldn't live with that. I can assign more staff to spend time with you for meals, conversation, whatever you like."

"How about that new assistant of yours, the man who called you when I woke up?"

"Darin Post? He's an engineer, and a good one, but I don't know what kind of conversationalist he can be."

"I think he's interesting," said Melody. "I'd like to get to know him better. He seems nice."

Her father smiled down at her. "Good looking, too," he said.

"I did notice that," she said.

Donovan Lane chuckled, and his eyes twinkled again. "You just said something funny."

"I did?"

"Yes. Your mom used to do that a lot. I'll talk to Darin, and see if he'll have a conversation with you sometime."

"I could use more books, and cubes for my holo set, too. I don't remember doing it, but I must have gone through everything in the room at least twice."

"Will do. If you feel up to eating I'll order dinner for you."

"Something greasy," said Melody.

"Not yet. Let's take it easy with something light, but ice cream for dessert."

"Thank you, Daddy. Love you."

Her father's eyes glistened again. He leaned over and kissed her on her forehead. "Love you, too, very much. I'll be back in the morning."

He left the room. Melody was alone again and immediately bored. She raised the head of the bed until she could sit up straight to watch holovision, but it was only sports and shows she had seen before. Staff arrived with a meal of thick soup, mashed beans and vanilla ice cream which she ate quickly. With her bedside remote she switched channels furiously, trying to find something new to watch. She finally gave up in disgust and switched the set off. If she dozed, perhaps she could find a pleasant dream to watch.

There was a soft knocking on the door to her room.

"Yes? Come in," she said loudly.

The door opened, and a face appeared. It was Darin Post.

"Oh, hi," she said.

"I hear that the daughter of my boss wants to talk to me," said Darin, "so here I am. Is this a good time?"

Melody gestured to a bedside chair. "Thanks for coming so soon. There are some questions I hope you can answer for me."

Darin sat down in the chair. He seemed nervous. "I'll do what I can, but I am the new guy here. What do you want to know?"

"Several things, but let's start with you. You're an engineer?"

"Yes, Mechanical. I was recruited out of the robotics lab at M.I.T to work directly with your father. Being part of Interface Systems Corporation was a dream of mine, and your dad is a robotics legend at M.I.T."

His enthusiasm was almost childish, she thought. "My father told me you're a good engineer."

Now Darin grinned. "I'll do my best for him. I've just received my project assignments."

"Am I one of them?" asked Melody, and was astonished when a look of horror appeared on Darin's face.

"He said you wanted to talk to me. I didn't think—"

"I'm sorry. I was making a joke, and I'm not very good at it. But I do have some questions I can't seem to get answers to, and maybe you can help me there. Do you know anything about me, my car accident, how I came to be cooped up here?"

Now Darin was suddenly guarded, and his expression was blank. "Well, Doctor Lane told me about your accident and the spells you've been having, and you being here so he can watch you closely. Sorry about your mother. I guess you were fairly young when it happened."

"I was thirteen, and that was twelve years ago. My continuous, linear train of memories ended twelve years ago. I have few memories since then, and when I get them they're snatches of things. I can remember a house in the countryside, and my father is there. I see a barn and a corral with two horses. I walk in a grove of aspen trees and seeds are floating around me on little parasols and birds are chirping, and suddenly I'm back in this room again. The car crash is a continuing nightmare for me, the terrified look on mom's face, and I remember her in ways that seem to be a sharing of her memories, not mine. Everything is all chopped up. I keep blacking out, and father says it was head trauma, and now he thinks the last problem has been fixed. I'm not sure I believe him. I can't even remember seeing a doctor here. Has my father said anything to you about my condition?"

"I've only been here a month," said Darin. "When I arrived he mentioned you, since I'd be working in the lab next door to your room. You'd been here a few days then, and he was worried. The room was closed off. Only a few people were allowed in here with your father. I've seen them a few times since then. A week ago your father was suddenly cheerful, said they had identified your problem and been able to fix it. He knew the exact day you would wake up, and made sure he was here for it. He wanted me here too."

"Why?" asked Melody, and looked at him closely. His face was relaxed, now, but he looked away from her as he spoke, and she wanted to see his eyes.

"I was pleased when you asked to speak to me, but since my lab is so close Doctor Lane had already assigned me the task of talking to you, getting you to talk and socialize again."

Now Darin smiled and looked at her again. "That has turned out to be an easy job."

He had such a wonderful smile. She managed a small one, and wished she could do better. "I have my gabby moments," she said. "It's nice to talk to someone besides my father. If I'm supposed to be sick, where are the nurses? One lady came in with a meal, and I probably won't see her again until morning. Give me a hand, please. I want to get up."

Darin was hesitant to help. "Are you sure you're ready? I—"

"I'm fine," she said, and held out her hand as she swung her legs off the edge of the bed.

Darin's hand was either very warm or hers was very cold. He held her hand until her feet were firmly on the floor.

"There," she said. "All steady, now. I want to see what my father was tinkering with."

Darin held her hand lightly as she walked slowly to the door of a neighboring laboratory where she found a table covered with chips and other electronic debris, and a short cylinder the size of a coffee can. "Oh, I remember you," she said, and pushed a button on the side of the cylinder. The device beeped, came to life with a shudder and began moving erratically around the table.

Melody shut it off. "This guy used to clean our floors in the country house. Dad was always tinkering with it, and mom complained it was always underfoot, but it saved her a lot of work. She knew that, and told me so when Father wasn't listening. He was always working on gadgets in the barn."

She paused, and looked at Darin. "See? I can remember things like that when I want to."

"It'll come back. You just have to be patient."

"I don't think so," she said. "Too much is missing, and it's all from the last twelve years. My earlier memories should also be affected if the problem was head trauma. Isn't there anything you can tell me, Darin?"

Darin shook his head, his eyes averting hers, and that worried her again. "Sorry, but I'm so new here, and I just met you. Talk to your father about it again."

"I've done that, and he gives me nothing new except reassurance that I'm getting better, whatever that means. I'm not saying anyone is lying to me, but I think I'm not being told the entire story, and I've had enough of it. I will not be cooped up in this place any longer. I only see the outside world through holovision, and I want to experience it and be part of it.

"I understand," said Darin.

"Not really," said Melody. "Look, Darin, I think you're a nice person, but my father has just sent you here to chat with me and make me feel better, and I thank you for that. My mind is totally weird. I'm imagining things that belong in science fiction. I have to have a truthful explanation for my memory gaps and blackouts and the strange dreams which seem to be memories that aren't my own. I'll give my father one more chance to give me an honest explanation. Tell him that. It must be soon, within a week, or I pack my bag and leave this place and throw myself into the real world. If I can't have old memories of recent years, I will make new ones I can remember."

"Wow, you even sound angry about it," said Darin.

"It's more like determined. Talking to you has stimulated my thinking. Maybe we can talk again before I leave."

"Please, let's do that," said Darin.

"Tell my father what I've said. Tell him I have to see him soon, and he'll have to be honest with me this time. I know I'm being misled."

"I'll tell him. Do you want me to go, now?"

"Yes. I have to get dressed, and try to get my brain to shut down so I can sleep."

"My lab is right next door. Give me a visit," said Darin, and he started towards the door to the outside hallway.

Melody looked into the mirror above her father's work table, and adjusted the tousled mass of dark hair that had crept down over her forehead in sleep. Brown eyes looked back at her over a nicely arched nose, but her full lips were pursed into a pouty look. A compulsion struck her without warning, and she couldn't resist it. "Darin?" she said.

He stopped by the door, opened it, and looked back at her. She put her hands on her hips, and posed for him. "Do you think I'm pretty?"

Again that beautiful smile. "Yes, I do, and you are also amazing."

The door closed, and Darin was gone. What can be so amazing about me, she wondered? I'll have to ask father about that, if he ever comes to see me again.

And the next morning, he did.

CHAPTER 2

It was eleven at night, and the weather was drizzly. The light from inside the Full Moon Bar added a glow to the mist in the narrow street. Twelve hogs were parked in front of the bar. Max Schuler had never been a Harley fan, but he looked them over before going inside.

It was loud, and there was lots of leather, not the usual crowd, bearded men with big bellies and a few women who looked like they could take an average guy down three out of four falls. Max hesitated at the doorway. He had a good job that required a low profile, so he was not looking for trouble, just a familiar place for a quick drink.

Len was tending bar and waved at him, so he went inside and found an empty stool at the crowded bar. Len didn't ask, just poured a double Black Jack with a squirt of soda, and pushed it across the bar to him.

"Different crowd tonight," said Max.

"Some kind of trade show down the street," said Len. "Haven't seen you for a while."

"An old client is keeping me busy. Could be long term, I hope, but the guy is kind of flaky."

Len smiled. "I won't ask what you're doing for him."

Max smiled back. "So I won't have to tell you. God, it is loud in here."

A bearded, leathered man whose buttocks spilled over the stool he was sitting on turned and gave Max a baleful stare. "Do you have sensitive ears, sweetie?" Five empty glasses were lined up on the bar in front of him.

"Excuse me?" said Max.

"Are we too loud for you? We're having a party in here. If you don' like it, get the hell out."

Max took a slow sip of his drink, and put the glass down. "Fuck you, biker boy," he said.

The big man turned and made a grab for Max's collar, but Max was quicker, his hand a blur, and the man froze when he felt the tip of the switch-blade touch his throat hard enough to form a little bead of blood there.

"If you don't want to die, go away and leave me alone," said Max softly.

The man gulped, his face flushed deep red. He leaned back carefully, stumbled a little sliding his big ass from the stool, and minced away without looking back.

"Sorry," said Max, and put the closed knife back into his pocket.

"No problem," said Len. "His drinking night was over anyway."

A soft hand on Max's shoulder made him jump.

"Hi, Maureen," said Len.

"Scaring off people again?" said the woman. She was in her forties, heavy makeup on a once pretty face, slender body; her arms and legs well muscled. "Want to scare me some?"

Max put an arm around her. "Still into that stuff?"

"You bet I am, big guy, and I have some new toys. Come home with me, and let's try them out."

"Let me buy you a drink first," said Max.

They had two drinks together, and caught up on news about their respective clients. Maureen's apartment was a four block walk away, and two flights up. She put her new toys out on the bed for his review.

Maureen undressed for him slowly, and watched his eyes. "No marks, now. It's bad for business. But you know how far you can go."

"I do, just as long as I can watch your face while I'm doing it."

Maureen lay down on the bed, on her tummy, and looked back coyly at him over a naked shoulder.

"Now don't hurt me," she purred.

Max laughed at the little joke they shared, and selected a two-inch wide heavy leather strap to begin his work.

CHAPTER 3

"Knock, knock."

The door opened slightly, and her father peeked around the edge of it. Melody was sitting up in bed, finishing the remnants of an omelet and toast breakfast brought by a sullen woman just after sunrise.

"Hi, Daddy. Come in."

He sat down in a chair at her bedside, and looked down at his hands in his lap. "How's my girl this morning?"

"Fine, but I didn't sleep well last night. I couldn't get my brain to turn off."

"You've been thinking a lot, I hear," her father said.

"Darin talked to you about yesterday."

"Yes. I wasn't surprised. This has been coming for a while, but I've been afraid to do it. I've been afraid of what it will do to you, our relationship, everything." Now he looked up at her, and she saw tears in his eyes again. She reached out and touched his wet cheek.

"I don't make tears like that. I guess that's another problem I have to understand."

Donovan smiled weakly. "We're working on it."

"And that's what we need to talk about honestly, without leaving anything out, Daddy. What is going on with me, and why are you hiding me away?"

"This place is safe. It has been safe for a couple of years. We've tried you in the outside world several times, and it hasn't worked out. You just don't remember it."

"I remember a house and a big barn and a workshop."

"My home away from home. I bought it after your mother died. It was my getaway from everything. Still is. I had you with me there three times. We were there when you fell asleep again at the breakfast table and I couldn't wake you up. I don't expect that to happen again."

"Because you fixed me," she said.

"Yes, I did, with a little chip the size of your fingernail. It's in a cavity above your left ear, but you probably can't feel it there."

Melody tried anyway, probing with a finger.

"It's supposed to regulate your sleep cycle, but the old chips kept crashing. I finally found a better one."

"So what else have you put into me that makes you hide me away?"

"That would take a long time to explain," said her father. "It has taken me twelve years to get this far with you, and I've had the help of some outstanding engineers and physicians."

"I've always felt I was badly hurt in the accident," said Melody. "I must have had brain damage."

Her father made a choking sound. "It was more than that, but here you are, my little miracle, thinking your way through things. I'm so proud of you, Melody, but this is very hard for me right now."

Melody only heard him subconsciously at that moment, but would remember it later. "I've wondered why I can't seem to cry or feel emotions like you do. I miss my mom, but it seems like she's with me all the time, sharing memories with me. Some are very intimate moments with you, Daddy. I've never said anything before because it's really weird. I don't want to be weird. I want all this fixed."

Tears were running down his cheeks. "It won't be fixed, sweetie. It's what you are. It's how I made you. I thought I had it all figured out, me, the guy everyone says is the greatest robotics researcher in the world. I've been backed up by a top notch staff of scientists and engineers who know all there is to know about synthetics. We had neural mapping and digitizing and muscular protein printing, and then the layered neuronal film production with digital imprinting. We thought we had reached a point where a kind of immortality for humanity was more than science fiction. It was a real possibility, but we didn't dare to go public with the idea. We were under attack by religious zealots who thought we were playing God even when we were only manufacturing robots as commercial and home-help aids."

Donovan Lane paused, and then reached out and put a hand on Melody's. "And then your mother was killed in that car accident. She had let me scan her so many times, always so encouraging. I thought I—"

"—You made a synthetic model of my mother?" said Melody calmly. What an interesting concept, she thought.

Donovan went on like he hadn't heard her. "She was an adult, so we had an exact template. The printing was splendid, came close to her exact weight, and all seemed well with the neuronal film assembly until we tried to turn her on. Nothing happened. The assembly, of course, was both memories and operating system in a parallel configuration. We think key parts of the operating system didn't grow together. We never figured it out."

Tears gushed from his eyes. "She never woke up. My Linda never woke up. And then, there was you."

He grasped her hand so hard it hurt her, and she grunted. Ah, she thought, here was a clue to her problems.

"Did you give me some of mom's memories?"

Donovan Lane lifted her hand and pressed it against his forehead. He was sobbing, now, and Melody had to concentrate to hear what he was saying.

"Melody—my baby—my only child—you died in that car accident along with your mother. You were both dead when help arrived. There was no chance for resuscitation. I lost both of you that day. I—I lost everything I had ever loved, and it drove me to do things I hoped I wouldn't regret later. When my renewal procedures didn't work with your mother's data I was devastated, and thought about abandoning the idea, but there was another person I had loved and lost and wanted desperately to have with me again."

"Me," said Melody, again calmly. Things were coming together nicely in her mind, for her thinking had been moving along lines similar to what she was hearing.

"You were young. Maybe that was the key. We tried the same procedure with your data, and it worked. The template was a twenty-four-year-old killed in a skiing accident. A picture of her at thirteen looked a lot like you."

"My data? How did you get that?"

"In your sleep, over several nights when you were twelve, and again when you had just turned thirteen. I mentioned it to you once, and you didn't seem to care. I don't think you knew what it was all about. With your mother, it was routine."

Well, well, thought Melody, it seems I am some kind of machine, a synthetic creature, maybe partially human. Fascinating.

"You've answered some questions for me," she said quietly. Melody felt no emotion, but some pleasure in learning new things about her that cleared up some mysteries.

Her father exploded in tears. "When you first woke up you said, "Hi, Daddy. What happened?" and I totally fell apart. I bawled for ten minutes and you just sat there with a quizzical look on your face like you did when you were a kid. I was a mess."

Now he let go of her hand, wiped his face and managed a faint smile. "My baby was back again."

"And here I am," said Melody. "This is all a surprise, of course, but now I understand some things. I just thought I had a lot of physical and mental problems related to the accident. I didn't realize that I was a machine."

"You are not a machine," Donovan said sharply. "Don't ever think that. The structure of your brain is non-human, and your organs are synthetic. The protein in your body, the muscles and tendons, was originally manufactured, but must be replenished in the usual way. You eat, process food and eliminate waste products in the usual way. You are a functioning human being in every way, and you are still my Melody. There are differences, yes. Right now you're not able to conceive a child, but we're looking at that issue. The problem is enormously complex. You will also remain the way you are for an indefinite time. There might be some aging effects, but we don't know what they might be. You might have a normal human lifetime, or much longer. You are the first of your kind, my dear, but there will be others soon. We're working on them now, and the work is kept absolutely secret.

Donovan leaned close to her, and patted her hand. "You seem to be taking all of this very well."

"Well, I'm human enough that I thought I was human. I do wish I had more memories since the accident, and not so many that aren't really mine."

"We've worked on you for nearly twelve years, sweetie, but you've only been physically activated, off and on, for a total of several weeks, and all of that has been here or at the farm."

"You put mother's memories into me, didn't you?"

"It was part of the research to see if another person's scans would be compatible with your network. I admit there were other reasons for doing it, all of them selfish on my part. Turns out the memories are a hundred per cent compatible, but the operating system side created a lot of glitches and we finally abandoned that work. Any remaining personality traits of your mother seem to be those that you learned from her as a child. If any of her memories really bother you we can open you up and find the neuronal structure we need to block. It's a tedious process, but we can do it."

Melody's eyes widened. "You can open me up? What do you do, remove a screw here and there?"

Donovan smiled. "I like the humor, Melody. It's you. People might call you a synthetic, but you are a human-based intelligence system, and as we speak you are evolving. You have several ports in your head, neck, chest, and the top of your spine. You can't feel them; they are seamless, and we open them with ultrasound well beyond the range of human hearing."

Fascinating, thought Melody. "Okay, but I want to keep mom's memories for a while. I miss her. I also want to get out of this repair shop and see the world. Am I ready?"

Donovan Lane hugged his daughter tightly. "I think you are. Get dressed. There are new clothes for you in the closet. I'm taking you on a tour, and then we'll have lunch with Darin. He really is your chief engineer right now, and for the long term if you two get along well."

"He's cute," said Melody, and her father laughed.

Melody got off the bed and her father embraced her again when she stood up. It felt awkward, and then he murmured into her ear. "Are you still my little girl?"

Something clicked in her head. "Yes, master," she growled, and Donovan held her at arm's length, looking astonished but grinning at her.

"Yes, you are still my daddy."

Donovan shook her lightly, still grinning. "Don't do that to me again."

"I'd really smile if I could," said Melody.

"It'll come. The emotions, too. Things are still settling in." He tapped his forehead. "Now, get dressed."

Several outfits hung in the closet. A red silk blouse attracted her, and a black skirt, and underclothes in black. There were high heels, but she chose the flats for comfort. She dressed, scrubbed her face with a wet cloth and ran her fingers through the tousled mass of her hair. There was makeup and lipstick in three colors there, but she left them untouched. She posed in front of the mirror. Nice, she thought. Red is a good color for me. I wonder how Darin will react when he sees it?

Her father returned. "Gorgeous," he said. "You will be noticed. Remember that only a few people know about you. Everyone will think you're a visitor. If asked, you are Delia Medford, daughter of Ronald Medford, one of our big investors."

"Am I rich?"

"Very."

"So now I'm an actress."

"Actually, your mother wanted to be an actress, and had the talent for it, but she married me instead."

Father took her on a tour. Her room was bordered by several laboratories behind closed locked doors along a long hallway in the west wing of Interface Systems Corporation. It was a campus of two story buildings connected in a hexagonal pattern spread over a square city block and surrounded by rolling hills and thickets of Birch and Elm. Tall buildings of the central city rose in the far distance, the reincarnation of what had once been the urban sprawl of Los Angeles.

"This wing is where all our company confidential work is done, and access is limited to less than a hundred employees," said Father as they walked the long hallway. "All the work on synthetics is being done here."

"Like me," said Melody.

"Don't let the word offend you. It doesn't describe the real you, but we use it to distinguish from normal robotics. In no way are you a robot, Melody."

"I am a thinking, partially human organism with many synthetic parts," she said.

"That's actually a pretty good description," said Donovan Lane.

They toured the development and manufacturing section of the campus. All was related to robotic systems for manufacturing and individual robots for household and commercial functions such as cleaning and landscaping, operating taxis and buses and subways in the inner city, and sales clerk duties in retailing.

"We are not the most popular company around," said Father. "Our products have cost people a lot of jobs, and the unions hate us. The religious people hate us mainly for the mannequin robots we make for transportation and retailing. They say we're attempting to make artificial humans and playing God. If they ever find out about our synthetics program I expect they'll try to burn the place to the ground. They don't have the same power they had before the Federal Government began taxing the churches, but they haven't lost any fervor in their activities."

No one approached them on the tour, but Melody noted many admiring glances from workers they passed, and it pleased her. It seemed they walked miles, and the sights began to blur together, the clanking of machinery, the smell of lubricating oil and polymer solvents. She felt her interest waning.

Father noticed it. "That's enough for now. Darin is waiting for us. We're having lunch in the cafeteria upstairs. What do you think of all this?"

"Very impressive," she said, and suddenly decided she was hungry. "But what I really want to see are the closed labs where the synthetics work is being done."

"Later," said Father.

They took an elevator to the second floor. The cafeteria was automated and self service, all meals free to employees and guests. They punched in their selections from a master board and their meals were trundled out on hot plates at an opening in the wall by the drink dispenser. Melody selected fish because she remembered liking it, though she wasn't sure if it was her memory or her mother's. The meal came with pasta and cheese sauce and a small side of broccoli, and she selected iced tea as a drink.

Darin was waiting for them at a table, and had begun eating. His face brightened when he saw Melody. "Wow, look at you," he said as they sat down.

"You like red?" asked Melody.

"On you it looks terrific," said Darin.

Father smiled. "You have an admirer."

"He's a tricky one, though. You knew all about me, Darin, and said nothing."

"Careful," said Father. "We're not in the west wing, now. Remember the old wheeze about loose lips sinking ships."

For this he received a blank look from Melody.

Darin just smiled at her, and Melody forgave him.

They had a nice lunch, and the conversation was light. Melody felt accepted and cared about. The revelation of her identity and origins did not concern her at the moment. She felt mostly human, and it was enough. But in future weeks it would not be enough.

Melody Lane was a synthetic human being with unlimited capabilities not yet explored, and minute by minute she was evolving.

CHAPTER 4

As spiritual leader of The Association Against Artificial Humanity, Jacob Cross was a resilient and enterprising man with decades of experience in manipulating an often dissatisfied and ignorant public. The success he had enjoyed as a young man preaching to the faithful from The Tower of Heaven on Channel 167 was a matter of timing. The country had experienced two depressions in a row, and there was general despair among the populace. People were working, the unemployment rate never exceeding six percent, but wages were poor and the rich got steadily richer. Jacob preached against all of it: the evils of wealth, the arrogance of the wealthy, and the slave wages of the workers. He told the people what they wanted to hear and they responded with gifts they often could not afford. Jacob thanked, blessed, and healed them dramatically with his own hands, and watched his accounts grow in Europe, Asia and the Cook Islands.

Jacob made one mistake during those years of his financial success. He preached revolution, but when it came with the election of both a socialistic congress and a socialist president his world came crashing down on him. The rich now paid tax rates of ninety percent, and that was good. Rigid controls were placed on banks and Wall Street in general, utilities were nationalized and all offshore accounts were subject to taxation. This was not good. Worst of all, the churches were redefined as profit making businesses, donations no longer tax exempt, and church incomes were suddenly taxed to the maximum. All churches suffered terrible losses of both followers and incomes. Their influence with government came to a sudden halt. For television evangelists like Jacob Cross, the followers disappeared and income became miniscule overnight. Overnight, it seemed, all religious programming disappeared from television, and did not reappear again until the advent of state-owned holovision twelve years later.

Jacob was indeed a resilient man. He licked his wounds and left the country, bought a small farm on the Cook Islands and lived there quietly for nearly twenty years, a country gentleman who entertained lavishly and gave generously to local charities for children. His accounts in Europe and Asia disappeared, reappearing in the Cook Islands under the names of various businesses and charitable trusts.

The small farm led to a grand estate in the hills. Jacob cultivated many important friendships during his years on the islands, for wealthy people played there. He became a friend to many corporate and banking leaders who yearned for the days before the socialist regimes with their regulations and high taxes, and their handouts to the lower classes. They yearned for the days when intelligence, ambition, hard work and a great deal of money set the rules and policies of a country and ruled it with a firm hand. They complained to Jacob Cross about this, and he listened, he sympathized, he told them things they wanted to hear. He suggested a revolution to them, as he had done once before for the enemies of his new friends. His new friends were much younger than he, and didn't remember the television evangelist from twenty years past. They began meeting in groups to formulate plans: deliberate product shortages, refinery shutdowns, new requirements for personal loans, massive layoffs to disrupt the economy, the blame to be placed on a socialist system run wild.

A government owned by corporate and fiscal leaders could be stable only with decent wages and full employment, and in the past twenty years technological advances had increasingly contributed to the employment problem. Automation in manufacturing had led to the loss of millions of blue collar jobs, was now creeping into construction, transportation and communication, even the fast food industry. The government had responded by creating more civil servant and public works jobs funded by increasing taxes, a process with no end in sight. Complaints were already being heard, and not just from the wealthy.

Robotics in medicine had become an issue with the religious right. Surgery was the least of it. Artificial organs had been developed: liver, lung, heart, all had been used, others being researched. What would be next? The brain? An artificial, immortal being without a soul? And the use of DNA engineering and its consequences were still being debated hotly after a hundred years. The scientists seemed to think they were God, and they were not. Jehovah would surely bring his wrath down upon them soon. Aside from considerations of financial gain, Jacob Cross now imagined himself as God's instrument. He came to believe that science, and scientists, had become the enemies of God. In particular, the medical-related sciences were pursuing technological advances The Lord had never intended for mankind to obtain. And at present, the work was being done without any opposition.

Jacob Cross saw an opportunity to provide needed opposition and disrupt the government for his new friends. He saw a way to win support from the working class by creating jobs taken from them by the machines. His friends would provide the working capital, plus a little something for himself, and the churches would surely contribute something to save the morality and the very soul of the country.

He began his new work by establishing the organization he called AAAH, the Association Against Artificial Humanity, and in doing so he heard about Interface Systems Corporation for the first time. ISC manufactured machinery for automated production, but was best known for research and development of prosthetics and artificial organs, and was rumored to be working on an artificial brain that could be interfaced to a computer. Surely this idea alone was blasphemy in the Eyes of God. What would come next? Artificial humans? Thus was born the title of Jacob's new organization.

The head of ISC was Doctor Donovan Lane, a man of great genius and reputation. He was also quite personable, and was regarded as an important public educator and advocate for science and technology. His connection to automated manufacturing, and its destruction of jobs, was enough by itself to make him a target for AAAH, but his research and development in medical areas made him a target for God's servants.

Jacob Cross prayed about it one evening, and asked for God's will.

Sometime in the night, he received his answer in a dream.

CHAPTER 5

Soft meadow grasses and patches of moss tickled her bare feet, and a light breeze cooled the skin of her face and naked arms. A trickling stream ran through the center of the meadow; she stepped into it and winced at the feel of icy cold water swirling around her toes. With the breeze came the scent of pine and lavender, and the musk from a young buck deer that watched her from the stands of Douglas fir surrounding the meadow. Melody relished the feel of all of it. She was deliciously alive. She loved the farm and all its surroundings, and hoped it would always be there for her.

She ran down the slope of the grassy hill, her long hair trailing in the wind. There below her was the white house with screened-in porch, a shed and tumbledown garage for cycles and four-wheelers, and the big red barn where her father had his workshop. She went straight to the barn. Half of it was filled with stacks of hay bales, and there were four stalls where horses had once been kept. They were now empty, as was the attached corral outside the barn. As Donovan Lane's business had grown and progressed, there had been less and less time to take care of the four Appaloosa breeders he had owned, and he'd finally sold them. Melody had seen pictures of the animals, and wished she'd been around when they were there. An instinct was growing within her, a desire to care and provide for something alive, something natural and organic, not synthetic like herself. She had discussed this with her father.

He was at his workbench along one side of the barn, tinkering with something held under a large magnifier. The bench was illuminated brightly by a panel of fluorescent bulbs above it, and the faint sound of a cello playing classical music caressed the air.

He looked up when she closed the door behind her. "Have a good hike this morning?"

"It's beautiful outside. You should join me sometime."

"Sometime. I'm getting close to finishing this, and you're going to be my guinea pig again."

She looked over his shoulder. With tweezers he was holding something the size of an aspirin tablet under the magnifier. "What is it?" she asked.

"Another engineering problem you have," he said. "We've been using drops regularly to lubricate your eyes because this engineer neglected to provide the system for it. We don't completely understand the mechanism behind tears, but it starts with a little gland above the eye called the lacrimal gland that makes the tears. There's also a little drainage system connected to it. The whole thing is activated through the limbic system and the hypothalamus. Tears are produced when the eye is dry or irritated, and emotional release, like crying, seems to be related to stress. I've given you the neuronal equivalent of hypothalamus and limbic system, but you need this little guy to substitute for a gland. A little neural net bundle around this, some programming, and I'm finished."

"When you put that thing in me, do you turn me off again? I think I've had about enough of that," said Melody.

"You'll be awake the whole time, I promise," said Father. "You did want to be able to cry, didn't you?"

"If it makes me more human you know I want to do it. I just don't like being turned on and off like a machine."

"Understood," said Father. "I can't guarantee you'll be able to cry as an emotional reaction, but I'm confident this device will at least protect your eyes and make them more comfortable, and we won't have to do the eye drops every day."

"That will give me more time to stare at the wall," said Melody.

"You're a lovely, twenty-six-year old woman with an incredible brain, and you can do anything you choose to do."

"I don't have any interest in science or engineering. I've been through some of your reference books, and they're easy enough to understand. The subject matter just doesn't appeal to me."

"Your mother was a people person," said Father, "sociology, psychology, the arts, that sort of thing. When I talked about my work she'd blink at me and smile, didn't understand a word I'd said."

"You said she wanted to be an actress," said Melody.

"Maybe. She did plays in high school, and took some lessons privately. She wrote dark poetry once in a while, and she loved theatre and holovision, but she never mentioned acting as a profession. Your mom was a housewife, and seemed to be satisfied with that. Why she hooked up with me is a mystery. She could have had any man."

Her father's voice faded, and she put a hand on his arm. He looked at her sadly.

"A piece of her is still with me, though, in you."

"I know. I feel her there every day. I really don't know what I want to do yet. I love reading, and I like the stories on holovision. It might be fun to be an actress. I would have to study the characters in depth, and see what makes them tick. I might even learn some things about myself."

"Could be," said Donovan Lane, and he looked thoughtful. "It's a tough business to get into, but I might be able to help. I know some people."

"You seem to know a lot of people," said Melody.

"Yes I do. You'd be surprised how many talented and famous people want me to scan them, to store some part of themselves for posterity outside of the body of their work. The ethics for using the library I have hasn't even been debated yet, but of course the permissions of individuals are required by me to use their scans in any way. I could cobble together outstanding talent for anyone with a brain like yours."

He wiggled an eyebrow at her.

"Right now I'll stick with what I have, and I don't know what that is yet."

"Okay," said Father, "but remember what I said. It'll be your call." He leaned close over the magnifier and used tweezers to adjust something on the tiny device he held there.

Melody leaned over his shoulder to look closely at it. "It has little legs on it," she said, and her cheek touched his.

"Those connect to the neuronal bundle once I program it. We'll run diagnostics tomorrow. That's enough for today. Darin is coming over for lunch so you can beat him at chess again. That boy can't get enough punishment. Someone else will be here, too. We have a surprise for you."

"Really? And it's not even my birthday yet. Exactly when is my birthday?"

"The certificate says December 19, 2284 at 4:10 A.M. in Los Angeles County Hospital. That's when you were born, that part of you that still exists today. You were home schooled, and there is a high school equivalency certificate. The death certificate has mysteriously disappeared from all public records."

"More friends in important places," said Melody, and father smiled.

Father put his toys away, and they walked back to the house arm in arm. Thick pea soup had been cooking since morning and they roasted two large franks to go with it, washing everything down with water. Melody knew her sense of taste was not yet up to human standards. She could distinguish sweet from sour, and little else. It was another problem Father was still working on. Digestion was not an issue, but Melody never pressed the capabilities of her system and avoided eating more than an ounce or two of meat at one sitting.

Darin arrived as they ladled out the soup. He always seemed glad to see her, was attentive, a good listener, and Melody felt stimulated when he was there. The first time they played chess he had beaten her, but it was probably the last time he would do that. One game was all the experience Melody needed and she had won every game since that first time. For Darin it was not defeat but triumph, she knew, because he had done work on the layers of neural net that made up her brain.

They played again after lunch, and Melody won three games in a row, the third game quickly. Darin shook his head in dismay.

"I've never seen that move before. Where did you read it? It must have been set up several moves before."

"No, it wasn't set up and I didn't read it. It seemed like the right thing to do," said Melody.

Darin looked at her father, and they both smiled.

"Some nice synthesis there," said father. "It's a good sign."

Melody didn't know what that meant, but figured it out later.

"That's enough for me," said Darin. "Thanks for the games, Melody. I think I'm getting better at it."

"Yes, you are," she said.

He stood up. "Got to go, now. I need to finish up some code for your upgrade and get ready for my date."

"Your date?"

"Marylyn Sommers in Marketing. We met in the cafeteria. She's a gamer geek like me. Nothing fancy, just a dinner and a show and then some gaming with mutual friends."

Melody felt a vague disappointment. "She plays chess?"

"Computer games, fantasy stuff, lots of action. I'll show you some time if you're interested."

"Oh yes," said Melody. "Please do."

"I'll have the code ready for Monday," Darin said to her father.

"Good. I'm finished for the weekend, so there won't be any surprises for you. We need to talk about a couple of scan additions, but I'll discuss it with Melody first," said Father.

"Okay, see you then. Bye, Melody."

"Bye," she said. She still felt a vague disappointment, unease, as if she was not connected to what was going on.

Darin left the house, and Father closed the door behind him. He walked over to Melody, who had remained sitting at the chessboard, and put a hand on her head.

"You're frowning. Is something wrong?"

She looked up at him. "No, I don't think so. I didn't know Darin had a girlfriend."

"Just an acquaintance, I think. Does it bother you? I know you like Darin."

"Yes, I do. I think you're wrong. I think he found a human girlfriend he shares interests with. It won't be the same as it is with me. He'll see the differences."

"Of course there are differences," said Father. "There are differences between all human beings. Melody, you don't see yourself from the outside. You're a beautiful, intelligent young woman, and nobody will ever think otherwise. Even those of us working closely with you, like Darin and I, can easily forget your origins. Stop worrying about it, and just be you."

"I'm trying, Daddy. I guess I haven't figured out who myself is, yet. I keep changing, and now you're talking about another upgrade. What is it this time?"

"Later," said Father, and waved a hand in dismissal "Look, I can see you're feeling down right now, and I had promised you a nice surprise, so I'm going to speed things up a bit. Give me a second."

Father went into another room, made a phone call and returned. "Our neighbor will be over in a bit. You remember Sid Henderson? We went over to see his horses one day."

Melody nodded. "I remember."

"We'll have some coffee with him. Help me clean up first."

Melody went to the kitchen with him where they cleaned up the dishes and residue of their lunch and got the coffee machine started. They were barely finished when the front door chimes played their merry tune and father went to answer the door.

Sid Henderson was a tall, raw-boned man who owned the ranch neighboring her father's. His leathery skin was burned brown by the sun, and his hands were gnarled from a lifetime of hard work under that sun. He was a widower, his children grown and gone, his everyday family the horses, dogs, cats and chickens that roamed freely together on his land.

"Hi, Melody," he said when he came into the room, and shook her hand warmly. "Getting used to life on the ranch yet?"

"It's nice out here," she said, and managed a faint smile. "I enjoyed seeing your place, with all the animals."

"Better'n the city," said Sid. "Peace and quiet, well, most of the time. You seemed to like the horses. You're welcome to come over for a ride anytime."

Ah, the surprise, thought Melody. "I'd like that," she said.

"Wish we could keep horses," said Father, "but we don't have the time for it, and Melody will probably move back to the city soon. That's where the work is."

They had talked about this, and it would happen as soon as Melody figured out what her work would be.

"Well, I can tell you from experience that living alone, even in the city, is a lot nicer if you have something to care about besides yourself. Having a pet to care for and nurture is good for the soul," said Sid.

"Unfortunately, a horse doesn't fit too well inside a city apartment," said Father.

"No, it doesn't, but I've got something else you might be interested in," said Sid. He turned and left the house without another word, and Father grinned at her. Melody was momentarily confused. Was this another surprise?

In a minute, Sid knocked on the door again and Father let him in.

Sid was carrying a cardboard box under one arm. He put it down on a coffee table in the front room and motioned to Melody.

"Let's see what you think of this," he said.

Melody walked over to him and looked down into the box. A small, furry, black lump was in one corner.

It moved, a tiny face appeared with pug nose and flopped over ears, and eyes the color of a sunny sky. It looked at her, and whimpered.

"You can pick her up if you like," said Sid. "She's still nursing, but you can feed her from a bottle."

Melody felt her heart quicken, and her hands trembled as she reached down to pick up the tiny animal, not much bigger than a large man's palm.

The puppy was very warm. She held it up in front of her. Blue eyes stared back from a coal black face. A small tail moved, beat lightly against her wrist. She brought it close to her face, touched its nose to hers, and felt a tiny tongue lick her face.

Melody felt a strange, new feeling inside her as she put the puppy against her cheek. The little tail moved vigorously, now, as did the dog's wet tongue, and it squirmed in her hands.

"She's a wolf hybrid," said Sid. "My Kitcha gave birth to five, and this little girl is the runt, but very active. She pushes her brothers out of the way at dinnertime. Not sure who the daddy is, but it must be Dagin, my Malamute. Otherwise I can't explain the blue eyes. Do you like her?"

"Oh, she's wonderful," said Melody, moving her face around as the pup kissed her frantically.

"She's an affectionate little gal, and she's yours if you want her," said Sid.

"Really? Oh, I do, I do." The strange feeling in her chest was now a tightening.

Sid handed some papers to her father. "Diet and care instructions are all there. The milk recipe is my own, and I brought along a baby bottle for starters. Better keep her indoors, or penned. If she gets loose she might never come back. Even with a hybrid, the wolf instinct is real strong."

The puppy now explored her neck, clutching at it with front paws. "Thank you so much. She's a wonderful gift," she said.

"Thank your father. He put me up to it. A single girl like you should have a pet, something to take care of and love. It makes the world brighter."

Melody learned against her father and showed him the puppy up close. He stroked its head with a finger. "She'll have a good home here," he said.

"I can see that," said Sid. "If you want to breed her someday, let me know. Not easy to find a wolf-cross with blue eyes."

Melody sat down on the couch. The puppy sniffed around, curled up in her lap and closed its eyes. Apparently it had had enough excitement for the day.

"Now you have to give her a name," said father.

Melody thought. The coal black coat of the pup made her decision simple. "I'll call her Ebony," she said.

"Ebony," she called, but the puppy had fallen asleep.

"Ebony with the sky blue eyes," said father.

"Momma and papa are both good sized," said Sid, "but the runt of the litter is likely to be smaller."

"I don't care," said Melody, and eventually Ebony would prove the man's assessment to be wrong.

That first night, Melody made up a little bed of pillows and a blanket and put it beside her bed for Ebony. That was fine until Melody was in bed and had turned off the lights. Two hours later she still wasn't sleeping because of Ebony's mournful sounds. She brought Ebony into bed with her on top of the covers, and felt her cuddle up tight against her covered body for the warmth. She lay awake a while, feeling a wonderful feeling inside her. Is this love, she wondered? And decided it probably was.

* * * *

Darin dressed hurriedly to give him more code writing time before his date. There were three projects to finish. The first was for Melody's new tear gland, and coding for the drainage sequence. The others were two new scans, one from an Anna Wilcox, the other from a name he recognized. Eleanor Dali had been a famous film and television star in the past century, known for her romance and damsel-in-distress roles, and the scan had been made at her request. Darin quickly wrote the simple program that layered the two scans together in a single neural sheet scheduled for installation along with the tear system in a single sitting. Darin assumed that Melody knew about it, but she hadn't mentioned it to him. He liked Melody. He enjoyed being with her. He could fall for a girl like that. But then, he reminded himself, she was a synthetic.

He finished his work, and hurried away for his date.

CHAPTER 6

Palm trees waved in bright sunlight over Rarotonga, and the resorts were all busy, the beaches full of bronzing tourists. A flotilla of private yachts lay a hundred yards off shore, and little rubber boats ferried their passengers to shore for another day of Cook Islands pleasure. Five boats converged on the same dock, where a swarthy man in a dark business suit waited with a line of golf carts behind him. He greeted each passenger and directed them to a specific cart. Most guests were older men dressed casually in colorful shirts and white shorts. There were two women, draped Polynesian style, and they were placed in the last cart of the procession.

The suited man led the line of carts along the beach and up into the hills outside of the tourist area. It was not a long trip; the island itself was only seven miles across. The road became narrower as they climbed to the interior of the island, the jungle closing in on them. They came to a gate which opened to admit them, and a few minutes later they approached a simple stone hut with a thatched roof, and a small barn with two horses as occupants. From this point there was a beautiful view of the sea below them.

Jacob Cross came out of the hut to greet his guests and pay special attention to the two ladies, making sure they were comfortable. He disapproved of board members bringing along their secretaries, but did not make an issue of identities. His security team kept close watch on everyone when they were in their own cities. Max was in charge of that, but now served drinks to Jacob's guests, walking among them in his business suit to serve a variety of piña coladas on silver trays, and smiling as best he could.

Max Schuler had been with Jacob Cross since before the demise of the evangelistic empire. Even then Jacob had employed a security team, and Max had quickly risen to the head of it. He was a block of a man with an ill-defined neck and huge hands. Small eyes so dark brown as to seem black peered from a square face with large nose and a small chin. His colleagues were quietly frightened of him. His record was foggy: five years as a navy seal, and eight more years of government security work, all agencies and job assignments classified. There had been two outstanding recommendation letters from the Navy.

Max Schuler looked like a thug, but he was smart, quick to organize, quicker to initiate strategic thinking, and people did what he told them to do.

Jacob did not question his methods. When a disgruntled employee discovered Jacob's skimming of church funds into offshore accounts and threatened to inform the believers, Jacob talked to Max, and within a day that employee disappeared from planet Earth, never to be seen again.

Jacob trusted Max completely, and regarded him as his partner.

Max served drinks, and there was informal chatter in the little hut, once a bar, and everyone relaxed in socializing. Nearly all attendees were well acquainted with each other, but no names were used. When it was time for lunch, Jacob pressed a button under the bar, and to everyone's amazement an entire wall slid aside to reveal a brightly lit hallway leading to exquisitely carved double doors, beyond which was an oaken paneled dining room with a long table set for fifteen. Beyond that space were several large rooms, lavishly furnished, only a part of the underground mansion built into the hillside.

Servants served a meal of fish and shredded pork, with a salad of greens and pineapple, and there was mango-flavored ice cream for dessert. Max acted as wine steward.

They adjourned to the boardroom, oak paneled, a single round table that seated twenty people. Each place was identified with either one or two letters on white cardboard teepees, and they seated themselves according to the teepees. The two women sat behind their masters, as did Max, taking notes on laptops.

"Good to see you all again," said Jacob. "We should do this more often."

Heads bobbed in agreement, and there were smiles. Everyone was nicely relaxed.

"Since this is our first formal meeting with everyone present I'm hoping to hear some favorable progress reports. Anyone care to begin?"

A man raised his hand.

"Ah, Mister C. What do you have for us?" asked Jacob.

"There will be fuel shortages for the next six months, but the supply of diesel fuel will be maintained. Diesel and home heating oils will be cut back in time for winter. The rationale is that new regulations and excess profit taxes are preventing expansion of our facilities. The same argument has been effective in explaining our shutdown of green energy development. We're beginning a new publicity campaign in the news media next week."

"Excellent," said Jacob. "I suspect there is a lot of truth in your rationale."

"There is," said Mister C.

"Well, we do appreciate your sacrifice. Anyone else?"

Four other people raised their hands and gave short reports. Layoffs were being reported as the result of higher taxes and increasing mechanization of production. Automated quality control had resulted in distribution slowdowns due to inaccurate reports of glitches in the system. Cutbacks in advertising were impacting the news media, including holovision, and were most hurtful in the pharmaceutical area without real damage to company profits. Such advertising had been used as a tax dodge in the first place, and was no longer allowed by the government as a tax deduction.

Jacob clapped his hands together. "These are wonderful strategies, gentlemen, and the fact that they are based on honest grievances makes them easier to believe and more powerful. I commend you."

Another hand went up. "Yes, Mister H," said Jacob.

"Misters C, FG, N, L and A speak for the rest of us, Mister Cross, lest you think we're not all active participants. All of us have implemented similar strategies. We appreciate that you have organized this group and given us a forum for planning, but I think now we would like to hear what personal strategies you have come up with to benefit our cause."

It was not what was said, but the tone of the man's voice when he said it. Jacob felt a slight flush of heat in his face, but swallowed his anger and smiled.

"Of course," he said, and managed to look kindly at Mister H. The man's eyes widened and Jacob guessed that from behind him Max Schuler was not giving the man a kindly look.

"You people put me to shame with your prompt action, but it's necessary for my plans to move more slowly. Remember that what I'm doing requires more intelligence related to things that might disturb the religious community as well as the unions, and in an indirect way. People have lived with automated manufacturing for a long time. It's the more recent advances in robotics that are affecting retail, communication and transportation jobs. All these little robots clerking in stores, and driving your cabs and trucks, even giving news casts, are raising havoc with good paying jobs for real people, and already there is an outcry against it. The next step is a synthetic human, a machine that can do everything a human can do in a work situation. We're talking about a soulless automaton to replace humanity. Doesn't that outrage you? It certainly should. Is man going to play God? Not if I can help it. Mankind has gone as far as he should with the machines. It must be stopped now."

Jacob took an extra breath to calm him. There was deathly silence in the room.

He smiled. "Well, you get the idea. We do need the support of the religious right. The problem is that talk about synthetic humans is just talk, gentlemen, but I happen to believe it. I think it is the next logical step in robotics, and I think it is being developed as we speak. Talk and rumor is no good by itself. I need proof that such machine intelligence is now being developed, or is already here, and I have a good idea about where to look for it. A company called Interface Systems Corporation has been producing human-like robots for years. My intelligence people tell me that until recently there has only been one plant on the west coast of the United States. This plant has been devoted to manufacturing as well as research and development, In the last year a new facility has been built high in the coastal mountains, disguised as a German company with the name Schutz Fabrik. It is a small facility, gated and heavily guarded. I'm certain it houses all the advanced research and development for the mother company, and I am making every effort to infiltrate it with people loyal to our cause. These are highly paid engineers and scientists, gentlemen. Surely you can understand there will be a price for their loyalty. There is a risk the intelligence we gain will not be worth the cost, but I feel the risk is minimal. The owner of the company, Doctor Donovan Lane, is a recognized genius in the field of robotics. The major product ideas have come from him, and I expect more to come soon.

"If our people can get close to him, we can follow his every move and exploit it to our advantage, especially if he does anything to produce an artificial human. He is working with federal money. That alone will help me inflame public outrage. With a good propaganda effort, we can enrage the public enough to burn the man to the ground and then get them to turn against those who have funded his work.

"We share a common goal, and that is the return of government control to the shakers and movers of our country. And I will use any means necessary to do that."

For a moment, Jacob hoped they might applaud him, but they did not. Some skeptical looks had disappeared, and he accepted that as a victory. It did not satisfy him.

They discussed meeting schedules. Some AAAH board members lived near each other, and had their own local meetings. Jacob pressed them to keep all board members informed of the outcome of those meetings. The group as a whole would come together three times a year for a general meeting. Working online was not considered, nor trusted. Any government awareness of their activities could result in immediate arrest and confiscation of property and businesses.

The meeting ended with another round of piña coladas, and then it was time for fun. Jacob had made exclusive reservations for all of them at Rico's resort and Golf Club on the south side of the island. There would be three nights and days of golf, surfing and tanning, and exceptional food at the five-star resort.

Jacob would not join them there, would never be seen with any of them. Only Rico, a trusted friend, knew who had made the reservations.

Jacob and Max took them back to the waiting golf carts and saw them off, waving goodbyes as the carts disappeared down the jungle-lined road.

"I think that went well," said Jacob. "What do you think, Max?"

Max did not look at him. "Mister H has an attitude problem that needs correcting. I'd keep an eye on him if I were you, sir."

Jacob patted the big man on the shoulder. "I'll leave that up to you. We'll need to show the board some results at the next meeting. How are the infiltration efforts going?"

"We've hit all the institutions with majors in robotics, but our focus is on MIT. We have applicant lists from all the job fairs. Interface Systems Corporation has hired at least six robotics engineers and several scientists over the past three years. We're trying to locate them now. We'll make our pitches, and I hope to have something positive for you within a month. You did say money was not an issue, didn't you, sir?"

"I did. Our colleagues are paying all the bills," said Jacob.

"I'm concerned about risks, sir," said Max, and glowered at him. "If a pitch is refused, there's a danger it will be reported to Donovan Lane. If he investigates he'll find the company we supposedly represent doesn't exist, and it might lead back to us."

"It could be a problem," said Jacob, "but I feel confident you have ways of convincing people it is not in their best interests to report our contact with them."

"And if that fails, sir?"

"I'm sure you know what must be done, as a last resort of course. It's not necessary for me to know the details."

"Yes, sir. I understand."

"You always understand me, Max. That's why it's such a pleasure for me to work with you. Now let us adjourn to the boardroom, where a pitcher of piña coladas awaits us. We need to discuss what must eventually be done with the brain behind Interface Systems Corporation, and that brain belongs to Doctor Donovan Lane."

They went back into the hut and the corridor beyond the wall, which slid silently shut behind them.

CHAPTER 7

Touring the synth fabrication laboratory was the most ghastly experience of her young life. Melody carried Ebony with her wherever she went, refusing to leave the dog home alone. Father allowed it. Solvent odors were the major irritant; Ebony wrinkled her nose and nestled close, mumbling.

"I'm not sure I should be seeing this," said Melody.

"I want you to understand the process," said Father. "Things can go wrong, and reactions must often be quick. It's enough for you to know the basics of construction. The entire lab is about to be moved to our new facility in the mountains. That's where you'll go for repairs and upgrades from now on."

"Why the move?" asked Melody, stroking Ebony's head. The pup had fallen asleep again. "This is conveniently close to town."

"Too convenient," said Father, "and too much open access here. Reporters are continuously sniffing around for stories about new products. The synth program must maintain secrecy, and we can't get it here. We're past the prototype stage. It's manufacturing and evaluation, now."

"And I was a prototype," said Melody.

"One of three," said Father. "The others are over here, both male. I haven't yet decided what to program them for."

He led her past protein vats and extruders to two tables on which lay two men, one slender and quite handsome, Melody thought, the other shorter and with heavier features.

"They're shut down, right now," said Father. "The darker haired guy might fit in security. He even looks like a cop. I don't recall where his template came from. The other guy, well, he is pretty. We've had a lot of fun with him when he was up and around. The man who sold us the scan and template was a party boy, and his gate swung both ways. Poor guy died from a blood cancer shortly after that. You might say this synth represents his immortality."

"Am I immortal?" asked Melody.

"We don't know, sweetie. You'll live for a long time, and you'll always be twenty-five. That can be another problem, unless you move around a lot. We're working on it."

"Can we go now? I don't want to see more of this, and it smells really bad in here," said Melody, and wrinkled her nose. Ebony stirred in her arms and looked up at her.

"Sure," said Father, "but there's more you have to see later. Maybe after your upgrade next week."

"So I can cry?"

"So you can take care of your eyes better. Nothing dramatic. We're having lunch with a friend of mine I want you to meet, and then we'll go home."

"I need to feed Ebony and take her for a walk," said Melody. "She likes to walk in the evening."

"Okay, let's go," said Father.

They left the laboratory and the building, and went to a company car Father had arranged for the day. Father punched in an address and they relaxed with soft drinks during the forty minute automated drive out of the hills and along a freeway until exiting onto a street that took them back up into the hills again. The road steepened, switching back and forth until both sides were lined with iron-gated and walled mansions in brick and stone.

"Wow," said Melody. "Who do you know that lives up here?"

"A very famous lady," said Father, and smiled. "She wants very much to meet you."

They stopped in front of a high double gate of iron decorated with gargoyles, a long driveway beyond it winding under overhanging tree limbs to a mansion in brick and cut stone. Father went to the gate and spoke into a little box there, and the gate opened. They drove up to the building, on their left a green lawn bordered by high walls and a myriad of roses planted in a vortex of plots. Two gardeners were working there.

They parked in front of the house. Father knocked on the front door with a huge knocker shaped like a dragon's head. Melody carried Ebony with her, refusing to leave her in the car. The door opened, and a tall man in a dark suit ushered them in, smiling. "She's expecting you, and very excited," he said.

The foyer was huge, a small fountain in the center of its marble floor, water sprouting from the mouths of angels flying. They sat on one of the couches surrounding the fountain, and the sound of falling water was both peaceful and mesmerizing. Above them, a broad staircase wound its way up to a second floor. The servant who had let them in climbed the stairs and was soon out of sight.

They waited only a minute before a woman appeared at the top of the stairs and began her descent. She wore a beige gown with a lacy, diaphanous cloak that trailed behind her, and her hair was coiled neatly into a bun at the back of her head. She descended the stairs with an attitude of drama, the poise and grace of someone royal.

Melody recognized her immediately, and gasped.

"Eleanor Dali," she said, and Father smiled.

Melody had seen most of her films on holovision, work dating back some sixty years when Eleanor Dali had been regarded as the most beautiful woman on Earth. At age eighty-two she remained strikingly handsome, her posture erect, azure blue eyes flashing. She extended a hand regally to Father, who kissed it grandly and with Polish style, one hand over his heart. Melody was astonished.

Eleanor turned immediately to Melody, and with an instinct that came out of nowhere Melody made a little curtsy to her.

"So this is your daughter, Donovan. You remind me of your mother, dear. So lovely. Your father has told me all about you." Her voice was deep, and husky.

Melody felt a shock and looked at her father, who raised an eyebrow and said, "She's a survivor, all right."

"I met your mother in a class before you were even born. I was doing some improv exercises as a special guest of Anna Wilcox when she had her Van Nuys studio, and your mother was one of her students. She had some real talent."

"I know she was interested in acting," said Melody, "but other things happened instead."

Eleanor put a hand on Melody's forearm. Ebony stirred and sniffed at her hand. Her fingers lightly brushed the pup's head, and Ebony yawned. "Life is joy, and sadness, triumph and tragedy. All of it is food for the craft, dear. All of it. Your father tells me you have some interest in acting."

"Yes. I love to watch holovision, especially the older films that don't have so much violent action and special effects. I love dramas and romances, the kind of things you used to do. I think I've seen most of your work, and I'm so honored to meet you. I can't imagine how my father arranged it."

"We'll get to that, dear. Let's sit down, now. Alas, standing is not my strong point these days."

They sat on a couch by the fountain, Father at one end, Eleanor beside Melody and turning to face her. Eleanor reached out to lightly stroke Ebony's head again, and the pup raised her head in response with a long blink of her eyes, seeming to enjoy the touch.

"Such beautiful eyes," said Eleanor. "Is she a mixed breed?"

"Ebony is a wolf hybrid. We think her father was a Malamute," said Melody.

"An exotic mix," said Eleanor. "I think she is appropriate for you. My Jeffy was a Pomeranian, but he died last year. I had him for eighteen years, and I should get another dog. It's not good to be alone, especially at my age. But enough of that. What I really want to know is why you are interested in acting. It's a very difficult profession to succeed in, even with talent. What is the appeal for you?"

Melody thought for a second or two, then "Well, I like to read. I love any kind of storytelling, especially with happy endings. I like the emotions, the reactions of the characters to each other, the way they reveal their inner selves."

She looked at her father. "Sometimes I don't really know who I am, and I pretend to be someone else. When I do that I think I'm really trying to understand myself. When I—"

"—Oh, Donovan, this is wonderful. She is wonderful. You have done a marvelous job. I have hope."

Father smiled. "It will only get better," he said.

Melody felt a touch of panic, having revealed an intimate thought to a perfect stranger. Father seemed to be relaxed, even pleased, while his synth daughter wallowed in confusion.

Eleanor sensed it, and leaned close. "I did say that your father has told me everything about you, dear, and I'm sure you'd like to know why he would do such a thing when you and some others like you are such a secret."

Melody was breathing rapidly and desperately wanted to flee from the house. Ebony looked up at her and whined. When Eleanor put a hand on Melody's arm again, the pup growled and burrowed into her mistress's lap.

"I will explain," said Eleanor. She took a deep breath and let it out slowly. Her eyes suddenly welled up wetly, and a tear ran down her cheek. "I lost someone, too, only it was not an accident. It was cancer. He was my only son, and it was my darkest secret, the result of a tryst with a man I will never name. I was a star, at the top of my craft, and a terrible parent. Nathan was raised by my servants, and I made up for my absence by spoiling him horribly. As a man, his life was adventure, travel and parties, with no meaningful work, but he was full of charm and claimed to be a budding actor, and everyone loved him. Then one day there was cancer, well advanced, and Nathan was only middle-aged. Despite his faults, a part of me was in him, and I loved him. I had never married. I had no one else. A friend of a friend told me about your father's work on scanning human consciousness and memories. I went to see him and we arranged a scan while Nathan was in the hospital. I remember the day when—"

Eleanor choked with a sob, and Father put a hand on her back.

"We thought a cure would be found someday. He had only months to live. The scan was done, and when he died I had his body frozen and stored at the American Cryogenics Facility in San Diego. It was a foolish thing to do. A few years later the company went into bankruptcy after many lawsuits and all the stored bodies were thawed out and allowed to decompose. It was a terrible scandal, and I was distraught. I went to your father again, and he offered me a solution in deepest secrecy."

Melody looked at her father. "You made a synthetic model of her son, and I think I know which one it is."

"You do?" gasped Eleanor. "It has only been a month or so since he—"

"Melody saw him in the laboratory while we were getting ready for another memory upgrade from the new file," said Father.

"He's quite young," said Melody, wondering.

"Nathan was in his fifties when he died," said Eleanor, "but I wanted him to follow in my footsteps, so he had to be young."

"I built him from a template from another young man who had also died from cancer. It was considered a donation for medical research," said Father.

"He's very good looking," said Melody.

"But only when I talk to him does he seem like my son. He looks so different. It was hard for me at first, but then he told me things he remembered, and it was the good things, the nice times we had together, and I was happy about what I'd done." Eleanor sniffed, and smiled wanly.

"We edited the original file carefully, and now we're loading a new one," said Father.

Eleanor reached over and clutched Melody's hand. "It is a new file you will share with Nathan, dear, and I hope you will choose to use it. The two of you would make such a beautiful couple on screen."

"I don't understand," said Melody.

"It's going to be your new update," said father.

"It's my legacy to both of you," said Eleanor, and now she spoke breathlessly. "My time is short. I had your father scan me the week after I met his new creation of my son. Nathan has received nearly all of the original file, but your father has edited out much of my personal memories to create a new file that will be yours if you want it. It contains all the memories of my classes with Anna Wilcox, my first work on the stage, the back street improvs, the endless screen tests and my countless days on set. It is the collective memory of all that has been precious to me for so much of my life, and I want you to have it. Meeting you and hearing your thoughts has made me desire it even more. You are lovely, Melody. You can be a star. If it's easier, think of it as my thanks to your father for giving my son back to me in a new form."

"Melody?" asked Father.

She sat there stunned, staring straight ahead. Ebony pawed at her arm, wanting to be petted again. "It's wonderful, like I'm dreaming, but I'm not dreaming. The memories I have now are sometimes like dreams, memories of things happening to other people and the original person I was, not the thing I am now. I wonder if I can do what you want, when I'm not really a human being."

Tears welled up in Eleanor's eyes, and her grip on Melody's hand was suddenly painful. "You are a human being, dear, and so is my son!"

"Melody, we've talked about this before. Forget your composition for one minute," said Father, "and try to look at yourself as others see you. In every respect, you are a fully functional human being."

"Not when it comes to emotions," said Melody.

"That will come with experience," said Father. "The only person you've really interacted with is me."

"But acting is dependent on emotional expression, and that's what's worrying you," said Eleanor. "I will teach you all of that by example, dear, in the privacy of your own mind, but of course you'll have to practice it: the open feelings of joy and sorrow, the subtext, all of it. I want to show you something, Melody. You are strikingly lovely, despite the fact your father has taught you nothing as simple as the use of lipstick or eyeliner. Come upstairs with me this minute."

It was an order. Eleanor pulled Melody up from the couch as Father grinned, and they all three ascended the long staircase to a second floor with a long hallway leading to an immense living room with picture windows looking out over the tops of trees to the high towers of buildings in the far distance. Beyond the big room were four bedrooms with adjoining baths, one corner of the master bedroom occupied by a broad vanity with mirror and a row of bright lights above it. Eleanor seated Melody at the vanity and ordered father out of the room.

Watching herself in the mirror was something magical for Melody as Eleanor worked on her: the powders, the blush, the contrasting colors on eyebrows and lashes, the dark red of her full lips. Eleanor hummed as she worked, and finally stood behind Melody, hands on her shoulders and peering closely at the mirror. "The tousled look of your hair isn't bad," she said, "but I'm sure my hair dresser would have other ideas. This is you, Melody, the way other people can see you if you wish it."

Melody had seen enough holovision to make comparisons, and when she looked into the mirror she saw an extraordinarily beautiful young woman, as beautiful or more than any holostar she'd ever seen.

"Now give me some looks," said Eleanor. "Change your face. You are surprised by something."

Melody widened her eyes.

"Now you are angry."

Melody narrowed her eyes, and stretched her face.

"Now you look at something in the far distance, and wonder what it is."

Melody relaxed her face, and focused on infinity.

"You see the differences as others will see them. Melody, you are a beautiful human being."

Eleanor turned, and shouted, "Donovan, come in here and see your beautiful daughter who will be a star!"

Father appeared, and stared. "Wow," he said softly. "That's all I can think of to say."

Melody suddenly felt warm inside herself. She held Ebony up beside her face so they were both looking into the mirror. "Do you recognize me, sweetie?" she asked.

Ebony wagged her tail, wiggled a little and licked Melody on her cheek.

Eleanor was glowing with pleasure at what she had done, and turned when her servant appeared in the doorway.

"Lunch is ready, Madam," he said.

"We'll be down in a minute," said Eleanor, and then she looked again at Melody. "I hope you enjoy it, dear. Your father suggested the menu when I expressed uncertainty about what you can eat."

"I eat anything," said Melody, "but in small quantities. I do use special supplements I take with water or juices."

"So I've heard," said Eleanor. "Does a small plate of chicken fettuccini sound good to you?"

"I love that dish," said Melody.

"I even have a special treat for your puppy," said Eleanor.

They went downstairs again to a dining room with a table set for four but large enough for fourteen. There was a garden salad and alcohol-free blush wine with the main dish, and a small orb of Italian Eis for desert. At Melody's feet, Ebony sniffed carefully at a dish filled with grains and chunks of meat, and then devoured it all in a minute.

"After your update, we must do this often," said Eleanor. "I do miss entertaining. So many of my friends have passed on. When you feel you're ready, we could do some readings together, practice some preparation techniques, even some improvisation. It would be good for Nathan, too. What I did wasn't only for glamour, fame and fortune, Melody. The work itself was everything to me. With you, and Nathan, I would be doing the work again."

"That would be nice," said Melody, though she wondered what the effects of her update would be. Was acting just the fancy of a young girl who watched too much holovision? Would the commitment be there, the zealous desire to do the necessary work with no guarantee of eventual success? She knew the statistics, a less than one percent success rate for talented people who wanted to be stars. Her own mother had been a casualty, had never come close to her young ambition, but still she had found a good life. What could be the harm in trying it?

"My upgrade will be soon," said Melody.

"The day after tomorrow," said Father, "and Nathan will be ready again the day after that. Maybe you can compare notes." He chuckled at his little joke.

Melody didn't think it was funny. What would it be like to talk to a synth like her? Surely it would be different than talking to father or Darin, and now Eleanor. The idea made her both anxious and excited.

"I would like to meet Nathan," she said, and Eleanor smiled. "I think it'll be interesting."

"Everything from here on out is going to be a learning experience for all of us," said Father.

"I think you see everything as an experiment," said Melody, "but for me this is all an adventure, finding out who I am and what I can do, and it will be the same for Nathan."

"Oh, this is so exciting!" said Eleanor. "We must get started right away."

There was no disagreement about that, and another lunch was scheduled two weeks in advance, giving time for Melody's update to settle in and opportunity for Nathan and Melody to meet for the first time in a laboratory setting.

At the front door Eleanor embraced Melody warmly, squeezing complaining Ebony between them, and then comforting the pup with a gentle hand.

"Thank you so much for everything you've done for me," said Melody.

"My dear girl," gushed Eleanor, "it is my pleasure. We are going to have such fun. I'll gather some wonderful material for it right away."

She waved to them, a lonely figure on the porch of the huge house, as they went back to the car, and she was still waving as the big gate with its gargoyle faces closed behind them.

CHAPTER 8

"This is nicer," said Melody. "There were terrible odors in the other place."

"It's all brand new," said Father, "and only research and development here. No manufacturing."

It had been a four hour drive south of Los Angeles and up into the coastal range where the Schutz Fabrik facility lay partially hidden in a box canyon. The three story oval-shaped structure protruded from the mountains by a hundred feet, showing only a small portion of the entire complex. Standing on an upper floor balcony one could see the shimmer of the Pacific Ocean in the distance.

Melody rested comfortably in a high-backed chair surrounded by instrument panels as father worked at the back of her head. She blinked her eyes experimentally, and felt moisture there.

"I think it's working," she said. "I feel liquid, and it stings a little."

"You'll get used to that," said Father, and he pried at something in the back of her head.

"What are you doing back there?"

"Opening a port. This seal is better than it has to be, but I'm getting it."

Melody had been oblivious to the installation of her tear gland and the plumbing that went with it. The procedure had taken over two hours, and father had 'turned her off' for it. She hated that term. Why couldn't he just say, "We put you to sleep," like you would say for a real human? It reminded her again that she was really a thinking machine, a synthetic recreation of a once living person, and not a real person at all. She didn't understand why it bothered her so much, why her irritation with it seemed to be increasing. Still, the irritation itself was a kind of emotion, a human thing, and that was positive.

She reminded her father of the proper phrase to use with her in the future. "Are you going to put me to sleep for the update?"

"Not necessary," said Father. "I want to see your immediate response when we connect up this time. There, finally I got it open. Your port needs a tweak."

Another reminder. "I bet you say that to all the girls," she said.

"Your jokes are getting better," said Father, oblivious to her sarcasm.

Melody let it go. At the moment it wasn't worth the bother, and she was distracted by Darin, who came into the room with a little box in his hand and walked up to her chair.

He smiled, and held up the box. "Here is your little piece of Eleanor Dali," he said, "all vacuum packed and ready to go. You can thank me later for the hours I've spent editing and coding this thing."

"You're putting that entire box into my head?" asked Melody, and was delighted by Darin's momentary confusion.

"She is being exceptionally clever today," said Father.

"Oh, I see, well, here, I'll show you," said Darin.

He opened the box and there was a hissing sound. He used a pair of tweezers to take two wafers the size of quarters from the box and placed them on an instrument stand to the left of Melody's chair. Each wafer had a pair of nubbins projecting out a centimeter from the edge, and both had a flat black surface.

"The housing is polymer, but each of those guys contains a stack of a thousand neurosheets painstakingly coded together by yours truly," said Darin.

"Don't believe him," said Father, reaching for one of the wafers with a pair of tweezers. "Most of the coding is already in the file, the interconnections of the neurons that form the memories. All he had to do was wire the layers together."

"A thousand layers," said Darin, smiling.

"And indeed it was a lot of work. It would be an impossible task in a human brain because memories are distributed all over the place," said Father, "but your brain architecture is far superior with centralized memory stacks and a nice impact and thermal shield to protect them."

Father patted her on the shoulder.

"Here we go, now. Let me know when you think or feel something new."

At first she only felt pressure at the back of her head. There was a click, and Father reached for the second wafer with his tweezers. "Anything?" he asked.

"Nothing yet," said Melody, and she closed her eyes in concentration, trying to relax. It was the first time she'd been awake while someone was working on her.

The first things she saw were her own old memories, the ones that were always there to haunt her: the face of her mother, smiling, saying something to her, turning to look ahead, a sudden look of terror on her face, and then a bright flash at the moment of impact. She wondered if that memory would ever go away, that last instant when she had been a living person.

Something else swam into focus. She was watching holovision, but the faces of the actors were blurred at first, and she moved closer to the images, but everyone was moving very fast and their dialogue was the random noise of a crowd, loud and raucous, so much so that she clapped her hands over her ears.

"Melody?" she heard Father ask, but his voice was faint.

The images of the faces cleared, and she recognized some of them as they flashed by, but none of them were Eleanor Dali. Those who were familiar were people she had seen on holo shows, she was certain of that. She put her arms at her sides and took a deep breath, let it out slowly, felt the beat of her mechanical heart slow, slow, slow as the jumble of images began to fade, only to be replaced by another.

It was a man's face, close up, a man she recognized from a show she'd seen. She concentrated again, but it was not a familiar scene, and she could not remember his name. She was in the scene with him, and they were lying in bed together, naked on top of the sheets, for it was quite hot in the darkened room and a fan was blowing warm air across them.

"Do you believe that I love you?" asked the man.

"Yes, I do, and I love you too, but the world keeps tearing us apart," she said, but it was not her voice. "It just isn't fair, and what we're doing isn't right. You are a married man."

"I feel guilt too, my darling," said the man, his face closer now and she felt his hands exploring, a tingle running through her body as he touched her here and there, his breath sweet. "But at this moment it seems right to me, as if heaven ordained for only this special moment when we are real with each other and act out our truth. Wherever the world takes me I want to remember this moment forever. I will always love you, Eleanor, and you will always be in my heart."

"Oh, my dearest," she said as they came together in a wave of heat, passion and sensation that—

"—Oh," said Melody. Her eyes opened wide and her heart was hammering hard. Moisture filled her eyes and she looked up, saw the blurred image of a face there. She reached out to it.

"Are you okay, Melody?" asked Darin.

She grabbed him by his collar, pulled him down to her and kissed him hard.

"Melody! What's going on?" yelled Father right into her ear.

It shocked her. She released Darin and blinked her eyes rapidly. Vision cleared. Father was leaning close to look into her eyes, and Darin was standing behind him, a foolish grin on his face.

"It was a memory, one of Eleanor's, I'm sure of it. I could feel all my senses at once. Oh, that was intense. Now it's gone. I'm not getting anything else."

She looked over at Darin. "Sorry," she said. "For a second there you were in the dream."

"Do I look like I'm complaining?" said Darin, and he blushed when Father scowled at him.

"Just the one memory? That's all you got?" Father's brow wrinkled with worry.

"There was more, but it was all jumbled together and moved so fast I couldn't pick anything out. Even the faces were blurred."

"Could have been formatting or partitioning going on," said Darin. "If that happened, they would be the first operations, and selective retrieval would come after that. The individual keys should be in there."

"How clinical," said Melody. "I've just had my first sexual experience, and you want to talk about formatting. The man involved said the name Eleanor, and we were naked, so it wasn't any scene from one of her productions. It was personal, and very intense, and I think I know what it might be the memory of."

"And that is?" asked Father.

"That is between me and Eleanor. Somehow you two got a personal memory mixed in with her professional work, and there might be more of them."

"That would not be good," said Father. "I made a promise to Eleanor about her privacy. This could blow everything about our deal with her, but we'll have to be honest about it. She'll have to be told."

Darin groaned, and put a hand to his face. "All that work," he said.

"Let me talk to her about it," said Melody. "The memory is a secret as long as it stays in my head."

Father looked at Darin, and there was no hesitation. "I'll call her today. She wanted to know the results right away. I'm not sure what to say."

"Tell her new memories are coming to me," said Melody, "but there is one I want to talk to her about privately. In other words, tell her the truth."

Darin nodded his agreement.

"Okay, I'll call her now," said Father, and he left the room.

Darin looked at her and smiled.

"What?" asked Melody.

"You're a good kisser," said Darin.

"Thank you, I think. How's the new girlfriend? Any progress?"

"That's a bit personal, Melody, but Marylyn and I are having some fun together. Her tastes aren't cheap. She likes the expensive restaurants and shows. No hamburgers and a holo for her."

"Better ask my father for a raise," said Melody.

"It's not that bad," said Darin, and his smile faded. "Feel any changes yet? We put a lot of stuff into your head today."

"Just that one piece of high drama. I do feel different, a bit apprehensive, or maybe I just don't like people probing around inside my head. Right now I'd like to go back to the ranch and take a nap."

"You're staying here overnight," said Darin.

"I know that. Maybe I'll have something to report to my brain technicians in the morning, but after I've had a full night's sleep, or downtime, or whatever. I'd rather be walking Ebony in the woods. I miss my dog."

"Sorry," said Darin. "Another day should do it. We'll join you for dinner, and talk about the meeting with Eleanor. Try to relax, even doze a bit. Maybe some new material will be retrieved in sleep."

"I'll work on that," said Melody.

Darin left the room. Melody turned on the holo and began flipping channels, but it was the middle of the day and there was nothing on except stupid talk and game shows. She gave up in disgust, turned off the set and sighed in sudden boredom.

There was a knock on the closed door to her room.

"Come in," she called, expecting to see Darin or father, who both had a habit of knocking politely before they entered.

When the door opened a man was there who seemed to be a stranger to her. At second glance, however, he looked vaguely familiar. He was tall and slender, with a mass of blond hair and startlingly blue eyes, a very handsome man indeed.

"I'm looking for Melody Lane," he said with a nicely resonant baritone voice. "I was told I should introduce myself."

"Okay, you've found me," said Melody.

"I am Nathan Dark," said the man.

The last time she'd seen him he was lying on a table awaiting the final stages of his activation, and his name was now familiar to her.

"Who said you should meet me?"

Nathan remained in the doorway. "My mother suggested it to me," he said. His voice tone was flat, without expression.

"Your mother is Eleanor Dali?"

"Yes."

"I've met your mother, and she has told me a little about you. Please come in." She motioned to an empty chair near her.

Nathan carefully shut the door behind him, crossed the room and sat down in the chair, hands in his lap, his back rigid.

There was an awkward silence as they stared at each other. It seemed an eternity before Melody finally spoke.

"Eleanor tells me you want to be an actor."

"Yes. I'm a student right now, but mother says I'm making progress. She suggested that you and I might work together to improve our craft in the future."

I thought my emotions were dull at first, thought Melody, but this guy beats that. "She also mentioned that to me. It could be fun."

"Fun?" said Nathan. "My intention is to be a professional actor, and I expect to work hard at it. I'm just getting started."

"So am I. I'm sure your mother is a good teacher. She was a wonderful actress herself."

There was a pause, Nathan processing what she'd said.

"A long time ago, she was famous for her acting. Mother and I had wonderful times together after my father left us."

Oh, boy, thought Melody. Where do I go from here?

It was decided for her after another long and awkward pause.

"I know what I am," said Nathan, "and mother told me that you and I are the same. Has this been a problem for you?"

"Yes. My memories have been confused. There are three people inside my head right now, and one of them is your mother. My mother is there, too, and myself when I was a young girl. Things get mixed up sometimes."

"You were young when you died?" asked Nathan.

"Thirteen. My father had scanned me before then as a part of his research. I was his first prototype."

"I'm told I'm the second," said Nathan. "I remember your father coming in to scan me at the hospital, and I still remember the pain. I was an old man, then. My current appearance seems quite strange to me."

It was all said in monotone, without a spark of emotion.

"My template was made by an artist, based on what the real me would have looked like at age twenty-six. I was told your template came from another person. Your mother wanted you to be young so you'd be more appealing to the holo studios," said Melody.

Nathan rolled his eyes, the first human expression Melody had seen him use. "Mother has been, and always will be in charge of everything around her. It was nice to be free for a while, but then I had to lose my health. I did not live wisely."

"But here we are again," said Melody, "not quite human, but close, and we have another chance at life, or existence, or whatever. How long has it been since you were activated?"

"In total, I have only been aware for a few days. I was awakened again just this morning."

"Clinically speaking, I'm a few weeks old," said Melody. "I was confused at first and felt like a machine when I was told what I am, but it's getting better. I feel more human already. It's important to interact with people, Nathan. If I'm a machine, then I'm a learning machine, and I'm discovering that I learn very fast."

"Do I seem like a machine to you?" asked Nathan.

Melody had a strange feeling for an instant. Later she would identify it as pity. "You look totally human, but your speech is without expression. I had the same problem at first, but I've improved quickly because I'm dealing with humans every day."

"I must do that, then," said Nathan. "I'm sure mother will arrange it."

"Didn't you say she wanted you and I to work together?" asked Melody.

"Yes, but that was in the context of studio training," said Nathan.

"So we can learn to be human by pretending to be human," said Melody.

There was a pause. "I suppose so," said Nathan finally.

"I'll probably be seeing your mother again soon. We have something other than acting to talk about. Would you like to visit her with me?"

Nathan thought, then looked at her and said, "No, I don't think so. I'd like to be by myself for a while, to think my own thoughts and try to unravel some things in my head."

"I understand," said Melody. "Later, then. It's nice to meet you, Nathan. It's nice to meet someone else who is like me. As synthetics we're few, and we should support each other."

"I've heard that term, and I think it's inaccurate. Our bodies are synthetic, but our brains and functioning are human-like, and we are self-aware. We are a mix of both."

"Hybrids," said Melody.

"I think that is more accurate," said Nathan.

"I'll remember that. It's certainly sounds better than synths."

Melody reached out her hand. Nathan looked at it, then reached out and took it gently in his. Melody shook his hand.

"Thank you for coming," said Melody. "I hope we can get together again soon."

"Yes," said Nathan. There was still no expression on his face. He stood up, turned, walked to the door without another word, opened and closed it behind him.

Well, goodbye to you, too, thought Melody. I think you're going to be a challenge, but you did say some things I like.

The following morning, Melody went to see the mother of the once-living person who still survived as the intellectual center of Nathan Dark.

* * * *

Melody had asked to meet alone with Eleanor, so Father dropped her off at the front door of the mansion and waited outside in the car. Lunch was ready to be served, so Eleanor's servant led her directly to the dining room where three places had been set. Eleanor soon arrived in a black robe decorated with huge red roses. She looked at Melody with furrowed brow, and seemed anxious.

"Isn't your father going to be here? His call sounded urgent. Has something happened?"

"I don't think so," said Melody, "but I wanted to talk to you alone about something, so Father is waiting outside in the car."

"Oh dear, this doesn't sound good at all, but we can't have him waiting outside in the sun. Jason. Jason!"

The servant appeared.

"Please go to the car outside, and bring Doctor Lane inside to the foyer for a cool drink."

"Yes, Madam," said the servant, and he went away.

"Now, what is this terrible thing you want to talk about?" said Eleanor, leaning close to talk just above a whisper.

Melody smiled broadly, something she'd been practicing and was getting better at doing. Eleanor smiled back at her faintly.

"It's not terrible," said Melody, "but it is a secret and it will be our secret. Before we get to it, I want to tell you I met Nathan yesterday. He came to my room after I'd had my updating, and we had a nice chat."

"Oh, how wonderful," said Eleanor. "I asked him to meet you soon. What did you think of him?"

"Well, he's new, of course. There are lots of hesitations when he speaks, and there's no expression yet. It'll pass with practice. We talked about that, and acting, about maybe doing some work with you."

"As soon as possible," said Eleanor, glowing now, and happy. "I've found so much material we can use. Some of it hasn't even been screened, all nice work but rejected by The Suits in the front office for some reason or two. They can be so exasperating, those people."

Eleanor paused, suddenly serious, and put a hand on Melody's arm. "It's all nice to think about, dear, but it's not why you're here. Now you must tell me about our little secret."

"It's something that happened in my update," said Melody.

"Oh no, didn't the memories come through?"

"Yes, everything from classes and backstreet improv through every feature you ever made. It was a jumble at first. I have to relax, even sleep, to pick out individual events, but it's coming along. I think it will take weeks to sort everything out."

"So what is the problem?" asked Eleanor.

Melody paused. Eleanor was looking worried again, and neither one of them had touched their lunch. It was a spinach quiche, and it was getting cold.

"We don't know what happened, whether it was a coding error or just an extremely powerful memory that forced its way into the file. After the update, I initiated recall and there was a jumble of things and then a powerful memory in great detail. It was not about acting at all, though at first I thought it was, it was so vivid, so emotional it brought tears to my eyes. It was a personal memory of something that happened to you, and a secret I'm sure you want to be kept secret."

Melody told Eleanor what she had experienced in complete detail, and the woman stared at her, stunned.

"I thought I recognized the man, and I remembered his identity later from a holocube sleeve illustration. He was Allister Grant, and you made three features with him."

There was a long silence. Tears welled up in Eleanor's eyes, and her fingers twisted together nervously in her lap. When she finally spoke, it was a whisper.

"We were in love," she said. "It was real, not inspired by some passionate scene on set, but he was married to a wealthy Gorgon who threatened to destroy his career if he ever left her. Out affair went on for nearly two decades, and to this day I don't think anyone ever really knew about it. We were clever people, Allister and I, and terribly discrete. Allister was his stage name, but to me he was Allen Smith, son of a postman in Hoboken, New Jersey, and he made me laugh. I had his love, and then he went and died before the Gorgon did. I've always hated her for that. Oh, excuse me."

Her servant had appeared again, and looked distressed. "Is something wrong with the meal, Madam? You haven't touched anything."

"I'm sorry, Jason. We were talking so much we forgot to eat. Could you warm the dishes up for us? And please bring me a box of tissues."

"Yes, Madam." Jason picked up the plates, and took them away.

Eleanor sniffed, and wiped her eyes dry with a hand. Her self-control had returned in an instant. "That memory you have is from our first night together, and it was a special night, more than we could imagine. It was the night Nathan was conceived. Alan did see him a few times. That stopped when Nathan was ten. Nathan might remember him as a friend of mine and a fellow actor. I told him his father left us when he was a baby. In a way it's true, and I want him to continue believing that, even in his—altered state."

"I will certainly honor that," said Melody. "I promise the entire memory will remain a secret with me, if you allow me to keep it. I think it's a beautiful memory, so powerful it refused to be left out of any file made. We could start over, make a new file, update again, but I suspect that memory will still be there."

Melody reached over and touched Eleanor's hand when tears welled up in the woman's eyes again.

"Please let me keep that memory, Eleanor. It will be safe with me forever."

"Yes, of course," said Eleanor, and she squeezed Melody's hand tightly. "It might even be useful to you, something to call up when you're doing a scene with real passion. We draw from life in our art, Melody. You must live intensely, and experience everything you can before you will truly portray the human condition."

It was a lecture. Eleanor was back, her eyes were dry, the look of sorrow gone. She patted Melody's hand.

"Your father is waiting, and we haven't had lunch. Did he send you here to talk about this problem?"

"No. I asked to do it alone. He knows the memory was personal, but not what it means. He was afraid you'd cancel your contract with him for both Nathan and me."

"Well, that's just silly," said Eleanor. "Two women have shared an intimate memory, and that's all there is to it. The poor man is waiting in the foyer, and worried about our chat. Ah, here we are. Jason!"

The servant had returned with their reheated food.

"Is there more?" asked Eleanor.

"Yes, Madam. I made enough for three servings."

"Then please make up another plate and invite Doctor Lane to join us. Oh, and bring us a bottle of the non-alcohol champagne while you're at it."

Eleanor turned to Melody. "Let us celebrate the memory. And when your father arrives I want you to look angry, as if we've been fighting."

They had begun to eat when Father arrived at the table. Melody had never seen him looking so anxious.

"Your servant said I should join you for lunch."

Eleanor glared at him, and Melody pursed her lips in displeasure, eyes flashing.

"Sit," said Eleanor, and gestured at a chair.

He sat down as Jason returned to slide a plate of food in front of him.

"I assume Melody has told you about our problem. It seems to be isolated, and I think we can—"

"—Oh stop it, Donovan, and stop looking like you're about to faint," said Eleanor, and then Melody broke into a smile. "There is no problem, and my little memory is safe with Melody. Now we need to put my scan to good use. Let's enjoy our lunch and then talk about coordinating what you want to do with Nathan and Melody so it fits what I want to do with them."

Father let out a long breath, but his face was still flushed. "Okay," he said.

A champagne cork popped.

They ate their lunch, and then talked for an hour about how their schedules would fit together.

CHAPTER 9

Darin came to work groggy, and had to jump-start with two large espressos in the cafeteria before he went to his laboratory. The previous night with Marylyn had ended wonderfully in her apartment, but when he finally got home there was a glow on the horizon and he'd had no sleep beyond dozing. He had time for coffee and a bagel, and then there was the three hour drive to San Diego and the Schutz Fabrik facility where all of his projects would soon be housed. For the time being he had a long commute three days a week and new apartment expenses to pay until company apartments were ready.

Donovan was pressuring him to move to San Diego. This meant leaving Marylyn behind just when things were getting hot with her, and he knew two guys in marketing who were waiting to pounce if he was out of sight. Both of them had more than enough money to satisfy Marylyn's exotic tastes in food and entertainment.

Melody was having coffee with Nathan in the cafeteria. Darin waved to her, and Nathan turned to give him a blank stare. No sense in bothering them, since the chats they had were part of their training, but Darin was tempted to join them. Since her first meeting with Eleanor Dali, Melody had been using makeup and doing things with her hair and was just flat out stunning all the time. She had developed a twinkle in her eye and some of her conversations were just, well, witty, maybe a bit naughty at times. She teased Darin about his expensive girlfriend. Once she had asked him in all innocence if he thought he was getting his money's worth, and then there was that twinkle in her eyes again. He might have attributed that to jealousy, but knowing what she was didn't make that seem likely. All that aside, he thought, if she was a real woman, I'd probably be crazy about her.

He left the couple with their coffee and went directly to his laboratory to work with Carl. The synth was sitting in an inclined chair, and turned to look at him when he entered the room.

"Hi, Carl. Ready for a big day?" Darin put his espresso on a table, and pulled up a chair next to his project.

"I suppose so. What do you have in mind?" asked Carl.

His name was Carl Hobbs. The name came from two random selections from the Los Angeles telephone directory. The template had come from the military with no names attached, and two scans had been used so far, both from unmarried police officers who had done it for the money and had allowed only their training and job experience files to be used. The result was a synth built for combat, with the training and experience for use in any security situation, all specs specified by Doctor Donovan Lane, its designer and creator. What it was currently lacking was an identity, a history, childhood memories, parents, friends, the joys and sorrows leading up to its training as an adult.

Darin did not know exactly where the files had come from, or who was involved with the scans. Donovan had only given him those details for Melody and Nathan. He'd once said that there were enough scans in his data base to make a small city populated only by synths, and that was enough for Darin to know.

Today was the day that Carl Hobbs would receive his complete identity.

"We're going to finish your brain today, Carl," said Darin.

"So I will be a real person?" asked Carl.

The intelligence was there, only the personal memories missing. Donovan had explained to Carl what he was, and he'd accepted it without confusion or emotion. His face was always relaxed, dark brown eyes peering out beneath heavy brows on a square face. Heavily muscled, with large hands, he had an aura of quietly controlled and possibly dangerous strength.

The data files were in two disks. A happy childhood was there, a military father, growing up on bases and then in a small town, a girlfriend, a sister, and people he could never find or touch, only a memory remaining. For Carl it would have to be enough, the memories considered irrelevant to the purpose for which he'd been created.

"You will see yourself more as a person," said Darin. "You'll have a history to remember and learn from. We've given you an exceptional brain, Carl, and you will learn very fast with living experiences. There are two people just like you who will help us to achieve that."

Carl nodded. "It sounds interesting," he said.

"So, let us begin," said Darin. He stepped behind Carl, opened the port at the base of his skull and pulled out a loading tray accommodating up to four disks. He loaded two disks into it with tweezers. One tap with the tweezers, and the tray retracted, and Darin closed up the port.

"Lean back and relax," said Darin. "It'll take a few minutes for the program to connect the disks to the proper layers and distribute the data. It'll come slowly at first, but let me know when you begin to sense something new."

Carl relaxed and closed his eyes, and in a few minutes Darin noticed eye movement beneath eye lids, as if the synth were dreaming.

"Are you getting something?" asked Darin.

"Yes. There are many people in different places. It's all blurred together. The face of one woman seems familiar. She is beautiful, and smiling at me."

"Could be your mother?" said Darin.

"No. I have no mother, and no father," said Carl dreamily. "I have the memories of real people, but they are not my memories. I am an artificial being, and you are giving me these memories to establish a sense of identity. I understand that."

"Those are human memories, Carl, and they will be as much a part of you as if you were born to them. You will see yourself as human in time, I can promise you that."

Carl opened his eyes. "I can accept that for now, Doctor Post, but I think that eventually I'm going to want more than that."

"And what might that be?" asked Darin.

"I will want to be like you, Doctor Post, a true, functioning human being in every way."

"We will make that our goal, Carl," said Darin, but as he said it and looked into the synth's dark eyes he felt hairs moving on the back of his neck.

* * * *

Father accompanied them to their first acting lesson with Eleanor Dali. Ebony was in Melody's lap and studying Nathan's face as they sat shoulder to shoulder in the back seat of the autocar. Nathan stared straight ahead. "I don't think she likes me," he said.

"She just met you," said Melody. "Hold out your hand so she can sniff it."

"She'll bite me," said Nathan.

"No she won't. Move your hand slowly, if it worries you. She's going to be with us a lot of the time."

Nathan moved his hand slowly, and then stopped when the dog's ears rose up. Ebony looked up at Melody, who patted her head and smiled. "Keep going," said Melody.

Ebony turned and sniffed at Nathan's hand, looked up at him. Her tail moved in Melody's lap.

"Touch her gently on the little knob above her eyebrows. She likes it there," said Melody.

Nathan did so, ever so gently, and Ebony blinked slowly, then wagged her tail.

"See, she accepts you," said Melody as Nathan rubbed Ebony's head gently.

"I hope so," said Nathan. "She is growing fast."

"I can feel it in my lap," said Melody. "Suddenly her feet are huge, and she isn't the little ball of fur I could hold in my hands."

"Hybrids can be very large. It's hard to predict how large, but size is in her heritage," said Father from the front seat of the car.

"We are hybrids," said Nathan suddenly.

Melody thought for a moment. "Yes, I suppose in a way we are."

"Not the same thing. Ebony is a DNA mix. That doesn't apply to you two," said Father.

"Dear Daddy always has a clinical answer to everything," Melody explained to Nathan. "He has trouble classifying similarities."

"Wow, that is profound," said Father, and smiled.

"Yes, it is," said Melody, and smiled sweetly back at him.

Nathan withdrew his hand, and Ebony mumbled, looked up at Melody and wagged her tail, a worshipful expression on her face.

"My baby," said Melody, and cupped Ebony's chin in her hand.

"Inseparable," said Father, and then he made the call to Eleanor to open the gate for them as they arrived at the mansion.

This time it was Eleanor who met them at the door.

"Come in, dears. Everyone is so anxious to work with you."

Everyone?

"Jason will take you to the study, and you can work there," said Eleanor to Father. She turned to Nathan and held out her hands to him. "Kiss, kiss," she said, and Nathan kissed her lightly on both cheeks.

"Hello, mother," he said, and Eleanor flushed with joy.

Father took Ebony with him, and the dog whimpered. Eleanor heard it and said, "Jason will bring you some lunch and a nice bowl for your doggy later."

She took Melody and Nathan to a set of double doors towards the rear of the mansion, and opened them dramatically.

It was a theatre, with a stage and wings, and five rows of plush seats facing the front. The stage was brightly lit, with three chairs at its center. The rest of the space was in gloom, the walls covered with folds of fabric, spotlights, now darkened, hanging from trellises in the ceiling. Several people sat in chairs along the walls, and Eleanor gestured at them. "You'll meet my associates later," she said. "We will be on the stage."

They climbed four steps to the stage, and Melody and Nathan sat in folding chairs opposite each other, their knees almost touching. Eleanor sat in the third chair, beneath which there was a stack of bound documents on the floor. She handed one to each of them, and leaned forward to whisper.

"We'll begin with a reading. The work should be familiar to both of you. Your parts are marked in color. Just read the words the first time through. Your audience knows nothing about you; you're just two young actors I'm working with because I feel you have potential. Now, turn to page one."

The title was 'Far into the Night', and the first scene was a bedroom argument ending in love making. The entire play came back to Melody in a rush, for not only had she seen it several times on holovision it was also a part of Eleanor's early memories of classes with Anna Wilcox. Nathan looked at her, and raised an eyebrow.

"Begin, please, and project to your audience, Melody. The first line is yours."

Melody was hesitant at first, her voice shaky with nerves, and Nathan's responses, while accurate, were flat and emotionless. Aren't we an exciting pair, she thought, but Eleanor didn't seem to mind, her only comments, "Louder, please," to both of them.

The scene ran twelve pages, ending with direction for a couple making passionate love on a bed. At least that part sounds interesting, thought Melody. I wonder what Nathan feels about doing that? She smiled at him, but he looked back blankly at her. Or not. Maybe he doesn't like girls.

"Any problems hearing the dialogue?" Eleanor called out to their audience.

"Loud and clear, Eleanor," said a male voice in the gloom.

"Good. Now we'll do it again, this time with some expression, some emotion, but don't force it. We will build in layers. Page one."

"I've memorized the scene," said Melody.

"Me, too," said Nathan.

Eleanor put a finger to her lips. "Too fast," she warned. "Just read from the page."

Melody understood. The entire play was hard wired into their memories before they'd even stepped on stage. Their audience would certainly wonder about that.

They did it again, and again, three more times, each time managing to get more expression of emotion in their responses, but it was an obvious struggle for Nathan. Eleanor coached them in character background and subtext, the latter a concept neither of them understood until later.

They came to the end of their final read for the day. Eleanor smiled. "Better," she said, "but it will get much better than that. The scene gets quite physical at the end, but we have no bed here. Nathan, you may kiss your co-star now. You are supposed to be in love with her."

"What?" said Nathan, looking stunned.

"I want you to kiss Melody, dear, gently and on the mouth. Show us a moment of tender love, please."

Nathan seemed paralyzed. Melody leaned forward and took his hands in hers, feeling a new excitement. "If it's a big chore, let's get it over with," she said and smiled.

Nathan blinked, looked at his mother, back to Melody, then leaned forward and kissed her firmly on the mouth.

"Assertive, yes, tender, no," said Melody, and chuckled.

"Again," said Eleanor, "this time slowly and lightly."

Their first contact seemed to have removed some inhibition in Nathan's mind. Melody helped by leaning close and this time their lips came together slowly and gently with light caresses, and both of them closed their eyes.

"You'll be doing a lot of that, and more, in the parts you play," said Eleanor, "and you will have to do it all in front of a grinning crew. It's not as easy or nice as it appears on screen."

"Still sounds like fun," said Melody, amused by the surprised look on Nathan's face.

"This is enough for today," said Eleanor. "I want you to meet my associates, now. They will play key roles in your professional development. We'll have some lunch, and then do your makeovers."

"Our makeovers?' asked Melody.

"If you're going to be stars in the industry, you must look the part. It will not be an ordeal, because both of you have good basics, and I have Jennifer and Lee working with us. The physical part is the easiest; your personalities will develop as we do The Work, as we call it. Come with me."

They followed her off the stage, down four steps into the gloom. Their little audience rose from their chairs as they approached, and Eleanor introduced them one by one.

"I want you all to meet my new protégés Melody Lane and Nathan Dark. Together you will be the team that lifts these dears to stardom."

Jennifer Anders was their hairdresser, a slender young woman with dark, brooding eyes and multiple piercings in nose and ears. She clasped Melody's hand warmly, but sneered at Nathan, eyes flashing.

Lee Dupres kissed Melody's hand grandly, then cupped Nathan's chin in one hand to study him in a creative pose. "Your hair color will have to change," he said.

Dennis Hopkins was a young holo director only six years out of university, and in search of hot properties. Eleanor introduced him as a young talent with enormous potential, and not afraid to do new things. Dennis smiled and nodded, but did not shake their hands.

Wallace Benson smiled and shook their hands vigorously. "I'm so grateful for this opportunity to work with you," he said. A nice looking kid, Melody thought, but he needed to eat more so his clothes would fit. Eleanor put an arm around him.

"First in his class at USC," she said, "and in two years he's already sold three screenplays. I was so lucky to get him on contract before the studios locked him into a staff position. He will create wonderful work, just for you two, some original, some from novels I have options on. It will be such fun."

Eleanor released Wallace, and then stepped up to a portly and balding middle-aged man who grinned as she kissed him on the cheek. "I've saved the best for the last. We've worked together for twenty years. This genius of a man got work for me when many people thought all I could do was retire.

This is my friend, my love, my agent. His name is Tom Lisco, and now he is your agent, my dears, and when you're ready he will be there to guide your careers. Tom, meet Melody Lane and Nathan Dark."

Tom shook their hands and smiled warmly, yet seemed reserved to them. "Eleanor has high hopes for you. Be ready to work hard, and listen to your teacher. She's a good one, and she has done everything in this business. I hope I'll be able to open some doors for you."

Melody sensed that at that moment, at least, Tom Lisco was not enthused about them. It was not likely that the first readings they had done onstage had impressed anyone.

Three other people were not introduced, and turned out to be drivers for those they had met. Those three did not accompany them to lunch in Eleanor's grand dining room and a wonderful Italian meal with chicken and pasta and a light blush wine. Eleanor dominated the conversation with tales from her working past, and deftly deflected personal questions directed towards Nathan and Melody, who said nothing during the entire meal.

After lunch, everyone left except Jennifer and Lee, who went upstairs to prepare for their makeover duties. Father was still working in the study. Melody wanted to check on Ebony, but Eleanor insisted they go upstairs immediately, and so they did.

Contrary to what they had been told, it was indeed an ordeal.

Their hair was washed, colored, streaked, styled, their nails filed and polished, eyebrows plucked, makeup applied with brush, pencil, pen, pad. Melody fell asleep twice while Nathan stared at himself in a mirror to watch the transformation.

Nathan's hair was now black, the shadowing around his eyes making him look brooding, with a hint of danger. Melody's hair, naturally dark, billowed above her forehead in a great wave that spilled down the right side of her face, her eyes lined in dark purple, her lips glossed in deep red.

Melody smiled. "Wow, that's beautiful."

"Yes, you are," said Lee. "This will be your look, on stage and off. It will require a great deal of maintenance."

"We'll always be here when you're working," said Jennifer.

"Every day?" asked Melody.

"Every day," Lee and Jennifer said in unison.

"That sounds tedious," said Melody.

"Part of the job," said Lee. "Bring along a book to read, and it'll go faster."

The man had no sympathy at all for her. Melody decided she didn't like him. Later, she changed her mind.

It was time to leave for the day, but they would be at it again at eight the following morning. Their regimen would be six days a week and they were required to arrive at six for makeup. The entire schedule seemed silly to Melody, since all they were doing was reading scripts on a brightly lit stage.

She had no way of knowing how rapidly the procedures would change, going from readings to action run through to performance with full sets and costumes. When asked about the accelerated schedule, Eleanor would only tap Melody on the forehead and say, "All the training, the basic education, is in there. Now you must practice the craft as if you are a professional, for that is what you will soon be."

They went back to Eleanor's study to retrieve Father for the trip home. When Father saw her he grinned and said to Eleanor, "Please introduce us. I don't believe I know these people. They are amazing."

Father kissed her hand, but at his feet Ebony suddenly ducked behind him and actually growled at her.

Melody was shocked by the reaction. "Ebony, it's me," she said, and knelt down. Ebony studied her for long seconds, softly growling, then sniffed at her outstretched hand and wagged her tail slightly. Melody picked her up and then the tail thumped soundly against her arm. "She didn't know me," Melody said, concerned.

"She sure does now," said Father.

"So sweet," said Eleanor. "My, but her feet are large."

"And she's getting heavy," said Melody, as Eleanor led them back to the front door of the mansion for their trip home.

CHAPTER 10

There had been weather delays, and the flight from Boston was a long one. Sheila Davidson was bleary eyed from the trip. She retrieved her luggage and exited the terminal. A white limousine was there, the driver looking like someone out of a gangster holo. He held a plaque with her name on it. She introduced herself and got into the car. There were refreshments, but she had barely finished a soda before they arrived at their destination. The neighborhood was old, with brownstone buildings a few stories high. The driver gave her a card for her appointment. Business Connections was on the third floor, room 304. She took a rattling elevator up, found the room and went inside. A plump, cheerful woman greeted her, asked her to sit, and disappeared into an inner office.

Jacob Cross was an old friend, her father had said, and had important business contacts that would help advance her career. She'd already signed the contract with Interface Systems Corporation, and had four days to find an apartment before beginning work there. Still, it was Jacob Cross, and not ISC, that had paid for her one way flight to Los Angeles, so an hour of her time was not too much to ask of her.

There were magazines and a Bible on a table in the waiting room. She hadn't done her morning reading on the flight out, so she picked up the Bible and opened it to a passage about humility that her father often read to her. With a new PH.D. certificate in hand it would not be proper to forget where she had come from, and the sacrifices that had been made for her.

The receptionist returned, and smiled when she saw what Sheila was reading. "It'll just be a moment," she said.

Sheila turned a page and read a few lines before being interrupted by a door opening, and someone said, "Ah, Doctor Davidson, it's so nice you could make the time to meet with me."

She looked up. A tall, elderly man came towards her, hand outstretched. She stood up, and shook his hand.

"Jacob Cross," said the man. "So nice to meet you. Last time we met was in church, and you were a babe in arms, and now here you are all grown up and a professional woman. That suit gives you a wonderful, executive look. I really like it."

"Thank you," she said. "My father said you were an old friend."

"Indeed. Rob and I go way back, to a time when things were much better than they are now. Come in, come in."

He led her into the inner office, and they sat together on a leather couch. There was a huge oaken desk, and bookshelves along one wall. Sunlight poured through large windows behind the desk. The other walls were decorated with surrealistic paintings in swirling colors, and of a tower disappearing into high clouds. The tower was surrounded by flying creatures like bats. Closer inspection showed them to be small angels.

"Your father is very proud of you," said Jacob.

"He taught me to work hard and be courageous," said Sheila. "He set the example for me, especially when life became hard for us. I'm sure you know what happened to us when the socialists took over."

"Alas, I do. Rob and I have kept in close touch over the years. He was one of my elders when I still had much faith in people. I too lost some of that when I had to start over in a new direction to put food on my table. But God has provided for me."

"We lost everything," said Sheila. "The new taxes killed his business. We lost the house. For a while we were hungry, until dad found enough book keeping and tax accounting jobs to support us."

"Praise God," said Jacob. "With all of that, doctor, here you are, a success."

"There was no money for college. Scholarships helped get me through the undergraduate program at Berkeley, but the government had killed all the grants programs for anyone who had ever had money. I worked thirty hours a week selling food in a deli, and it took me six years to get my undergraduate degree."

"Summa cum laude," said Jacob.

"And no social life," said Sheila. "Graduate school at MIT was a different story. My research assistantship paid for everything. There's still lots of support for science and engineering."

"Especially robotics engineering," said Jacob.

"Yes, especially that. I had six job offers before I'd finished my thesis."

"So you'll be working for ISC right here in Los Angeles. What made you choose that company over the others? Money?"

"The offer was generous, a bit more than the others, but the work will closely parallel what I did for my thesis, and much of that is based on the original research of Donovan Lane, who owns the company. It was an easy decision to make."

"Will you be doing original research?"

"Development mostly, here in L.A. It's the manufacturing division. I'll be working on bionet adaptation to production automation and some other applications. I did that for simple machines in my thesis work. I can compress entire computer systems down to the size of very tiny chips."

Jacob smiled broadly. "How marvelous. Rob's little girl has turned out to be a genius. Someday you'll be doing new basic research like your boss Donovan Lane."

"That would be nice," said Sheila. "They have a new basic research facility in San Diego. It's called Shutz Fabrik. All the work there is company confidential, so they couldn't tell me about it."

"Secret work," said Jacob. "I'm a supporter of basic science, but I always worry about secret work. There aren't any controls about what's being done."

"Well, industry is very competitive, and new product development has to be kept secret until patents are established," said Sheila.

"I worry more about new basic research directions that involve moral and religious issues, like the old arguments about cloning and genetic engineering leading to, you know, customized human beings made to order," said Jacob, and he frowned.

"I'm opposed to that," said Sheila. "I believe in science, but there are limits to how far we should go with it. My father taught me there are things God does not want us to do, even when we are capable of doing it. We must follow God's will in the work we do."

"Your father was wise to teach you that, and now you have the opportunity to do it. Robotics has advanced so rapidly. Many human jobs have been lost in manufacturing."

"The hope is to free people to do other things. It has been difficult because people can't afford to get the new training they need. That is the fault of our government," Sheila said firmly.

"I agree with that," said Jacob, "but there are also jobs being lost in areas other than manufacturing, and ugly rumors about robots that look and behave like humans and might even be the recreation of a human."

"That's speculation, of course, but it's possible," said Sheila. "I don't see that happening in my lifetime."

"But would you oppose it?"

"Absolutely. If we did that, we would be playing God. I would not take part in it."

"Even if it were done in secret?" asked Jacob softly.

"Ah, I see what you mean, if it was company confidential work. I wouldn't want to lose my job, but I'm afraid I'd have to blow the whistle on that one."

"Let's hope you never have to make that decision," said Jacob. "I wish you the best in your chosen career, Sheila, and I want us to stay in touch. Here is my card."

Jacob handed her a business card. "Give me a call if I can ever be of help. I would be more than happy to arrange consultantships for you. It's part of my business, and some consulting on the side can make a lot of money for you in a few hours each month. Your father was so close to me he was like a brother, and I want to do everything I can for his lovely daughter."

"You're very kind. Thank you," said Sheila.

They stood, and shook hands again. Jacob escorted her to the door. "Use that card, now, and keep in touch. Let me help you if I can."

Sheila left the office feeling elated. She was moving to a new city, but was not alone. A close friend of her father would be watching out for her, a man who shared her father's faith. God did indeed work in subtle and mysterious ways.

The idea of consultantships also appealed to her.

* * * *

Max called a few minutes after Sheila had left. "Anything new?" he asked.

"I might have something with long term value," said Jacob. "The daughter of one of my former elders just left the office. She's a Ph.D. just hired by ISC. She's also a believer and not government friendly. It's just what I want, but she's in the manufacturing division and what we need is people in Schutz Fabrik. If anything controversial happens it will be there."

"My news is good, then," said Max. "I didn't have any luck until I went back a year to an MIT job fair and followed up on the interviews there. ISC hired three people, two of them with undergraduate degrees in Mechanical Engineering, the third with a PH.D in robotics. His undergraduate degree was in Engineering Physics, and he was hired as a Senior Research Scientist. I'm working the consultantship angle, and contacted his parents. They told me he's working directly with Donovan Lane. We can't get closer than that, Jacob. I have his e-mail. He's young, probably ambitious. I'll see if I can entice him to an interview."

"Don't move too fast," warned Jacob. "We don't want to scare him off. Our opportunities are more limited than I'd hoped for, and our colleagues will be expecting a positive progress report at the next meeting. We have some detractors there, Max."

"Detractors can be dealt with," said Max coldly, "but we'll have something for them, even if we have to make it up."

"You share my thoughts," said Jacob.

"I'll contact this young scientist right away. His name is Darin Post. Let me know if you hear anything about him."

"I will do that," said Jacob, "and good luck."

"Good luck to both of us," said Max, and they ended the call.

* * * *

It was testing day at Schutz Fabrik for the synth they called Carl Hobbs. Darin had installed the wetware the night before. The handgun was a nine-millimeter high capacity weapon now outdated by its fully automatic cousin, and more complex for operation and disassembly.

While Darin took notes and timed him, Carl took the weapon apart and reassembled it properly in just over a minute. He loaded up two magazines with fifteen rounds each in twenty one seconds, the strength of his fingers far exceeding those of a human's. The firing range was a single pipe at shoulder height, stretching twenty five yards beyond the laboratory wall with a cable system for the turning target at the end of it.

Darin tested Carl's system by having him shoot fifteen-round semi-auto strings over time intervals of ten minutes, twenty, ten and five seconds. The results were all the same, bench rest-sized groups 1.26 inches in diameter and centered on the target.

"You are a shooting machine, my man," said Darin.

"A better barrel bushing and properly swaged bullets would make the groups smaller," said Carl.

"This is more than enough accuracy for your applications, Carl."

"And what might those be?" asked Carl. "Will I be used by the military?"

"Possible, but not likely," said Darin. "I think Doctor Lane is grooming you for private, personal security until everything has been tested out with good statistics."

"I will be someone's bodyguard?" asked Carl.

"Probably. We'll see. We're not in a hurry."

"Will I be required to injure a human being?" said Carl.

"I don't know. We haven't added anything to your system that would prevent it, but the criteria for such action will be strict. We haven't addressed it yet. Would it bother you to hurt someone?"

"Yes, I think it would," said Carl. "My memories of humans are kind ones. It seems to me they are all members of one family, and I was once a part of them."

"You're only partly synthetic, Carl, and we've given you special abilities such as quickness and great strength. If it makes you feel better, think of yourself as an enhanced human."

"I will. Thank you for saying that, Doctor Post. Sometimes I get confused about what I am."

"Eventually what you want to be will be decided by you," said Darin. "You're an artificial intelligence capable of learning very quickly. The way you're constructed, your intelligence is enhanced even more than your physical abilities. Try not to get a big head about it."

There was a pause, Carl thinking, then, "I see, it was a joke. I do understand arrogance, Doctor Post, but the concept seems irrelevant to me. It serves no purpose."

"A little bit can lead to self-confidence," said Darin.

"I have that," said Carl. "I'm quite capable of following instructions, and I have the basics needed to develop independent judgment with experience, when it is provided."

"That will come soon," said Darin. "You'll be working with two other people who are like you, and they are more experienced. You'll learn from each other. Our hope is that all of you will eventually learn how to be completely human, Carl, because all of you might live for a long time."

"I look forward to that," said Carl, his voice flat and devoid of any emotion. It was a characteristic Darin had noticed in all three of the synths immediately after activation. But it was a transient effect that went away with social interaction, and seemed related to the original human personalities at their cores. Melody had changed the fastest, her core a thirteen-year-old teenager with a gregarious mother who had a wicked sense of humor, as near as Darin could tell. Nathan was coming along, too, and had his mother alive to guide him. Darin still couldn't imagine Melody and Nathan working together as actors. He desperately wanted to observe one of their classes, but still had not been invited to attend.

"One more test, Carl, and then we'll call it a day."

"May I read after we're finished?" asked Carl.

"Of course. What are you studying?"

"Criminology," said Carl. "It seems appropriate for what I've been designed to do. An interesting subset is criminal psychology. That's what I'm reading now."

"I'm not sure police work is what Doctor Lane had in mind for you," said Darin, "but I'm sure he'd approve of your reading. Let's go do a little gym work now."

"That is for physical conditioning, Doctor Post. Is there something about my physical structure that needs development?"

"Not at all. We're doing a strength test."

The gym was a short walk from the firing range. Darin led Carl to a heavy bag hanging from an iron frame. Two male employees were on treadmills, and glanced at them curiously. There were two universal machines bordering a bench press and dead lift area in the room. Darin motioned for Carl to stand close to the heavy bag, facing it.

"Here is the scenario. A person you're guarding is attacked by a knife-wielding assailant, and you intercept him. The man is needed for questioning, so you don't want to kill him, just stop him with a single punch. Please demonstrate that for me in attack stance. I will count down from three. Okay?"

"Yes," said Carl, turning slightly, hands beneath his chin, and dropping into a slight crouch. Muscles in his back bulged hugely beneath his jacket.

"Ready, then. Three, two, one—"

Carl's right arm snapped forward little more than one foot and struck the heavy bag at chest level. There was a thump that reverberated throughout the room, and the metallic screech that was the tearing of a heavy suspension bracket made of iron. The bag, now shaped like a peanut, flew ten feet before crashing into a wall and scattering a row of medicine balls on a shelf there.

Carl looked worriedly at Darin. "It was only half effort, but I think this was more force than you requested."

Darin laughed. "You might say that. No need to question the assailant, that's for sure. And we need a new bag."

"I'm sorry, Doctor Post," said Carl.

"Don't worry about it. It's a parameter problem, and we'll adjust your operating system before we turn you loose on humans in combat exercises."

The two men on treadmills had stopped walking, and were staring at them.

"Show's over, guys. Just testing our new security man. He's a former Seal, so don't mess with him."

Darin laughed, and the men laughed back, but Darin wondered if he'd made a mistake in doing the test with witnesses present. Lane would probably chew him out for it.

He left Carl in his room and wrote up a complete report on the tests, including the presence of observers at one of them. Before leaving for the day he checked on the synth one more time, found him reading at a table in the library and taking notes. Darin had to remind him to eat something. It was another problem with newly activated synths, since they required nourishment but had yet to develop any sense of hunger or taste.

It was a twenty minute drive home to his San Diego apartment. There was a call from Marylyn, who was desperate to see a new Raglione ballet at The Forum. He got online and spent four hundred dollars for two tickets to the event.

Darin dialed a meal into his kitchen automat and paid a utility bill for the Los Angeles apartment, then opened a letter from a Business Connections Associates after being tempted to trash it. A man named Maxwell Schuler offered him the opportunity to establish lucrative consultantships that would only take a few hours of his time each month. Schuler wished to arrange an interview with him soon and there was contact information at the end of the letter. Darin circled it with a pen and read the letter again as he ate his meal.

The letter gave a range of income he might expect from consultantships. The numbers were very large.

CHAPTER 11

"If I were human I would call it a nightmare, but since I'm not human and only a strange kind of machine what should I call it?" Melody heard the sarcasm in her own voice in the darkness of her farmhouse room. As a synthetic she did not truly sleep, but drifted into a kind of twilight, a state of total relaxation. The countless files in her exceptional brain were then reorganized, formatted, some discarded from the day's experience, others placed in areas of instant recall. Unlike a human, Melody had instantaneous access to any file in her mind, and without a defined hierarchy of importance her thoughts would be a continuous jumble of confusion.

Strong impressions with emotional content had a nasty habit of interfering in her mind's order, and this one had been recalled and disposed of when she was near complete consciousness. She sat up with a jerk, her breathing quickened, and she was immediately angry with herself. Next to her, Ebony raised her head and whined, licked Melody's hand when she touched her pet reassuringly.

"I should never watch holovision news at bedtime," she said.

There had been a report of a union demonstration at the gates of ILC, placards waving, protest shouts of 'Down with robotics! Machines are job stealers! What are next, artificial people?' This was the second demonstration in as many weeks, and had come without warning. She knew Father was worried about it.

Somehow the news report had combined with her own concerns to produce a new scenario that had shocked her into full consciousness and brought back her paranoia about being a synth, and hating it.

"Nathan doesn't have this problem. Why me?" she mumbled.

In her reverie, she had been performing "Romany and Deiros" on stage in white silk, arguing with her lover over his roving eyes when suddenly someone in the front row of the audience stood up and pointed at her. "That woman is a phony, a synthetic! She isn't an actress at all. Can't you see that? She's a cold machine, playing her part without emotions, and we're all paying for it. Stop it now!"

There were catcalls from the audience, and then a barrage of fruit and wilted vegetables thrown at her, and Melody wondered why people would bring raw foodstuffs to a play, and then a green melon hit her in the shoulder to drip red goo all over her silk dress and she was totally awake and gasping.

Immediately she could see where it all came from. The classes with Eleanor had just finished, and one more meeting was coming up to finalize strategies for the careers of both Melody and Nathan. Eleanor still wanted them to work together whenever possible. In their final class they had been doing 'Romany and Diros', and at one point Eleanor had stopped the play, taken Melody by the elbow and quietly said, "You know the script so well, dear, but you need to work on inflection and show more emotion in your responses. What you're doing is too dry."

Melody was stunned by that, felt she'd been improving, but knew that emotional displays and subtext were her weak points. At her core were two passionate human beings. Father had fashioned tear ducts for both her and Nathan, and it was Nathan who could cry while all she could manage was a misty-eyed look when she thought about Ebony being hurt.

Now she was angry. "What in the hell is wrong with me?" she asked the darkness.

She got out of bed and went down to the kitchen to make a pot of tea. Warm liquids always seemed to clear her mind. Ebony padded along behind her and sat beside her at the table. No longer a ball of fluff, Ebony was showing new muscle and sat on her haunches with her chin in Melody's warm lap.

Father came down a few minutes later, looking sleepy. "What's up?" he said.

"Bad dream," said Melody. "I'm being psycho again."

"How so?" Father grabbed a cup and poured some tea for himself.

Melody told him about the scenario, and how she'd connected it to the newscast and what Eleanor had said to her.

"Haven't noticed it," said father. "I can see you're angry right now, kind of a slow burn like your mom used to do."

"But she could cry," said Melody.

"Sure could, especially when she wanted something and was having trouble getting me to agree to it." Father smiled at a memory.

"I cannot cry," said Melody. "Your mechanical tear-maker isn't working, or there's something wrong with me."

"Nothing is wrong with you. Your eyes are all teared up right now, and you're not sad, you're angry. What are you angry about, Melody? It's getting worse. I've noticed. Ebony has noticed. That's why she hangs so close to you all the time."

Melody looked down at the black head in her lap. Blue eyes rolled upwards, and regarded her sadly.

"So what are you mad about? Don't you know?"

Melody thought about it. There was a long pause.

"I don't like what I am," she said.

"I've heard that before," said father. "I thought you were over it. There has to be more to this."

"Lots of things," said Melody, and she felt her face flush. "I remember being a real person, a girl having fun and then the memories stop and I wake up as a machine. I remember my mother. I can hear her voice, and feel her touch, and I miss her. I miss her a lot! That little girl I remember had a father, and I know it's you, and I call you Father, but aren't you really my creator in a different way? Sure, I have human memories, but my brain is a stack of disks you invented, and my body is a sack of water and protein deposited onto a titanium skeleton. I can't stop thinking about that! I want to be human!"

Father stared at her in horror. "Wow, when you dump you really do a job with it. I've never heard this from Nathan, or even Carl Hobbs, and he's brand new. Maybe it's because their cores are from older adults, not a young teenager like yours."

"You're being analytical again!" screamed Melody.

Tears flooded father's eyes. "I know you miss your mom, and so do I. God, I think about that woman every day. No, you don't look like her, but I see her in the way you talk, your mannerisms, even your temper."

Tears rolled down father's cheeks, and his voice shook. "I lost everything I loved in that accident. I had a technology, and I used it the best I could to keep just a little piece of the people I loved. I did the best I could, Melody. You are all I have left!"

Father made a strangling sound, and buried his face in his hands. Ebony whined, and at that instant Melody felt something break inside her. There was no pain, more of a sudden pressure in her chest that moved upwards and into her head, and suddenly her vision was a blur and tears were streaming down her face in salty rivulets she could taste. A strange sound came out of her mouth, and she was shaking. Ebony whined again and barked as Melody stood up and went down on her knees in front of father, burying her face in his lap as they clutched each other in a shuddering embrace.

"I'm sorry, Daddy, I'm so sorry. I love you. I really do. I don't know what made me so mean."

"I know, honey," said Father, his face pressed down against the crown of her head. "It made me crazy for a long time, until I had you. Now you're everything I love, all rolled up into one person. I don't think I could go on without you. There would be no justification for my life."

Father cupped her chin in his hand. His eyes were red and swollen, but he smiled at her faintly.

"Hey, you're crying," he said.

"Yes, I guess I am. Your tear duct thingy is a go."

"There was more to it than that," said father.

Melody smiled and put a hand on his face. Ebony was suddenly there, wedging in between them and licking their faces, her tail wagging frantically.

"I think I've just learned what makes me sad," said Melody. "Eleanor will be pleased."

"I wish I could tell you how to feel more human," said father. "Maybe Eleanor or Nathan can help you with that. I think Nathan's having to deal with his core's real mother has helped him."

"He complains about it sometimes," said Melody. "He doesn't like being controlled by her. He wants to be free."

"It's a familiar problem from his memories, and it helps tie him to his core. My new guy Carl comes from military and police scans, and he is definitely the best adjusted of the three of you."

"I haven't met him," said Melody.

"Maybe you should. Darin is working with him today. I'm sure they won't mind a visit. We're up, and we are awake. Let me fix you an early breakfast."

"Okay."

Ebony sat on her haunches, tail wagging, and tongue lolling, and turned her head back and forth to watch them.

"Ebony, too. I'll heat up the leftover stew. We'll have farm fry: eggs, potatoes, bacon and cheese gimished."

"Yum," said Melody. "I can taste the bacon."

"We're celebrating a breakthrough," said Father.

Melody agreed with him.

* * * *

The ISC track was behind the plant, an amphitheatre nestled back into the foothills of the coastal range. Employees were encouraged to use it, and also the gymnasium, where there were handball and basketball courts, changing rooms and showers. The track circled two tennis courts, where games were in progress. It was a Saturday, but still a working day for scientists. Darin sat in the top row of the ten-row bleachers to watch Carl warm up on the track.

"Hey, Darin! Mind if we join you?" Donovan and Melody stood at the base of the bleachers, looking up at him. It was Melody who had called.

"Sure, come on up. You can see better from here. Carl is just getting started."

Donovan and Melody climbed up to join him. Darin was again struck by Melody's appearance. God, she is lovely, he thought.

"So when do we start seeing you on holovision?" he said to her.

"Just as soon as Eleanor's agent can find us some jobs," said Melody. "I'll probably start out by selling soap."

She sat down beside him. Her musky, wonderful scent enveloped him. "Is that Carl out there on the track?" she asked.

"Just warming up. He's following a program, increasing intensity each lap for forty laps. We do it five times a week."

"Ten miles," said Melody. "Why? Our internal chemistry gives us the muscle growth we need. Why the exercise?"

"Exercise enhances the chemistry. Carl is bigger than you, and he eats a lot more than you do. We want the chemicals going to the right places."

"I don't have any trouble with that," said Melody.

Darin looked at her and smiled. "No, you don't."

"Oh how nice. You're flirting with me again," she said.

"And you're teasing me again," said Darin.

"She does a lot of that," said Father. "When do you think Carl will be ready for field work?"

"He's probably ready now. We'll need something simple to start with. His decision making ability is limited at this point, but it will grow rapidly as he encounters new situations. Too much too soon could cause a breakdown and put him in a do-loop mode. He'd just shut down if that happened."

"Poor machine," said Melody, and Darin saw Donovan frown at her. Melody was looking repeatedly at her watch, now. Carl had increased his running pace, and she was lap-timing him.

"He runs without effort. That last lap took eighty seconds. How fast can he go?"

"I've seen him do fifty seconds in the last of forty laps, and he wasn't tired from it."

"Well, we do have our advantages," said Melody. "I should try it sometime, if it isn't too sweaty."

"You actors are all hot house plants, looking pretty but not moving around much, I think," said Donovan, teasing.

Melody didn't respond to the dig, and looked again at her watch. "Wow, he is really pounding it now."

"Seven laps to go. I really don't know yet how long he can keep up this pace," said Darin.

Carl ran the final seven laps in a full sprint, then walked, hands on hips, taking deep breaths for a few strides before leaving the track and walking towards them. He came up the bleacher in four leaping bounds and sat down in front of them, face glistening with the perfumed perspiration characteristic of a synth.

Melody wrinkled her nose at the odor, but smiled and put out her hand. "Hi. I'm Melody. You are quite an athlete, sir."

Carl shook her hand. "Carl Hobbs, ma'am. I've heard of you. You're an actress." He smiled, and it was a nice smile, Melody thought. Carl did not have leading man looks, but was powerfully constructed on a six-foot frame with large arms and huge hands. Dark eyes peered at her beneath heavy brows in a round face, and he had a large, finely arched nose which she thought was his best feature. It gave him a somewhat regal look.

"How did I do today, Doctor Post?" asked Carl.

"Couldn't ask for more," said Darin.

"I'm probably on a plateau," said Carl. "It'll get better. A pleasure to see you here, Doctor Lane. It has been a while."

Donovan shook Carl's hand. "Your progress has been excellent. Are you ready for some field work?"

"Ready for anything you want, sir. Just say it, and I'm ready."

"Your enthusiasm is impressive," said Melody. "How do you do it?"

Only Carl did not seem to hear the sarcasm in her voice.

"I've enjoyed my training very much, but now I want to put it to good use. It's my reason for being what I am. Don't you feel the same way?"

Melody's eyes flashed, but she was instantly calm again. "Sometimes," she said, "but not always. Maybe we can talk about it when the time is right."

"How about right now?" said Father. "You two take a walk around the track and get to know each other. Could be you'll be working together someday. Who knows? Anyway, Darin and I have something to discuss in private."

"Oh, oh, more secrets," said Melody.

"We'll remain here," said Father. He gestured for Melody to leave with Carl, and her face flushed again with anger.

"Dismissed, sir," she said, and stood. Carl held out his hand, took hers and led her down the bleacher levels to the ground and out onto the track.

"You are angry," he said, as they began walking.

"I don't like being told what to do like that," she said.

"I believe our creator wants us to have a conversation," said Carl.

"Creator? That man is my father. Over half of my core comes from his dead daughter, and I'm all that's left of her."

"Interesting," said Carl. "I can understand the emotional attachment you must have with him. I don't have such a thing. My core is a mix of two or three people, and all of it is tactical training experiences. There's only a trace of family memories or other relationships. Doctor Lane is my creator, and nothing more. I will develop my own relationships and memories as I live my life as a synthetic being."

They were walking briskly, now, Carl swinging his arms, and Melody struggled a bit to keep up with him. "Don't you have any problems with being a synthetic?" she asked.

"Why? I am what I am, and was born to it. I've been given exceptional abilities; have interesting things to do, and a promise of tasks even more interesting. What more could I want?"

"I want to be human," said Melody, and then, "Could you please slow down. I'm not into sweat."

Carl slowed for her. "Sorry. Exercise is good for my chemistry, and helps me think more clearly."

"I get that by walking my dog, and it's not as fast as this."

"Ah, you have a pet for companionship," said Carl. "I've been thinking about that, but right now I spend all of my time with Doctor Post. Pets require time and attention. Maybe when my training is finished I'll get one. Do you have a large dog?"

"I think she will be large, but she's only half grown now. She's a wolf-husky mix. I named her Ebony."

"You have affection for her?" asked Carl.

"Yes. I like to have her with me. I miss her right now. I care about her."

"You love her," said Carl.

Melody thought. "Yes, I suppose I do, if you interpret love as caring."

"I think it's a good definition," said Carl. "There is also romantic love, which involves feelings I haven't experienced. I expect to understand that in time."

"As an actress I play with that in my work. I have to use all human emotions, and I'm not very good at it yet."

"The way we've been constructed, learning of any kind comes quickly for us. I'm sure you will excel in your work. Mine has not yet been defined for me, but all my training and core is related to military service. I'm sure it will be interesting."

Carl's voice droned on, as if rehearsed. "You are so positive," said Melody. "I wish I could be that way."

"Another thing you will overcome. Our cores are different, so our development proceeds in different ways and different speeds. I'm enjoying our conversation, by the way."

Said without expression, it was a revelation to Melody. "Me, too," she said. She smiled at Carl, but his face was a blank.

"They're still up there talking, and we've done two laps. How many more should we do?"

"Are you tired or uncomfortable?" asked Carl.

"Not really, no."

"Then let's do two more laps before we interrupt them. We have given them enough time for us to talk. They think they are being clever."

"I hope we'll have a chance to do this again," said Melody.

"We will. I suspect they have other plans for us in the future. What do you think of this exercising we're doing?"

"It really does help you think more clearly," she said.

They walked two more laps and talked about their core backgrounds and training, and at one point Carl said something that Melody would always remember with fondness for a new friend.

"You worry about not being truly human, but this is hard for me to understand. From what I've seen and heard, the emotions you show and the feelings you describe, you are human in every way and there is much I can learn from you."

It made Melody feel wonderfully warm inside to hear that.

* * * *

Melody was in a good mood during the drive to Eleanor's palace that afternoon. They had picked Nathan up at the plant. His left ocular had been giving him problems with random bouts of blurred vision, and the problem turned out to be a partially detached lens which was replaced. They sat shoulder to shoulder in the back seat of the autocar, Father in his usual front seat position to approve route changes suggested by the autopilot in the heavy traffic they were experiencing.

"It was nice to meet Carl Hobbs," said Melody. "He told me some things I needed to hear. It made me feel better about myself."

"I thought he might," said Father. "Of the three of you so far he seems to be most at ease with his identity. There's a hard discipline in his military core. Everything is an assigned task, or an order to be obeyed."

"Oh, I think there's more to him than that," said Melody.

Father smiled. "Do you like him?"

"Yes."

"I haven't met this person," said Nathan.

"You will. He'll begin his field work soon. Maybe when you two are famous holo-stars he can be your bodyguard, and fight off your fanatical fans."

"I'm sure that will happen soon," said Melody.

"That's what Eleanor has in mind. You're graduates, now, her protégés, and she has a lot of influence. That's what this meeting is about." Father wiggled an eyebrow at them.

They were twenty minutes late, and Eleanor met them at the door. "Where have you been? Our colleagues have schedules to keep," she said angrily.

"Bad traffic," said father. "The car got here as fast as possible."

They went straight to the theatre, and the people sitting there in a circle of chairs on the stage. Tom Lisko, Dennis Hopkins and Wallace Benson were there, and one man they hadn't met. Eleanor sat down with them in the circle. Father sat in the front row of the audience seats to watch.

"Hello again," said Melody, and gave them her brightest smile.

"We've been looking forward to this," said Nathan, and looked beautiful for them as a leading man should look under the direction of Eleanor Dali.

"You both look terrific," said Dennis, and he turned towards Eleanor. "Madam, you have done a superb job with these young people. They are definitely camera ready."

"And they can act, thanks also to Eleanor," said Tom.

Eleanor blushed with pleasure. "The talent was there, and the craft came swiftly. I've never seen such rapid progress, and I want their careers to develop at the same rate. The industry needs new faces, and here they are for you. What do you think, Mister Goldsmith?" She suddenly straightened, as if startled. "Oh dear, I haven't introduced you! Melody, Nathan, this distinguished looking gentleman is Daniel Goldsmith, Chief Executive Officer of Global Studios. He is a star maker."

Melody didn't think the man looked so distinguished. He was short, plump, and balding, and there was sheen of perspiration on his forehead from the hot lights above the stage. "Nice to meet you," she said, and smiled sweetly. "Likewise," said Nathan, and he leaned over to shake the man's hand.

"My pleasure," said Goldsmith. "I see the potential, Eleanor, and I understand you have a plan. Let's hear it."

Now, we're finally getting down to business, thought Melody.

"Eleanor and I have worked out some things," said Tom Lisco, "and I've already circulated publicity photos and bios to several agencies and studios, including Global. We are selling a couple, a package of two people, beginning with some advertising, a few guest appearances, then a series and major productions based on a script Wallace Benson here has completed and is ready to market."

"It's a Gothic romance, with Melody Lane as the heroine in danger, and Nathan Dark as her lover," said Wallace, twisting his hands together. "The story begins—"

"—Not yet, Wallace," said Tom. "Dennis will arrange a pitch meeting."

"I've read the script, and it's what we've been looking for, Daniel," said Dennis. "We need new faces to light up the screen, as we used to say. Those new faces are in front of you."

Goldsmith grunted. "Call my secretary. Has anyone else seen the script?"

"No, sir," said Dennis. "Right now it could be your exclusive property, provided that Melody Lane and Nathan Dark have the starring roles."

Goldsmith grunted again. "Are they under any contract?"

"Not at present, sir."

Why don't you ask us? thought Melody.

"My secretary will schedule the meeting," said Goldsmith, and then he turned towards Wallace Benson.

"Be ready to pitch your script, son. I'll give you fifteen minutes."

“Yes, sir,” said Wallace, and blanched white. For one instant, Melody thought he was going to faint.

“Whatever we do, Melody and Nathan work together,” said Dennis. “To the public they are a couple, on and off the holoscreen. Maybe they are lovers. The public will wonder. Two beautiful people, always together, even in their work. Always on set, kids.” Dennis smiled at them.

Melody leaned against Nathan. “What do you think of that, lover?”

“It’s a surprise,” said Nathan, and everyone laughed, even Daniel Goldsmith.

At the moment, Melody and Nathan were not amused. Even from her place on the stage, Melody could hear Father chuckling in his audience chair

“I’ve arranged an audition with Newberry staff and executives in the morning. Their advertising appears everywhere, and the initial exposure should be a good start,” said Tom, and he turned to Melody and Nathan. “Tomorrow we play with the nice people in Beverly Hills.”

“Selling soap?” said Melody, sarcasm dripping.

“No, dear. You’re going to sell diamonds.”

* * * *

Within the three dimensional projection shown inside the homes of a hundred million watchers, two incredibly beautiful people sit in low light at a table next to a window looking out at breaking waves under the light of a full moon. They are gazing at each other, the man in tuxedo, chiseled features, a five o’clock shadow, beautiful yet somehow dangerous looking, the woman in a sapphire, sleeveless gown, porcelain skin glowing in moonlight, a fine-featured face and billowing hair that can only be described as supernatural. They have finished eating, a few crumbs left on their plates, a few sips of wine remaining in crystal goblets. Soft, angelic music plays in the background.

The man reaches across the table and takes the woman’s left hand in his. A close-up of the woman’s face shows misty eyes and an expression of love that makes hearts ache. With his other hand the man removes a small box from his pocket and places it on the table to open it with thumb and index finger. Inside the velvet-lined box, now in close-up, is a platinum ring set with a solitary canary-yellow diamond two carets in weight. The camera pans back to the woman’s face, her eyes widening, tears welling as she first sees the ring. A wide shot; then, the man removes the ring from the box, hesitates, and slips it onto a finger of the woman’s left hand. Not a word is said, but there is a musical swell, another close-up of the woman’s face, a tear running over her cheek as she smiles and makes a single nod of her head. The camera pulls back as the music swells again, and text overlays the image, saying, “If you love each other this much, then begin your life together with a Newberry diamond.”

The advertisement appeared two weeks after Melody and Nathan auditioned for it, and within a few days after that Tom Lisco was buried in inquires about his two new clients.

CHAPTER 12

The meeting with Darin Post was short and disappointing. Max felt foolish about having had such high expectations for it. He'd done his homework on the man. Darin had been at the top of his graduating class, had been personally selected by Doctor Lane to be a close research associate. Their interests overlapped; part of Darin's thesis work had been directed by Lane. The thesis, titled, "Sequencing Neural Net Manifolds in Parallel Computing Systems" had even mentioned possible applications to artificial intelligence.

Jacob was desperate for evidence of work on artificial humans, was certain ISC was involved with it. Even the slightest tangible evidence of such work, especially if government funded, could be used to inflame the vocal, radical religious right and instigate the disruptive furor his board was looking for.

Max had made further inquiries about ISC personnel through Sheila Davidson, who was proving to be a loyal informant and had been quickly promoted to a group leader position in Manufacturing Design. She reported that Darin was not aloof, was generally liked, but was known for his expensive tastes. He had an upscale apartment in the hills, and drove an expensive sports car in private outings. He had a very expensive girlfriend, a budding ISC executive in marketing who had come from wealth and graduated from Harvard. Max had also obtained contact information on the girl, who had been likely attracted to Darin by his position, ambition and generosity.

All the elements had been there for a successful interview with Darin Post. But it had not turned out that way, from the first minute on.

Darin arrived on time, waiting less than five minutes before being ushered into Max's office. His handshake was tentative, his smile faint, and he was guarded and suspicious from the moment he sat down. He wanted to know how Max had heard of him, and why a robot geek was so interesting. Max was a skilled liar and well prepared. He told a tale about university contacts and connections to start-up companies with young entrepreneurs in robotics. Darin remained quiet while Max made his pitch, rattling off company names and the lucrative consulting rates they were willing to pay.

"With your background and experience, there are lots of new companies that would like to pick your brain to help them get started," said Max, and immediately had reason to regret saying it.

"I suppose they'd all like to know about the work I'm doing at ISC," said Darin, and his eyes narrowed.

Max was quick, but felt his face flush. "Not at all. I assume you've signed a confidentiality agreement with your company. You would never be asked to dishonor that. In fact, this interview will never be known to have occurred, by anyone, including ISC, even if you make a commitment to join our consulting team. Does ISC have a policy on moonlighting? That could be a problem."

"I'm not aware of any such policy," said Darin. "What do you charge for your service?"

"You pay nothing. Companies choose you from our brochures, and pay us a twenty percent surcharge on what they pay you. We are only a brokerage for services, and we do everything with complete confidentiality. Even without moonlighting policies, we have found most companies are biased against employees who also use their talents elsewhere. We certainly don't intend to cost you a position you already have."

"So it's all done secretly," said Darin.

"Absolutely," said Max.

"Well, I guess that's one problem I have with all of this, that and the fact that I only recognize a few of the companies on that list you showed me. The work could be interesting, and the money sounds fine. I appreciate your interest, but I think I'll pass on this one. I have more than enough to do at ISC, and I think I'll just concentrate on my efforts there."

Max swallowed hard to contain his irritation. "Your work there must be extremely interesting for you to pass up this opportunity. I suppose it's all company confidential?"

"It is," said Darin, standing up. "Well, I don't want to waste any more of your time. Do you have a card?" Darin took a card from his wallet, and slid it across the desk.

Max smiled, and picked up the card. "Sorry, I'm fresh out. I'll send one to you. I will be in touch from time to time. You might even change your mind. Thanks for coming in."

They shook hands, and Darin left the office. Max sat back down and looked closely at the business card.

"Asshole," he said.

That had been yesterday, and now he had to tell Jacob about the interview. Jacob would not be happy, and it was not good when Jacob wasn't happy. Max coughed, took a deep breath, and called Jacob on his cell.

"Yes?"

"Bad news, sir. Darin Post wouldn't sign."

"Why not?"

Max summarized the interview in complete detail. "He seemed hostile from the get-go."

"Give him a month, and contact him again. Donovan Lane might have known about the interview, and sent him in to check us out. Have Sheila ask around about it. She's doing some good things for us, and ISC likes her. That'll have to be enough for now. The board meeting is in an hour, and I want you there. Bring your pocket recorder."

"I'll be there," said Max, relieved.

"You might have another problem to solve for me."

"I understand, sir," said Max.

The meeting was in Burbank on the fifth floor of First Merchants Bank building. Jacob had rented the entire floor for the afternoon, and they were given access to the private elevators in the back of the building. Half of the sixteen board members attended, but they were the hard core of the membership, and it was the first time Jacob had not used his plush Canary Islands home for the meeting. Max arrived early, and ushered people into the room as they appeared. Two men had again brought along their secretaries. Jacob tolerated it. The women seemed to be loyal to their bosses, their inclusion likely involving more than business.

Jacob made his grand entrance, and sat at the head of the long table. He summarized his union contacts and the resulting demonstrations in Washington and at the gates of ISC. He mentioned an agent moving up in the hierarchy of the company. Information on secret research would soon be available.

"I don't think so," said Mister H, the CEO of an English engineering conglomerate. "All we're getting are rumors and speculations. I don't think anything is going on seriously in making artificial humans. The technology isn't there."

"But it is there," said Jacob. "We see that in the refereed publications from university research. It's the applications that are being kept secret. All we need is evidence of one government sponsored study, even in progress, and we can blow our socialist empire to pieces with the public outrage.

"Speculation," said Mister H. "People might not even care. The demonstrations can help, and we should focus on those. We don't really need you for that, Mister Cross. We can bribe union officials and politicians as well as you can."

"If you have the contacts, which you don't, and I am a citizen, which you are not. Foreign interference in our government is not taken lightly in this country, Mister H."

"I agree," said Mister S. "We need to keep a low profile to the point of being invisible. We represent everything the people of this country despise."

There were nods of agreement around the table. Mister H saw them, and shook his head in disbelief, and suddenly recovered. "Very well, I'm a minority voice, but I stand by what I say, and there is another thing troubling me that should trouble all of us. That thing is an accounting of your expenditures on our behalf."

"That is forthcoming," said Jacob.

"You said that at our last meeting, and two quarters have passed us by. You do have an accountant, don't you? We should have two reports by now. All of us have contributed substantially to your operating fund for AAAH without even seeing your articles of incorporation. We have shown faith in you, Mister Cross. Now, please, show us how our money is being spent."

"I didn't feel quarterly reports were necessary, but they have been prepared. I'd planned on an annual report, but if you wish I can send you the two we have ready right away. Hands?"

Every hand went up around the table, and Mister H smiled nastily. "This should be interesting. Thank you," he said.

"Other reports, please," said Jacob. His face was relaxed, but Max knew that internally the man was raging.

There were reports of layoffs and production slowdowns due to taxes and increased mechanization, all of it generating publicity to stir public sentiment, but the process was slow, and the government quick to retaliate with talk of excess profits by the companies and government tax incentives for mechanization.

They adjourned for cocktails, and a large buffet had been arranged for them. Mister H made a show of leaving right after cocktails, citing an important business meeting he just had to attend.

At the door, Jacob shook the man's hand, complimented him on his honest and direct contributions to their meetings, and waved a fond goodbye.

The others were already lined up at the buffet table. Jacob turned to Max, and his voice was the soft growl of a predator.

"I want that man dead, dead, dead, and I don't care how you do it. See to it, Max."

"Yes, sir," said Max.

* * * *

In the second floor prototype laboratory housed in Schutz Fabrik, Donovan Lane stood over a vat to watch the deposition progress of a new synth. In a bath of pinkish gel lay a titanium skeleton bristling with fine wires connected to a master board mounted above the skull. With a myriad of different electrostatic potentials applied, condensation of protein complexes out of the gel bath took place at different rates, but was not slow, the elements of tendons and muscles visibly growing as he watched. Under construction was a female form, and Donovan had taken special care in its design, for it would eventually be the reproduction of a friend's dead wife.

Donovan had played university club rugby with John Harper when his Linda and John's Jilian had been their girlfriends. Overnight the men were like brothers, and they carefully scheduled wedding dates two years later so they could each serve as best man at the other's wedding. After graduation they had kept in close touch, Donovan heading west to seek his fortune, John staying in the east to join the FBI as a forensics chemist. Linda and Jilian had also remained close, but it was Jilian who was first to die, killed by a sinister cancer that produced no tumors, a spidery thing that was all through her before it was discovered. Two months before Jilian's death, Donovan had scanned her, trying to give his best friend some hope, but his synth technology had not yet been proven. They grieved together, and grieved again when Linda was killed seven years later.

Synth technology had restored a part of Donovan's loved ones to him, and now it was his best friend's turn. In the vat over which he watched, the body of what would be Jilian Harper was beginning to form.

Donovan watched for a while, and then went to three other vats where synths were in advanced stages of formation. There was one female, and two males, all made from artist rendered templates, and with no scans yet assigned. There were only a few application approved scans left in his stock, including his own and Darin's. They had been making bi-monthly updates since Melody's awakening, a supplement to the protection of the work they were accomplishing together.

Donovan checked the progress of the synths. These three would be ready in a few weeks, so he still had plenty of time to figure out what to do with them.

Darin arrived in late afternoon after driving his sport car at high speed down from Los Angeles to San Diego. He seemed tired.

"I thought I'd never get out of the plant," said Darin. "The gates were blocked by a demonstration, and we had to call the police. Who all is behind this crap? I know the unions are involved; there were local 42 and 68 signs all over the place. But some guy was on a platform yelling about us playing God and making artificial parts for people. That doesn't sound like union to me."

"We do make artificial limbs, and hearts," said Donovan. "It's no secret, and all of it is hand work, with no automation."

"Not just that," said Darin. "He was yelling about making artificial brains programmed to do our bidding. Where is he getting this stuff? Do we have a leak somewhere?"

"I don't see how. There's only a small staff for the synth project," said Donovan, "and all of them have signed confidentiality agreements."

"Not worth much if the money is right," said Darin.

"I believe in our people," said Donovan.

"I think you should consider doing an investigation: records, phone calls, bank accounts, anything you can get."

"I think that's extreme," said Donovan.

"I have my reason, Donovan. I've been approached."

"What?"

"I've been approached by a company offering me lucrative consultantships on a part-time basis. They interviewed me yesterday."

"Oh, dear," said Donovan. "Are you unhappy about your work here, Darin?"

"Absolutely not. I was curious about a pitch they sent me, and went to the interview to see if it was real."

Darin told Donovan the details of his interview with Max. "The guy was slick, but he didn't look like a business man, and I doubt if half the companies on the list he showed me even exist. He was subtle about it, but I think he wanted to know exactly what I do here."

"Hmmm," said Donovan. "It could be corporate espionage. It's known to happen through consultantships with disgruntled or recently terminated employees. I pick your brain and pay you handsomely, and then say goodbye forever. Proving it is difficult. I could call Better Business Bureau and see if the agency is legitimate."

"The office door said 'Business Connections'. He didn't have a card to give me, but he has my card. I turned him down flat, but he said he'd be in touch again."

"Ah, hah. I think I'll have Carl check out the company. He enjoys investigative work, and it keeps him busy. Darin, I want to be sure you're happy here working for me. If there's anything I can do to—"

"—I'm totally happy here, with the work and with you. I was nervous about telling you about my interview, but I trusted you to understand. I can't dream of another position I could like more than the one I have right here," said Darin.

"I'm glad to hear you say that," said Donovan.

They shook hands on it.

* * * *

For six months there was barely enough time for rest, even for synths. The first Newberry advertisement had gone viral, and the agency had brought them in for two new ones for their campaign. Offers had flooded tom Lisco's office for advertising jobs; Melody and Nathan sold wine, jewelry, sexual aids and bedding, appearing as a wealthy and sophisticated couple in sensual and exotic settings. Off screen they were now regularly seen in shops and the best restaurants, dressed expensively and often in intimate conversation. Rumors were circulating about these two rising young stars, as yet undiscovered by studios, and the public heard all of them. It was then that Tom received the first studio inquiries offering scripts for minor parts and with auditions to follow. For nearly a month, Melody and Nathan spent their afternoons reading, their photographic memories absorbing everything in one scan. Auditions were arranged for mornings.

The job offers began to come in, but most were for single characters, not a couple. Tom had sent them to all auditions for the experience, but he had his orders from Eleanor. Melody and Nathan could only appear as a couple, and finally two offers came in that matched the requirement. Both were from holovision; there was a murder mystery in a detective series, and a romantic series about young, upward bound executives. Nurse Melody was stalked and tortured before Doctor Nathan risked his life to save her from the clutches of a deranged patient. And corporate executive Melody discovered love with intern Nathan in a scene viewed by half of the holovision audience.

"She has the face of an angel," said one reviewer.

"I cried hot tears," said another.

There were pictures and articles in the fan magazines, and letters poured in.

Tom got a call from Daniel Goldsmith at Global studios. "I'm hearing good things about that young couple you're representing. You know, the ones Eleanor touted to us. I assume they're not contracted yet. You said you'd call me first."

"That I did, sir," said Tom. "We've accepted no exclusive contracts for them so far."

"Well, I'd like you to accept one now. That young writer I met at Eleanor's place has come up with a pile of things I think are just right for your clients."

"You mean Wallace Benson? I remember he was working on something for you."

"Not then, but he is now. I hired him as a staff writer for the studio after I bought a screenplay from him, and he's working on spinoffs. There's enough material here for a series and several major productions, Tom. It's all based on a story called 'Ariel's First Love', and everything takes off from there. I'll send it to you. I want Lane and Dark to read it right away. The thing is perfect for them; I'd call it gothic romance, but there's more danger to it, some perversion even, film noir scary stuff. If they'll agree to it, I'll offer an exclusive for them, with artistic approval on any project. I'll pay top dollar, Tom. Top dollar, more than the union will ever get for them."

The man was nearly shouting. Tom could imagine him sprawled across his desk, sweat glistening on his bald head. "Sounds good. Send me some copies by courier, and I'll have Melody and Nathan read them right away. We'll get back to you in a couple of days."

"Don't talk to anyone else," said Daniel.

"That's a promise, sir. I'll read the script, too. In the end, Melody and Nathan will make the decision. I'm just here to advise, and vet contracts."

"We both know better, Tom," said Daniel. "Give me some help here. I can show my appreciation down the road a piece."

"I'll give the best advice I can, sir. It's nice to be working with you again," said Tom, and they ended the conversation.

At least it'll be nice until we get down to money talk, thought Tom.

And two hours later, four copies of 'Ariel's First Love' arrived at his office, delivered by motorcycle.

PART 2. STARDOM

CHAPTER 13

"Carl has something to tell us," said Donovan. "Meet us in the conference room in fifteen minutes."

"Give me an hour," said Darin. "I'm loading Jilian's wetware, and you wanted that finished today."

"Okay, an hour, but be there. Carl has found something important."

Darin punched the desk set off and went back to his work. The synth sat upright in a low-backed chair. She was slender, a long face, quite pretty, he thought. The hair cap had been removed, and three ports were open in the back of her skull. The operating system was in place. The quarter-sized disks were lined up for insertion. Each contained tens of thousands of neural net layers that were the memories and personality of Jilian Harper, the deceased wife of John Harper, Donovan's best friend. Darin inserted them in sequence, one woman's being on twenty-seven disks. It was always an unsettling time for Darin, giving life to a mannequin.

The boot command was on the final disk. He inserted it, closed the port and sat down to wait for the ten minute process to finish. It was right on time. The synth opened her eyes, and blinked.

"Hello, Jilian," said Darin.

"Where am I?" she asked. "Is this the hospital?"

"No. It's a research facility. You're quite safe here. Can you answer a couple of questions for me?"

"Yes, but what am I doing here? I was in bed, and the cancer was—"

"—Just a bad memory," said Darin. "What is your name?"

"Jilian. You called me that." The synth looked around, confused.

"I mean your complete name, first and last."

"Jilian Harper. What's going on? Why am I not in bed?"

"What's your husband's name, Jilian?"

"It's John. Where is he? I want to see him." The synth's voice rose in volume.

"Later. He'll be called. We just woke you up. What are your children's' names?"

"We don't have children. Are you a doctor? This doesn't look like a hospital to me." Now she was getting excited.

"You need more rest. Next time you wake up your husband will be here." Darin reached over and pressed a tiny bump at the base of the synth's skull.

"I want to see John right—"

The synth's eyes closed, and her head slumped forward.

"Looking good," said Darin, and he wiped the synth's face with a moist cloth before leaving her sitting there while he went to his meeting with Donovan and his synthetic investigator.

They were waiting for him down the hall in the Schutz Fabrik boardroom. There were coffee, and little cookies on a plate. Darin smiled when he saw Carl eating a cookie. "Hey, Carl, how does that taste to you?"

"There's sugar, and cinnamon, and a bitter nut, perhaps almond," said Carl.

"We do good work," said Darin, and poured some coffee for himself.

"How did it go with Jilian?" asked Donovan.

"She's up and running, seems coherent, the usual confusion and anxiety. I turned her off before I came here."

"That's a little insensitive, Darin," said Donovan, and frowned at him, then turned to Carl.

"What he meant was—"

"—I understand, Doctor Lane. Doctor Post has put Jilian into sleep mode until familiar people can be with her. This will minimize her anxiety. I would ordinarily associate the phrase 'to turn off' with an electronic device or a machine. Strictly speaking, that does not apply to Jilian and me, or the others like us."

"That was my point," said Donovan, still frowning, and Darin felt heat rush to his face.

"I'm sorry," said Darin. "I didn't mean it in a negative way."

"I didn't have a problem with it," said Carl, and he pushed the plate of cookies across the table towards Darin. "Have a cookie, Doctor Post. They're quite tasty."

Donovan smiled. "All is forgiven. So tell Darin what you told me."

Carl sat down, and put a folder on the table in front of him. Darin sat across from him, while Donovan paced the room.

"You wanted me to investigate 'Business Connections', and I have done so in depth. It is a legitimate business, registered with the business bureau, and has tax identity numbers at city and state levels. Federally it is listed as a subsidiary of Cross Enterprises, which has its home office in the Cook Islands and has paid no federal taxes since its incorporation nearly two years ago. I think that in itself might be of interest to the IRS, especially since a charitable trust is also run by Cross. It was opened over a year ago, but I've been unable to find any record of donors, or donations received. It is the trust title that caught my eye, Doctor Post. It is called 'Association Against Artificial Humanity', and I think that makes it of great interest to us."

"Wow," said Darin. "Does it ever. Who do we know in the IRS?"

"There's more," said Carl. "I did not stop there. The head of Cross Enterprises is listed as Jacob Cross, age sixty three, an American citizen born in Detroit. I have made a broadband search for information on the man, using public and government records. I must say the information processing system you have given me has greatly reduced the time necessary to do this search. Fortunately, Jacob Cross is not a common name, and filtering was simple."

"So what did you find?" asked Darin, feeling a little impatient.

"Twenty years ago, Mister Cross was investigated by the Treasury Department for fraud. No charges were ever filed. He was a television evangelist and operated a church called 'Tower to Heaven'. At its peak, the congregation approached half a million people, and many were donors. There were complaints, and church accountants were subpoenaed. The books were a maze of deceit, but masterfully done, and the best tax agents could not find enough concrete evidence of fraud to press charges. Some believed the station and its advertisers were even involved. There was enough pressure, however, to make Cross close down his operation. Now it appears he has another way to do business. I've identified his accounting firm and the banks he is using in the Cook Islands. With your permission, I can get all his financial information for you."

"You can do that?"

"Of course," said Carl. "It is a matter of trial and error at extremely high speed. It is also illegal."

Donovan stopped pacing, and grinned. "I think it would be safe. I'd also like to run this by a government friend before we do it. I think Cross is behind some of our problems. My friend has contacts with Treasury people; maybe he can open up a new investigation. I don't understand why Cross would personally pick on the robotics industry. It seems his focus for demonstrations is primarily on ISC. It's also apparent to my grant monitors. They are being publicly accused of funding synthetic human research."

"Which is exactly what they are doing," said Darin.

"But it's all top secret!" said Donovan. "I'm worried about losing grants. We have a leak, or this guy Cross is making lucky guesses. It's only an extrapolation of all the work we've done on artificial limbs and organs."

"May I proceed with my investigation of bank and accounting records?" asked Carl calmly.

"Start with the banks. I have to talk to my friend."

"Would that be John Harper?" asked Darin.

"Yes," said Donovan. "He can't help us directly, but he knows people who can."

And at the moment he will be in a most grateful mood, thought Darin. "He'll be here tonight to see Jilian," he said.

"We'll wait until morning. I'd hoped to get Melody here to help Jilian enter her new world, but I swear my daughter is working seventy hours a week now. She can't be here for even an hour. God, her mother would be so proud. But I remember when Melody was in the state that Jilian is in now. You and I will have to do the job."

"Tomorrow morning it is, then," said Darin. "Do you need me to meet with John Harper tonight? I've made other plans. 'Firebird' is being danced at The Pavillion, and I have tickets for Marylyn and me."

"Excuse me," said Carl. "If you don't need me for anything else I will be in my quarters, working on our new project."

"Thank you, Carl," said Donovan, and Carl left the room.

"I'll meet John at LAX. We're having dinner at Leo's at six. Why don't you and Marylyn join us? My treat. I'd love to meet your lady. We'll keep the conversation non-work related."

"I think she'd like that. The performance is at eight, and it's not far from Leo's."

"Good," said Donovan. "Six o'clock, then. Now let's take another look at Jilian. I want to run a couple of diagnostics before we wake her up again."

They left the conference room, and went back to work. Before they were finished for the evening, Carl Hobbs had already broken the account number, user id and password leading to one of the bank accounts for Cross enterprises in the Cook Islands.

* * * *

Marylyn's blond hair was a billowing mass surrounding her face. Her toned arms, wasp waist and attractive curvatures were all emphasized by the little black dress she wore.

"You look nice," she said, adjusting Darin's tie and then kissing him ever so lightly on his lips.

The evening was clear and warm, and Darin had the top down on the Audi. Marylyn leaned her head back, eyes closed, and let the wind tousle her hair on the drive to Leo's. Darin gave the attendant a five dollar tip and the Audi was whisked away to a safe place.

Leo's was packed, the noise level high, and the delicious aerosols from grilled steaks and ribs filled the air. Marylyn was immediately impressed by the gilded walls and red tablecloths. Donovan waved to them from an archway leading to a second, quieter room, and they followed him to a corner table in the back.

A slender man in a grey suit rose to greet them, and Donovan put a hand on his shoulder. "This is my friend, John Harper. John, this is my colleague

Darin Post and his friend whom I haven't met yet." Donovan smiled nicely as Marylyn held out a hand to be kissed or shaken.

"Marylyn Sommers, and it's so nice to meet you, Doctor Lane. I'm in Marketing, but we've never met before."

Donovan shook her hand, and Harper smiled after shaking Darin's hand. His eyes were moist. "Thank you," he mouthed silently, and they all sat down.

They all had a drink, and Donovan ordered a red wine with the meal, their steaks ranging from Marylyn's choice of rare to John's medium well. The salad course arrived quickly, and there was a small loaf of bread with an olive oil dip. There was small talk about the weather and the traffic.

"I can't believe I'm having dinner with the big boss," said Marylyn, apparently thrilled, and everyone smiled. She turned to John Harper, who was seated next to her.

"Are you a robotics engineer, Mister Harper?"

"No, I'm a forensics chemist. I work for The Federal Bureau of Investigation."

"I've seen holo-productions about that kind of work. It sounds exciting. Is your wife a scientist?" Marylyn pointed at the ring on John's left hand.

John hesitated, looked at Donovan, who showed no reaction. "No, she's a school teacher, fourth grade. She had other business, and couldn't make the trip with me to see Donovan."

"We go way back," said Donovan. "I was best man at their wedding."

Darin realized he'd been holding his breath. He raised his glass in a toast. "To old friends, wherever they are."

Their glasses clinked together.

The rest of the meal was free of tension. Donovan told stories about adventures he and John had enjoyed in college. Marylyn listened with rapt attention as John recalled some mysteries he had solved for the FBI. She smiled brightly when Donovan asked her what she liked to do when she wasn't selling products for ISC.

"I love to travel," she said. "I've been all over the world, since I was a little girl. My parents had the travel bug."

"And the means to do it," added Darin.

"I was raised in the Hamptons. My father's company designed and manufactured medical instruments. I love the arts: theatre, opera, and ballet, all of it. We're seeing Stravinsky's 'Firebird' ballet tonight."

She reached over and put her hand on top of Darin's. "I'm so glad I've found someone who shares my interests in the arts."

Everyone smiled.

Later, when Darin and Marylyn left the restaurant, Donovan and John remained behind to talk, over another round of drinks.

"That was nice," said Marylyn. "I really enjoy talking to ambitious, successful people who accomplish something with their lives."

They enjoyed the ballet from their seats in the Golden Corral area of the orchestra section, and had drinks during intermission. Still another five dollar tip to retrieve the Audi, and they were on their way back to Marylyn's condominium for a nightcap and perhaps more.

"What a wonderful evening," said Marylyn, and put a hand on Darin's face.

"Yes, it was, and it's not over yet."

She smiled, and lightly caressed his thigh. There was a pause, then, "Oh, I forgot to ask you about that consulting opportunity you told me about. I didn't want to bring it up in front of Doctor Lane."

"I went for an interview, but it wasn't for me," said Darin.

"Why not?" said Marylyn, and furrowed her brow in disappointment.

"The whole business sounded shady. I hadn't heard of the companies they represented. I think they wanted to pick my brain about my work at ISC."

"Is that bad?" said Marylyn. "What are you doing that could be so important to them? It's all public record."

"Not all of it. I can't talk about my work. You know about confidentiality agreements. You signed one."

"Yes, but everything I sell is publicly advertised."

"That's manufacturing. I'm in research and development. It's why I'm always running down to San Diego when I should be up here with you."

Marylyn's hand explored his leg. "Maybe we could rent an apartment there, instead of you living at the plant."

"Maybe, but they're expensive."

"That's why I'd hoped you'd take advantage of consulting opportunities to make a lot of money for only a few hours a month. It could be our fun money."

She squeezed his knee, and smiled.

"Maybe another opportunity will come along. The whole thing smelled, Marylyn. I didn't like the interviewer, either. He looked more like a thug than a businessman."

"We'll have to wait, then," said Marylyn, and took her hand back from his knee. "I'm disappointed, Darin. I thought you were more ambitious."

"I am ambitious, but I'm also selective in my dealings with people."

Marylyn sighed, and was silent all the way back to her condominium. Darin escorted her to the door, expecting more to come, but she put her arms around his neck and gave him a sorrowful look.

"Not tonight, Darin. I'm tired, and I want to get to sleep right away. Call me in the morning, say ten. Let's have breakfast here."

"Okay," said Darin, masking his disappointment. "Sleep tight."

She kissed him long and soft on the mouth, and went inside.

Darin dragged his enraged libido back to the Audi, and drove home.

Inside her condo, Marylyn deposited her purse on a table, and made a call on her cell.

"Hi, this is Marylyn Sommers. You asked me to call back at the end of my evening. No, he's not here. I'm alone. He's really not interested. It sounds like your man made a bad impression on him. There wasn't much I could say to persuade him. I feel badly about accepting all those tickets from you, Mister Cross. I have nothing for you. Well, if you try again I'll give you my support, but Darin is strong-willed and very secretive about his work. Yes, we had a nice time tonight. Doctor Lane was there with an old college friend who's a chemist for the FBI. John Hopkins. His wife was busy, and couldn't be there. Nice man. Oh, Mister Cross, you shouldn't. I've done nothing for it. Of course I love the opera. Oh, my goodness, thank you so much. Certainly, call me any time, and I promise not to tell Darin. My hope is you'll discover a situation he'll find acceptable. Thank you again, Mister Cross. Good night."

Two season tickets for box seats at the opera is so generous, on top of everything else. They must want Darin's services very badly, she thought, and then she went straight to bed.

* * * *

The party was held in the Mission Hills home of a friend of a friend of Jacob Cross, and all core board members attended. The sprawling estate was on the top of a hill, accessible by a steep, gated driveway winding up from a narrow main road with steep grades and switchbacks. Occasional turnouts offered views of city lights and deep canyons along one side of the road. Harold Skrin, known as Mister H to his fellow board members, rode in an auto-limousine with Mister S and his secretary Janet, a slender brunette with tanned arms and generous breasts. They chatted about the scenery and drank champagne from a bar dispensing four varieties, all of which they sampled.

The festivities were in full swing when they arrived. Harold blamed himself for their late arrival, and Mister S had been generously accommodating about it. Harold hadn't initially planned to attend, but then his flight had been rescheduled, and there was packing to do. He was attending the party for appearances sake, and would have to leave early.

Music from a three piece band filled the air, and there was the odor of grilled meats and wines. People were lined up at a buffet table, and a self-service bar was lined with bottles and glasses. A glass-lined refrigerator was filled with beers. Sliding glass doors opened to green grass bordered by rock gardens and sculptured hedges. There was a swimming pool, and a few people were splashing around and throwing a large ball back and forth.

Janet smiled when she saw that, and excused herself to change into her bathing suit.

"Wait until you see her," said Mister S, and he wiggled an eyebrow evilly. "She stores her suit in that little purse she carries."

The drinks were delicious, the food excellent, the conversations inane and boring. Jacob Cross and his shadowy associate Max were nowhere to be seen all evening. Harold managed to smile and keep up his end of triviality production until ten o'clock, when it was time for him, alas, to leave. He'd generally had a nice evening, and the opportunity to see Janet in her astonishing bathing suit. A good secretary is hard to find, especially one available for business trips

His host, whose name Harold had quickly forgotten, called an auto-limousine for him, and the attendant programmed it for the airport, Terminal C. Harold was the sole occupant of the limousine as he went down the driveway to the main road. The parking attendant watched it leave, and made a call on his cell phone.

* * * *

Halfway down the hill, Max had parked his van on a small dirt turnout against a wall of rock. Beyond the other side of the road were only air, and a six-hundred foot drop to the canyon floor below him. Five hundred yards behind him he had blocked the road with a barrier announcing road closure due to a rock slide. The sign was unlikely to be necessary at this time of night for such a short time, he thought, but then you never know.

One at a time, Max unloaded three generator powered spotlights and tripods and carried them uphill around a corner to where a generous turnout was located as a viewpoint. He placed a spotlight in each lane facing uphill, and another on the fringe of the road opposite the turnout. The generator was on wheels, and he rolled it to the corner and then connected it to the spotlights by a strip and a single, heavy duty switch. The generator purred to life, and there were three, short test flashes of the spotlights.

He waited. The night was very dark, and cool. The call came, and Max held the switch in his hand. It was only a few minutes. There were flashes of light on hillsides as the auto-piloted limousine made its steep descent around curves and switchbacks. Suddenly there were two headlights coming around a curve twenty yards up the hill. One heartbeat and Max closed the switch, illuminating the limousine with three blinding spotlights.

The limousine, sensing imminent collision, had no time to brake, could not go straight or to the left, choosing in a millisecond to steer around the vehicle light on the right and swerve back again without knowing the available space was inadequate for such a maneuver.

The limousine sailed off into the night and dropped six hundred feet to the canyon floor, exploding on impact.

Max did not hear the terrified screams of Mister H. He watched the car burn for a moment. Satisfied, he loaded all of his equipment back into the van and drove downhill to retrieve the road barrier he had placed there.

It was a ninety minute drive back to his apartment, and the work had made him hungry. He stopped at the golden arches for a burger and fries, and made a call on his cell phone.

"It's Max. The job is done. Accidents do happen."

"Thank you, Max" said Jacob Cross. "I can always depend on you. If we have any other dissenters, this should calm them down. I have something else for you and your marvelous database connections. There's no hurry, it's just some personnel information I need, but it's with the FBI. The man's name is John Harper. He's a chemist for the agency. See what you find out about him. It might be useful."

Max wrote the name down on a napkin. "Will do. Anything else?"

"No, that's it," said Jacob. "You are my right hand, Max. Good night."

"Good night, sir," said Max. He finished his meal and was home before midnight. He watched some holovision, went to bed, and immediately fell soundly asleep. If there were dreams, he didn't remember them the next morning.

CHAPTER 14

Melody and Nathan sat shoulder to shoulder in the back seat of the limousine. It was the biggest night of their infant careers, and they were both terrified. For appearances there was a liveried driver, and Tom Lisco sat next to him in the front seat.

The special screening of the Global holo-production 'Ariel's First Love' was at the Fox-Newberry theatre only a mile from Mann's, and the attendance was by invitation only. All the major players in the Hollywood industry, directors, producers, studio executives and their spouses, had accepted invitations, if only out of curiosity. Global Studios had not produced a new star in a decade, and some of the shakers and movers were wondering if Daniel Goldsmith had lost his touch.

The public had not been invited. Rumors of something new had trickled into the media, rumors of a romantic gothic series featuring two new stars named Melody Lane and Nathan Dark. No bios or photos were available; for the public, it was all a great mystery.

Melody and Nathan had been on set for sixteen weeks, six days a week. The two hour pilot would be shown at the special screening, but three regular episodes had been done and were being finished up in post-production. Everyone knew that a poor audience reaction to the pilot would not bode well for the entire project, including the future careers of the featured actors.

"What if they hate us?" asked Melody.

Tom Lisco laughed. "I've seen the previews. They'll love both of you. Relax, and enjoy the evening."

There was more to Melody's fears than Tom realized. Of course she wanted to see the project succeed. A lot of people did, a lot of people whose lives depended on having the work. She wanted her performance to be perfect. She wanted her performance to be so human that her audience would laugh and love and cry with her. What she did not want was the audience knowing that in the big projected three dimensional images floating above a dark stage, the writhing figures making love there were really two machines trying to look human.

Her fear on set was constant. What if there was a glitch in her wetware, and she suddenly shut down, eyes open, catatonic? What if, in the middle of a love scene, she suddenly began babbling about entropy production in free space? Not one person on the set knew what kind of creatures they were dealing with. Nobody questioned the stamina of leading actors who did not sweat under hot lights, or complain about odors or sudden distractions, actors who could memorize an entire script overnight and keep up with all the changes. It seemed that people were too busy to notice.

Sometime soon, Melody reflected, someone would have to be taken into their confidence and trusted to keep their secret. Eleanor had told no one about them. Melody had talked to Father about it, and they had agreed that Director Hopkins was perhaps the best choice, but it would be best not to approach him until it was clear the project with him would be continuing. And the time to find that out was now only hours away.

Melody nudged Nathan with her elbow, and he looked at her. "Are you nervous?" she asked.

"Of course," he said. "I've really been enjoying the work, and I don't want it to go away."

"Me, neither," she said, and nudged him again. "With practice, you've become a pretty good kisser."

Nathan smiled. "I've had a good mentor and teacher to help me through the agony of it."

"Why thank you, sir," said Melody.

I wonder if he feels the little stirrings I feel when we kiss, thought Melody? Father had told her he hadn't yet figured out a reliable way to simulate sexual stimulation for them, but he was working on it. For Melody it was a warm, fuzzy feeling, likely brain-centered.

"I like pretending to be someone else," said Nathan. "It has helped me to understand myself better."

I'll bet it has, Melody thought, and it made you reinvent yourself away from Eleanor. "Me, too," she said. "If things don't go well tonight, I'm going to start sleeping in until six."

"I like the routine," said Nathan.

For Melody, routine meant up at five, thirty minutes of running, pick up at six, make up and reading at six-thirty, a not-so-good commissary breakfast at seven-thirty, on the set eight to six with thirty minutes for lunch, director review and then home by eight with enough time to play with Ebony and then off to bed.

Six days a week.

"I don't like it," she said. "I'm neglecting my dog. Ebony hates it. I wanted to bring her along tonight, but the suits wouldn't let me. They said she might intimidate the wrong people."

"They actually thought it was a good idea, but not for tonight," said Tom. "They said a starlet who has a wolf for a pet is good publicity."

"She's a wolf-husky mix," said Melody.

"A big one," said Nathan.

At eighty-five pounds, Ebony's back was now nearly to Melody's waist when she stood next to her. One look from those sky blue eyes stopped people in their tracks if they approached too quickly. Her coal-black coat had grown thick, and there was a quarter-sized white triangle in the center of her forehead to invite a soft rub.

"When you're a star, you can walk her on the red carpet, but not to-night," said Tom. "Try to relax, now. We're almost there."

Both of them tried to relax, and failed, and then suddenly they were there.

There was no fanfare, no red carpet, and no throng of anxiously await-ing fans. A few people in tuxedos and gowns were entering the theatre as they pulled up in front of it, above them a brightly lit marquis announcing 'Private Showing'. The driver opened the door for them and they got out of the car. Tom walked behind them as they headed towards the lobby, arm in arm, and suddenly father and Eleanor and a nervous looking director were there, all smiling.

"Follow us. We're in the balcony. Wallace is already there," said Den-nis. As director he would be the first to go on stage after the showing. They followed him to an elevator which took them one floor up. The few people in the lobby didn't even glance at them. They were seated together in the balcony, front row center, just above a rack of spotlights. Wallace grinned feebly at them, and looked ready to be sick.

There was nobody with them in the balcony, but when Melody looked over the edge she saw that the orchestra level was packed with men in tux-edos and women in a rainbow of formal gowns. She saw a few people look-ing up at her, and jerked back in her seat.

Nathan sat next to her on one side, Dennis on the other. "After the show-ing, an usher will come to get you and Nathan to join me on stage. You won't have to say much, just be yourselves. We're going to have a good time," said Dennis.

Before Melody could answer, the lights were dimming and the audience was silent, and then, from projectors in a black floor, the forty-foot spherical hologram of the production appeared above the stage.

Music that Melody had not heard before swelled in volume, a melody soon to become known as Ariel's theme, touching the emotions of millions of viewers. For the next two hours, Melody and Nathan watched themselves in horror, noting every awkward pause in dialog, the weakness in sub-text in close-ups, the ridiculous poses and use of hands in emotional scenes. Melody did catch Nathan grinning at her during one love scene, had even known on the set that it was going well.

There was only one audience reaction, a gasp when Ariel was dragged by her lover from the edge of a cliff after she had fallen there in a fugue. And in the final scene when Nathan, as Ariel's lover thought to be dead, returns to her first as an apparition and then is found to be real, Melody's eyes filled with tears, but she heard nothing from the audience.

I feel it inside, she thought. Why can I not project it? There was no reaction, and I thought I was doing so well.

The lights came up with the end credits, and there was polite applause from the audience. Dennis patted her shoulder, and hurried up the aisle. Father smiled at her, and Eleanor gave her a thumbs up. Wallace looked very worried, now, and stared glumly ahead.

"Well, nobody walked out," said Melody.

"I'm satisfied," said Nathan, "but there were some small problems."

"I saw a lot of problems, big and small," said Melody.

There was no time to grieve. An usher came to get them, and they followed him to the elevator and down to a hallway taking them backstage where they saw Daniel Goldsmith standing in the wings. The man didn't seem to notice them, and Melody swallowed hard, taking Nathan's hand in hers for comfort. Dennis was onstage, talking to the audience, and suddenly he was looking at them and stretching out his hand.

"And here, ladies and gentlemen, are the stars of our production, Miss Melody Lane and Mister Nathan Dark. Please give them the welcome they deserve."

Oh, dear, thought Melody, and stepped out onto the stage hand-in-hand with Nathan.

The applause was thunderous.

Melody looked out and saw half of the audience standing, and others were rising from their seats. In the front row, a woman was wiping her eyes with a handkerchief.

Dennis gave them each a hug and they waved to the audience as the applause continued. "What do you think of that?" asked Dennis.

"Wow. Thank you so much," said Melody. They bowed, and the audience quieted as people sat down again.

"These two are the most professional people I've ever worked with," said Dennis, "and this is just the beginning for them. They are now under exclusive contract with Global Studios for a series and three major productions, and hopefully much more."

Melody raised an eyebrow at Dennis. They had signed no such contract yet, but suddenly she knew it would be signed before the evening was over, and that was all right with her.

Nathan did not change expression. He would go with the flow, as he always did.

"People will want to know how you became so accomplished so quickly," said Dennis. "Where did you study?"

"Well, we both had drama classes in school," said Melody. When we were human beings, she thought.

"More recently, we did a lot of class work and repertory under the direction of Eleanor Dali, and we really owe everything to her," said Nathan in his wonderfully resonant voice, and he pointed up towards the balcony.

People looked up at Eleanor, who now stood, waving to them, a huge smile on her face.

"Star of stage and screen long before holovision, ladies and gentlemen, and now she passes her craft on. Thank you so much, Eleanor, for giving us these young people," said Dennis, and the audience applauded again.

"And standing next to her is the author of our original screenplay, Mister Wallace Benson. Thank you, Wallace," said Dennis, clapping.

Wallace stood, beaming at last. The applause was lighter, but sincere. What do they think we could do if we didn't have a good script to work with, thought Melody?

"Another question from our audience," said Dennis, pretending there had actually been one. "Have you known each other a long time?"

Melody couldn't help herself. "Since birth, I think," she said, then thought, Oh, I shouldn't have said that.

The audience laughed.

"There seems to be a strong feeling of intimacy in your scenes. Are you a couple?"

"We're just good friends," said Nathan, and the audience laughed again.

Dennis gave them a sly look in reaction to their little conspiracy. "Okay, we can accept that for the moment, can't we? Besides, it's time to celebrate this wonderful evening together. Melody and Nathan, thank you for your inspiring performance. Ladies and gentlemen, please join us for a champagne reception in the lobby, and a chance to meet our new stars. Thank you for coming, and good night."

There was steady applause as they left the stage and were intercepted by Goldsmith. "The contracts are ready to be signed," he said.

"I am so surprised," said Melody, but she smiled at him.

When they reached the lobby a champagne reception had miraculously appeared; there were lines at two self-service bars, and three handsome young men in white coats were scurrying around the room with trays of filled flutes. Dennis led them to a place near the front entrance where Wallace was waiting for them, and the four of them formed a reception line where they spent an hour smiling and nodding and saying thank you to their guests. Young men or old, all seemed timid meeting Melody, while women played nervously with hair, gown or jewelry when they stepped up to meet Nathan. Wallace was having the best night of his life, and said so. Father hugged Melody tightly. "My baby," he said. Eleanor hugged all of them, and cried when Nathan hugged her back.

Few people introduced themselves, but Dennis made introductions for some of them, all studio executives, producers, and investors, and then there was Angela Heath, president of the Performing Artists' guild. Angela reminded them about union requirements for working, and the schedule for dues. Dennis shut her up by saying everything had been arranged for payments through Global Studios, and Angela went away.

No media people had been invited, but Global had prepared a news release, and had staff there taking videos and photographs that would be on the net before the evening was over. Goldsmith only appeared once in the lobby to have his photograph taken with all of them. He disappeared early in the evening, and Melody wondered why. Weren't there contracts to be signed?

Father and Eleanor excused themselves and left in the same limousine an hour before the reception ended and the last of the guests had wobbled out the doors. It was just the four of them, now, and Melody wondered what was next when Dennis led them to a new limo and driver pulling up in front of the theatre.

"Are you hungry?" asked Dennis.

"Hungry and thirsty," said Melody. "All they had was champagne."

It would soon be common knowledge that Melody and Nathan never consumed alcoholic beverages. The excuse was that alcohol blurred the senses, and lowered the quality of their work. The truth was that father had warned them both that even a small amount of alcohol could mess up the cross-linking in the neural net layers in their special brains. "Blue-screen, anyone?" he'd said, another one of his terrible jokes. Neither of them had found it amusing, and it was making their social life more complicated. People didn't really understand.

"Nicky's has the best burgers in town," said Dennis. "Nothing fancy, but we'll have privacy this time of night."

It was a ten minute drive from the theatre. They pulled up to a diner that looked like an old Pullman car without wheels. It was nearing midnight, but the waitress and cook seemed busy and there were four men eating at the long counter. There was a heady odor of grilled meat in the air. The cook waved to them, and his customers turned to gawk at the three men in tuxedos and the beautiful woman in a formal gown who were just dropping by for a late night hamburger.

They went past the counter to the end of the diner where there was a private, glass enclosed room with two tables. Daniel Goldsmith was sitting at one table, on top of which were three folders and ink pens. "I've already ordered," he said, "for all of us. Let's get this done first, and enjoy the food."

Their contracts were long, but had been vetted by Tom, and signature pages had been tabbed. Tom's initials were on every page. Nathan showed no reaction as he read quickly and signed. Melody gulped once when she got to the compensation page and realized she was signing a nine figure contract for three years of work, and promised extensions.

The waitress brought a selection of drinks: sodas, vanilla smoothies, and coffee. Melody chose coffee, black. They finished signing; Goldsmith put everything in his briefcase and shook their hands, relaxing for the first time that evening. Their meals, identical, arrived at midnight, a double burger with bacon and cheese and a special, secret sauce. There was a side of onion rings. Melody's sensors appreciated the aerosols and flavors of grilled meat. She couldn't taste the onions, but enjoyed the crunchy feeling in her mouth.

Suddenly it was over. Goldsmith said goodbye and left in his own autocar, his hand firmly grasping his briefcase. The rest of them piled back into the limousine for the drive home. All of them were sleepy after the big meal. Wallace went to sleep in the car, having managed to drink considerable quantities of champagne before eating.

Melody and Nathan got out first at their apartment building, rooms rented for them near Global Studios during production. They would now be expected to find their own housing. Dennis hugged them. "See you on Monday. Time to start earning the big bucks," he said.

Nathan was on third floor, Melody on fourth. They hugged in the elevator. "We're rich," she said.

"Only if we have time to spend it," said Nathan, and smiled. "I wonder if they'd pay anything at all if they knew our secret. I'd like to talk about that. Can we have lunch tomorrow?"

"Sure," said Melody. "I'll bring Ebony along. It'll be good for our image if the place we go to is expensive enough."

They both laughed at that.

Melody hurried down the hallway to her one-bedroom suite of rooms with its white rugs and furniture, and deco art. Ebony had been left alone for seven hours since the housekeeper had left, but it had been routine during production and she always seemed patient about it. Still, Melody always worried what Ebony might do if she had a snit.

She let herself in and turned on the front room light. "Ebony!" she called, and waited. A few seconds later, the animal came out of the bedroom, yawning, her tail wagging vigorously. Melody got down on her knees to hug her dog, her love, her attachment to the real world. Ebony yammered a little greeting, her face pressed against Melody's, and they went back to the bedroom for Melody to undress and get into bed for a night of twilight sleep.

Ebony slept in the lover's place next to her.

* * * *

"It's Max. I got that information you wanted. It was all in the federal data base. John Harper is a forensics chemist for the FBI, all lab work, so he probably can't do anything for us if that's what you're looking for. He's been with the agency for nearly forty years. Looks like he and Donovan

Lane were classmates at MIT. No children, and his wife died from cancer twenty one years ago."

"He didn't remarry?" asked Jacob Cross.

"No record of it," said Max.

"Then why would he tell our girl his wife was busy and couldn't take a trip with him?" asked Jacob.

"I have no idea, sir. His wife's name was Jilian, and she's been dead a long time."

"Well, I think we need to look into that," said Jacob.

CHAPTER 15

Melody's life changed dramatically overnight. Someone at the special showing had taken many short clips of the production, and then posted them online. By the following evening all the clips had gone viral, and were the talk of holo-fandom all over the world.

She was suddenly a superstar, and so was Nathan. They discussed their new status at lunch. Already they had learned the value of hats and sunglasses in public, after being stopped by several excited holo-watchers in their own rooming house.

"What do you say?" asked Melody.

"I just say thank you, and hope they enjoy the series, and then I run. Is anyone watching us now?" said Nathan.

"I don't think so, but I'd rather be outside on such a sunny day," said Melody.

They were sitting in a booth in a back corner of the room. A waitress had taken their order, and didn't seem to recognize them.

"What did you think of last night?" asked Nathan.

"Hectic, but nice. I was so nervous at first, but then the nerves went away. I actually had fun, Nathan. I didn't even think about you know what until this morning."

"You mean our little secret?" said Nathan.

"Exactly. All the attention, the money, the work, it could all go away overnight if we're found out. That's always going to be in the back of my mind."

"Nothing will happen as long as we're good actors."

"Maybe. We should talk to Father about this, and find out what the real dangers are. My imagination is too good at making up stories about it," said Melody.

"Mother never seems to worry about it," said Nathan.

"Eleanor was so proud of you last night. She cried half the evening, and especially when you gave her that big hug."

"She's proud of both of us," said Nathan. "Both of us are her creations."

"We owe a lot to our creators," said Melody. "Sometimes I forget that. I still have trouble separating out the human and non-human parts of myself."

"We need both. They work together. It's what we are," said Nathan, "and with upgrades, we'll be even better."

"My daddy's promise," said Melody, and then she peered over the top of her sunglasses at him. "He says he'll have that special something ready for us soon."

"That might help in some of our scenes, but otherwise I can't see the value of it," said Nathan, and he took off his sunglasses. "I also think these things make us too obvious here."

Melody removed her sunglasses, and smiled. "It sounds exciting to me. Aren't you even curious?"

"No, not really. Sex is purely a human activity, and we're not constructed or programmed for it. We can't reproduce, so what's the point?"

Melody leaned over and hit Nathan's forearm lightly. "Fun, Nathan. You've heard of fun, haven't you?"

Nathan actually smiled. "A good book is fun for me. I think Ariel's naughtiness is rubbing off on you."

"I love her," said Melody.

"So do I, on the set." Nathan paused, and looked suddenly serious, but then the waitress arrived with their omelet and hash browns with biscuit breakfasts, ordered for lunch.

The pretty blond, in her twenties, put their plates on the table and crossed her arms nervously in front of her.

"I can't believe I'm serving you here," she said. "I saw the clips of your performance last night, and you were both incredible."

"Why thank you," they said in unison, and Nathan added, "The series begins next Thursday at eight. Hope you enjoy that, too."

"My husband saw the clips with me, and I must say he was inspired. We had a very good time last night."

The girl blushed as she said it, then tore a blank sheet from her order book and put it on the table in front of them. "Could you please sign that for me? I promise not to tell anyone else you're here."

They signed, and the girl rushed away with a broad smile on her face.

Nathan shook his head. "As I was about to say, I hope you realize our lives have just changed in a big way, and not necessarily for the better. The studio owns us, now. Everything we do will be orchestrated by them. Everything. Our privacy is a thing of the past."

Melody patted his hand. "We'll find the time for it, Nathan. I'm not going to give up our little chats like this one. It's just you, me, and Carl right now. We're the only ones who can really understand each other. You are a friend, Nathan, a really good friend, and I'm not giving that up either."

Nathan squeezed her hand. "Same for me, but we keep telling people we're just friends, and they don't want to believe it."

They laughed. "Showbiz," said Melody, then, "I don't know what I'm going to do with all that money."

"Me neither," said Nathan, "but I'm sure the studio will find people to help us figure that out. One thing for sure, we won't be in that rooming house any more, and it has been peaceful there."

They finished their brunch, and walked arm in arm back to the apartment building that had been home for half a year. They hugged in the elevator and went their separate ways. Ebony gave Melody her usual enthusiastic greeting, and stayed close or in physical contacts with her the rest of the day and into evening when it was time for bed.

Melody read and relaxed, then skimmed the script of her fourth episode to be produced in the coming week. She had memorized her part in one sitting, and now made notes in places where a bit of improv might lighten up the flow a bit.

She found the clips of her performance from the previous evening, and watched them, unimpressed by the small format, but astonished by the over thirty million views received on the net. The gushing comments astounded her even more, letters of love and lust about twenty minutes of holo.

Life had indeed changed for Melody Lane and Nathan Dark, and it would begin on the following Monday, a working day on set.

* * * *

For Melody, life was quickly routine with work, work, work, six days a week, and Sunday was for everything else. It was a frantic, exhausting pace, with barely a moment to relax, or just to sit and stare at the wall. Gradually she learned how to deal with it, finding ways to work relaxing moments into days planned to the minute for her. Sleep was not an issue. Unlike humans, she did not require deep sleep for regeneration or cerebral reorganization. Twilight sleep, a kind of slowing down to a fugue state, was enough for her as long as she got at least three hours of it each night. Daily meals were quick snacks, since her nutritional needs were mainly satisfied by the special liquid protein supplements that father had designed for all his synths. A clear plastic bottle of the sweet smelling, white liquid was always near her when she worked.

Exercise was important to her, and started her day, running on the treadmill at home and going through a rapid series of movements with light weights that produced pleasantly warm sensations in her muscles and maintained the shapes and curves the studio expected of her. Occasionally she ran with Carl, when he was in town, but most of his time was spent at Schutz Fabrik in San Diego. She wished otherwise, and was growing to like the burly man with the quick mind, despite his still flat personality. Father said he was grooming Carl for security, but Melody could not see him in that role unless it was for intelligence analysis. She could not see a trace of potential violence in him.

After the second of her temper tantrums, which Melody had learned to act out nicely, the studio reluctantly allowed her to bring Ebony on set each day. Dennis had no problem with it, but it was a precedent The Suits fought against until Goldsmith intervened. Ebony helped by being the perfect observer, sitting quietly by the director's chair to watch the action, or sleeping in the pile of colorful pillows provided for her. At first the crew was nervous around Ebony. She was now large enough to be impressive and had the steady, blue-eyed gaze of the wolf in her. She did not bark or whine, but held herself with dignity, always alert, and at first meeting there was a definite aura of danger around her. Gradually the crew relaxed, and even made her a big doggy dish embossed with her name and a gold star, and kept it filled with water by her throne of pillows.

There was only one incident that marred Ebony's presence on set, and nearly led to her forced exile. It was the first rehearsal of a bedroom scene where Ariel is confronted by her dark lover Eric over her secret investigation into his questionable past. Melody and Nathan were partially clothed for the scene, and the lighting was dim for it. Later, Melody wondered if Ebony had mistaken Nathan for someone strange to her. The middle of the scene was suddenly loud, and violent, Eric shouting at Ariel, striking her and throwing her onto the bed, then climbing up on top of her.

There was a low, menacing growl from the darkness off set, and everyone froze.

Ebony didn't charge, but stalked into the light, her back and head low, hair bristling, her lips pulled back in a horrible snarl that only a true wolf could imitate, and her growl promised mutilation and death.

Nathan rolled off Melody to one side of the bed as Ebony jumped up on the other side and took a step towards him, a splatter of drool staining the bed covers.

Melody screamed, "Ebony, stop! Bad dog! Off garbage! Ebony, it's Nathan!"

Ebony's jaws snapped shut, and she jerked upright.

"Off the bed! Lie down! Bad dog, Ebony!" Melody pointed towards the darkness.

Ebony whined pitifully, turned and jumped off the bed, then crept out of the light to her mound of pillows and flounced down there to sulk.

"Off garbage?" asked Nathan.

"It's what I said to get her off things when she was a puppy," said Melody.

"That is not going to happen again," said Dennis. "If it does, the dog is gone forever. Five minutes, people, and then we'll try it again. Melody, do something with that animal. Contract or not, I won't tolerate this kind of disruption."

"Sorry, so sorry," said Melody mournfully, and then she rushed to comfort her dog. Nathan was right behind her. They kneeled down to pet chastened Ebony who seemed to know what her mistake had been. "It's all right, honey. See, it's Nathan here. You know Nathan."

Ebony whined, and licked Nathan's hand.

In the end, Dennis forgave her, and she was allowed to stay, and she never again made trouble on the set, even though at times it was a stranger, and not Nathan, who now menaced Ariel. At such times she would watch alertly, and her muscles would bunch, and some crew members would hold their breath, but nothing happened.

Even so, nobody ever forgot that low-slung stalking beast with the unearthly snarl and a growl that made bone vibrate.

On the one free day of her week, Melody did her morning run with Ebony in a local park. Occasionally there were other runners as the sun rose, and once in a while a person sleeping on a bench. Nobody ever approached her during the runs, not with Ebony there. The dog had met Carl a few times, and seemed to like him. When he showed up for a run she would put her front paws on his thick chest and rest her chin on his shoulder for one of his neck rubs. She seemed to sense gentleness in him, and Melody thought it was sweet to think of a synth that way. It was almost as if Ebony thought he was human. She certainly thought Melody was.

Sunday was clothes washing day and the cleaning up of her little apartment, until the publicity campaign got going and the studio took her shopping for an expensive place to live. They had opened bank accounts for her, obtained credit sticks and established pre-paid accounts for her in clothing stores all over Hollywood, the valley, and down Rodeo Drive. They had loaned her a lovely, red Mercedes convertible for her personal use, but she only used it on Sundays. The rest of the week it was studio-owned autolimos that picked her up and delivered her to and from work, all very convenient.

At first, the studio dressed her as one would dress a doll. A lady from wardrobe, known only as Harriet to Melody, went shopping with her and ran up bills of tens of thousands of dollars to fill the standard-sized closet in her apartment. There was everything from ball gowns to blouses and tight sweaters to slacks and even a bathing suit, all of it designer brands, and nothing off the rack.

The same was happening to Nathan. They rarely saw each other outside of work, now, but still had breakfast together to share complaints at their hideaway café on Sundays.

There was a run-up of publicity before the holovision series began, and now even their evenings were no longer sacred. There was a deluge of clips on the net and hourly holo-ads on four channels, and the couple had to appear together on talk shows four times in as many weeks. It was particularly hard for Nathan to smile so much. It wasn't natural for him, but necessary. Countless female and more than a few male fans were already in love with him.

At the core of publicity was the mystique about Melody and Nathan as a couple. They were seen having lunch at little known cafes, for privacy, of course, but in a short time those cafes were suddenly popular. They shopped Rodeo together, always seen carrying labeled and colorful bags of their purchases, and often gazing fondly at each other. The paparazzi were quick to identify their favorite haunts and began following them when they appeared. Melody and Nathan quickly tired of their demands for poses, and the chaos they created around them. When they complained to Tom, he showed them their pictures in hand-picked junk tabloids, and pointed out that Global Studios had not paid one dime for the publicity they generated.

The series 'Ariel' pilot debut was only a week away when they were both forced to move out of their simple, but comfortable apartments. Two of their Sundays had been taken up following around a studio-appointed realtor who showed them one condominium after another in the Hollywood Hills. The requirement was for something simple yet spacious, not too ostentatious, but well above the tastes of the common man.

They each paid cash for furnished condominiums perched on hillsides with decks for views and enough space for four people. It was a ten minute walk between their properties.

The move itself was simple enough: clothes, books, a few personal items. Everything at their old apartments had been owned by the studio. They moved on a Sunday morning, and were settled by evening. Ebony walked around half the night to check out her new territory, even after Melody had gone to bed.

The premiere of the series was on the following Tuesday, eight o'clock, prime time, a two hour pilot episode that ran two hours without advertising and was sponsored by Global Studios at horrible cost.

Melody's new family was with her at home to watch it in her entertainment room with central holo-stage and surround sound. Father and Carl had come up from San Diego to see her new digs. Eleanor came over with Nathan, and they all had hot dogs and hamburgers on the deck. When it was time, and the condo tour was over, they retired to the entertainment room with bowls of ice cream to watch the show.

Halfway through the show Melody knew it was working, because she was crying and so was Eleanor, and even Nathan was getting misty eyed. She was watching other people, not herself, not Nathan, people desperately in love, but trapped in a dark and dangerous world.

There was a crescendo of music as the pilot ended, and then a preview of the first regular episode in one week. This was followed by an announcement of the feature production due in theatres later in the year.

There were hugs all around, even for Carl, who seemed perplexed by it and didn't respond. And father had brought a bottle of gourmet grape juice for celebration.

Eleanor analyzed every scene for them and pointed out some flaws. They listened politely, and she was happy being a teacher again. Nathan worried about her because she'd been having some fainting spells and he'd finally forced her to see a doctor. Nothing was found, but the doctor had told Nathan privately that his mother might be having some circulation problems that needed watching.

Father and Carl were the last to leave. It was nearly eleven, and tomorrow was another early start for Melody's working day.

"Are you still running?" asked Carl.

"I have my treadmill," said Melody. "The nearest track is at a high school near the bottom of the hill."

"Let's meet there at seven next Sunday for a run. We need to talk."

"Oh?"

"We'll discuss it then. It's something your father and I have been talking about."

"Okay," said Melody.

"I might be early," said Carl, and held out his hand.

Melody shook his hand. "Glad to meet you," she said, kidding him. "No more hugs for you tonight, I guess."

Carl looked blank, didn't seem to understand her humor. "Good night, Melody," he said.

Melody hugged Father again, and they left her. She went out onto the deck and watched their car meandering back down to the city.

So, what have you and Father been talking about, she wondered?

Ebony was waiting for her in the bedroom when she went inside.

CHAPTER 16

There was a bright glow on the eastern horizon, and Carl was waiting for her at the track, a dark figure sitting in the bleachers. He hopped down six rows to meet her, with surprising ability for such a muscular man.

"Hi," said Melody, stretching her arms above her head.

"Thanks for coming," said Carl. "I know you're busy, but we need to talk."

They walked briskly for a lap before jogging. "I'm making a personal judgment here," Carl began, "without consulting your father. He has given me a security advisory position as a part of my training, but I'm taking the position more seriously than he might think. Things are happening that you need to know about. Your father won't tell you, because he doesn't want you to worry. He would not be happy if he knew about our conversation this morning."

"I know about the demonstrations," said Melody. "They're getting uglier lately. It's all about robotics causing job losses for union people."

"That is the official reason, and the unions are most sincere about it, but they have been inflamed and encouraged by another group that cares nothing about job losses. I think we have identified the group behind it, a group calling itself the Association Against Artificial Humanity. It is funded through a charitable trust"

Melody felt a shock. "Artificial humans? That's us, Carl. How could they know? We're the best kept secret around."

"I doubt they actually know we exist, but the speculation is logical. Your father has pioneered so many developments in prosthetics and artificial organs, and then came his work on neural nets and biological memory systems. To speculate about artificial humans is only to extrapolate the science he has published. But the subject itself is offensive to the religious and right-wing elements of the country, and we believe it is being used to motivate them in a plot to disrupt the current government they despise for its socialistic policies. We've identified a coordination of demonstrations and work stoppages involving layoffs in robotics and other manufacturing companies across the nation."

Carl began to jog, and Melody hurried to catch up with him. Two people, a man and a woman, had joined them and were running half a lap behind.

"We have identified three CEOs who contribute to the AAAP charitable trust, and there are likely more. The trust is handled by a former tele-evangelist and known con man named Jacob Cross. His motivation is likely money; we know that trust money is being siphoned into his own accounts in the Cook Islands."

"You keep saying we," said Melody. "Who is we?"

"Myself, and the FBI, through a friend of your father. There are also some treasury people involved now."

"Do they know what you are? Did Father tell them about you?"

"No. I initiated everything with some research I did for your father. One FBI man knows about me, but his former wife is also a synth, you see, and he is grateful to your father for it."

"I remember," said Melody. "Her name was Jilian. Father wanted me to counsel her when she was first activated, but when I finally had the time she'd been released. I felt badly about it."

They passed the other couple on the track, and both people looked at them strangely.

"Government people are so secretive; they must trust you a lot to let you work with them."

"Not exactly," said Carl.

"What?"

"I'm not exactly working with them. I do research. My skills are in rapid search and analysis. I search out records, break codes and passwords, and your father passes on my summaries for government verification. He refers to me as his advanced computer systems."

"How is that legal?"

"It's not, but there doesn't seem to be any problem with it yet."

"Carl!"

"The government does its own investigations, but there are codes and assigned agents, and poor communication between them. Their reports are simple to obtain."

"You could be arrested for spying! Father, too. Does he know what you're doing?"

"Of course," said Carl. "I'm only sharing the secret with you because I think there is potential danger to all of us, including your father. The existence of synths must not be revealed. People will not understand. The AAAH group must be stopped, and disbanded. Your father only sees the dangers of political disruption, and possible loss of his research funds. I am thinking about our existence as a new species. Melody, we could be destroyed!"

They passed the other couple on the track again, and both people were startled by it.

"But what can we do about it?"

"For now, only what I'm doing, but we must all do nothing to reveal our existence. You have suggested to your father that Dennis Hopkins should know what you and Nathan are, in case something goes wrong at work. Don't do that. That knowledge cannot be spread. Even Doctor Post has been contacted with a false job offer in the hopes of getting information from him. We know that Jacob Cross and his AAAH associates were behind that. They are hunting, and getting close. With proven evidence of our existence, the support for their cause would explode."

Melody suddenly noticed she was getting warm, and they were coming up on the other couple again.

"Carl, I think we're running too fast. We'll be noticed."

"You're right," he said. They slowed, but it was too late. They had already passed the other couple for the third time in as many laps.

"Where do you guys get all the energy?" shouted the man.

Melody just turned to smile brightly, and pumped a fist up into the air.

Carl didn't miss a beat. "My hope is that the government will shut down Jacob Cross' fraudulent operation and disband AAAH. If they fail to do this, we'll have to take action ourselves," he said.

"That sounds sinister. What kind of action?"

"Whatever is necessary," said Carl, and they slowed to a walk again. "There is another thing to discuss. Your father feels that as your stardom brightens you might find it necessary to have a bodyguard. He would like you to consider me, if that need arises. I would be interested in that position, if it's acceptable to you."

"If the need arises, the studio has agencies they work with for that," said Melody.

"They are human. It would be safer to be protected by your own kind, certainly in terms of identity security."

Melody smiled, and leaned against his shoulder. "You really want to be my protector?" she said softly, kidding him.

Carl looked straight ahead. "Of course. I'm well prepared for it, and I do enjoy being with you."

"Thank you, Carl. That was sweet. I'll consider your offer, if the need arises."

The other couple caught up with them, and wanted to talk. There was a polite exchange of pleasantries involving running and exercise in general, but they managed to get away without having a real conversation.

* * * *

The viewing public fell in love with both of them.

According to fandom, Nathan Dark was born to be the hero with a checkered past. His chiseled features and deep-set eyes, combined with a quiet, dark and brooding personality, suggested dominance and danger to the scores of women and more than a few men who fell hard for him.

Melody Lane was the consummate damsel in distress, beautiful and fragile yet somehow stoic and brave. In weeks, she was a fantasy queen with the male population, and the lesbian community quickly adopted her as their pet. There seemed to be no middle ground in fandom, when it came to Melody Lane or her character. People either wanted to save her, or ravish her.

Fan writings online equally expressed both persuasions. Artwork that appeared bordered on pornography, according to the religious right. But Melody's real shock came when she discovered that some entrepreneur was marketing a full-sized silicon doll of Ariel with great attention to anatomical detail, and complete with sets of underwear and fetish clothing. Melody complained to Global Studios, and they later sued, settling out of court for a substantial fraction of the profit for the very popular product, which continued to be marketed.

Melody's paranoia about being discovered as a synth returned with a vengeance. Father and Carl had to talk her down from it again. Nathan was not helpful; he found all the fuss quite amusing, and was always on stage when they were in public.

They were followed by paparazzi and fans wherever they went. At first they were polite, but that changed quickly, the public seeming to adopt a feeling of ownership of its newfound stars. There were times when Nathan and Melody were both amazed by the rudeness. They were stopped, hemmed in and jostled on the street. Meals were interrupted for autographs and unwanted conversations. The studio was not helpful or even sympathetic. It was all good publicity, they said.

The little café near their old apartment building became their only retreat for meals. By prearrangement, the owner there closed and locked the doors after their arrival, and put them in a secluded corner to enjoy his cooking.

Within a month after the pilot episode, the paparazzi found out where they were living and began loitering in the neighborhood. Neighbors complained, and the police were called, but it was like batting away flies on a hot summer day. The insects just kept coming back again and again, waiting for that one opportunity for a photograph that would put food on their table for much of the year.

Fans lurked day and night, and grew bolder with each passing week. A few knocked on Melody's door, seeking autographs or a snapshot. She made the mistake of giving one autograph, and was punished by the plague of interruptions that followed. Finally she called the police when she heard a fan attempting to jimmy open a first story window. She signed a complaint, and the young man was arrested. After that, the police ordered regular patrols of the neighborhood, but there was little else they could do.

Melody was frightened for her safety. She called the studio, and a search began for bodyguards who would accompany Melody and Nathan when they were out in public. She called Father, and talked to him about Carl.

"He could live here, daddy. I have plenty of room, and Carl would have lots of quiet time for his research while I'm working. I've seen it firsthand; people keep their distance from me when Carl is around. Nathan isn't having the same problem as I am. His fans fill his mailbox with cookies and perfumed love letters, and he thinks it's cute. And I can't even leave the house to walk Ebony anymore."

"Okay, okay," said Father. "Tell you what, come down to the Schutz plant next Sunday, say ten. I have an upgrade for you, and then we can load Carl's things in your car so you can drive him back to Los Angeles."

"Yes!" said Melody.

"You and Carl will still have to make the San Diego trip for upgrades, and a few will be coming up soon."

"Not a problem," said Melody. "Thank you, Daddy."

"Still my little girl," said father. "You always call me Daddy when you want something badly."

"Only if I know I have a good chance of getting it. See you Sunday," said Melody.

That night she went to bed feeling better, and safer, knowing that her friend Carl Hobbs would soon be there.

The following Sunday she made a leisurely three hour drive in her Mercedes on the coastal highway to San Diego, and up into the hills to the sprawling campus of Schutz Fabrik. The weather was clear, and she kept the top down, listening to classical music all the way. Ebony sat in the back seat, occasionally leaning out to let the wind flop her ears. People in other cars stared at her when she passed them, and a car full of teenagers hooted and whistled at her. She arrived at the research complex before ten, and the guards at the gate let her right in. Both were armed with handguns and rifles, and the high, wire fence around the buildings was now electrified. There had only been a few small demonstrations at the gates of Schutz Fabrik, but it was obvious to Melody that her father was preparing for something much worse.

She parked her car in the visitor's lot by the administration building and Ebony accompanied her inside to register as a guest. Everyone wanted to pet her dog, and Ebony accepted it in her own, dignified way, relishing the attention. The badge given to Melody allowed complete access to all the buildings in the complex, and had been authorized by her father. Still, as a visitor, she had to be accompanied by a staff member wherever she went. A secretary came to fetch her, an older woman named Betty who had transferred down from the L.A. plant. The woman had worked there for over a decade when the company was still young, she said. She took Melody through three second story passages and up an elevator to the fourth floor of building C, where all the company confidential and government classified research was being done.

Father was waiting for her in one of the laboratories, and Carl was with him.

"How was the drive?" asked Father.

"Slow. There was lots of traffic, but it's a beautiful day. How are you, Carl?"

"I have my things packed. I hope they fit into your little car," said Carl.

"The trunk is empty," she said.

"I have a small suitcase, my computer, and a bag for some books and my research materials," said Carl.

"Wow, you are a collector, aren't you?" said Melody.

Carl didn't catch her joke. "I collect information, and it occupies no space to speak of."

"So you'll be able to turn your new room into a track," said Melody. "I'm glad you're coming back with me, Carl. I'm going to feel safer with you there."

Carl nodded politely.

"He's not field tested, Melody, but this will be a good way to see if there are any wetware glitches we need to address," said father. "Carl will contact me regularly with his own opinions on how things are going, and I want you to tell me if anything happens that seems strange to you. You're both exceptionally fast learners, but in the field things can happen so fast that you're reactions can be sabotaged by lack of normal instincts and experience. That's what I'm looking for."

"Okay, we'll be watchful, like we always are," said Melody, and smiled.

Father shook his head. "I don't need to remind you, and you're not a little girl anymore. God, you were already like that at thirteen."

Melody sensed some sorrow in his voice when he said it.

"Well, as a going away present, I have something new for both of you," said Father.

"You said something about updates," said Melody.

"We're trying some new things with sensory interfaces that might be useful to both of you. I did the adaptation, but the original work was done by a very bright wetware specialist in L.A. for use in quality control. I'm trying to get her transferred down here for AI research. You might even be working with her someday."

Melody thought about what Carl had said regarding security. "Is that safe?"

"All our employees have had thorough background checks. When you're recruiting talented people, sooner or later you have to trust them," said Father.

There was no arguing with him, but she didn't agree, and she knew how Carl felt about it. He was looking at her, but remained mute.

"Have a seat. It'll only take a few minutes," said Father.

They sat down in low-backed aluminum swivel chairs in the middle of the room. The floor was mostly bare. There was a line of cabinets and a rack of instrument panels up against one wall. Father left them for a moment, and came back pushing the rack of instruments. A cluster of wires hung out of a port on one side of the rack.

"Are you shutting us down for this?" asked Melody. It was a process she had truly grown to hate, a kind of consensual death that reminded her of what she was.

"Don't have to. This is going into a new slot." Father tapped her head. "You have a lot of empty space up there."

"Why thank you for saying so," said Melody.

Melody heard a hum, felt pressure at the back of her head, and was blinded by the great mass of hair that had been slid forward over her face for port access. There was a click, and then father was inserting wires into her head and checking instrument panels. "One of these days I'll get around to converting all this stuff to PC," he said.

Another click. "There, it's done."

"I don't feel anything new," said Melody.

"You won't, not now, but you'll tell me about it when it happens," said father, and he turned to Carl.

"I do love a mystery," said Melody, and watched father open up two ports on the back of Carl's head. "I always feel weird watching this. It's like a scene out of an old science fiction film I remember. Frankenstein lives again, and we're it."

"You're just being dramatic," said father. "It's not like that at all." He inserted two narrow chips into the back of Carl's head, closed the ports and opened up another one for a diagnostics check. "Feel any tingling in your hands?" he asked.

"No, Nothing," said Carl.

"Good. We're done. Have a good trip north. I'll be up there again in a few days." Father closed up the port, and pushed the instrument panel back up against the wall. They followed him back to the lobby, and Melody turned in her badge. A secretary had brought out Carl's bags, and was waiting for them. Ebony sat obediently by the receptionist's desk, her tail thumping the floor hard when she saw them. The receptionist smiled. "She's such a sweet dog. Everyone wanted to pet her."

You are such a con artist, thought Melody, but didn't say it as Ebony nuzzled Carl's hand. Now I have two protectors.

Carl's worldly possessions fit easily into the trunk of her car, and Carl seemed to enjoy the classical music and minimal conversation during the drive north. They managed to avoid the rush hour by minutes, and Carl commented on the lovely view as they climbed up the hill to her condo. Melody looked ahead, saw two parked cars she knew were paparazzo's, and four people who were probably fans were sitting on the curb across the street from her dwelling.

"Oh, boy," said Melody, "here I am, bringing a new man home with me in my open convertible. This will give them something to talk about. Let's see how quick they are."

She activated the garage door as she approached the condo. Car doors opened, and men with cameras tumbled out, nearly running in front of her. The fans stood and waved, and Melody waved back. The paparazzi raced across the street towards her garage. She pulled in and stopped, and had the garage door closed before they even reached her driveway.

"What was that all about?" asked Carl

"Welcome to Hollywood," said Melody.

* * * *

Doctor Sheila Davidson truly enjoyed her work at ISC, but found it becoming routine as her first anniversary approached. There had been a substantial raise in salary with her promotion to group leader. She only had six people to supervise, but none of them had advanced degrees, and it was simple to break down projects into individual menial tasks they could handle. She kept the most challenging work for herself, and enjoyed the complimentary assessments of her results. She had followed and admired the work by Donovan Lane since she had taken a seminar course from him at MIT. She had read all his published work, and kept files of it for reference. Her own thesis had been an extrapolation of that work, and now she used all of it, but always in applications to manufacturing processes with large machines. Many of the programs she worked on had much to do with the coordinated motion of mechanical parts doing repetitive tasks. These were not thinking machines, vast parallel processors that could generate new programs as they evolved. Lane's development of auto-car systems and the cute little robots that sold lingerie were a step closer, and his biological operating systems had made it possible.

This was the kind of work she really wanted to do, and she boldly made that known to her supervisor on several occasions after group leader meetings. She was not unhappy, she said, but felt she could contribute more to the company by developing new, compactified codes for use in biological operating systems.

Finally, she enjoyed her evenings at home by writing up a fun code for an automated grocery clerk who would make jokes about various items as he checked them out, and made up new jokes based on the shape and color of the items. She presented it to her supervisor, and asked if there would be any interest at Schutz Fabrik for its use. Schutz Fabrik was where she really wanted to be. That was where the basic research was happening, and where the future of robotics was being generated.

She was almost surprised when her supervisor came to her one day to say that Schutz Fabrik had been quite impressed by her work, and had sent a representative to talk about it with her. A private lunch had been arranged in the conference room.

She was nervous about the meeting, and wanted to make a good impression. She did not consider herself to be an attractive woman, and was an introvert, preferring to interact with individuals when possible. She hoped the Schutz Fabrik representative would be someone from research, and not administration.

When she entered the conference room it was empty, but two places had been set for lunch at the long table. She sat down, and waited only a moment before a girl came in with salad plates and a large pot of coffee, smiled at her and departed. She waited another moment, wondering if she should begin eating, but the door opened again and a man entered the room.

She turned to look at him and inwardly gasped, recognizing him immediately.

It was Donovan Lane. "Sorry I'm late," he said, and extended a hand as she rushed to push her chair back and stand.

"Sheila Davidson, sir," she said, and shook his hand. "So nice to meet you. I've read all your papers."

"We've met before," he said, looking closely at her.

"I did a seminar with you in my fourth year. 'Coding DDY for Dummies', you called it."

"I remember," said Lane. "You gave something on compactification. Did you publish it?"

"It was part of my thesis, sir, and yes, I published it in the Journal of Applied Science."

"Well, here you are now, and some nice evaluations of your work for us have crossed my desk. I hear you'd like to join the Schutz Fabrik family to do some basic research."

"Yes, sir," she said, and then the serving girl arrived again with their lunch of chicken cordon bleu, scalloped potatoes and string beans.

Lane took a bite, then, "We had more fun with that code you submitted to us. We have a robot we call Elmer, because the engineer who designed his face was a Bugs Bunny fan. We use Elmer to test all the systems we use for automatronic sales, and tour buses, and we loaded that program of yours into him and spent half an afternoon laughing. The more terrible the joke, the harder we laughed. It's brilliant work you did for Elmer, and it's the kind of innovative work we're looking for in the Schutz Fabrik division. Everything we're doing there is cutting edge."

"That's what I want to do," said Sheila. "the work I've been doing here has been interesting, and I've learned how my recent work can be applied to large scale manufacturing, but I want to go beyond that now, and I want to stay with the company."

"Hope you don't mind an illegal, personal question, but are you married or engaged?"

"No, sir, there are no attachments."

"I had to ask. A job offer would not depend on your answer, but it's a concern with us. Some of our projects last for decades, and the grants we get often depend on the quality and the records of our researchers. We can't afford to lose good people."

"If the work is what I want, I will certainly make a long term commitment to it," she said.

The girl arrived again with their desert, a small dish of a chocolate gelato, and she poured coffee for them.

"I wish I could tell you what projects we have ongoing, but nearly all of it is government classified or company confidential. I can tell you that what you did for Elmer is useful to us and your qualifications fit with what we do. You'd have to move to San Diego. Our people work all hours, day or night, as the project demands. We have no regular shifts to speak of."

Sheila smiled as brightly as she could. "It all sounds wonderful, and exciting."

Lane smiled back. "If it was up to me, I'd offer you a position right now, but I keep everyone in the loop at R group when it comes to research personnel decisions. I'll circulate your file, and talk to some people, and give you a call by the end of the week." He took another sip of coffee, stood up and shook her hand again.

"I'll look forward to your call," she said.

"Nice to meet you again. Thanks for your work with us. Elmer thanks you, too."

"I hope to get a chance to meet him," she said.

"Maybe you can make up more of those terrible jokes together," said Lane. He grinned, chuckled, and left the room.

Sheila sat there for a few minutes, sipping coffee and reflecting on the excitement of working with a man whose work she had admired for so long. With his brilliance, she could participate in expanding the frontiers of robotics to unimagined limits, just as long as those limits did not exceed those governed by her faith and moral judgment.

The following Friday, Donovan Lane called to offer her a position as Senior Research Associate at Schutz Fabrik, and she accepted it.

On Saturday, she made a call to Jacob Cross to give him her good news.

CHAPTER 17

They finished dinner, and John retired to the front room to watch some holovision. Audrey finished putting the dishes into the turbo-wash, and was wiping down the sink when the cell remote buzzed in her ear.

"I would like to speak to Jilian Harper, please." It was a male voice.

"There's no Jilian Harper here," she said. "You must have a wrong number."

"Isn't this the John Harper residence?"

"Yes, it is, but—oh, dear. You must be looking for John's first wife. Jilian died a number of years ago. My name is Audrey. John and I have been married for over a year, now. What is your name? John is here. Maybe he remembers you."

"Bill Summers, Mrs. Harper. Jilian and I were schoolmates before she met John. I had a little crush on her at the time. I never met John, but I knew they'd been married. I just wanted to say hi, a voice from the past. I'm so sorry to hear she has passed, and I'm very sorry to have bothered you. Goodbye, Missus Harper."

"Goodbye," said Audrey, but the connection had already been broken.

She went to the front room and told John about the call.

"Do you remember him?" asked John.

"I never knew a Bill Summers in any grade. It must be a prank, or just a call to see if we're at home. Should we report it?"

"Don't bother. The police can't do anything about it. Are you sure you don't remember a guy who had a crush on you?"

"Jilian would remember, and she doesn't," said Audrey, "but I remember the first crush I had, and it was you." She leaned over him, where he sat in his chair, and put her arms around his neck.

"Sometimes I forget your name in public. Old habits die hard, hon. You'll always be my Jilian," said John.

"You're Jilian and Audrey's first love, too," said Audrey, "as long as they live, and that could be a long time. Have you thought any more about getting that scan?"

"Can't hurt anything to do it. Donovan said there's no cost for us. I should tell him about tonight's call. Something smells about it. I'll call him tomorrow. Why don't we both meet with him? Maybe you can meet Melody, if she has the time. You two can compare notes on the new lives."

"I'd like that," said Audrey. "Why don't you call Donovan while you're thinking about it?"

John made the call, but Donovan didn't answer, so he left a request for a callback. The two of them watched holovision for a while and then went to bed, cuddling each other as they fell into their respective deep and twilight sleeps.

* * * *

Jacob Cross broke the connection, and sighed. "Well, that didn't go anywhere. He's recently married again. You'd think the FBI would update his records more often. We're chasing ghosts, Max. I think we'll have to get creative, and make things up. The tabloids will print anything we send them, right? It's all speculation anyway, right? Those people don't care, but damn it I wish we could get something real to report." He slapped his hand hard on the desk, rattling the ice cubes in his drink against the glass.

They were sitting in the dark, the only light coming in through the glass door panel from the hall outside. The building had closed for the night, and they would have to let themselves out through the back alley entrance.

"If there's anything to find, your girl at Schutz Fabrik should find it," said Max.

"Maybe, but she's brand new there, and I doubt they'll show her very much so soon. We're on a time schedule, Max, and I need something now. I need something dramatic. Another year of donations, and we can cut and run. The board is quiet for now, but they won't be quiet for long. I sense suspicion after the death of their mouthy colleague. The demonstrations are only a nuisance. They need to become violent. I want violence, Max. I want blood on the hands of the government. That is your specialty, Max. Give me blood.

"Any restrictions?" asked Max calmly.

"None, as long as the finger points to the government or the unions. I want to see evidence of a civil war in the making, and people die in civil wars, Max. I'm sure you can handle that."

"Free hand?"

"Free hand, anything you decide, and anything you need. I'll pay you in cash, no questions asked."

"Okay," said Max.

"I'll do the press stuff. Here it is. If artificial humans don't exist now, they're in the works. Some might be among us right now, and Lane is making them. They might even be famous people. My girl at Schutz mentioned something that might be the best thing I have from her so far. Everyone at the plant is thrilled about Donovan Lane's adopted daughter becoming a huge holo-star. Isn't that interesting? Lane had a daughter, but she died with her mother in a car accident, and now he has an adopted daughter, as a single dad, by the way, and she just happens to have a monumental acting talent to make big bucks in the holo-industry. Can you see the story, Max? Daddy has the technology, and makes a synthetic version of his dead daughter for whatever reason. Hell, it could be sexual. And now worshipful fans pay good money to watch a performing robot."

"You're making all of this up," said Max, smiling.

"So what? People believe what they read in the tabloids. It doesn't have to be true."

"If it was true, and Lane could make a synthetic holo-star, what else could he make?' Max shook his head.

"Who cares?" said Cross. "It's gotten to the point where I don't have time to care, or prove anything, but I'll tell the world it's all true, and the tabloids and the net will support me. If that doesn't inflame the faithful and all the other moralists out there, then society as we know it is doomed. That is the message I will bring to them, Max. We are riding all together on the highway to hell."

Jacob's voice had risen to a crescendo in his fervor.

"Amen," said Max. I'm working for a lunatic, he thought.

* * * *

It was the first love scene she had done since returning with Carl from San Diego. The lights were low on the bedroom set, and they lay half-naked on their sides, hands exploring. The dialog was a near whisper as Nathan described the dangerous opponent he would be facing in the early morning duel. Perhaps it was their last time together, and Ariel's tears wet her cheeks. Cameras moved in close, a crew of six only a yard away, gawking at them. Their lips came together softly, brushing a soft caress that the fans were crazy for, but then it suddenly changed.

Melody let out an exhalation of breath through her nostrils, and moaned. She grasped Nathan's neck and pulled, her mouth opening wide, her breath coming in gasps. It went on for seconds, Nathan going with the flow, the crew leaning forward, astonished.

"Cut!" shouted Dennis, and clapped his hands together.

Nathan pulled back, and blinked rapidly. "Woof," he murmured, and grinned at her. Melody's breath still came in short gasps. Delicious warmth was spreading throughout her chest, and a wonderful tingling in her neck had now reached her shoulders.

"Wonderful, Melody, you nailed it," said Dennis.

Now there was polite applause from the crew.

"Authenticity, that's what I want, and you found it. Both of you are shining. Makeup! Twenty minutes, people. We have twelve more pages to do."

They blotted each other with towels, and then the makeup girl scrubbed and dusted them.

"Did you really enjoy it that much?" asked Nathan.

"Did I ever," said Melody, and she rolled her eyes at him. The makeup girl smiled, and left them.

"Daddy gave me a new upgrade when I was in San Diego," she whispered. "Now I know what it was for. My daddy is a naughty man."

Melody rubbed a finger lightly over her lips, and her eyes widened. "Oh, my God, I can do it to myself. This is going to be fun!" She tilted her head back, and laughed.

"If you say so," said Nathan, watching curiously. "Right now, I'm feeling neglected."

Melody giggled, and punched him in the shoulder.

"I felt that, and it wasn't pleasant. Tell your father I demand that upgrade."

Melody leaned against him. "I think my weird sense of humor is rubbing off on you."

"Unfortunate, but true," said Nathan.

There were no more love scenes for the day, only dialog and a long close-up of Ariel gazing into the distance with deep subtext. Dennis was happy about the day, and rushed off to editing. The limousine arrived after makeup had finished cleaning them up, and took them back to their condos on the hill. Both of them were in good moods, feeling satisfied with the work they'd done that day.

Ebony greeted Melody politely at the door, sitting on her haunches, tail thumping. Carl came out of the kitchen. He was experimenting again, had added an extra topping to the store-bought pizza he had cooked for them. Melody made up a salad, and they ate together. When it came to food, everything was an experiment. Father had developed his liquid supplement to satisfy all their nutritional needs, and allowed them to do the rest of the food studies. Synth metabolism seemed to handle anything in limited quantities, but benefited most from oils and greasy foods.

"They know I'm here," said Carl, "but it doesn't seem to make much difference. I caught the same kid looking in the front window this morning, and when I went outside he just laughed at me and ran. There was the usual pile of love letters on the porch this afternoon, and I never saw who left them. I suppose I could sit by the window, and watch all day."

"Don't bother," said Melody. "The studio is supposed to be hiring a couple of guys to watch the house and follow me around. Those aren't just love letters, Carl. Some weird and lonely people are out there, and I've become their fantasy. I'm Ariel to them. Some of those letters describe some rather dark scenarios about playing with Ariel, and she doesn't even own a whip."

Carl looked at her blankly.

"Fetish stuff: ropes, whips and chains, that sort of thing," she said.

"Interesting," said Carl, and Melody wiggled an eyebrow at him.

They finished the pizza, and cleaned up the kitchen. Carl went to his room and Melody remained in the kitchen to spend what was left of the evening to go over the next day's pages. Bedtime would come soon.

Her cell extension buzzed, and she touched her ear.

"Melody, it's Nathan. Something terrible has happened. Mother's servant just called me. She collapsed at the dinner table, and he called for an ambulance. They're taking her to Valley Hospital. Can you drive me there?" His voice shook with pleading.

"I'll be right over," she said, and broke the connection. "Carl!" she called. She told him what had happened, grabbed a coat and went to the garage. The top was still down on the car. As the garage door opened she saw people walking across the street towards the driveway. She gunned the engine, and backed out fast. People jumped out of the way, and one man made a rude gesture. Tires squealed when she accelerated. Nathan's condo was a hundred yards down the hill, and he ran out to the curb as she pulled up. As he jumped in, headlights of a car by her condo went on.

"Buckle up," she said, and Nathan was slammed back into his seat as she accelerated. It was a Grand Prix drive down the hill, and traffic was light on the 405. It was a forty minute drive to the hospital, and Nathan only said one thing. "She's been having fainting spells lately, but they found nothing wrong. Nothing."

They went straight to the emergency room entrance.

"You have a patient named Eleanor Dali. She was just brought in," said Nathan to the receptionist.

"She's in OR," said the receptionist. "Have a seat. Someone will come out to get you."

They sat down and waited. And waited. It was nearly midnight when a gowned doctor came out to see them, a mask pulled down around his throat.

"Are you Nathan?" he asked.

"Yes. I'm a close friend of Eleanor's."

"She said your name when she was brought in."

For one instant, hope flickered, and then died.

"I'm sorry. She had a massive aneurism, and she went into cardiac arrest on the table. We tried very hard, but couldn't revive her. Someone will come out to ask about arrangements, and we have a chaplain on the floor if you'd like to talk to him."

Nathan stared straight ahead, and looked stunned. Melody gripped his arm tightly. "That won't be necessary," he said. "May we see her?"

"Give me thirty minutes. Again, my condolences for your loss."

"She was a famous actress," said Nathan dreamily.

"I know," said the doctor. "I saw her films when I was young. I'm glad to see someone here for her. She was quite a lady."

The doctor went away. Melody put an arm around Nathan's waist, felt a shiver, and squeezed him. He looked at her with dry eyes, but said nothing, and suddenly a nurse was there to escort them. She took them through double doors, past a nurses' station and down a long hall to a darkened room, and there was Eleanor Dali lying peacefully in bed, as if asleep. They stood at the bedside for a long time, and then Nathan reached down and touched his mother from another life.

"She's still warm," he said, and when he looked at Melody she felt tears coming, and Nathan saw it.

"I can't cry," he said. "What's wrong with me?"

"You're in shock," said Melody, and sniffed. "It's not real, yet. We owe so much to her. I'm glad she lived long enough to see our success. She was very proud of us, Nathan."

"I know," he said, and then his voice cracked. "I wasn't a good son—in my other life, I mean. I did things that—that made her ashamed of me. I still don't understand why she wanted me back. I—just—wasn't—worth it."

Melody hugged him hard. Tears finally gushed from his eyes, and streamed down his cheeks. He sobbed, and Melody cried with him as they looked down at the peaceful face of the woman now gone from them.

Something suddenly occurred to Melody. "You know that my father has a fairly complete scan of Eleanor. Do you think you would want to—"

"—We discussed it," said Nathan. "She said she wanted no part of it, that one long life filled with good memories was enough. I will honor that."

"Okay," said Melody, and she hugged him again.

They were interrupted by a soft knock on the open door. A man in white shirt and tie stood there.

"Hi, I'm Allen Bishop, the chaplain on call. Can I help you in any way?"

"I'm not a religious person, but a prayer would be nice," said Nathan.

"Are you the children of the deceased?" asked Allen.

Yes, in a way, we are, thought Melody. She elbowed Nathan softly in the ribs as he paused to answer.

"No, we were both acting students and protégés of Eleanor's. We became very close friends of hers," said Nathan.

Allen was taking notes. "There are no children, or close relatives who can make arrangements?"

"Not as far as we know, but like I said we were close, and I know she made pre-arrangements with Forest Lawn for cremation. I don't know which funeral home she named, but the Forest Lawn people will know."

"I'll make a call for you in the morning," said Allen. He stepped up to Eleanor's bedside and took their hands in his.

"Now, let us pray," he said, and they bowed their heads.

If there is a God for humans, is there another God for synths? wondered Melody.

It was a nice prayer, thanking God for the long life of a woman beloved by so many, and whose work would be remembered far into the future.

Melody did not have awareness of Gods, but of a creator who had been her true father in another life. He had given her a new life, and a piece of her mother, and a piece of the woman they now prayed for. In a strange way, Eleanor would live on in Melody, including the memory of a secret love that would never be revealed, even to the product of that love.

She would also live on in the long, long life of her new son.

They thanked Allen for his comforting, and he went away. A nurse told them they could remain until morning if they wished, but they only stayed a few more minutes, arms around each other's waists.

"I'm glad you're here," said Nathan.

"Me, too," said Melody.

"I've never felt so miserable. People talk about heartache, and I can remember that from a previous and disappointing existence, but this is worse. I feel impotent, with no hope for any future, like there's no longer any reason for me to be here."

"You're grieving, Nathan." Melody reached up and wiped a new tear from his face with her finger. "When people die, their loved ones grieve for them."

"But it's a human reaction, not something programmed into a neural net," Nathan said bitterly.

"Neural net or not, we're grieving, and that shows love and caring and sorrow and anger, and everything humans experience. I think that makes us as human as human beings can be."

Nathan choked again."But it hurts," he said.

Melody drove him home, put him to bed and stayed with him until he had drifted with quiet sobs into sleep. At three in the morning there were no paparazzi or fans to hassle her when she got home and garaged the car. Carl was still waiting up for her, and Ebony was sound asleep on the bed. She had tea with Carl and talked about the evening and started to cry, and then suddenly Carl hugged her, and in his arms she felt very comfortable.

Five days later there was a memorial service for Eleanor at Ester Funeral Home, and the who's who of Hollywood attended. A few close friends attended the internment of Eleanor's ashes in her Mausoleum niche at Forrest Lawn. Melody and Nathan, father and Carl were there. Darin was absent. Marylyn had made other plans for him that didn't include a funeral.

The service was short, with an invocation, a prayer, a blessing for a life well lived. A few people spoke, including Melody, but Nathan remained seated.

The four of them stood together, holding hands as the service ended, and Melody was suddenly aware of something she hadn't consciously realized before.

This is my family, she thought.

CHAPTER 18

The studio didn't ask for her input on the candidates, and she had no say about the hiring decisions. It seemed to Melody that they had gone out on the back streets of the city and hired two thugs to protect her. Off the set her life had become intolerable, and fame was a curse.

The first season of the series had finished at the top of the charts, and the two completed episodes of the second season were being touted everywhere months before their debut. Production had begun on the big feature for theatres, and the schedule called for six weeks of filming. They were working day and night, and Melody had great admiration for the stamina and dedication of the human cast and crew who did not share her advantages. She and Nathan had the script memorized and modified to their liking in three weekend evenings together in his condo, just before his move. Under pressure, neither of them required more than two hours of twilight sleep each night. They did not share the difficulties faced by their human colleagues, but understood them.

Their problems were off the set. The popularity of the series had driven fandom into a frenzy, and encouraged improper and even insane behavior by the fringe group of disturbed people always lurking there. The police had grown weary of breaking up unruly groups of fans and paparazzi constantly around her home. As intimidating as Carl was, he was resentful at spending his time chasing people off her front porch and away from the windows.

"I'm trying to organize intelligence about people more dangerous to you than your fans," he complained. "Life would be simpler if you moved to a gated community or got yourself a mansion like Nathan's. You have the money for it."

She knew he was right, but didn't want the hassle of moving when she was so busy at work. Not just yet, but she was looking.

In her will, Eleanor had left everything to Nathan, including her gated mansion high in the hills with other such properties. There was a private neighborhood security patrol to police the area. Melody, Carl and a small truck had moved Nathan to his new home in two Sundays of packing and driving. The entrance to the neighborhood was gated, had a kiosk with a guard who vetted every visitor for entrance. There were no paparazzi or passionate fans to contend with, only the perfumed letters that began arriving again after the few days it took fandom to identify his new address.

It was Melody who had the problem, and the studio that finally took action. On a Wednesday, when her filming ended early around four o'clock, she was called to the office of Daniel Goldsmith himself to discuss her security concerns.

When she entered his office, Goldsmith smiled at her from behind his expansive desk and gestured towards one side of the room. "Meet your new bodyguards," he said.

Melody looked at the two men sitting on a couch, and her first instinct was to run away. They looked like thugs.

"Gentlemen, meet Melody Lane, your new client and a very important asset of Global Studios. Melody, meet Misha and Andrus."

The men stood. Both were over six feet tall, swarthy looks and shiny, black hair. They had probably shaved that morning, but needed another one. They wore suit and tie, but their jackets were open to accommodate enormous stomachs, and Misha had no obvious neck. They stepped forward, holding out hands the size of dinner plates.

"Misha Zahn," said the first thug. His hand enveloped hers and squeezed carefully to avoid crushing her titanium bones.

"Andrus Meyer," said the second thug, and did not shake her hand for more than a heartbeat.

Melody turned to Goldsmith. "Well, they are certainly intimidating. Exactly what will they be doing for me?"

Both Misha and Andrus scowled at her. "We're guards, not servants, ma'am," said Misha.

"I understand that. I don't need you in my house. I have Carl for that. Outside the house is another thing."

"You already have a guard?" asked Misha.

"He's a friend, and very capable of protecting me," she said primly.

"Melody, these men have been hired by my office to answer your complaints. I'm not asking for your approval," said Goldsmith. "They will take turns making sure unwanted guests do not set foot on your property. One will be with you publicly wherever you go, and both will accompany you and Nathan on any activity I deem to be studio publicity. That's the deal."

"Okay. I guess I asked for it, just as long as we don't have to be buddies," she said. "I don't need a chauffeur or shotgun; I drive my own car when I'm out by myself, and they can follow me.

"It's your buck," said Misha, smiling nastily at Goldsmith.

"Whatever you want, Melody. I just don't want to hear any more complaints," said Goldsmith. "They'll also follow the limo to and from, and set their own strategies."

"We'll take good care of you, ma'am," said Andrus.

I bet you'd like to, she thought. Both men were all but undressing her with their eyes.

"Okay, we're done here," said Goldsmith. "I just wanted you folks to meet. You're on the payroll, guys. There will be a job review in a month." He looked straight at Melody. "Play nice with each other, and remember you all have the same boss."

"Yes, sir," said Melody, and saluted him.

"That's overacting," said Goldsmith.

Melody blew him a kiss, and left the room.

Misha and Andrus were scowling again as the door closed behind her.

* * * *

Carl was not happy about the new bodyguards. "Don't you know anything about their background or experience?"

"Goldsmith didn't tell me anything. I wasn't asked, Carl. I'm just hired help."

"Well, that's not accurate," said Carl.

"You know what I mean. Anyway, they won't be in the house. Outside, they'll follow me around, discretely, I hope. When Nathan and I are out on one of our publicity dates, they'll be an obvious presence. People won't come near us. Both guys look like Mafia muscle. The must total six hundred pounds as a pair."

"I could have served as your escort," said Carl quietly.

Melody detected disappointment in his voice. "You've taken care of me here at home, and you have your research duties for my father. We talked to him about this, remember? He wanted to ease you into field work a step at a time. Your wetware is primarily military, Carl, and we're not in a war."

"I'm not sure about that," said Carl, and then he looked straight into her eyes. "This has nothing to do with your father's plans for me, Melody. I want to keep you safe."

Melody had a strange feeling. "Oh, Carl, that's a sweet thing to say. I really appreciate it."

"And I really mean it," said Carl, his gaze intense. "You are still a captive in this house. You used to walk Ebony any time you felt like it, but now you have to awake her before dawn to do it. For once, let's take her for a walk before the sun goes down."

"There are people out there."

"They won't bother us. I promise."

Ebony was on the bed, half asleep, but jumped up, thrilled, when she saw the leash in Melody's hand. They changed into their running clothes, and when they appeared on the porch there was clapping from across the street, and two paparazzi got out of their cars. Carl walked over to talk to them. Melody thought the swagger of his wrestler's body looked cute from behind. At first, the predatory photographers were crouched and ready to sprint, but then Carl said something and they relaxed. He talked to them for a minute, and they got back into their cars. The few fans on the curb just waved and smiled, and Melody waved back.

Carl came back to her. "Okay, let's go."

"What did you say to them?"

"I promised them a posed photograph with Ebony when we return. They were very nice about it. No force was necessary."

Melody smiled. "No thugs, you mean."

"Exactly," said Carl, and they began to walk, Ebony tugging hard on the leash. After three blocks, they gave the dog her wish, and began to run, finally leaving the street to follow a dirt trail that looped up behind and around the hillside neighborhood. They ran hard for an hour, and when they got back to the house their faces were glistening and Ebony's tongue lolled wetly from her mouth. They posed for the paparazzi as the sun reached the rim of the hills, and Melody signed autographs for two female fans who shyly approached her.

Minutes after they entered the condo, Melody noticed that the paparazzi and the fans had all gone away.

Ebony went straight to bed, and in an hour was snoring. There was cold chicken for dinner, and Carl made an interesting salad out of lettuce and cucumbers and lots of olive oil, a regular staple for the synth metabolism.

"The run tonight was wonderful, Carl. Thank you. I've been turning into a hermit."

"Understandable," said Carl. "Your long hours at the studio and then publicity appearances at night fill your entire week. Sunday is your only free day, but you can grab an evening hour during the week, too. Let's run at least twice a week, like we did tonight. Promise me."

"Okay, I promise."

"Now I also have work to do. I have a new FBI update on Jacob Cross to go over"

"You hacked their files again?"

"Yes, but they know I'm doing it. They are not stupid people, and they appreciated the access I gave them to all of Cross's Cook Islands accounts. Our relationship is unofficial, but the work has been stimulating."

"Happy hunting," said Melody, and smiled, surprised when Carl smiled back at her.

"Thank you for trusting me, Melody" said Carl, and then he turned and went to his room.

Melody sat at the table a while, and reflected on her day. The issue of her security had been dealt with, but she was not happy about being followed around by men who looked like thugs. There was also a deep, subtle feeling that in the past hour or two her relationship with a fellow synth known as Carl Hobbs had suddenly changed.

It was a nice feeling, and when she went to bed that night, she thought about it again while she absently rubbed her lips softly with a finger.

A nice feeling indeed, she thought.

* * * *

It was the first production glitch she had experienced, and it brought out the worst in everyone. The two day delay in filming should have meant two rare days of private time for her, but no, father had to call and make her drive to San Diego again. She only relented because Jilian was going to be there, and Melody still felt badly about not being there when the woman had first been activated.

At first it was a script problem, but not for Nathan and Melody. Supporting cast members thought their lines were illogical and out of character. Dennis encouraged occasional improv from his leads, but not at the wholesale level, and only when Wallace Benson agreed to it. It was a union thing. There was a mini-revolution on set when one-scene characters began making up their own dialog as they went along, and suddenly Dennis and Wallace were both screaming and actors were stalking off the set while Nathan and Melody looked on, astonished. Dennis threatened firings, and there were tears, and then dear Wallace saved the day by agreeing to do a rewrite and there were hugs all around.

Dennis declared a two-day kiddies' recess for things to cool down, and Wallace disappeared into his closet to write and rewrite some twenty pages of new material.

Nathan and Melody washed up, thrilled about the unexpected free time, and were heading to their limos when Father called.

"John and Jilian are here," he said, "and there is someone I want you to meet. Can you come down on Sunday?"

Melody told him about her unexpected recess.

"That's even better. Come down tomorrow, and it'll save motel expenses for them. Bring Nathan and Carl. This is for all of you."

Melody agreed to it, because Jilian rarely came out west, and because the trip might keep her Sunday free.

They took the Mercedes, top down, Nathan in the front seat with Melody, Carl and Ebony in the back, and there was room for their toothbrushes and a few small things in the trunk.

"Are you ever going to buy a car?" Melody asked Nathan.

"Why? I have you and the limo to drive me around. Besides, I don't know how to drive."

"Seriously, Nathan, you're supposed to be a learning machine. Buy a car, and I'll give you driving lessons for a dinner at Leo's."

"Melody is a good driver, but she drives much too fast," said Carl.

"I flash my lights at slow-pokes in the fast lane, too," said Melody.

Nathan's eyes twinkled. "I'll consider it, but for now just get us safely to San Diego at less than warp speed."

"What is warp?" asked Carl, and Nathan had to explain it to him.

They arrived at Schutz Fabrik in time for lunch with father and the Harpers. Father had arranged for them to spend the night in quiet apartments in the plant, had called Goldsmith to argue privacy for their trip. Misha and Andrus had been left behind them this one time, and would not be lurking around during their visit.

At lunch they mostly talked about their problems on the set, and Nathan's new mansion, and the evening runs with Carl and Ebony on the trail behind Melody's condo. John and Jilian looked radiant, a happy couple reunited by science. When lunch was over, Carl went somewhere with John to give him a confidential report to carry back to the FBI, and to discuss their progress in the matter of Jacob Cross. Nathan remained with father for casual conversation while Melody went away with Julian for an overdue conversation about life as a synth.

"Try to be back by three," said Father. "We have things to discuss, and there's someone I want the three of you to meet."

They found a corner table in an employees' lounge, and poured coffee for themselves.

"I'm so sorry I couldn't be there for you when you awakened," said Melody. "Things were just getting started for me at the studio."

Jilian reached over and patted her hand. "I understand. You've done so well. I appreciate you taking the time to come here today."

"I still remember when I was awakened, or activated, whatever. It was a very weird experience."

"I was very confused," said Jilian. "Doctor Post tried to help, but he didn't seem to know what to say to me."

"He does have a lacking in the bedside manners department. Father was better at it when he woke me up, but then he had a good idea about what was going on inside my head."

"One minute I was in pain and dying in bed, and the next I was sitting in a white room with a nice looking young man smiling at me."

"Dreamtime," said Melody. "I had both my memories and my mother's, all mixed up, and no images matched when I looked in a mirror. It took a while to realize it was me I was remembering, and not some other person. Within a day, I was doing better at it."

"John came in the evening and explained everything after I was awakened a second time. As soon as I saw him, everything was better. We'd had a long life together, but a simple one, no children or grandchildren, just us. My confusion went away in a day."

"So how have things been since then?" asked Melody.

"Our lives are like they were before the cancer and the hospitals." Jilian smiled. "John and I met in grammar school. We were best friends before we were lovers in college, and then married. It's like we've been together forever. We don't go out much. We read, watch some holo, and by the way, we love your show. Ariel is so sweet and vulnerable. Even old people can become romantic watching her deal with her men."

"You get romantic feelings?" asked Melody.

"Oh, yes. At our age we don't do much more than cuddle, but we do a lot of that."

"I cuddle with my dog," said Melody.

"I don't have the physical feelings, the arousals I had when I was human, even as I got older. Your father says it's a shortcoming he's working on," said Jilian.

"A lot about sex is brain centered, and he's tried some new wetware on me," said Melody. She rubbed a finger over her lips, and rolled her eyes. "Oooo," she murmured.

"Really?" Jilian smiled, her eyes widened in surprise.

"Sensory systems, particularly for touch and smell, are also on his list of improvements, but wetware is important."

"Would your father try something on me?" asked Jilian.

"Ask him. Another problem I had was an identity issue, but I think I'm over it. I saw myself as a machine, and not human. It took me a while to accept that I'm both."

"I haven't thought about it much, and neither has John. Well, he hasn't said anything to indicate it. I have talked to him about getting a scan done. I'm not going to age, and John is."

"Father doesn't know that for sure," said Melody. "Our bodies can wear down, but can be replaced, and so can our brains as long as a scan exists. We're not immortal, but we can be recycled like old cans."

Jilian chuckled. "John isn't sure he wants to live that way, but we're talking about it. In the meantime, we're together again."

"That's sweet," said Melody. "I haven't found anyone who makes the ground move for me yet, but I think I'll know when I find him."

"There are millions of men in love with you right now," said Jilian.

"They're in love with Ariel, not me."

"I think Ariel is you, deep inside. That's why she's so real," said Julian.

"Maybe, but I had a good teacher who taught me how to become the character I play."

Jilian shook her head. "It's more than that. I envy your talent. You are amazing. Think of all the young girls who want to be just like you."

"And to know what I am? That thought terrifies me. I am not some programmed, mechanical robot, but that's the way people would see me if they knew. In their eyes, I would no longer be a human admired for creativity, but a technical marvel. It would ruin everything. That's why the security of the synth program must remain absolute."

"As it is with John and our friends. Jilian is dead, and I am the new wife, but in the privacy of our home I'm still Jilian. To our friends, it's Audrey. If they knew what I am, they just wouldn't understand.

Melody looked at her watch. "You can be sure of that. I've enjoyed this, Jilian. You've adjusted faster than I have. We need to meet the others, now. Be sure to talk to my father about you-know-what."

"Oh, I will," said Jilian. She smiled coyly, and they hugged.

They went back to the conference room and found father and Nathan still chatting there. They had another cup of coffee and then Carl and John arrived.

"We have made wonderful progress," said Carl, and he looked pleased with himself.

They chatted individually for another hour. There were no secrets between John and Jilian. After a discussion they asked father about an interesting new update for Audrey. Father clapped John on the back, and declared both of them to be naughty.

Nathan shared something that shocked Melody at first, and then worried her later. "I told your father about this, but he wasn't surprised and said I should share it with you, since it might impact what we do."

"Is he giving acting advice, now?"

"No, no, it's just that I have this friend, a friend who has become rather dear to me."

"You have a girlfriend? When and how did that happen?"

"Not a girlfriend, it's a guy, and I met him at the studio. He wants to move in with me, and I'm considering it."

Melody was struck dumb. "Oh," she managed to say, then, "anyone I know?"

"Maurice Duval," said Nathan.

"The art director? Oh, my God, he is so cute."

"I think so," said Nathan. "It scares me some, but your father reminded me that the original me had a sexual gate that could swing both ways. I can even remember a couple of minor incidents that mother covered up because she was so ashamed of me. It was one reason why I felt I was not a good son to her. I don't feel that way now, Melody."

"Archaic silliness," said Melody. "You are what you are, and the danger is suppressing it. You can go nuts doing that. So, you have a boyfriend."

"He's been coming to my house to watch old films. We cannot be seen in public together."

"Good thinking. It would blow our image, and Goldsmith would go through the roof. He might even fire us."

"I thought of that. We can be very discrete, but Maurice wants to move in next week. If anyone ever finds out about it, our story is that he lives independently in my guest house while he looks for a place of his own."

"Okay," said Melody. "I'm happy for you, Nathan, but I should be disappointed. I still think you're a wonderful kisser, you know."

Nathan smiled. "Do you think I'm faking that, especially after the surprise in your update? I love kissing you, Melody, and I enjoy being with you for our publicity shows in public. Remember what I said about my gate?"

"Yeah, I heard," said Melody. "Both ways" And then she hugged him tightly for a long time.

Father came up to them while they were still embracing. "Someone must have said something really nice," he said.

"We were talking about girlfriends, and boyfriends, and gates," said Melody.

There was a pause before Father figured that out, and then he said, "Just be careful about it."

"Father knows best," said Nathan, and Melody gently slapped his shoulder.

"Both of you come with me; I want you to meet someone."

"Have John and Jilian left?" asked Melody.

"No. We're all meeting in the conference room. Carl, too."

"Did John talk to you about a scan?"

"We'll do one to satisfy Jilian for now, but he's not keen on being reborn. It's common. Darin feels the same way, but the scan is in his contract."

"How about you?" asked Melody innocently.

"I do monthly scans. If anything happens to me, and there's someone around to do it, you can bring me back anytime as long as you make me extremely handsome and virile. I have too many projects left to do to even consider dying. Speaking of virility, I have a new update for both of you."

"Another secret?" asked Melody.

"Yes. You'll love it," said father, and he winked at them. "We'll do it before you leave in the morning. Right now I want you to meet the person who has done some of the work. Be careful what you say. She does not know about the synth project."

Everyone was back in the conference room, and there was a woman Melody had never seen before. She was tall and slender, and wore a form fitting business suit, her dark hair tied in a bun at the back of her head. The heavy-rimmed glasses she wore gave her a severe look. In seconds, Melody gave her a mental makeover and decided the woman would be attractive if she ever worked at it.

Father took them straight to that woman, and introduced them to her.

"Melody and Nathan, meet Doctor Sheila Davidson, our new Senior Scientist at Schutz. Sheila, this is my daughter Melody, and her holovision co-star Nathan Dark."

Melody caught Davidson's quick glance at Nathan, and saw her blush.

Sheila shook their hands, and smiled faintly. "What a pleasure. I've heard so much about you from friends who watch your show."

"Have you seen it?" asked Melody.

"No. I never watch holovision. I'm one of those people who take work home. The work is my entertainment.

"Sheila has already accomplished some marvelous results for us," gushed father, and Sheila's face reddened.

"Thank you, sir," she said.

"What is your area?" asked Melody.

"Primarily coding for parallel processing, but here I'm adapting that for use in the marvelous neural net matrices Doctor Lane has developed. I'm also working on new sensory chips for automated production. The chips sense things like pressure, friction, heat and cold, even light and electromagnetic forces. They are also coupled, so one sensor produces a sensation in another. It's all very technical to describe, but I do the coding for the applications."

"How wonderful," said Melody dryly, and looked at father, who was grinning at her.

Oh my God, this is the person who wrote the code for my recent update, and probably the one we're getting tomorrow, thought Melody. She's writing code for sex, and doesn't even know it. Oh, that is kinky. Naughty daddy. Naughty.

"We're expecting big things for Doctor Davidson. She was a lucky find for us," said father.

"I'm sure," said Melody. "I hope you enjoy working here, Doctor Davidson. Don't let my father work you too hard. He's a taskmaster, but underneath he's really a nice guy, except, of course, when he's grouchy.

"Thank you," said Sheila. "It's nice to meet you all, but I have work to do, so please excuse me."

"If you get a chance, watch our show," said Nathan.

"Oh, I don't think so. My friends call it gothic romance, and that's much too bawdy for me. My parents never approved of such things, but I know it's very popular. Good luck with the show."

Sheila left the room without another word.

"Well, that was abrupt," said Melody.

"Conservative upbringing," said Nathan.

"If she only knew what she was doing," said Melody. "Oh, that is poetic. Daddy, you are evil."

"There are lots of applications that have nothing to do with your desires, dear," said father.

Carl came up to them, and Melody grasped his arm. "Did you meet her?" she asked.

"Very intelligent, but cold," said Carl. "She doesn't seem like a happy person when she's with others."

"Really?" said Melody. "I didn't see that."

"She doesn't look you in the eye," said Nathan.

"That I did notice," said Melody.

John and Jilian went back to their overnight apartment, and father took Nathan on a tour. Carl and Melody went back to the lobby to retrieve Ebony, who had been waiting patiently by the receptionist's desk, always looking cute and being spoiled by attention. She needed a walk, and Melody leashed her.

They were halfway to the big double doors leading to the outside, when their world rocked beneath them.

The explosion was terrible, a low frequency boom they could feel in the pits of their stomachs. A pressure wave rolled across the tiled floor as a visible ripple. Vases and books fell off tables and shelves, and the big picture windows at first bowed inwards and then rattled for seconds.

They looked outside. A few people sat on the ground by the gate, hands covering their ears, looking stunned. Three people were still running down the street and away from the gate. Yards from the gate, flames flickered from the blackened remains of a van, and gate guards were approaching it cautiously.

"Car bomb," said Carl. "Doesn't look like anyone was hurt. That van was sitting there empty when we arrived."

The few protesters who had been near the gate hurried away. There were no bodies in the van. Carl played security officer for Shutz Fabrik and joined police in looking over the van. Evidence was found for a C4 explosion set off by a timing device, and placed to minimize injury or loss of life.

Late in the evening, the van was towed away. Father was visibly shaken by the event. They had planned to go out for dinner that night, but ate at the plant instead.

During dinner, father received a call from ISC security in Los Angeles. A backpack bomb had gone off at the gate of ISC earlier in the evening, blown a six foot gap in the fence, and killed seven people.

The press was blaming the radical elements of union protestors.

* * * *

The heat had been left off all day, and the apartment was cold. Sheila went straight to the thermostat and adjusted it. There were no messages at her workstation, and she put two files there for a little homework later in the evening.

She nuked a frozen dinner in the microwave and allowed herself a fruit yogurt for desert, then spent an hour doing some code rewrite from the file she'd brought home. She'd learned a long time ago that doing technical work right up to bedtime meant no sleep at all that night. Instead, she spent half an hour on her treadmill and then watched holovision for an hour before bedtime.

The entire Ariel series was in her cube collection, and she chose a recent favorite where Nathan Dark, as Count Ruelo, rescues Ariel from a dungeon in the castle of her rejected lover Ivan Knifebender, and flees with her while the castle burns to the ground. The closing scene with Ariel making love to her count in the tall, sweet grass of a meadow was one that Sheila could not put out of her mind, and she lived it once again before sleep.

Nathan Dark, as Count Ruelo, had become her fantasy man, a gentle yet strong man who gave his love unselfishly and without thought of return.

Sheila was in love with the character, and the man who portrayed him, and today she had met the man.

She thought he was even more beautiful in person.

"God, please forgive me for my lust," she prayed, and went to sleep that night in Nathan's arms, feeling his soft caresses, and the warmth of his breath against her cheek.

CHAPTER 19

The news wasn't any better the following morning. Holo-news suggested the explosions might be due to radical union actions, but then the unions retaliated, quickly claiming no responsibility and blaming ISC for a violent attempt to drive protestors from their gates.

There was coffee in the conference room before breakfast. Nathan and Melody would then get their updates and make the drive north again with Carl and Ebony in the back seat

"One of my federal contract monitors called me this morning," said Father. "He had the nerve to ask me if we were responsible for the explosions. The union has taken their claim to congressional representatives. My funding is in danger, if this continues."

"It has to be Cross," said Carl. "He's stepping things up, but I wonder about the reason for violence. He might be responding to what Doctor Post said to him, but no evidence for the federal investigation should be visible to him yet. The IRS will soon be requesting an audit, and his board members have been identified. The CIA is monitoring his international correspondence and has a watch over the Cook Islands property. I suspect that Cross has abandoned subtle tactics in favor of explosions and deaths to please his supporters. To a man, they are known to be advocates of a return to the old capitalistic state, and destruction of what we have now. That's what the government people think, and that's what got the CIA involved. This is not about ISC or artificial human research; it's about destabilizing the government. We can't do much until our government decides to strike back."

"That's not encouraging," said Father. "You're telling me I'm a pawn in a political game, and someone else has to move me."

"Yes, but only if you wish to stay within the law," said Carl softly.

There was a long silence. Everyone looked at Carl.

"Any suggestions for going outside the law?" asked Melody.

"Of course," said Carl. "My purpose is our security, and I make no moral judgments. If I'm defending myself from an attack by a poisonous reptile, I do not attempt to capture it. I cut off its head. Cross and his board of radical capitalists are the reptile. I could easily come up with a plan to eliminate all of them."

"Carl!" said Melody.

"It's certainly a dramatic idea, as long as I don't have to go to jail for it," said Nathan, and he laughed.

"We can't do that, Carl. We're not criminals," said Father.

"I know it's not the moral thing to do. It was just a suggestion. My hope is our government will soon act to take Cross and his organization apart. In the meantime, all we can do is guard against attack."

"Agreed," said Father. "For now, let's get your updates done so you can get out of here. Darin is waiting for us."

'Darin? I haven't seen him in a while. Is he getting enough sleep at night?" asked Melody.

Father understood her. "Yes, he is still involved with Marylyn. She really keeps him going, but manages to get him to bed on time."

"I just bet she does," said Melody, and father raised an eyebrow at her.

"Jealous?"

Melody snorted. "Not likely. I thought he was a nice guy when I first woke up, but now I don't think he cares much for us vat people."

Father snickered. "Vat people, is it? That's a new one."

Melody rolled her eyes at him.

"Darin has had some problems separating human from artificial, but I think he's improving. Be patient with him," said father.

Darin was waiting by the same chair in the same laboratory when they filed in behind their creator.

"Hi, stranger," said Melody.

"And how is stardom treating you?" asked Darin. "Hi, Nathan. I have an update for you, too, and for Carl."

"Me?" said Carl.

"Oooo, and it's a surprise," said Melody.

"That's right. None of you will know what you're getting. That's part of the evaluation process," said Darin.

Melody winked at her father, but he didn't wink back.

One by one, they sat in the chair, and Darin opened up their ports to receive the updates. There was one chip for Carl, and two each for Nathan and Melody.

Darin adjusted Melody's hairpiece. "There, all finished. Enjoy."

"Try not to drive so fast on your way home, sweetie," said Father, and he hugged her, and then shook hands with Carl and Nathan. "I'll be here all week. Darin and I have six new projects underway."

Six new synths, you mean. I wish I was a mouse in the wall to see what you're going to do with them, thought Melody.

They said their goodbyes and piled into the car, Ebony thumping her tail in anticipation of the wind in her face. Melody was in an obedient mood, and kept her speed below ninety all the way home. They dropped Nathan off at his mansion on the hill. The gates opened for them as they approached the property, and Melody let him off at the house. She was surprised when the front door opened, and Eleanor's old servant was standing there.

"I have the money for it, so I kept him on. He's been a big help," said Nathan. He grabbed his little bag and gave Melody a peck on the cheek. "See you on set," he said, and climbed the stairs to the porch. Melody drove away, but glanced in her rearview mirror to see another man appear in the doorway.

Nathan was hugging him.

When Melody reached her condo, there were no fans or paparazzi waiting for her, but Misha and Andrus were having lunch in their car across the street. They didn't even wave when she appeared.

She garaged the car, and closed the door. Carl went to his room and Ebony headed straight to the bedroom and her designated spot on the bed. Melody emptied her little travel bag and poured a glass of grape juice.

The mail had piled up below the slot in the front door. Melody gathered it up and sat down at a table to sort through it. There were a couple of bills, the rest of it the usual fan mail. She read and discarded a few of them before one envelope caught her eye. It was post marked Costa Mesa, her name and address printed in large letters and a magic marker border in black had been drawn around the edge of the entire envelope. She opened it up, and was startled by the page it contained, a sheet of paper covered with pasted in letters from magazines.

"You're going to die, bitch.

"You're going to die slow and hard.

"You'll never see it coming."

It was definitely not a fan letter, and Melody's breath quickened.

"Carl!" she called out.

* * * *

He felt like an evangelist again.

"Gerard, you are the public conscience for our nation, and you have to do something to make them aware about what is coming or might already be here. First machines, then legs, arms and hands, that is not so bad in itself, though God does expect us to endure suffering for our sins and find ways around our shortcomings."

Jacob's voice rang with the hot emotion that had once galvanized his followers. Gerard Elis, the editor in chief of 'Real Truth' had known him since his evangelistic days, had been a follower and a deacon in the church. These days his own preaching and revelations were earning him a handsome income from the sales of his weekly newspaper in grocery and convenience stores across the nation.

"God is in us, Gerard. He shares his love, compassion and intelligence with His Children, but we have usurped his authority over us. We defy the natural laws He has established, and go our own way as if He does not exist, and the depth of our sin increases each day. We defy death, seek immortality, and strive to become Gods ourselves. Artificial organs, whether heart, lung or liver, were the beginning, and now every organ has a substitute. Muscle and nerve fibers are now replaceable, and the rumors of an artificial brain are more than rumors, Gerard. It's all happening at ISC and its affiliate Schutz Fabrik, and I have information sources there. Artificial humans are not conjecture, my friend. They walk among us now.

"You should look for people with special abilities, and I have a suggestion for you. There is a new holo-star named Melody Lane who has taken the entertainment industry by storm. She is said to be the adopted daughter of Donovan Lane, who is the CEO of ISC. That is interesting in itself, because I've been unable to examine any adoption records for her. I've been told the adoption was private, and the records are sealed. The woman has appeared suddenly, and with incredible abilities. She is beautiful and alluring, but is she real? Could she in fact be an artificial creature created by Donovan Lane to replace his real daughter who died with her mother in a car crash over a decade ago? That, at least, is public record. Think of the impact of such a story, Gerard. Think of the public interest.

"Yes, I'll send you what I have right away. If it's true, the woman is an abomination, a symbol of human arrogance in playing God, and you can do something about it. Soon, Gerard, it must be soon, before Donovan Lane builds an army of these things, and who knows what could happen then?

"Thank you, Gerard, and God bless you for the work you're doing."

Jacob broke the connection, and smiled. "Well, that should start some drama for the board."

He auto-dialed his cell, waited, and then, "Max, I'm just checking in. did you send the tickets? Good. I'll give her one last chance. It doesn't seem to be going anywhere; I think she's given up on changing his mind, and she has nothing else we need. Nothing new from our other girl out there? I didn't think so, but we've got her in a very good place. Things are moving along, now. Your theatrics have helped. Keep it up, Max. Another few months and we can disappear. Yeah, I've been thinking about that, too, maybe somewhere off the west coast of Greece. That's the dream, Max. Good night."

* * * *

Marylyn called out from her upstairs bedroom, "I'll be ready in a few minutes, hon. The tickets are on the dining room table."

Darin walked over to the table and found the tickets. Tonight they would see Giselle at The Center. They had both seen that ballet before, but the seats were suburb, and the tickets hadn't cost him the usual three hundred dollars. A freebie they were, one of several they had enjoyed lately. Marylyn had told him they were perks for season memberships.

An open envelope near the tickets caught his eye. It was not stamped, and taped edges indicated it had been torn off a package. Darin was shocked by what was written on the envelope in neat, block lettering: 'Compliments of Jacob Cross. Enjoy, and keep in touch. (760)734-8971.'

Darin's face felt hot, and his hands were shaking when Marylyn descended the stairs, a purple vision in her strapless gown. She took one look at his face, and frowned.

"What's wrong?"

Darin held up the envelope. "What the hell is this?"

"It came with a package," she said, and then stepped close. "Uh, oh, I've been found out." She gave him a submissive smile.

"Did the tickets come in this?"

"Yes."

"Free from Jacob Cross. Do you know who Jacob Cross is?"

"He's the man who tried to recruit you for consulting jobs. He thought I might be able to get you to change your mind." Marylyn twisted her fingers together, and looked down at her hands. "I thought it was a wonderful job opportunity, and you refused it."

"For good reason, as it turns out. What other things did he send you besides tickets?"

Now the tears came, and her voice shook. "Little things, some jewelry, some undies, some of the things you've said you really like. Have I done something wrong, Darin?"

Darin's voice had risen in anger, but he felt badly about it and softened. "I don't know. Did you talk to this guy? Did he ask you any questions?"

Marylyn stepped closer, put her arms around him and buried her face against his chest. "He called twice, and I called him once. He wanted you so badly, said you were brilliant and wanting your talents. He asked, but I couldn't tell him what you do at ISC. He thought I would know in Marketing if you had any pending patents. There was nothing I could tell him."

"Anything else?"

"He asked casually about our social life, our favorite restaurants and cultural events. I did tell him about our dinner with Doctor Lane and Mister Harper, but there were no questions about it."

"Well, it's going to stop right now," said Darin, his anger beginning again. "Let me tell you about this guy. He's a charlatan, and a fraud. He might be involved in the troubles we've been having at the plant, and the government is after his ass for tax evasion and anarchist activities."

"Oh, dear," said Marylyn, "but how was I supposed to know that?"

"You couldn't, but you could have at least been honest with me."

Anger turned to rage as Darin took out his cell phone and punched in the numbers on the envelope. His rage was hot, his hands shaking again. He felt like his head might explode.

The call was answered immediately.

"Yes?" said a man.

"This is Darin Post with a message for Jacob Cross."

"You must have a wrong number," said the man.

"Do not call or contact Marylyn Sommers again. We know who you are, and who you have been clear back to your evangelism days. We know about your Cook Island business, and the little band of anarchists you're working with. Start running now, because the government is coming after your ass, and we hope to see you in prison soon."

"If I could, I would pass your message on to Mister Cross, whoever that might be," said the man, "but you do have a wrong number."

The man hung up. "Wrong number? I don't think so," said Darin, but as his rage subsided he suddenly felt panic about some of the things he'd just said. He breathed deeply to control himself again, and Marylyn looked terrified until he held her tightly.

Affection overcame anger, and he forgave Marylyn's innocence when she tearfully asked for forgiveness and understood his outburst. They made up with a hug and a kiss, but their enjoyment of the ballet was dampened by the memory of things said in the heat of anger that evening. Darin worried all night about what he had said, but in the morning, honesty forced him to tell Donovan about the call he'd made.

Donovan was very unhappy about it.

* * * *

Jacob clicked off his cell, and let out a deep breath he had been holding for several seconds. "Well, that was interesting," he said to an empty room. "It makes my investment in tickets and trinkets all worthwhile."

He auto-dialed his cell again, and waited two seconds.

"Max, it's me again. I just got an angry call from Darin Post."

He gave Max the details of the call.

"I'll be surprised if it's true, especially about the off shore accounts, but they seem to know something. We have new enemies, Max, and I'm taking the cap off the list of targets you can consider. No advice is necessary from me, my friend. I'm sure you'll be your usual creative self. It's time to begin cleaning our house."

Jacob went to bed that night briefly reviewing what Darin had said, but then dismissed it as the words of a dead man, and fell into a deep, peaceful sleep.

CHAPTER 20

Melody received her third death threat when the premiere of 'Ariel's Conquest' was a week away. It was the same as before, the same message pasted together with words cut from magazines, and a black border around the face of the envelope.

Melody cried when she opened the envelope, and Carl was suddenly furious, an emotion he hadn't shown before.

"The police, the studio, even your father have done nothing to effectively address this. It is not a prank, and it's affecting your life," he said loudly.

"There's nothing they can do," said Melody.

"You don't leave the house, except for work. We haven't had a run in two weeks. I don't mind walking Ebony, but it's not the same for her, and hiding out is not healthy for you. You have duties, like the premiere."

"I'm not going," said Melody, and sniffed.

She was startled when Carl yelled at her. "You can't do that! You can't ruin a career because some sick human is sending you nasty letters. I'm here to protect you. I think you trust me, and I'm tired of your father talking about field testing and then doing nothing about it. I will accompany you to the premiere. Tell him that, and I want you running again, starting right now."

"It isn't evening yet," said Melody.

"I don't care. Ebony is waiting. Get the leash."

His behavior stunned her, but there was something comforting about that. "Is that an order?" she said softly.

Carl lowered his voice, and touched her arm, his brow furrowed deeply with concern.

"Yes, it is," he said softly, and Melody was moved by the way he said it.

Melody got the leash, and Ebony leaped from the bed when she heard it rattle. The animal had seemed lethargic for a week, even with the nightly walks with Carl.

Misha and Andrus watched them from their car as they left the street and ran up into the hills.

"Back at it," said Andrus. "Wonder why they quit doing it for a while."

"Who knows about rich people," said Misha.

* * * *

The limo swerved left out of the traffic pattern, and then looped back up over the freeway to Wilshire West. Melody and Nathan didn't react to the sudden move, but Tom Lesko gasped, and clutched at his stomach. First the death threats, and then publicity deadlines, and now the event was finally going to happen. "I shouldn't have had desert after dinner," he said.

Melody leaned against Nathan, uncrossed her long legs and pushed herself deeper into the cushioned seat. "Take a pill, Tom. We're the ones performing tonight."

"And I'm here to orchestrate," said Tom. "You have fun, and I watch over The Property."

"That's us," said Nathan. "I'm sure Global couldn't survive a week without us."

"That's truer than you realize," said Tom. "We're coming in, now, so bring up your glamorous selves. There's one aisle through the crowd, and that's the most likely danger zone, if there is one. Nathan will lead with a hostess. Melody, you take Carl's left arm and my right. No autographs this time, we're going straight inside."

"Yes, sir," said Melody, and gave him a mock salute that drew the hint of a smile from him. "I hear and obey, sir."

"That'll be the day I relax," said Tom.

The limo swerved again, and slowed. Through tinted polymer, Melody could barely see the theatre, and the crowd of expectant fans packed at the entrance. This time Father was there, and Darin with his lady Marylyn, and then there was Carl, waiting to protect her.

With Melody's tears, Carl's argument with Father had been short. "It's just for an evening, and not complicated," said Father. "I suppose we can give Carl a try. Misha and Andrus will also be there."

Her family was coming together for this wonderful evening, and she was thrilled. For the moment, it was easy for her forget that among her countless fans, one did not wish her well tonight or any other night. One only wished to share in the experience of her death. And he doesn't even know what I am, she thought.

Laser beams scribed pulsating patterns on the surrounding towers of steel and glass, and 'Ariel's conquest' was lit up in meter-high letters on the theatre's marquee. As they came close, laser beams found them, and played over the car. There was a sea of faces sprouting a forest of waving arms.

The limo stopped, the door opened, and there were screams and cheers from the crowd. Ariel's Theme burst forth from huge speakers above the marquee, music from a scene with Nathan and Melody entwined on a beach of black sand. Melody had gone deep inside herself for that scene, and father had tried something new. Placed behind her left ear, a synaptic multiplexer had picked up the signals of her emotional reactions during the scene. Post production had then mixed these in real time with the sound track. Audience testing had revealed enhanced reaction to that particular love scene, and it was attributed to the modulated music track they'd listened to. Fandom comments worldwide had verified their feelings that it was not just beauty that made Melody Lane the number one holostar in the world; it was the depth and intensity of her soul.

Nathan got out first, and waved. A beautiful, young starlet took his arm and went with him on the red carpet walk to the entrance, swerving expertly to avoid the many hands reaching for them.

"Wait for Carl," said Tom. "Let him take your hand."

The noise was deafening, and Melody squinted in the bright lights. A black-gloved hand reached for her; she took it gently and exited the limo. Carl Hobbs stood tall beside her, his face without expression, his eyes covered by dark glasses giving him an alien look. He smelled like musk with a hint of polymer varnish, and his arm was as hard as stone when she grasped it.

Tom Lesko exited right behind her, and Melody hugged his arm, smiling serenely as she drowned in the plaintive melodies of an Ariel in love.

People screamed, and wept. Bodies strained against thick ropes bordering the red carpet leading into the theatre. Police stationed along the way pushed them back. Carl moved quickly, pulling Melody and Tom into a near trot. Misha and Andrus were right behind them. Dressed in tuxedos, they still looked like thugs.

Father waved to her, and Darin grinned. Marylyn gave her a thumbs up. Hands reached out to her. She smiled back, but couldn't see many faces in the bright lights. Ahead of her there was suddenly a scuffle. Someone had broken through the rope barrier, a young man in baggy pants and a loose-fitting woolen shirt. A policeman grabbed for him, but missed. The man sprinted towards her, holding out something sparkling with colors in his hand. His eyes seemed glazed, and his mouth hung open in a crazy grin.

"Carl," said Melody Lane.

Carl's right hand shot out like a piston, and hit the man in the throat. The man fell heavily at Melody's feet, gurgling. The thing in his hand bounced once, and came to rest. It was an artist's paperweight, filled with swirling colors.

Misha and Andrus hauled him roughly to his feet. The man coughed hard, his face tinted blue. He looked at Melody with the saddest eyes she'd ever seen, and pointed to the colorful glass ball at her feet.

"I wanted to give Ariel a piece of my art," he croaked, "but they won't let anyone get near you."

Tom leaned over, and picked up the paperweight as police pulled the man to one side. He caught the man's eye, and gestured to show him his gift to Ariel had been received.

Carl pulled them ahead, but Tom pulled back. "God damn it, Carl, slow down," he growled. "Do you realize what a mess you just made?"

"He was protecting me, Tom."

"By striking an over-zealous fan in the throat? You violated a fundamental rule, Carl. Donovan said you were ready for this, but you're not. You'll report to him in the morning for reassessment."

Melody stared at Tom in horror.

Carl was mute. They entered the theatre: plush, red carpet, a crystal chandelier hanging from a high domed ceiling, and there was a spiral staircase leading up to balcony level. People rushed to them: producers, directors, and a few of Melody's peers. Nathan was waiting for them, and Melody saw his eyes suddenly widen.

Melody felt a shiver pass through Carl's arm. She looked up at him, saw his mouth opening and closing without sound. His entire body began to shake.

"Oh, no," said Melody.

Tom took one look, and rolled his eyes. "Shit," he said softly. "Just what we need. He's crashing. Andrus, go outside and bring Donovan Lane back with you quickly."

Andrus rushed away while Tom held Carl up until they got to a couch.

"I think the poor man is having a seizure," said someone nearby.

Melody went up the stairs to her balcony seat with Misha as her escort. She looked back in time to see both Father and Darin pushing their way forward to where Carl sat twitching on the couch.

Misha smelled of tobacco and sweat, and his arm was like a tree trunk. Nathan sat on one side of her, a silent Misha on the other. Tom joined them half-way through the show, leaned over to whisper that Carl had been loaded safely into a van for transport to Schutz Fabrik.

The audience cheered at the end of the show. Tom joined Melody and Nathan in a reception line afterwards, and helped to hold them up under the barrage of questions and compliments they received.

As the evening waned, Melody had one moment alone with Tom, and she steered him into a corner, holding him there with a firm hand on his chest.

"How did you know about Carl?"

"You mean what he is, what you and Nathan are? Since the beginning. Eleanor told me about Nathan, and Donovan figured I'd better know all of it. I'm your manager and agent, Melody. I have to know these things. Tonight would have been a scandalous disaster if I hadn't known what was going on."

What he said made sense, but Melody was angry with her father for betraying their secret and then not telling her about it.

She made her feelings be known to him when he called the next morning to tell her Carl was resting comfortably at Schutz Fabrik after being cleared of a crippling logic loop, and then rebooted for further service.

* * * *

It was good that their argument was over the cell, for father could not see her face and realize how angry she really was.

"Who else have you told about us?" she asked.

"Nobody new, not yet, but it'll happen. It has to, Melody. So far it's only a handful, like Eleanor, Tom and the Harpers, people directly involved with the program. Eleanor told Tom on her own, but I've had to trust him, and he has earned that trust."

"I think it's dangerous," said Melody.

"What's going on right now with Jacob Cross is dangerous. I'm sure he's behind the explosions. What if he decides to begin attacking us personally? He could target Darin or me. He might even go after you, might be doing it now with those death threats. Who knows? I have to think about the company, too. If something happened to both Darin and me, who could carry on the work? There's only one person I know who could handle the core wetware work, and she is new to the company."

"Oh, God, not that Davidson woman," said Melody.

"Why not? The woman is a genius," said Father.

"Just a feeling. She seems uptight and arrogant to me."

"That's not technical, Melody. I'm not talking about revealing secrets related to you, or Nathan or Carl, but she should at least know we're working towards synth development in the near future. I'd bet money she already suspects it."

"Well—" Melody began.

"—Sheila is doing all your coding and wetware work, Melody. Do you think she actually believes it's running a production machine somewhere?"

"Probably not, if she's as bright as you say she is."

"Okay, then, I'm also going to tell her about what's going on with Jacob Cross. Up to now that has been kept from everyone in the company, and she should be worried about facing it. If Sheila is suddenly in charge, it will likely be due to something Cross ordered."

"That's very pessimistic thinking, Dad," said Melody.

"But possible."

"I guess."

"Then you'll understand why I'm talking to her this afternoon about being just under Darin in the need-to-know department."

"I don't like it, but I'll hope it's the right choice. There's another thing we need to talk about."

"Carl," said father.

"Yes, Carl. How is he?"

"Well, you know how it is with fuzzy logic. You're living with it. The fault was really mine. When he moved into your place, I upgraded his protective reaction specific to you, and left out the fuzziness, which in this case meant common sense. Carl could only see that guy coming at you fast, and what was in the guy's hand didn't matter. He took action, and then got yelled at which served as a negative feedback that put him into a weird do loop, and suddenly everyone around you was coming after you, and he flat out crashed trying to keep up with all the stimuli. I've fixed it, but he'll be more fuzzy, now, more docile."

"I want him back," said Melody.

"I don't think that's a good idea. I can use him here for research, and he won't be much good as a bodyguard anymore."

"He wasn't just a bodyguard, daddy. He was my companion."

"Oh," said father, then, "Ohhh," again. "You like him."

"Yes, I do."

"That's interesting."

"As a scientist or as a father?" said Melody.

"Both. That does put a new wrinkle on things. Tom won't support it. He wanted Carl thrown back into the vat."

"Tom works for me, not the other way around," said Melody.

"He can raise hell with the studio, or quit, or both."

"Let him. One word from me, and he's gone. He has nothing to say about my personal life. If he lifts a finger to oppose this, I will get a new agent, and so will Nathan, I promise."

Melody heard the chuckle. "That one came in fast, and just under the chin. I'll warn him. Carl should be ready in a week, and I'll drive him back."

"I'll be in the studio suites by then. I'm doing interior renovation, and having a gate and walls put up around the property. I bought out all the other condos here to make one big compound. I think you'll like it. The pool and tennis court are also mine. I'm rich, Daddy."

"Yes, you are, but you're still my little girl. Love you."

"Love you, too," said Melody.

She looked outside, and saw Andrus and Misha asleep in their car. There was a faint banging sound as workmen began tearing down walls to connect all eight condominium units.

Eventually, it would be a nice place for the three of them to live: Melody, Carl, and their pet dog Ebony.

Melody had plans for them.

* * * *

When Sheila Davidson arrived in her office, there was a note on her desk asking her to see Dr. Lane right away. She skipped coffee, and went to his corner office at the end of the long hallway.

"Good morning, Doctor Davidson," said Margot, Lane's receptionist and office manager. "Go right in, you're expected."

Sheila knocked softly on the inner door, opened it, saw Lane at his desk. He smiled, and stood up.

"Come in. Coffee's ready, and I have blueberry muffins," he said.

He served her coffee black. She took a muffin and sat in a chair in front of his desk. Lane sat on the edge of the desk to talk, and sipped coffee.

"Sorry about the short notice, but I think it's urgent we talk about something," he said.

Oh, God, have I done something wrong? thought Sheila.

"First of all, in just a short time you have become a very important member of my research staff," said Lane, and immediately Sheila felt better. "You are one of three people I trust to work with the compressed files and coding we use for our biological and neuronal sheet systems we're building. I include myself as one of the three. You have done your work without question, and we have misled you about the true purpose. I think you have a right to know what it is. The work is very secret, and I trust you to keep it that way. Do you have a problem with that?"

"No, sir," she said, and shivered with anticipation.

"You know about my scanning techniques that go back over a decade. Most of that has appeared in the open literature."

"The technique, yes," said Sheila, "but nothing about formatting or applications. There are lots of discussions and rumors about that."

Lane smiled. "I've heard some rumors, and one will soon be true. It only became possible after we finalized the neural net technology and developed the coding for all the cross linking which, by the way, you are still working on to this day."

"You have developed a human-like robotic system," said Sheila, and held her breath.

Lane smiled again, and spoke softly. "More than that. We're quite close to producing a being with a lab synthesized body and a brain of neural net layers into which are downloaded the memories and personality, the operating system if you wish, of one or even more human beings. We are very close. The first prototypes are already in process. I'm not sure what to call them. Cybernetic organisms? AI systems? Synthetic humans? We call them synths, for short."

Lane leaned over and looked closely at her. "No gasps of surprise? Are you stunned? What do you think about this?"

"I'm a bit surprised, but not much. It's a logical extension of your previous work. I didn't think it would happen so quickly."

Internally, Sheila was boiling with emotion. She fought hard to keep it from appearing on her face. She could not allow him to see her concern, or her fear.

"When do you anticipate the synths being operational?" she asked calmly.

"A year, two years tops. We're fine tuning, now, developing new sensors, compressing the brain architecture."

"What a shame it's kept secret. This is Nobel-prize work," said Sheila.

"Oh, we're applying for all the basic patents as we go along," said Lane, then, "Sheila, there's another reason I'm telling you all of this. It's not just because I respect you as a scientist. There are only three of us who are at the core of this work. If something happened to even one of us, the entire project could be in jeopardy."

Sheila frowned. "I don't understand."

"Don't you know about the demonstrations, and the recent explosions?"

"The union violence, yes. Do you think our lives are in danger?"

"I do, but not from union activists. They are all pawns in the trouble we're having. I need to tell you about a man named Jacob Cross, who is behind all of this."

For one instant, one tiny instant, Sheila lost control. Her eyes widened, heat came to her face, and tiny beads of perspiration were suddenly on her forehead, cooling the skin there. Her heart was pounding so hard she could hardly breathe. Lane saw, she knew he saw it. She swallowed hard, took a deep breath and let it out.

"There's a conspiracy against us, and we weren't warned?" she gasped, as if that was the reason for her reaction.

"We now have concrete evidence we didn't have until now. Let me tell you about Jacob Cross."

For the next twenty minutes, Sheila listened to the story of an evangelistic zealot who had stolen from his own church, and then preyed on conservative religious believers to create a fund he could steal from again. He was a con artist and a fraud, now in league with antigovernment conspirators, and probably responsible for explosions that had killed innocent people at the gates of ISC.

After twenty minutes, it was enough. Tears came to her eyes, and she was crying. Her body shook with her sobs. "I didn't know," she said. "My father was a member of his church."

Lane put a hand on her shoulder, leaned close. "Did you know him personally?"

Sheila fought a war with faith and loyalty, and for one moment put her war with faith aside.

"He contacted me when I first joined the company. My father respected him, and has very conservative opinions. I didn't even know his church had been closed down. He wanted evidence of artificial human research funded by the government, and just asked me to keep my eyes open, and I said I would. He's called me three times since then, but all I could tell him were rumors."

"Now you have more to tell him," Lane said softly.

Sheila bristled. "I'll tell him nothing. He's a charlatan, and has used people of the faith for his personal gain. He has betrayed God, and for that he'll be punished."

"You sound like a person with strong beliefs," said Lane, nearly whispering, now.

"I am a Christian, and God is in my life," said Sheila.

"And does your God have a problem with the work you're doing for us?"

Sheila thought quickly, and told a partial truth.

"No, I don't have a problem with the morality of my work," she said.

It's the application I have a problem with, and I must now pray for guidance, she thought. God will understand, if I'm trying to do the right thing.

"If the man calls again, I'll say I have nothing new for him. Maybe he'll give up, and leave me alone."

"Or we might use you to feed him misleading information. Would you be willing to do that?"

"Of course. Do you still want me to be with the company?"

"You've been honest with me, Sheila. Yes, I want you with us. Nothing has changed."

Sheila burst into tears again, her chest aching. "God bless you," she sobbed.

"He already has, in many ways," said Lane, "and I really believe He approves of the work we're doing, using all the tools He has given us."

It was like a benediction. Sheila's tears stopped as if a valve had been shut. "That was a nice way to say it," she said.

Donovan Lane gave her a tissue, and used another one to help dry her eyes.

CHAPTER 21

Misha and Andrus were not happy with the new arrangement. "What happens if he has another fit, or just goes nuts? He could kill you with a squeeze before we could react, and then we'd get the blame for it," said Misha.

"I'm willing to take that chance," said Melody.

"If he attacks you, I'll blow his head off, and I won't wait for your permission to do it."

"Fair enough," said Melody, but she shuddered at the look in Misha's eyes. She could question his odor and competence, but not his dangerous look.

Now, in the quiet of her Global guest suite, she felt safe again. The suite covered half of the twentieth floor of the Global building, and had a distant view of the ocean. Up the beach, the Santa Monica shopping ring looped far out to sea. The walls and furniture were in beige, and there were full spectrum tubes in ceiling panels to supplement the sunlight even in daytime. Melody snuggled in deep pillows on a sofa, a pile of freelance scripts in her lap, a few placed to one side, many scattered on the floor after her rejection.

Misha and Andrus patrolled the outside hallway while Carl made random rounds inside the suite. Carl moved silently, but always there was a telltale odor of musk, polymer and oil in his presence. Melody looked up as he entered the room to check the sliding doors to the balcony. Father had returned him to her just that morning, and it was the first time for just the two of them in the room.

"Talk to me, Carl. I'm tired of reading these things. Most of them are awful."

"One moment, Melody," said Carl, his voice a mellow baritone that seemed new to her. He checked the balcony, the area above and below it, then closed the doors and sat down stiffly in a plush chair facing her.

"What do you want to talk about today?" he asked, face blank.

"What? I want to talk about you. How are you feeling, now? I still don't really know what happened to you."

"Will you teach me today?" He stared at her vacantly.

"Carl?"

"I am happy, here. I am fulfilled by my tasks. My reward is the completion of a task. I've been given a reset pulse, and it modulates my powerpac. I am energized."

"Stop it! You're scaring me!"

Now Carl grinned at her. "Still here, but I am sorry I let you down. I didn't have any control over it. One minute I was doing my job according to instructions, and then I was being chastised for it, and then it seemed everyone was coming after you. I don't remember anything after that."

"Father said you had a logic loop problem."

"A do loop, yes, but at that point I couldn't do anything. Doctor Lane fixed it, called it a minor glitch, but it didn't feel that way to me. He's telling people he's made me mellower, but he hasn't done that at all. If anything, I have more freedom of choice, now. Doctor Lane called me fuzzier."

"I like fuzzier," said Melody. "It's closer to human. I missed you, Carl. I'm happy about you being back with me."

"I missed you, too," said Carl, and an awkward moment passed while they just sat and looked at each other.

"Have you received more letters?" Carl finally asked.

"Yes, every two or three days, same message each time. Someone is ruining a lot of magazines. I didn't even open the last one, just threw it in the trash. My mail is picked up at the post office while I'm here, so the hate mail is still going to the old address."

"Whoever is sending them could still know you're here," said Carl.

And two nights later he was proven correct when a black-bordered envelope was slipped under Melody's hallway door. Melody screamed for Carl, and yelled at Misha and Andrus on their ear cells while they investigated the intrusion on a highly secure floor.

An elevator had come unannounced from ground level, and Misha and Andrus had moved independently to intercept it, coming in from different directions. In the meantime, they discovered that someone had gained roof access to the elevator shaft and a service tunnel, and had dropped into the hall from an air return vent while Misha and Andrus met an empty elevator.

The entire operation had happened in less than a minute.

Melody read the letter, and it was different this time. In one instant, she went from fear to fury.

"He even knows what I wear to bed! He says I should wear the purple teddy when he comes for me. He wants to have sex, and then watch my face while he slowly strangles me! Why can't anyone catch this guy?"

"He's clever," said Carl. "He got by three of us."

"One of you stays by my door, then, instead of chasing empty elevators! I want a gun!"

"No," said Carl. "You don't have training, and it could be turned on you."

"Not a good idea, ma'am," said Andrus, and Misha nodded in agreement.

"So I'll sleep with a knife under my pillow!"

"If it makes you feel better," said Carl. "Try to sleep. The three of us will watch very closely tonight."

"Right now, that's not comforting," said Melody. Parading in front of them, she went to the kitchen, selected a large butcher knife and a small cleaver for protection, and headed for the bedroom.

"Privacy, please," she snarled at them, "and I'd better see all of you outside my door in the morning."

* * * *

Back in her bedroom, Melody began to relax again. Suddenly, Carl's body filled the doorway. In low light, his eyes glistened.

"My protector," said Melody, and smiled.

"Yes," said Carl.

Melody yawned, and stretched like a cat. "I want to have nice dreams tonight. This has been a terrible day."

"I'll be right here until you sleep," said Carl.

"I miss my dog. I miss her warmth next to me," Melody said sleepily.

"I'm sure she's having fun at the ranch for now," said Carl. "Pets just aren't allowed in this building. No exceptions, even for you."

"Stupid policy," she said, drifting off.

Her eyes closed, and Carl felt her slip away, her brain still active, but going into a different state to reorganize and refresh. He'd watched her do this many times, and wished he could follow her into her dreams. She'd given him a special soundtrack made just for him, sweetly modulated sound allowing him to duplicate her route into slumber. Once there, though, a part of her special mind moved in random fashion, flitting here and there while another part remained totally awake and ready for instant response to stimuli. Carl was amazed by the mix, but so far had been unable to duplicate the random part for himself.

Melody's patient teaching had brought him to a point where, a few minutes each day, he could lie down and consciously shut out all visual and audio stimuli to review the events of the day, positives and negatives, and then build alternative scenarios to better fit his assigned asks. The change had been gradual, but he felt it. It was as if, a few minutes each day, he was reinventing himself.

Melody's breathing was now slow and deep. Carl pondered the day's events, and remained alert. Something wasn't right. Something wasn't the way it seemed. He'd built several scenarios for the delivery of the latest threatening letter, and one of them disturbed him deeply. If true, it could mean that Melody was still in immediate danger.

Carl did not do his assigned random checks of the suite that night. Instead, he stationed himself in a dark corner of the front room near the double-door entrance.

He did not have to wait long for something to happen.

It was well after dark, and the police who had been called about the break-in had left. There was no background noise to interfere with Carl's acute hearing. Misha and Andrus remained at their station by the doors for about an hour, and then began wandering the halls again to relieve their boredom. Their attention span seemed short, even by human standards. Carl listened carefully, but the men spoke softly, and were often far enough away to exceed his audio detection limit.

The elevator came and went several times for no apparent reason, and Carl heard a door open and close twice, but otherwise it was only Misha and Andrus engaged in inane conversation, and not paying attention to their duties.

Well after midnight, it was suddenly silent outside the suite, but only for a while. Minutes later, Carl could hear snoring. Melody's human guards were asleep again, and quite impotent. Carl resisted the temptation to go outside and awake them in a frightening way, not to injure them, but to encourage their wakefulness. They were, after all, Melody's first line of defense.

Sometime later, in the darkness of his corner, Carl heard a faint thud and felt a transient vibration in the floor. There was a sustained scuffling sound after that, and then the elevator arrived, a sharp note signaling the opening of the doors. The doors closed, and there was a whine of the motor running the elevator. Silence again, then a scraping, ripping sound, metal on metal. Carl left his corner, took several steps towards the doors, and listened again.

There were more scuffling sounds, something hard being dragged on the carpet outside the room. There was a metallic rattle, and then Carl heard a distant tone, as if a great bell had been struck, a hollow sound with overtones, fading quickly. Carl stepped up to one side of the doors, his audio sensitivity ramped to a maximum.

At first there was nothing, though he continued to sense weak, transient vibrations in the floor. A soft scratching sound from low on the door was followed by a moan, and it was human. Carl felt a single shock pass through the floor, and he reached for the door latch, his left arm cocked and ready to deliver a lethal blow.

Nobody was there. The chairs by the doors were empty. The long hallway was empty. The doors to the elevator were open, but it was dark inside, and someone had ripped the air-return grate from the ceiling again, and thrown it against a wall, damaging the wallpaper.

Carl stepped outside, closed and locked the door behind him. There was a red spot on the carpet by the doors, and two faint grooves in the carpet fabric ran off towards the elevator. He followed them, nanoscale parallel processors busily building scenarios in his head as he scanned his surroundings.

He noticed that a door nearest the elevator was slightly ajar, and decided incorrectly that it was not important.

Three feet from the open doors of the elevator he saw the black cables supporting it. He peered over the edge. The elevator cab was far below him, probably at ground level. There was a click behind him, and he started to turn around.

Something heavy slammed into him, knocking him headlong into the elevator shaft. His arms and legs flailed wildly. In the three seconds of his fall, his brain reviewed nine different scenarios of what was happening now and soon after. He chose one as his right hand caught a cable and squeezed tightly. The only variable now left was the identity of Melody's assailant. His hand crushed down on the cable, slowing him rapidly, but he crashed onto the top of the elevator cab with considerable force.

A body was there, a human body crushed and broken by a long fall.

It was Andrus.

Carl dropped through the ceiling hatch of the elevator, found the controls smashed, and pried open the doors in one move with his bare hands. A guard at the front desk in the lobby gave an astonished look at the ripped and torn metal of the elevator doors, and yelled as Carl sprinted away towards the stairwell.

* * * *

Melody heard a sound, and was instantly awake. "Carl?" she asked, but there was no answer. It was cold when she got out of bed in her underclothes. She went to the closet, slipped into a silk robe, and heard the front door open and close.

"I'm up, Carl. What's going on?"

Still no answer, but Carl often waited to reply when he was finishing a task. Melody pulled up her hair, and tied it into a tail as she walked out into the front room. "I heard a noise," she said.

She was two steps into the room when someone grabbed her roughly from behind, a strong arm encircling her and a fat hand clamping down tightly over her mouth. The man's breath was hot in her ear.

"Your boyfriend is gone, and he ain't coming back. Time to party, bitch. Let's see if you're wearin' that purple thing I like so much."

It was Misha.

Melody twisted, and tried to drop out of Misha's grasp, but he pulled her up again, her feet leaving the floor and banging ineffectually against his massive legs. He grabbed her right wrist, twisted her around, and tried to pull her right arm up behind her, but the arm wouldn't move for him. "Stronger than you look," he growled. "This'll be more fun than I thought." He lifted her again, and began backing towards the bedroom.

She moaned, and let herself go limp as they reached the bedroom. Misha's grip slackened for one instant as he began to change his hold on her. She suddenly kicked backwards off the door jam, and slammed him into a bedpost, then twisted away and sprinted towards the front room. Misha caught up with her halfway to the doors and grabbed her by the hair, jerking her back so hard her skullcap came loose and she was dangling from his hand by a thin sheet of polymer.

"What's this?" asked Misha. "What the fuck is this?"

The doors shattered into splinters as Carl came crashing through them like some out-of-control tank. In the last second of his life, Misha seemed surprised by the sight of him as Carl caught him by the throat in one hand, swept his huge body up in a high arc, and drove him head-first into the floor like a spear.

There was a sickening crunch and a snapping sound as Misha hit the floor, and then silence. Light streamed in from beyond the destroyed doors. Melody fumbled at her skullcap and the dangling mass of hair, and tried to put it in place again, but it wouldn't stick.

She looked at Carl, and whimpered, and he held out his arms, and she stepped into his embrace, pressing a cheek against his chest.

"You okay?"

"No."

"Sorry I was late. I fell into the elevator shaft, and had to take the stairs back up."

She was miserable, and her eyes were full of tears, but she laughed anyway.

Carl held her for a long time. She let the skullcap dangle, and put her arms around him until her breathing slowed, and only then did they call the police.

With Carl's help, and a glue bird, they got the skullcap back in place just before the police stormed the suite with automatic weapons and armor. Carl just shook his head at the sight of them.

A sergeant examined Misha's crumpled body, and looked at Carl. "You the one who took his gorilla down?"

"Yes, sir," said Carl.

"He was attacking me," said Melody, and held Carl's arm.

"Man, did you ever body slam him. This guy is huge. What do you bench?"

Carl thought. "Five-twenty-five, and a hundred pound pull band on top of it."

"Right," said the sergeant, not believing him. "Anyway, this guy is toast, and it's self defense, but I'll still need statements from both of you."

"He killed another man. You'll find him on top of the elevator cab at ground level," said Carl.

"Okay, so you relax for now, and I'll send someone in for a statement while we go over the area."

There was no more sleep for Melody that night, and tomorrow was a working day. On the couch, she managed to doze in Carl's arms for a couple of hours. Tom and her father were called by the police at her request, but Father was in San Diego, and so it was Tom who showed up at three in the morning, looking disheveled and sleepy-eyed.

The investigation took all night, and while Melody was putting herself together for work, and Carl was cooking sausages and eggs, Tom told them what the police had found.

"Looks like he was trying to set up Andrus or even Carl as the killer. They found a quick acting drug ampoule on Misha's body. We'd find him stoned unconscious, and the two of you or maybe just Carl in the bottom of the elevator shaft with Andrus. The guy must have been a real woman hater."

"I will never hire another human to be my bodyguard," said Melody. "Their behavior is ruled by their glands."

"Please don't say that to the police," said Tom, and Melody stuck out her tongue at him.

The three of them ate an early breakfast together, and the police finally left before dawn. Melody had managed to pull herself together again, and the studio limo would soon arrive to pick her up. Melody and Carl sat down on a couch, and sipped coffee.

"You've had a hell of a night. The studio will understand if you cancel out for today," said Tom.

"There is no way I will allow a human goon to interfere with my work," said Melody, and Carl nodded as she leaned against him.

Tom smiled. "You are a tough one," he said, then, "You know, you two look cute sitting there together. You look like a couple."

"Two synthetic peas in a pod," said Melody.

"We are friends," said Carl, without expression.

"Whatever," said Tom

The limo arrived, and Melody went off to work. It wasn't until the following evening that Nathan, Dennis and his crew learned what had happened to her. They had shot twelve pages of script that day, and everyone agreed that she had performed perfectly.

CHAPTER 22

It was a report meeting, and only the domestic board members had accepted invitations to attend. These men had the most to gain from any disruption of the socialist government ruling their economy. Jacob worried about the waning interest of his four international members. Perhaps it was fear caused by the death of their British colleague. They were not stupid people. The entire board had been most agreeable after the supposed accident. Their questioning was no longer aggressive, and they now deferred quickly to his judgments, but Jacob recognized a danger in this. He could not read their minds, or predict what they might do next without his knowledge. Payments to his accounts still continued, and the banks still insisted there had been no breaches in their security. That could change overnight. What Max had told him was likely true. Lane had knowledge of his existence, and would make trouble for him, might use his government connections for a clandestine investigation the banks could not detect.

This thought was reinforced by a call he made to Doctor Sheila Davidson in preparation for his board meeting. Perhaps she would have some positive news for him this time. Her cell beeped three times before she answered it.

"Doctor Davidson, Jacob Cross here, just calling to see how you like your new position."

There was a pause, and then, "It's fine. I don't have anything new for you except the old rumors. I don't think I'm going to be of any use to you. Maybe you shouldn't bother to call me again."

Jacob heard hostility in the tone of her voice. "I'm a patient man, my dear, and I'm sure your faith will guide you in exposing anything that goes against the will of God."

"I have prayed about it, Mister Cross, and I'm happy here. Doctor Lane has been good to me, and trusted me enough to give me a lot of responsibilities. I owe him for that. Do you understand?"

"I do," said Jacob, "and I admire loyalty. The day might come when you have to weigh your loyalty to God against your loyalty to a man, and I'm sure you will do the right thing. I will keep in touch."

"Goodbye, Mister Cross," she said, and broke the connection before he could answer.

"Well, that's disappointing," said Jacob Cross to an empty room. "The poor girl has been turned, and made herself a dangerous loose end. What a shame. I really liked her father."

The meeting, this time, was in the Burbank Black Building, a boardroom rented on the third floor for only an hour, and private parking in the basement of the building. Eight members attended, men Cross considered to be the core of the organization. Box lunches were brought in with turkey sandwiches and chips, and there were coffee and tea in dispensers for them. Cross outlined the article soon to appear in tabloids accusing ISC of synthetic human research, and there was a discussion of possible lawsuits. The initiator of the discussion, a Mister M, was quickly convinced that no such lawsuits would be forthcoming. Mister M also questioned the necessity for the bombings at the gates of ISC and Schutz Fabrik, and was worried about where the finger of blame would be pointed.

Cross was ready for that one, and summarized the right wing reactions in the media and online. The explosions were government attempts to discredit the unions. They were meant to scare people from investigating the criminal research going on at ISC and Schutz Fabrik, and the cover-up went up through congress to the office of the president.

"We did not have to lift a finger to get this publicity," said Cross, smiling. "If anything, there is a demand for more bloodshed to fuel the outrage."

"And who does the killing?" asked Mister M.

You, again, thought Cross. "We have expert resources for that work. There is no way it can be tied to us. There is an old saying, gentlemen, about breaking eggs to make an omelet, and our project is the omelet."

Mister M nodded, and the others were silent, but nobody in the room looked directly at him for several minutes after that. Cross had a crawling feeling in his stomach when the meeting was over, but then as everyone was leaving the room Mister M turned to smile at him and gave him a thumbs up, and the crawling feeling went away.

Well, I guess he needed a few minutes to think about it, thought Cross.

He could not read the man's mind, of course, and that was unfortunate, for in giving the thumbs up, Mister M had suddenly made an important decision regarding his own future with the organization known as AAAH.

* * * *

Max had not attended the meeting because there were final preparations he had to make for tonight's mission, but Jacob had called and asked him to meet in the basement parking garage.

Max parked his car facing the elevator door, and waited. Several board members came down to their cars and drove away while he hunkered down out of their view. It was twenty minutes after the last of them had left that

Jacob appeared, and Max flashed his headlights at him. Jacob walked over in the gloom of the garage, and got into the front seat with him.

"How did it go?" asked Max.

Jacob told him about the meeting, and the conversation with Sheila Davidson.

"Do you want me to add her to my list?" asked Max.

"Your list?" said Jacob, and smiled.

"Enemies, objectionables, whatever," said Max. "People you don't want to have around."

"I wasn't aware of a list. Who is currently privileged to be on it?"

"Doctor Post, Doctor Lane for sure, maybe his daughter."

"The actress?"

"If you say so."

"I don't say anything, Max. The decisions are yours to make about anyone who might prevent our early retirement, and I am feeling some pressure about that."

"I have something planned for this evening," said Max.

"I don't need to hear about it, Max. I trust you to do good work."

Max saw a strange glint in Jacob's eyes, and felt a shiver. There was now little doubt in his mind about the sanity of the man who had promised him a fortune.

He had been busy for three days after weeks of observation and another week of planning. Both ISC and Schutz Fabrik used a fleet of rented limousines for managers and top executives, but in Los Angeles Donovan Lane often used his own car, and his limo use was unpredictable. Darin Post sometimes rode with Lane, but not always, so Max focused on their travel routines at Schutz Fabrik, where both men always used limousines for travel to and from the workplace. Alas, they were never in the same vehicle together, which was a complication, and their selection of a particular limo seemed random. The solution was an umbrella approach, installing remote activated explosive devices on each of the six limousines in the fleet, with a mother board to pick and choose which target to destroy.

Bomb placement was straightforward. Max assembled six brick-sized devices with trackers and stub antennas that could be magnetically attached beneath the dashboard of the vehicles. Each Thursday, the rental agency hired crews to wash the limousines by hand, including the interiors. It was a different crew each week, men looking for work lining up early in the morning for a job. Max joined their ranks, and the evening before his planned shift he stored the thirty-pound case holding his devices behind packing crates near the washing area. The following morning he was first in line for work, volunteering for interior vacuuming and scrubbing. One device stored nicely under his loose clothing. As he went from one car to another, cleaning rags were replaced and another device picked up. Interior front windows were sprayed, and in less than ten seconds a device installed beneath the dash. In three hours he had placed all six devices, and written down the license plate numbers of each vehicle. And at the end of the shift, he received forty-five dollars in cash for his work.

Back in his motel room, he put the mother board of his transmitter in a box and wired it to six toggle switches which he labeled with the license plate numbers, and then attached a nine volt battery to the complete assembly, leaving one wire disconnected to conserve battery life. He relaxed, then, watched some holovision, and took himself out to dinner with the money he had earned that day.

But Jacob did not want to hear any details about what he was doing.

"You sure you don't want to know my targets for tonight?" asked Max.

"I assume they are on your list," said Jacob. "Good hunting."

"How much longer before we disappear?"

"Maybe a month, after the next meeting. I'm giving a big party for them in the islands."

"Do we leave together?"

"No, we'll meet somewhere. I haven't decided where, yet."

Max smiled nastily. "You wouldn't want to disappear on me, you know. I'd feel better if some of that money was in an account with my name on it."

"I'll see to it, Max. You can trust me."

"Oh, I'm sure I can, like you can trust me to do what I have to do if something happens to my retirement plans."

Jacob laughed. "I hear you, Max, and it's no concern. There's plenty for both of us in those accounts. Another month and it's ours."

"Okay, and as a bonus I'll add Davidson to my list."

"Whatever you think best, Max. I need to get back to the office, now. Have fun tonight. I'll look for something in the media."

Jacob patted Max on the shoulder, got out of the car and disappeared into the gloom of the garage. Max waited for a few minutes, but no other car left. Finally, he drove back to his Hollywood apartment to assemble the package for his evening performance.

His targets for the evening were Darin Post and his lovely girlfriend Marylyn. Nothing personal, just business, killing by remote. The thrill only came when he was allowed to use his hands or a weapon close up so he could watch the face of his victim, and such opportunities were rare.

Every Friday, Darin took the mag-rail up from San Diego, and his girlfriend was there to meet him at the station with her shiny, black BMW. Every Friday, she drove them to a restaurant for dinner, and then to some venue for expensive entertainment. Marylyn, it seemed, was always an expensive date. Saturday until Sunday, the couple disappeared into her high rent condo before Darin again was taken to the mag-rail station for his trip back to San Diego.

It was their routine, regularly timed and predictable, that was so appreciated by Max.

He was at the station before Marylyn arrived, and she parked in her usual spot. He enjoyed a fast food burrito while they waited for the train to arrive.

Darin came out of the station with a small bag, and waved when Marylyn flashed her lights at him. There was a ritual of hugging and kissing when he got into her car.

Max followed them back to Marylyn's building, and waited patiently while they did whatever they did before dinner. When they emerged, Darin was still in his business suit, and Marylyn wore a classic 'little black dress' that quickened Max's breath, even at a distance.

He followed them to Angeny's Steak House on Wilshire, and a valet took their car to the service parking area out of view behind the restaurant. Max parked along the street, and strolled to the darkened parking area with his bag draped casually over a shoulder. There was no fence to obstruct his entry. In less than two minutes, he found the BMW and slid beneath it to put his package in place just forward of the gas tank, fastening it there with three strips of duct tape. He returned to his car, and waited for just over an hour and a half before Darin and Marylyn came out of the restaurant. A valet went to retrieve their car.

The tragedy of Max's evening was that the car was out of his view until it pulled up in front of the restaurant.

The valet was a twenty-two year old man who attended school days and worked two jobs evenings to support himself. Speed meant good tips, and he was in a hurry. Car rows were separated by concrete curbs to prevent cars backing into each other. The valet remembered backing the BMW into its space. He was wrong. He put the car into gear and lurched forward, banging his head on the ceiling as the car bumped and rattled its way across the curb in front of it, and then a second one a few inches beyond. The scraping sounds beneath the car nearly stopped his heart, but beyond the curbs there was silence. Shit, thought the valet. Maybe they won't find out until they get an oil change. He delivered the car, and the man gave him a five dollar tip.

Across the street, Max watched them get into the car. Darin drove, and when they passed by, both were laughing about something. Max held the detonator in his right hand, and watched their car in his rear view mirror. A reliable range was no more than three hundred yards. He waited two seconds, and pressed the detonator.

There was a huge explosion off to his left and behind the restaurant, sending up a shower of sparks and wispy flames.

Max watched the fading tail lights of the BMW.

"Well, that's not good," he said to himself.

He drove away quickly when people began pouring out of the restaurant to see what had happened.

CHAPTER 23

They argued about it for an hour by cell, but in the end Carl had his way. He resolutely refused to leave Melody even for a day, so Darin and Donovan took the mag-rail up to Los Angeles for their meeting.

After the attack by Misha, Melody had refused to stay in the suite provided by the studios. She cited the lack of security there, but those close to her knew the primary reason was to find a place that would welcome Ebony, for she missed the dog terribly and often said so.

At her own expense, Melody rented the entire top floor of the Bristol Hotel two miles from the studios, and on a little hill that offered a marvelous view of the city. Security was minimal. The reception desk was partially obscured from the entrance by a sundries' kiosk, and after ten in the evening there was no receptionist, and the doors were locked. Occupants had keys, and visitors could be rung up by using the intercom panel by the doors. The hotel was old, but clean. There were three suites on the top floor, and Melody had rented all of them, leaving the connecting door open day and night. Carl spread his work out in one suite, Melody and Ebony spending most of their time in another, and they had converted the third into a kind of gymnasium, with a huge kitchen and sauna. The entire space totaled that of her new home, but that would be under renovation for at least the next sixteen weeks.

Melody and Carl drove in her Mercedes to pick up Darin and Father at the mag-rail station. It was dusk when they got back to the hotel. She garaged the car in the basement, and they took the elevator up. At the fourteenth floor the elevator stopped, and Melody had to insert a special key to take them to her suites at level fifteen. The doors to a connecting stairway were always kept locked, and the key to that was only in Melody's possession. Father liked what he saw, and was satisfied with his daughter's security precautions.

Ebony greeted them all with enthusiasm, and went back to her place in the bedroom to await her dinner. Carl had become a proficient cook, and a stew had been in a slow-cooker several hours before their arrival.

"I get home so late," said Melody, "and I'm not very good in the kitchen. It started out as a hobby for Carl, and now I'd probably starve without him."

They sat down at a linen covered table with settings of silver, and there were gold-bordered plates and crystal glasses. Carl opened a bottle of red wine and poured for their guests. The aroma of beef stew and fresh baked bread filled the room. Carl disappeared into the kitchen and came out carrying a bowl of food for Ebony's dinner. A moment later he placed large bowls of stew and flat noodles in the center of the able, and then added a plate of buttered, fresh bread. "Serve yourselves," he said, the turned down the room lights to half intensity, and finally sat down. He raised a glass of juice he'd poured for himself.

"To friends," he said.

Melody raised her glass. "And to family," she said, and they drank.

Outside the big picture window, the lights of the city sparkled in the distance. Stew was ladled onto noodles, and bread was passed around. For the human guests, the wine was a perfect complement to the meal, and Carl promised them ice cream when they were finished eating.

Donovan and Darin sat at the ends of the oval table while Melody and Carl sat facing each other, and Donovan watched them throughout the meal. He watched the little glances between them, the raised eyebrows a signal of something unsaid but understood, the hints of smiles, and he remembered what Melody had said to him during an argument.

"He's not just a bodyguard, he's a companion," she'd said.

And now I think he has become much more than that, thought Donovan.

My little girl, my Melody, first dead and then returned to me in a new form, and I worried, I worried a lot about whether or not it would really be her, and how much of her mother I would see in her, and it's all there, everything I'd hoped for in the core of the being I created. She is so beautiful, and I owe no apologies for doing what I did, not to anyone, even God. And Carl, my man, what a change in you. You were made for battle, a new warrior caste with pure military experience in your core. That part remains, but there is something new, a calmness, a gentleness when she is present, a light in your eyes when you look at her. I didn't think it possible, but you have somehow reinvented yourself. I've been focused on the physical. There is something I haven't duplicated, something that goes beyond the physical body and brain structure to produce a human being, and yet it is there in these two people.

"Carl, you are a terrific cook," he said.

"Thank you, sir. I enjoy doing it. Would you like some ice cream? I have vanilla, and several sauces to choose from."

"Absolutely," said Donovan. He reached over to pat Melody's hand, and did his single eyebrow wiggle at her. "He's a good guy to have around, isn't he?"

"Absolutely," said Melody, and gave Carl a beautiful smile.

The conversation suddenly turned serious when Melody turned to Darin, and asked, "How are things going with Marylyn these days?"

Carl served them little bowls of ice cream, and jars of sauces were passed around.

"Pretty well. We just had that one blowup about her getting sucked in by Cross. She really thought she was helping me. I'm still kicking myself for shooting my mouth off on the cell. I hope I didn't start something. Do you read the newspapers?"

"Never," said Melody. "It's too depressing."

"I read the headlines," said Donovan.

"You probably missed a short article on the back pages last weekend. Someone set off a bomb in the valet parking lot of Angeny's Steakhouse. It blew a three foot crater in the asphalt."

"More bombers," said Donovan. "More crazy people."

"Maybe, but Marylyn and I had dinner at that steakhouse the night it happened, and Marylyn's car was parked in the valet lot. We were gone when the bomb went off, but it must have been pretty close to when we were there."

Everyone was exchanging glances.

"You didn't hear anything?" asked Carl.

"Probably a coincidence," said Donovan. "That doesn't mean we shouldn't be cautious. I wouldn't put anything past Cross, once things begin to close in on him."

"You remind me that I have an announcement to make," said Carl. "We now have a defector to work with."

"What?" said Melody.

"He's a defector from the AAAH board. His name is John Modrin. He contacted the FBI and will help bring down Cross's operation if he's given immunity from prosecution. He's a corporate head of a software engineering firm in New Jersey. So far, he's given us meeting places and times, and the identities of the active board members. He says Cross is behind the bombings at our plants, and is planning new bloodshed, but he had no specifics. The board members fear Cross; they think he murdered one of their colleagues. They also fear an associate of Cross named Max Schuler."

"That's the guy who interviewed me about consulting jobs," said Darin. "He's the one I said looked like a thug."

"Likely so," said Carl. "John Modrin says he attends some meetings when decisions are to be made, but not others. He says nothing, just watches them. They are intimidated by him. It sounds like he's an enforcer for Cross. The FBI has not found him in any data base, and we have no photograph."

"I remember what he looks like," said Darin.

"Perhaps we can do a sketch together," said Carl. "I have a program for doing it digitally."

"Does it take long?" asked Darin.

"It shouldn't," said Carl. "We can do it tonight, if you wish."

"Okay," said Darin.

Carl turned to Donovan. "Sir, I can think of several ways John Modrin can be useful to us, but some of them require he be scanned. Would you be willing to do this, if the FBI will allow it?"

"To get more information out of him?" asked Donovan.

"More than that, sir. I have many photographs of the man, and recordings of his voice. I'm thinking we might make a synth of him for infiltration purposes. I'm sure the FBI won't risk him personally for that assignment."

"Good idea," said Donovan. "I have seven blanks ready, and five of them are male. It'll take two days to print the features, and another for uploading. Send me what you have, and we'll get started on it."

"I have all the material in the next room," said Carl.

"We'll need FBI permission first," said Donovan.

"No, sir," said Carl. "They only need to know about the scanning and any relevant information you get from it. Synthetic human beings do not exist. They are only speculation."

"You're right. Let's hope they approve the scanning," said Donovan.

Melody set her coffee cup down hard on the saucer. "This conversation is really making me squirm, guys. I'm glad Nathan isn't here. All this talk about blanks and printing and uploading. Doesn't it bother you, Carl? It sure bothers me. I was once a blank, as you so delicately put it, and then I was printed up like a big doll and clever things loaded into me. I don't need to be reminded of it. God, I hate that kind of talk!"

"Not again," said Donovan.

"The longer we exist, the more human we feel. I'm sorry, Melody. I was insensitive to bring the subject up in your presence," said Carl.

Carl looked contrite, his brow furrowed, and Melody gave him a sweet smile. "Of course you're forgiven," she said.

My, my, thought Donovan. "Let's lighten it up. Carl, you and Darin can work on the sketch and I will have a nice chat with my daughter," he said.

They agreed. Carl led Darin to his suite, and Donovan adjourned to the front room to sit on a plush, white couch there. Melody sat down next to him, and he grinned at her.

"What?" she said.

"So, you and Carl are now a couple."

There was a pause, a serious expression on Melody's face. "Yes, I guess we are."

"Do you love him?"

There was another pause. "I care about Carl, and he cares about me. Is that love?"

"Probably," said Donovan.

"I hope you're not wondering if a synth is capable of loving," she said.

"I don't doubt that for a second, and I hope you're not wondering whether or not a human can love a synth. I love you, Melody, because you're my daughter, and I know you love me."

"Well, I'm glad that's settled," she said.

"I do wonder about something, though," said Donovan. "It's personal, but I'll ask anyway, as your father, of course. Do you two ever have what we might call romantic relations?"

Melody raised her eyebrows in mock surprise. "Does daddy want to know if we ever have sex?"

"Well, I did give both of you some sensor and wetware updates that could be useful in that department. Nathan, too. Consider it a technical question, if it makes you feel better about answering."

"I don't have a technical answer. We both like touching, leaning against each other while we read. We cuddle, like the time after Misha attacked me. I love that. He knows I get all tingly when I rub myself softly, especially on my lips. He did it once when I was feeling playful, and I nearly cried with pleasure. But we're both so busy, my work day so long. We just don't have much quiet time together, and when we do we usually run, and since the incident with Misha, Carl has been giving me defense lessons every morning. He says I still haven't discovered my real strength, but when I hit that big bag it swings pretty far. I will never allow myself to feel as helpless as I felt when Misha picked me up."

"You have Carl here."

"Not every hour of the day and night, and he wants me to be able to defend myself. My father gave me an exceptional body, he says, and I need to know how to use it. Woo, woo."

Donovan laughed. "I'm still working on improvements," he said.

Carl and Darin returned to the room, and Darin passed around a digital sketch showing a face with heavy brows, small eyes, a prominent nose and cleft chin. "This is Max," he said, "as close as we could get, and it's pretty close."

Melody took one look, and said, "A thug if I ever saw one. We could use him on the show. No wonder your interview was so short."

"Don't underestimate him; he's Cross's right hand, according to our informer. I doubt if Cross would trust a stupid man in that capacity. I also suspect he has some talent with explosives. Keep an eye open for this guy," said Darin. "He could be anywhere."

Carl handed a file to Donovan. "Here is the material on John Modrin. It should be all you need to finish up a synth, and I've already warned the FBI about the advisability of doing a scan. I'm sure I can have that arranged for you in a day or two."

"We'll get right on it," said Donovan. "We should get to bed. Tomorrow begins early for all of us."

"We have you in the south bedroom," said Melody, and pointed. "Your bags are there. Carl will drive you to the station. I'll be out of here at six."

They stood, and Melody hugged her father. "Be careful," she murmured.

"You, too," he said.

Melody hugged him tightly, feeling his human warmth, smelling the spicy odor of the soap he used. There was a strange, disquieting feeling in the pit of her stomach.

"I love you, Daddy," she said.

"And I love you too, sweetie," he said, and squeezed her.

They went to their rooms, and straight to bed.

In the morning, Melody and Carl were up at five for an intense workout in their home gymnasium, and then a light breakfast. The studio limo arrived for her at six, and the rest of them left half an hour later as the sun came up to begin a new day that would be long remembered.

* * * *

Max Schuler had been living out of his car for four days, waiting for just the right moment to reveal itself.

Schutz Fabrik was nestled in one of three shallow canyons running in parallel up into the hills above the city. There was only one road running up to the plant. A guardhouse and barrier had been erected a hundred yards down the road from the main gate to keep protestors at a safer distance from potential trouble, and there was no place anywhere along the road where Max could hide his car. A topographic map showed him a narrow road up the neighboring canyon to a cell tower at the top of the hill, and numerous groves of trees where he could keep his car out of view from the road.

Limousines rented by Schutz Fabrik came and went as necessity arose. They could only be identified by their license plates, and even with good binoculars it was necessary for Max to get within two hundred yards of the main gates to see the plates clearly. In an ideal universe his targets would all be in the same car at the same time, but Max had no illusions about ideal universes. He was playing a statistical game, with people in different cars at roughly the same time, and a single moment in which to make his strike. There would be no second chance for his plan to work. His first target was Lane, followed by Post, and Davidson a distant third. Davidson often used her own car, and Max considered her unimportant for the moment. There were other ways to get to the woman. Lane and Post often left work around the same time, but at varied times until after dark. Usually, but not always, they used separate limos. He had learned all of this from ten days of observations before he'd even wired the limousines with explosives.

He had now waited four long days and evenings for the moment of his strike to arrive.

Each morning he left his motel room before dawn and drove up the canyon towards the microwave tower to hide his car in a grove of trees. Each morning he loaded his backpack with water, some food, his binoculars and the box with six death-dealing switches, and made the climb over the hill to an isolated grove of trees and thick brush some two hundred yards from the gates of Schutz Fabrik. There he remained in a little hollow he had dug out, until well after dark, constantly observing the target area, and constantly ready to unleash destruction in seconds.

Incoming vehicles could not be targeted, since the occupants were not visible, but did show who arrived that day. For two entire days, Donovan Lane and Darin Post had not even shown up at the plant, and Max wondered if they had moved to ISC in Los Angeles, in which case his entire plan was a failure. But at noon on the third day, Lane and Post appeared, getting out of the same limo at the front entrance of the Schutz administration building. It had happened quickly, Lane out of the front seat, Post the back, before Max had a chance to react. The explosion would be focused in the front seat area. Once the occupants were out of the car, the chances of fatal injuries would be slim. Max needed the cars to be moving, the occupants securely inside.

Max was now alert to the possibilities for the day. He waited patiently, staring through the binoculars at the loading area, the deadly little box of switches in his lap.

At exactly six in the evening, he was rewarded by the appearance of Lane and Post at the front entrance. His heart jumped when he saw Sheila Davidson come out of the building behind them. She began talking to Post as two limos moved towards the entrance. Lane got into the front seat of the first limo, and Max could clearly see the license plate. He looked down briefly at the box in his lap, found the correct switch and put his finger on it. When he looked again, Davidson had turned to walk back into the building, and Post was stepping towards a limo turned partially in towards the building. For one horrible second, Max realized he would not be able to see the license plate. Lane's limo was already moving quickly towards the gate, would be out of range in a few seconds at most. One target was certain, the other less so, and Max had spent a lot of time assembling and placing the explosives.

"What the hell," he said, and threw all six of the switches in rapid succession.

He burst out of cover, and ran up the hill as the six explosions erupted flame and debris inside the gates of Schutz Fabrik.

* * * *

The call from San Diego came in early evening when Melody and Carl were preparing dinner. Another episode had been wrapped that day, and Dennis had sent everyone home early. It was a luxury they enjoyed every two to three weeks, and always took advantage of. They had done an extra run with Ebony, and then spent some leisurely time in the gym that left them both hungry.

Carl was preparing a spinach quiche, while Melody chopped vegetables for a salad. Ebony was pacing back and forth in anticipation of dinner when the cell buzzed in the next room. Melody had taken the cell extension out of her ear for her workout, and left the kitchen to answer the call.

Carl heard her answer the call as he finished preparing the quiche. There were some muffled words, and then silence. Carl moved to deposit a mixing bowl into the sink.

Melody's scream was ear-splitting, a shriek that went on and on. Carl dropped the bowl, shattering it to pieces in the sink. Ebony yelped, and fled the kitchen, heading towards Carl's office.

Carl rushed to the living room. Melody stood in front of the couch, hands pressed to the sides of her head, the cell lying at her feet. When she saw him, her shrieks turned to racking sobs, her entire body shuddering, and tears rolled down her cheeks. Carl grabbed up the cell from the floor.

"Who is this?" he demanded. "What's going on?"

"Is this Carl?" It was a woman's voice.

"Yes."

"This is Sheila Davidson. We've been attacked at the plant, car bombs in the limos, and they all went off at once as we were leaving for the day. Doctor Lane is dead, and Doctor Post has been badly injured. I was there, too, and just missed getting hit by debris."

Carl could barely hear her over the sound of Melody's sobbing. She sat down on the couch and put her face in her lap, grasping her knees. Ebony came into the room, and hesitated before walking over to nuzzle her mistress' hand.

"You're in charge, now," said Carl. "Where did they take Darin?"

"Saint Elizabeth Medical Center. It's in old town. He's still in surgery. I'll be there in half an hour."

"We won't come down tonight. They will forbid visitors until morning at the earliest. I have to take care of Melody first, and we'll be there in the morning. Are you okay?"

"No. I'm still shaking like a leaf, but I'm not hurt. I'll ask the medical people to look me over."

"Good idea. You're needed, Doctor Davidson. There are things we have to do."

"I understand that. I'll see you in the morning," said Sheila, and she broke the connection.

Carl sat down on the couch by Melody, and put his arm around her as she sat up again. Her shrieks and sobs were now moans, a terrible sound that distressed him even more than the sound of crying. Her eyes were closed and puffy, cheeks soaked with tears, and her fingernails raked at the fabric of the couch.

He turned her towards him, and Ebony whimpered, put her big head on his knee. Carl squeezed Melody tightly, and felt her arms go around him, her face pressing into the crook of his neck. There was really nothing he could say or do, except to hold her in her terrible grief.

He turned her face, and brushed hair from her forehead, lightly ran a finger over the wetness on her cheek. She opened her eyes, still moaning, and the look in her eyes made him ache all over. He touched her lips with a finger, and then leaned over a little to touch his lips to hers, a light brushing once, then twice, then again as he felt her strong arms tighten around him.

The moans became soft sobs as she turned her face against his neck, and he whispered into her ear.

"I promise you, Melody, there will be consequences for this. There will be justice."

The sobbing suddenly stopped, and then there was a long silence. Melody squeezed his back hard with one hand, her other hand sliding up to the back of his neck. She pulled back to look at him, and her expression was disturbing. The color of her eyes had gone from blue to deep violet, and her voice was a raspy whisper.

"I don't want justice, Carl. I want them dead. I want all of them dead. Will you kill them for me, Carl? Please?"

He shushed her, squeezed her tightly to him, and she began to sob again. Minutes later, she seemed to have exhausted herself, and was dozing. Carl picked her up and carried her into the bedroom, Ebony close behind. He put Melody on the bed, and lay down beside her, encircling her with one arm. Ebony jumped up, lay down on the opposite side of Melody and pressed up warmly against her, and the three of them went to sleep that way to end their terrible day.

PART THREE: CONSEQUENCES

CHAPTER 24

It was one in the afternoon before a nurse came out to say they could go in for a visit. Darin had been removed from intensive care, and taken to a room at eight that morning. Carl and Melody had been with Sheila in the lobby since eight, and Nathan arrived with Maurice Duval in tow. Maurice would not be privy to their conversation with Darin, and planned to do some shopping in old town.

When Sheila met Nathan for the second time, he kissed her hand grandly, and she made no effort to hide a blush.

She can light up like a Christmas tree, thought Melody. I should talk to her about a makeover.

Maurice nodded a greeting to all of them. When he left, Sheila asked, "Who is that man?"

"Art Director for my show," said Melody. "He and Nathan are good friends."

"How good?" asked Sheila.

"Very good," said Melody, and smiled.

"Oh," said Sheila, with obvious disappointment.

A nurse took them to an elevator, and they went up to the third floor. Darin's room was at the end of a gloomy hall, but they found him sitting up in bed and spooning red Jell-O out of a glass. His head was wrapped in bandages, and there was an obvious bulge from a thick chest wrapping. He waved to them as they came into the room.

Melody's eyes teared up when she saw him, and her sorrow returned in a rush. Darin took her hands in his, and looked down at their entwined fingers.

"I'm so sorry about your father, Melody. There was no warning, no chance to get him out of the car. I'm lucky to be alive. I was just opening the back door when the bombs went off. The door took most of the shrapnel, but I got the rest. I think they cut a pound of metal out of me, but none of it penetrated deeply. I was a bloody mess, though. I heard you scream, Sheila."

"I ducked behind a column, but a jagged piece of metal hit it inches above my head. I saw your body go flying," said Sheila.

Darin turned to Melody. "How are you doing?"

"Lousy," she said, and wiped at her cheek. "We don't have to speculate about who's behind this. What are we going to do about it?"

"I called the FBI this morning," said Carl, "and they're moving ahead with an audit, but there's nothing else they can do right now except send John Modrin to us for a scan, and we need to do that right away."

"What good will that do? They should arrest Cross for murder, or at least inciting violence, and pick up that Max guy who works for him."

All of them could hear a dangerous anger in her voice. This was not the Melody they were used to.

"There's no evidence for that," said Carl. "They wouldn't be able to get a warrant. We, however, do not have such restrictions. There are things we can do if we're willing to act outside the law."

"Such as?" asked Melody.

"I can't discuss that here, not in the presence of Doctor Davidson. There are certain facts she doesn't know, and especially with Doctor Post incapacitated she has to be a part of any plans we make."

"Oh," said Melody, and everyone looked at Sheila.

"What?" she said.

"We all knew it was coming," said Darin, "and Donovan trusted her completely. He told me that. I'm going to be in here at least a few days, and Sheila will be it for new wetware and programming. She has to be told, and this is a good time to do it, since we're all here."

They all looked at each other. Lips pursed in agreement.

"I don't understand what's going on," said Sheila.

"So who wants to go first?" said Darin.

"I will begin," said Carl, and gestured to two chairs near Darin's bedside. "Please sit down, Doctor Davidson, and be more comfortable."

She sat down, and Carl sat next to her. He leaned forward, looking serious, while the rest of them watched anxiously.

"You are an intelligent, professional woman, Doctor Davidson, so I will be direct and to the point. The rumors you've heard about the development and manufacture of synthetic human beings are based on truth. Artificial intelligence systems in human form do exist. The first prototypes are with us now, and several are nearing completion in the laboratories of Schutz Fabrik."

Sheila looked shocked at first, with a quick intake of breath, but then she smiled. "I knew it," she said. "I knew he was close. Even the work I was doing pointed to it, all the new sensors, the neural net layering and compression, and all of it parallel processing. I was supposed to be working on small machine applications, but it seemed excessive to me."

"These are not machines," said Carl. "They are functioning human beings with synthetic bodies and cores uploaded from real people, some of whom are deceased."

Sheila scowled. "The man you are fighting would call them an abomination, a sin against God, and my father would agree with him."

"And what do you think?" asked Melody.

"Once, I might have agreed with my father, but now I'd have to tell him he's wrong. Melody, your father and I often talked about the rumors and about the good things that could be done if the rumors were true. I don't think he had sin in his heart, and he told me once that God guides us in doing what we do. I believe that, now. I've done work on the prototypes, wherever they are. I would like to meet them, and do more."

"That can be easily arranged," said Darin, smiling, "since you and I are the only two people in this room who can be classified as truly human. The first prototypes are right here in front of you."

Sheila gasped, and sank back into her chair. She looked at Melody first, and Melody gave her a little wave as a tear ran down her cheek.

"Hi, I'm Melody Lane, and I'm a synth," she said. It was a joke they occasionally made about themselves. "I died with my mother in a car accident when I was thirteen, and Daddy brought us back. An artist figured out what I'd look like at twenty-six, and here I am, with mom inside me, too. It gets a little weird sometimes."

Now Melody looked at Darin. "I love my dad, and I want him back."

"We'll talk about it later," said Darin. "Nathan?"

"Me, too," said Nathan, and looked straight at Sheila. "I died in my fifties from a wild life of excess in drinking and other pleasures. My mother was a famous actress, and still wanted me back. I like to think I've done better this second time around."

"That is most certainly true," said Melody, and hugged him.

"That leaves me, the boring one," said Carl, trying unsuccessfully to be amusing, because there was nothing his audience saw that was boring about him. "I was uploaded from military-experienced people to engage in police and security work, but I've discovered a skill in doing related data analysis."

"He has saved my life," said Melody, "but I'm still trying to lighten him up a bit."

"There is one other synth that's operational," said Darin, "but that person isn't relevant to what we're doing here."

"You're all so real," said Sheila, astonished. "I would never have guessed."

"We are real, and there is nothing to guess about. This is not science fiction. Now, what are we going to do about Jacob Cross?" said Melody.

"If he's like my father, then he hates the concept of you, or any other science he thinks goes against the wishes of God," said Sheila. "His reasons for attacking us go deeper than his relations with anti-government conspirators. He will not stop with the death of Donovan Lane."

"He will if we kill him first," said Melody softly, and everyone stared at her.

"I tend to agree with you," said Carl, "but I don't think it's the first step for us. Cross is not planting the bombs, it's his colleague Max, and right now we only know he's nearby. He is the physical threat to us, and we have to find him."

"You once said something about cutting off the head of the snake. Well, that snake is Jacob Cross," said Melody.

"For now, we'll let our government go after him. The IRS will demand an immediate audit, and we're ready to track any bank transfers or even freeze accounts. We have a complete list of AAAH board members, and their affiliations. A story will soon go out to all the media, exposing their activities and relations with Cross, and his history of tele-evangelism fraud will be exposed again. John Modrin tells us there is already considerable discontent on the board, and only fear has kept them in line. With exposure, the hope is they'll all break and run. They could all be facing lengthy prison sentences."

"For murder?" Melody asked, her voice cold.

"This is only part of the plan, Melody," said Carl. "Please be patient."

"John Modrin will be scanned, and his synth will attend AAAH meetings to keep us on top of their activities, but it won't be for long," said Darin. "Things should crumble quickly."

"For now, John Modrin is on his way here for a scan, and we have a new synth to prepare," said Carl.

"I can do the wetware from the scan in a few days, but I know nothing about prepping the body of a synth," said Sheila.

"If I can get out of here in a few days, I can have the feature printing done in two days," said Darin. "We could have the synth ready in a couple of weeks."

"A week would be better," said Carl.

"Not possible," said Darin, and Sheila nodded agreement.

"John doesn't know when the next board meeting is. We'll have to get lucky," said Carl. "I'm circulating the sketch of Max Schuler to all the local police agencies, and eventually it'll be nationwide and even circulated by Interpol. We'll have to hope for some luck there, too. None of us are safe from him."

There was a short silence, and they all looked at each other. "Well, that's it, then," said Darin. "This has been a terrible couple of days. Melody, again, I'm so sorry."

"I have to make the arrangements, now," said Melody. "I'll let you know when the memorial service is, but you'll probably still be here."

"Marylyn will attend for me," said Darin.

"Please invite me," said Sheila.

"Of course," said Melody, and gave her a hug. "You're a part of our family, now."

Sheila wiped her eyes dry when the hug ended.

Carl and Melody picked up Ebony in a room off of the lobby, and left right away. Sheila went back to work, and Nathan waited for Maurice to return from his shopping.

The drive back to Los Angeles was at high speed, and mostly in silence. Carl dozed when it was clear that Melody did not want to talk, her face grim as she steered in and out of traffic.

Back at the hotel, there was no time for an afternoon run. Melody made several calls to a funeral home and Memorial Gardens to finalize the cremation, service and internment of what remained of her father.

She did not eat dinner that night, but allowed Carl to lead her into their home gymnasium for a stress relieving workout. There, as Carl watched silently, she hit the big bag so hard that it fell to the floor, and they had to replace the chain it had been hanging from.

* * * *

It was eight in the morning when John Modrin arrived to be scanned. Two FBI agents accompanied him, and were allowed to be present during the process. The technology was public record, and all the synth work was on another floor. The agents had not been told about it.

Sheila met them in the lobby. John was a distinguished looking man with a nice smile, neatly barbered, and wearing a tailored suit. It was hard to see him as a traitor, or as a coward jumping ship to avoid prosecution, but that is the way Sheila saw him. He tried several times to start a conversation with her, but failed, and she only responded to questions or concerns about the scan.

John was worried when he first saw the apparatus, a chair surrounded by racks of instruments, and a large hemisphere bristling with cables running in all directions like a fan.

"Will this hurt?" he asked.

"You won't feel a thing, but the process takes two hours, and I'm giving you a relaxant to reduce background we need to filter out. You might even sleep a little," said Sheila. "Don't worry. Your protectors are here to assure your safety."

John scowled. "You seem hostile to me."

"I don't even know you, but I know what you've been up to. I don't have to like you to do a proper scan. Just sit down here, and try to relax."

She hooked him up, and gave him two capsules to take with water. When his eyes closed, the machine was already recording the life experiences of John Modrin, most of which she would later edit out and multiplex with his voice print for a simple task Carl Hobbs had revealed to her.

Timing would be crucial.

* * * *

The memorial service for Doctor Donovan Lane was held at North Hollywood First Methodist Church, and all pews were filled. Donovan himself partially attended in a tall, red urn placed on the altar. Melody, with Carl and Nathan at her sides, sat in the first pew with Sheila and Tom. Marylyn arrived late, and sat in the back of the church. The reverend Douglas Turnbull said nice things about the deceased, and led them in prayer. Several people spoke, including Melody, who sobbed at times, but managed not to fall apart, and she was grateful for that.

The paparazzi were kept at bay outside the church, standing across the street with a hundred or so fans of Melody and Nathan. They snapped their pictures with telescopic lenses as their prey excited the church, and a few of them followed the caravan to Northside Memorial Gardens.

For Melody, the experience in the mausoleum was surreal. There were Melody, Nathan, Carl, Tom and Sheila to watch the box of ashes go into its niche, two rows up from the floor. The row was also occupied by two other boxes, one bearing the remains of a beloved wife, the other for a thirteen-year-old daughter named Melody. That's all that's left of the real me, thought Melody, but here I am again. Is this reincarnation?

Nathan had graciously provided space for a reception, and paid for half of the catering expenses. When they arrived, the big circular driveway was jammed with cars. The front doors were open, and they went inside to greet a talkative crowd surrounding the buffet. Talk was light, and Melody found it comforting. Life does go on, she thought, especially when there's hope that an ending isn't necessarily an ending, but then she had yet to discuss that issue with Darin.

When people had voiced their sympathies for their hosts, and the food supply was thinning, they began leaving, and soon it was only the few of them relaxing in the big living room as the caterers began cleaning up the mess of plates and cups scattered around the house. Maurice had been a shadow during the reception, but now he came out of the kitchen and sat down close to Nathan on a couch.

Melody smiled at them. They looked so relaxed and natural sitting there, their shoulders touching. Melody had speculated about their private life together, and wondered if she could ever get Nathan to tell her something about it. Sheila watched them also, little glances now and then. Melody was certain the woman had a terrible crush on Nathan, but then who wouldn't? As for Sheila, it was Doctor Davidson, now, in charge of technical operations until Darin was back, a religious woman with conservative values, but still a woman who desired a man. Melody decided she liked her. Maybe we can do something about that hair, and the awful suits you wear everywhere, she thought.

Dinner that evening was the remains of the buffet, and they went their separate ways at dusk. Nathan and Maurice waved goodbye to them from the front doors.

"I think Maurice is living in the house, now," said Melody to Carl. Freeway traffic was light at this time of night, and she drove leisurely in the slow lane.

"He is," said Carl. "Maurice showed me their bedroom. They have a nice collection of what some people might call erotic art there."

"Really? How did you manage that?"

"I didn't. Nathan asked him to show me the room, and wanted my opinion about the art. He said he wanted a man's point of view, and that didn't make sense to me."

"And what did you think?" said Melody softly.

"The art was nicely rendered, but the subjects were all men, and I didn't think it was particularly interesting."

Melody laughed. "Straight as an arrow," she said.

"What?"

"Nothing, but now I'm dying to take you to an adult bookstore, and see what you like there."

"Okay," said Carl, and Melody laughed again. For that one moment, it had been a wonderful distraction for her, the grief pushed to the back of her mind, but now it returned.

"I feel empty, right now, like a big piece of my life has been torn away."

"He was my mentor and teacher, my creator," said Carl. "We'll talk to Darin, and see what can be done, but right now we have problems threatening our existence, and we have to deal with those first."

"I understand that, Carl. I'm thinking about the future after that."

It was late when they got home, and Ebony greeted them at the door. She was still trustworthy about being left alone, sleeping on the bed, never making a mess. Melody fixed a late dinner for her, and they watched holonews for a while. There was mention of Donovan Lane's funeral, the highlight being the attendance of his grieving daughter Melody Lane, famous holo-star. There was also a review of the circumstances of Lane's death, and the investigation underway. The sketch of Max Schuler was shown, requesting public aid to locating the suspect in the case.

"All it will do is make him harder to find," said Carl. "We'll have to get him to come to us."

Melody leaned against him on the couch. "Time for bed. Life does go on, and the limo will be right on time in the morning."

"Sleep well," he said.

"Carl?"

"Yes?"

"The night I heard about my father, and you carried me to bed. That was a wonderful and comforting feeling for me."

Carl looked at her as she reached out and clasped his hands in hers.

"Do you want me to carry you to bed?"

"Yes, and I want you beside me all night. I want us to dream together."

His look was serious and intense. "You want us to be intimate, like what you and Nathan do on your show? I'm not built for that, Melody. There are things your father didn't include in my design. I want to please you. I do care about you very much."

Melody touched his cheek. "I know that, sweet, and I care about you. We can touch, and explore, and kiss. That's enough."

Carl stood up, and there was just a hint of a smile on his face as he held out his arms to her. "Whatever you wish," he said.

Melody let out a little squeak, and jumped into Carl's arms. He swept her up as if she were a feather, and carried her into the bedroom. He'd expected to lie down with her fully clothed, and was astonished when she rolled from the bed and took everything off, clothes thrown in every direction, and then she leaped on him, pushing and pulling.

Carl gave her the freedom she wanted, though in his core there were no memories of sexual experience. His feelings were strong, but he did not recognize them as love as she undressed him, and then they were pressed together and she was guiding his hands and touching him all over, and after a few minutes he decided it was all very nice indeed, and he kissed her, and that was even more wonderful.

After a while they just lay together, embracing tightly. Suddenly, Ebony whined, and they looked down at the end of the bed to see the dog resting her chin on the covers there. She had been watching them, and now they could hear the thump of her tail against the floor. Carl patted the bed at Melody's back, and Ebony yipped, jumped up and took her place beside her family, and in a few minutes all were soundly asleep together.

* * * *

Sheila couldn't sleep that night. The sight of Nathan and his boyfriend at the Lane reception wouldn't allow a retreat from her consciousness. She found it repulsive on two levels. She had read her bible since childhood, and knew the opinions of the apostle Paul regarding two men lying together. What would he think about a man lying with a synth? Melody, Carl, all her colleagues, human or synth, had been so kind to her, yet she found herself struggling again not to see them as abominations in the eyes of her Lord.

She prayed on it, but for three nights sleep eluded her. On the third night she asked for an answer, and dozed. When she awoke, she felt peace within herself, and the answer was clear.

Synth or human, they were all God's children, and were loved by Him. There was no evil in the love of one being for another.

CHAPTER 25

The entire week was stressful for Jacob. It began on Monday, when he received notice the IRS was going to audit all of the AAAH accounts. He'd anticipated the eventuality of an audit, but not so soon, and he'd only been able to siphon off a portion of the monies into his Patmos account. The island was half an hour by helicopter from the Turkish coast. He had purchased a cottage there, ten acres of land with a vineyard and an acre of olive trees that would bring in a modest income each year and give him some status and protection in the local community. He could be satisfied with a quiet retirement and a simple life after years of unrewarded religious service, and work with capitalistic anarchists to fulfill his mission against intellectuals who sought to replace God.

Jacob did not consider himself a greedy man, but the money was there and he deserved it. The three accounts had totaled just under three million dollars, and there were bills to pay, some legitimate, and one to his consultantship subsidiary that Max had handled. Max had done wonderful work for him, and expected an equal share of the holdings, but alas, it would not be so. The man had been a loyal servant, and still had work to do, and Jacob would encourage him in the doing of it. With a few pen strokes, he closed the consulting firm, wrote a two hundred thousand dollar check to Max, and mailed it to his post office address in Los Angeles. Another withdrawal of seven hundred thousand was wired to Patmos, through banks in Athens and Istanbul. He would let the government have what little was left to find, as a kind of restitution for their auditing efforts. Before the audit even took place, he would be gone, disappeared, an escape by air, car, bus, ship and helicopter through Istanbul down to Ephesus and then to his little island. His documents included American and Greek passports of high quality, all made by an old friend and servant of God's church.

He had not heard from Max since the elimination of Donovan Lane. The man was professional, and would remain deeply underground for a time. He would certainly surface soon enough to inquire about his share of their holdings. He might even find his check to be a cause for concern.

The killing of Donovan Lane was Jacob's major victory. Whatever Max had planned now was secondary to it. Perhaps he would even be killed doing it, and Jacob would never have to worry about Max ever finding him again.

This was on Monday, and Jacob felt he had a good handle on things, everything moving according to his schedule.

On Wednesday, an expose article appeared in the Los Angeles Times, accusing him of fraud and complicity in a plot to weaken the government of the United States. The names of all board members were there, with the identities of their companies, and estimates of the funds they had contributed to the AAAH. The article would ordinarily have been deserving of an immediate suit for slander. Unfortunately, the article was factually true to the letter.

The e-mails and three cell calls came in before noon that day. His board members were terrified, and ready to jump ship. The one supporter was Mister M, who urged calm, and asked for a meeting soon so that they could discuss a counter-strategy. By the end of the day they had set a date for another meeting in Burbank the following Wednesday. The three overseas members made it clear they would not attend. The killing of Donovan Lane had also made them fearful of possible links to the board, and the negative impact of right-wing public opinion of their cause. Jacob made it clear in return that if it became necessary to dissolve the organization, all board members would be expected to attend a final meeting in the Cook Islands, at which time remaining AAAH funds would be refunded to them.

By the end of the day, his nerves were on edge, and his heart was beating erratically. Three glasses of wine helped to calm him, but he was still uneasy. The rational part of his mind saw the beginnings of a crumbling in his organization sooner than he'd planned for. He'd known from the beginning that it couldn't last, but it had served his purpose nicely. He felt a need to talk about it, and Max had always been there to listen. He called Max again, but there was no answer. This time he left a long answer, quickly summarizing what had happened with the IRS and the press, the newly scheduled meeting, and the check he'd sent to the post office address. He wished Max well in whatever he was doing, blessed him for what he had done, and hoped to see him again at the next meeting. At that meeting, he said, they should make their final plans for disappearance, and get started on the arrangements.

Jacob felt better when he ended the call. There had been enough truth in it to satisfy him.

* * * *

Max listened to the message, and shook his head, smiling. Empty cartons from a Thai restaurant were scattered on the table in front of him, and he took another sip of beer.

"More lies, old man. I can hear it in your voice," he said out loud, "and if that check isn't in my box in the morning, I'll know I've really been screwed. If it is there, whatever happens, at least I can allow you to keep on living. Chasing you around the world won't pay me anything."

But in the morning, Max went to the post office, and the check was there. "Well, well," he said, testing the check's edge with thumb and forefinger, "Maybe I've been wrong about you. The least I can do for this is finish the job you wanted done."

By noon he had cashed the check, put twenty thousand in his account and obtained a bank draft for the rest, using that to purchase gold certificates on the open market and at a discount. Max did not plan to retire. He had contacts in Europe and the States, and was certain about employment opportunities of a temporary nature. In between jobs, his life would be simple and relaxed, a little house in a small Costa Rican village, with bird song, and fruit hanging from trees, all close enough to a city for some exciting, social fun.

This was his dream.

In the meantime, there was work to be done. One target was still in hospital, and watched too closely now. One was constantly protected by a bodyguard. The third one, Sheila Davidson, lived alone and was vulnerable. First things first, he thought.

He would worry about the other two later.

* * * *

Sheila worked day and night on the wetware coding for John Modrin. Only a part of his scans had been used, that part dating back to his college days, and up-to-date through his membership in AAAH. She decided he was not an evil man, but greedy, a man who desired more than society would allow him, and so he had gone to war to change that. He had not expected killing, or violence of any kind. He had not expected dealings with a man whose agenda was anti-science fostered by religious dogma. It was science, in fact, that had built his empire in manufacturing technology. Sheila could forgive him for that. The man had gotten himself involved with bad company, and was making some amends by allowing himself to be used against them. Still, Darin and Carl had little trust in the man. John would never know about the synth representing him, might guess it was a cleverly disguised human when the time came.

It was networks within networks. The main thrust of her coding was the cross-linking of two hundred sheets of polymer, each with the millions of self-linked neural net layers of molecular thickness that came out of the scanning process. The rest related to speech and sensory centers, and included her own recent work. Sensory and audio data was not part of the scanning process, and had to be obtained from separate tests before multiplexing into the final matrix. Exact reproduction of speech, with its rich structure of overtones, was still imperfect, but getting close. It had not been an issue with synths such as Melody, since her vocals were simply taken from an unknown human source and there was no effort necessary to match any previous speech pattern. In this respect, what Sheila was doing was something new. She was expanding the frontier of a new science, and she was excited by it.

For nearly a week, she worked day and night, eating quick meals in the cafeteria, sleeping on a cot in the laboratory four nights in a row, and then Darin returned from the hospital and told her she had to stop doing that.

His head was sill wrapped with a wide bandage, and he winced when he turned certain ways, but he seemed to be doing well, and was working twelve hour days after his return.

"You have to get away from this a while each day," he said, "or you'll burn to a cinder. Believe me, I've been here. Go to a show, a party, anything. Have some fun."

"I relax at home," she said, feeling defensive. "I read, and watch holovision. I've enjoyed watching Melody's show."

"Melody likes you," said Darin.

"Really?"

"Yes, really. She thinks you're pretty."

"That can't be so."

"She told me that. She also said she'd like to change your hairstyle, and take you shopping for something besides your business suits, and I don't think she was kidding about it. Don't be surprised if you get a call from her. Now, let's get to work. You need to see the synth lab."

He took her upstairs, and for the first time she saw the stages of synth production, with final products there ready for printing. When she entered the laboratory, her senses were flooded with the odors of solvents and cooking polymers, and five glistening forms in coffin-sized vats were something out of a horror film for her.

"I know this will be difficult," said Darin. "You've been honest with us about your religious background. Try to remember that a body is just a body, a vehicle, whether it comes out of a womb or a vat."

He tapped his forehead. "What's important is what's up here, the personality, the memories, the who of what we are, the consciousness, the soul, whatever. We don't even understand it, but it's up here somehow, in our heads, and when we make a synth, that part comes from a real human being."

Sheila looked down at the faceless form in a vat, and wrinkled her nose. "I'll have to admit that seeing this for the first time is disturbing, but it's mostly the odors in here. I've told all of you I have no problems with the concept. I accept what you just said. There are no religious issues for me here."

Darin smiled. "And I shouldn't bring it up again?"

"That is correct," said Sheila, and pointed. "Is this the synth I'll be working with?"

"Yes. It's being kept warm and moist, and is ready for printing. Modrin's features have been programmed into the printer, and we have added the rest from stock data."

"The rest?"

"Certain male characteristics considered generic."

"Oh."

"Someday we hope to make them functional."

"Interesting." Sheila tried hard not to blush, but failed.

The big 3D printer was in an adjacent laboratory. A pneumatic lifter lifted the synth from the vat and carried it to the printer, where there was a cradle it fit into. Streams of warm air and moisture bathed the blank as the printer head lowered and began spewing its special fleshy polymer a layer at a time over the entire length of the blank. It was a slow process, one that would take two days to completion, and Sheila stayed only long enough to see the beginnings of a nose, a chin, eyebrows, even nipples and the hint of generic features Darin had mentioned. Two cells the size of a child's toy block would then be inserted into the base of the synth's head and become the receptacle for the chips that Sheila was preparing.

"He was a genius," she said softly. "All of this came from one man's mind."

"Pretty much," said Darin, "but I've made some contributions, and so have you."

"How do we go forward without him?" asked Sheila.

"That's a good question," said Darin. "It might be difficult."

There was a pause, and then Sheila said, "Melody wants her father back."

"I know," said Darin. "The problem is she probably wants him back exactly the way he was, and we can't do that."

"Why not? You have his scans."

"The man is dead and buried. He was well known, and photographs of him are everywhere. His death is public record."

"Different body, same man. We just talked about that."

"I don't think Melody will accept it," said Darin.

"I think she will, and the company needs him," said Sheila.

Darin nodded, and Sheila left him to think about it when she went home to relax.

Max followed her home.

* * * *

It would have been a better day if Melody had kept her temper in check.

Wrap-up day was the day they all looked forward to twice a year, and this one was at mid-season. There would be a two week break in shooting, although the series would not be on the air again for an additional ten weeks. The wrap-up party was always special, and big boss Goldsmith never missed it.

Nathan spent the day in a water tank, clinging to the mock-up of a sinking ship while techs with huge fans and water buckets blew rain on him as he was apparently drowning in the fury of a storm. Melody's Ariel had it little better, standing at the edge of a cliff made of boxes, and staring out at a green-screened sea horizon while rain poured on her with great force and added to her grief as her lover drowned in the waves. By the end of the afternoon, both of them were soaked, frozen, and shivering violently as the fans were turned off and the weather cleared, and then they heard the wonderful words.

"That's a wrap, folks," shouted Dennis. "Time to party!"

Actors and crew cheered and clapped. Nathan and Melody hustled to the locker room for long, hot showers, and returned to the set wrapped in soft, fluffy robes for the party.

The caterers had been waiting outside the aircraft-hanger-sized Studio B, and now the big doors opened and two trucks drove inside. A dozen men and women spilled out of the trucks, and set up a buffet line in minutes. There was an outstanding selection of junk food for all tastes: hamburgers, hot dogs, deep dish pizzas, pies, and tubs of ice cream. No diet was spared, all the actors and crew stuffing themselves like starved animals.

And then Jennifer Anders, Melody's makeup artist since her first day on set, came in waving a small newspaper above her head.

"Hey look, everybody! Our Melody Lane is a robot!"

Melody would later swear her heart actually stopped for two or three beats. She felt dizzy and lightheaded for one instant, and then her pulse was suddenly racing, and she couldn't take a breath.

"What is it?" shouted someone.

"The new issue of Real Truth. Melody, you and Nathan are on the front page with a bunch of robots from old films. There's a big article inside. You didn't tell us you're an alien," said Jennifer, and waved the paper in front of Melody.

Nathan looked closely. "It says robot, not alien. The headline is 'Human, or Robot?' And I'm in there, too. Who thinks up this crap? Don't they worry about lawsuits?"

Nathan sounded indignant, while Melody struggled to escape a state of panic, and finally found her breath.

"That's exactly what we'll do, and put them out of business! I've seen this rag at grocery store checkout counters, and there's no truth in them!"

"The article talks about artificial humans being made by your father's company," said Jennifer. "There's nothing about robots."

"That is slander! Our company has a big team of lawyers who will fight this and put these bastards out of business!"

Melody's face was hot, her forehead pounding, and she felt a pressure behind her eyes, and then someone said something that changed her reaction.

"Is she serious?" someone said softly.

Oh God, I'm making an idiot out of myself, she thought, and turned to Nathan.

"You know who is behind this," she said.

In reply, he put a finger to his lips, a quick gesture that nobody seemed to notice.

"Nobody takes this stuff seriously," said Jennifer. "It's all entertainment, Melody. It's fun."

Just then, Daniel Goldsmith walked up to the buffet line to join their party, and Jennifer waved the paper at him.

"Have you seen the article about Melody and Nathan?"

"As a matter of fact, I have. I'm a subscriber," he said, and picked up a plate.

"You have got to be kidding us," said Melody.

"Not at all. I've planted some articles in there myself, but not his one. I thank whoever did it. I can't get this kind of publicity for a million dollars a minute on the open media. This rag is read by tens of millions."

This did not make Melody feel better. "It's making a bad joke about my father's company, and the timing couldn't be worse. To me that's slander. All we have to prove is malicious intent."

"Oh poop," said Goldsmith. "The readers won't remember your father's name or his company five minutes after they skim the article. Chill out about it. Your father was a great man. History will be good to him."

No support for her wrath was forthcoming, and she had lost dignity. Her reaction to recover came automatically, without thought. She took two staggering steps towards Goldsmith with her arms outstretched, and her speech was a lisp. It had worked once in amusement, why not again?

"I hear and obey, mathter."

Everyone laughed.

"That's good," said Goldsmith. "Do that at your next public appearance, and show everyone what a good sense of humor you have."

Now Melody smirked at him, as people continued chuckling. "Your sarcasm has been noted," she said, hands on hips.

In seconds, it was as if nothing had happened. Everyone filled their plates, stuffed themselves, and drank large quantities of beer, Nathan and

Melody both abstaining as usual from the alcohol for reasons people no longer pressed them to reveal.

The limos arrived, but only Nathan and Melody used them, and the revelry had grown quite loud by the time they left. The party was a substitute for dinner, and Carl had anticipated it, cooking only for himself. By the time she got home, Carl had finished eating and was working on a rough script for the John Modrin synth they would soon be putting into the field.

Carl was his usual calm self about the article in Real Truth. "So soon after your father's death, the article is insensitive. I expect a negative response from the public, and it'll be forgotten news in a week. Cross is certainly behind this, but he has run out of options to please his board. They just don't have the same agenda, and all his pretending has caught up with him. Are you finished for the season?"

"For two weeks. Why?"

"I was going to handle this script transfer by cell. Let's drive to San Diego so I can do it face to face, and you can spend money in old town."

Melody stepped up close to him. "Maybe we could rent a motel room this time, and have some privacy?"

Again there was that faint smile. "Maybe we could," he said.

And they did.

CHAPTER 26

Darin was waiting for them in the printing lab. "What held you up?" he asked.

"Carl did the driving this time," said Melody. "He-is-a-very-cautious-driver," she said slowly, and smiled.

"All relative," said Carl, "since you like to drive just under sound speed. Ebony was still able to flap her ears in the wind."

"Ebony?" said Darin.

"She's in the lobby, as usual, being cute and drawing attention, as usual," said Melody.

Darin turned to Carl. "Do you have the script with you?"

"Yes, but it's not polished like the version I e-mailed you for the upload. This is more conversational, less detailed for the interview."

"Okay, let's do it. Melody, do you want to sit in on this? Sheila is here."

"Sure," said Melody, "and I want to talk to her afterwards."

The room next door to the lab was a reception area and lounge with plush sofas, chairs, and a table with a p.c. and large monitor on it. A man sat in one of the chairs, and stood as they entered the room. He was tall and slender, distinguished looking with graying hair and startling, blue eyes. He smiled, and extended a hand.

"Carl, Melody, meet John Modrin," said Darin.

"Carl Hobbs, sir," said Carl, and shook the man's hand.

"And you are the famous Melody Lane," said John, taking her hand gently in his. "I've enjoyed several episodes of your show."

"Thank you," said Melody, impressed. There was a nice lilt to the man's voice. She was a bit surprised that he said nothing about her father.

"We thought we'd have a chat with you before the meeting. That's next Friday, correct?" said Darin.

Carl was shuffling papers in his lap. "How many people are expected to attend?"

"Oh, maybe five board members, including myself. I've been in touch with the others, but they really feel it's a waste of their time. They never really were part of what I'd call the hard core. It's the domestic people who have the most to gain. Jacob will be there, of course, and maybe Max. He doesn't attend all the meetings, and everyone is more relaxed when he isn't there."

"Does Jacob sense that?" asked Darin.

"Oh, yes. He's quite perceptive, and likes us to be afraid when there are decisions to be made. He has a powerful personality, and I must say I admire it."

"Does he know that?" asked Darin.

"Like I said, he is perceptive," said John. "I'm sure he knows that I do not approve of violence, and that our agendas are really not the same, but I accept him as our leader, and openly support him in any way I can."

"That's good," said Darin. "We want you to continue with that attitude, even when the others demand the organization be dissolved."

"That is likely to happen at this coming meeting," said John. "The others are at their wits end. They see no progress, and the press reports have badly frightened them. Things have come to a head rather quickly."

"It's very important to have that final meeting in the Cook Islands," said Carl. "Do everything you can to encourage that, as we've discussed previously. We want everyone to be there."

"I understand," said John, "especially for the hard core." He looked up towards the door. "Oh, hi, Doctor Davidson, I didn't see you come in. It's nice to see you again."

Sheila sat down in a chair next to Melody, and nodded to her. "Good to see you too, John. Are you ready to go to work?"

"Yes, I am. Do you have anything new for me?"

"Just a tweak. It'll only take a second. Please continue with your conversation."

"Some quick things," said Carl. "I don't recall who Mister S's secretary was."

"Oh, that's Diane, a lovely lady, and she wears red a lot."

Sheila stepped behind John Modrin, and extended a forked tool to open a port at the back of his head. She took a chip from a plastic holder, and held it close to the port.

"So she likes red. What are your favorite colors, John?"

"Oh, I do love red, but also orange or hues mixing the two. I like earth colors."

In one motion, Sheila pulled a chip from the port and replaced it with another. "I'm sorry, John, I didn't hear that. Tell me again what your favorite colors are."

"Well, my real favorite is red, but I love oranges and mixtures of red and orange. I love earth colors."

"Thank you, John," said Sheila, and she closed the port at the back of his head.

"Much better," said Darin.

"It's pretty much right on," said Carl.

Even Melody had noticed the change in John's voice, the timbre now deeper than before.

"I envy your upcoming trip to the Cook Islands," said Sheila. "Tell me about Jacob's house there and the view from that big porch."

They listened while John Modrin's synth gave a detailed description of Jacob Cross' exotic home on the hill, and the wonderful views he'd seen from there. Carl again shuffled papers, making comparisons with the previously uploaded script.

"It's all consistent," he finally said. "I think he's ready to go to work. He'd been away from the stress when we scanned him, was a lot more animated when he first came to us. Cross might notice that, but I don't see what we can do about it," said Carl.

"His reaction to pressure should be enough," said Sheila. "It's never going to be perfect."

"Then it's a go," said Darin. "John, you have a job for Friday. Just follow our instructions, and come back here after the meeting."

"I'll do that, Doctor Post." John stood up. "Nice meeting you folks. Maybe we'll see each other again sometime." He reached down to shake first Carl's hand, then Melody's, and walked out of the room.

"Where is he going?" asked Melody.

"Back to the printing lab. We have some touching up to do on his hands and chin," said Darin.

"Are we done here? I want to talk to Sheila before we leave."

Sheila looked surprised.

Carl fumbled with his papers. "We're rushing too fast here. I have things to clarify with John. I can do it while you're working on him."

"Come on, then," said Darin.

"How long is it going to take?" asked Melody.

"Maybe two hours," said Carl.

"Make it three," said Melody. "I want to take Sheila shopping."

"What? I can't—"

"—Of course you can. Your work here is finished. Isn't that so, Darin?"

"For today it is," said Darin, smiling. "Better do it, Sheila. You don't get many chances to shop with a holo-star."

"But I don't need anything," Sheila protested.

"Wrong, and wrong again," said Melody. "We will make a list, and use my credit card. Call it a gift for the wetware you've written for me, the new sensor aps, you know. The fun stuff. Have you been to old town yet?"

"No."

"Dear God, Darin, you've insulated her from society with all the work. Shame on you."

Darin laughed. "Better get your purse, Sheila. Have a good time. You've earned it."

"Three hours," said Carl. "I'll wait here."

Still bewildered, Sheila went to get her purse, and followed Melody out to the lobby where Ebony, surrounded by three lovely admirers, greeted them with a thumping tail. When she saw the leash her tail thumped harder. It was a sunny day, and Melody put the top down on the Mercedes. Sheila sat in front with her, Ebony on her cushion in the back, and they drove out of the hills and down to the quaint shopping area of town at shoreline.

"This is a very nice car," said Sheila, and there was a faint smile.

"The studio keeps nagging me to get a better one, something more in keeping with my, ahem, status, and I keep refusing them. This was my first car, and I'm comfortable in it, and I like to drive very fast."

"I notice that," said Sheila.

"You have a car?"

"Yes, a little two-door, nothing like this, but good mileage, and practical."

"Yuck. I don't like practical. Life is too short."

"Not for you," said Sheila.

"We don't know that, yet. Our bodies shouldn't show aging, but there's no data yet. We haven't been around long, so it's too early to tell. My father was making all sorts of tests on us. His main concern was our brains. He was worried about deterioration of cross links between layers. Our brains are based on chemical bonds, and those bonds aren't going to last forever. If something goes wrong, we'll get a new brain with a new upload, and we have to keep our scans up-to-date. Father had been doing it quarterly, and Darin will continue that practice."

"Your father was such a nice man," said Sheila.

"I'll get him back. He just won't look the same."

"It must be hard to suddenly wake up and find out that you're not, well—"

"—Human?" said Melody. "Yeah, it's weird, but then the brain takes over, and you suppress all the rest. There were sensory problems, and those have mostly been solved. You helped with that. We cannot reproduce, and the parts associated with that are only decorative. I do not keep a copy of 'The Joys of Sex' or 'The Sixteen Paths to Heaven' in my library, but I do wish I had the need for it. Nathan and I sure have a lot of fun playing at it for our audience. He is one heck of a kisser."

Sheila said nothing, but blushed.

Melody steered onto the freeway, and darted into the fast lane when she saw the slow lane was blocked ahead. "I saw that," she said.

"What?"

"The blush. I've seen it before. You have a crush on Nathan. Well, join the club. He's a beautiful man. Right now, he prefers the company of men, but that could change any time. He's kind of complicated that way. Do you have a boyfriend?"

"I don't date," said Sheila.

"Why not?"

"I don't have the time. Besides, all the guys at work are married or close to it. I don't do the bars, and the men I've met casually aren't interested in girls with brains."

"They do if they're properly packaged," said Melody, and flashed her lights at someone poking along at eighty, a hundred yards ahead in the fast lane. "In case you haven't noticed, you're a pretty girl. Does the company actually require you to wear black business suits with no style?"

Sheila smiled. "No, but it seems to be the standard for female professionals."

"Well, we're going to change that," said Melody, and jerked the steering wheel as she hit the accelerator and crossed over three lanes of traffic just in time to catch the exit ramp to old town.

Sheila gasped, and grabbed the edge of the door with both hands.

"There are some wonderful shops here, and we have the time to do all of them. And then we need to talk about your hair."

There was a central parking garage; they parked at second level, and took an elevator down to the street, Ebony proudly leading the way at the end of her jeweled leash.

"What do we do with your dog while we're inside the shops? It's hot out here today."

"They all know me here. Ebony goes in with me. No dog, no sale," said Melody.

Ebony was a hit in all the shops, her blue eyes and friendly manner attracting everyone. It was a novelty to see what looked like a large, black wolf in an expensive clothing store.

At first, Sheila was reluctant to buy anything, since Melody was paying the bills, but Melody kept on calling it payback for services rendered, and finally warned her in a friendly way about possible consequences for offending a major holo-star. Sheila finally got into the spirit of things at Elisa's, a designer dress and jewelry shop, and tried on several things, including a knit, short-sleeved sweater that fit her like a glove.

"My God, girl, you have a wonderful figure. Why have you been hiding it?" Melody clapped her hands, and the salesgirl nodded and smiled.

Sheila turned around slowly in front of a mirror, hands on hips, and her face seemed to glow.

A peasant skirt, designer shirt and shawl came next, and they left the store carrying two colorful bags. It was the same at the next store, and the next, and now they were carrying four bags between them, Melody attaching Ebony's leash to her waist belt to free both hands. People gawked at them in the street, a few smiled politely, recognizing Melody, and all moved subtly aside to make way for the creature accompanying them.

Their last stop was at Iver's, a fashionable shop known for its wide variety of sizes for off-the-rack clothing. "You must have a little black dress to show off that figure of yours, and a string of small pearls to go with it," said Melody.

Sheila tried on three dresses, and discovered she was a perfect size three. Melody applauded again as Sheila turned in front of a mirror, looking amazed at the sight of herself. "You see how this one emphasizes your arms and legs. You can have all the brains in the world, and the men will still go crazy about this one. It'll turn them into little boys."

They headed back towards the parking garage, Melody occasionally looking back over her shoulder as she had done all afternoon, but Sheila didn't seem to notice it.

"There is one more thing, but we don't have time for it," said Melody. "Your hairstyle is neat, but plain. It should attract the eye to your face. There's a good salon here, but I have a better idea. I want to do a makeover on you at my home, and you will be my guest until next Monday. You need a vacation, and Darin will allow it. I'll do your hair and makeup, and teach you some things, and we'll have some fun, so please say yes."

Sheila did not dare to interrupt the torrent of words, but smiled. "Yes, if it's not inconvenient. Do you really have the time for this?"

"Only on rare occasions, and I need something creative to do besides reading bad scripts I don't want to do. I have worked with some of the finest hairdressers and makeup artists around, and I know the craft. We'll talk to Darin, and you can pack a little bag, and we'll drive you back to Los Angeles and return you on Monday, and nobody here will know who you are."

Melody turned and smiled brightly, her enthusiasm melting away something inside Sheila that made her so careful about structuring her life.

"Okay," said Sheila, and Melody patted her shoulder.

The drive back to Schutz Fabrik seemed shorter this time. They found Darin and Carl still in conference with their new synth, but it ended quickly, and Melody told Darin about her plans with Sheila.

"Monday is fine," said Darin, "but we need you here then. Carl has come up with another application for Modrin's synth, and we'll need new wetware for it."

"I'll have to be back here Monday anyway," said Carl, "and I'm not leaving you alone up there."

"Fear rules," said Melody. "Okay, let's go. I want to be back before dark. You can drive."

"It will take longer," said Carl.

"As long as we're back before dark. I'm sure our guest will appreciate the slower pace."

"I can understand that," said Carl, and he looked at Sheila, who shook her head and grinned at him.

They first drove Sheila to her condominium across the street from the beach. It was a windy day, but a few people were under umbrellas out on the sand. The street was narrow and one way in front of the building, and there was underground parking with an entrance kiosk manned during the day and night by two retired police officers named Fred and Mike. Carl and Melody waited in the car while Sheila took an elevator up to her second level unit to pack a small bag.

"Seems like a secure place," said Melody.

"It isn't," said Carl. "You just disable the guy in the kiosk, and wait here until she comes down again. No place is safe against someone who knows what he's doing."

"What about our place?"

"That one, too; it's even easier. We don't even have an active reception desk after dark."

"Oh, you're just trying to make me feel safer," said Melody, and jabbed him in the shoulder.

"I'm saying you should not rely on others for your protection. Not even me, so be alert, and ready to protect yourself. Why do you think I've been working with you on self-defense?"

"Okay, okay, I get it, but I'll never be fast enough to outrun a bullet."

"You will, if it never has a chance to leave the barrel," said Carl.

"Smarty," she said, and leaned her head against his shoulder.

Sheila came down a few minutes later with her little brown travel bag, and got into the back seat to give tail-thumping Ebony a light hug. Ebony had taken to Sheila immediately, and made part of the trip home with her big head nestled in Sheila's lap. The number of people in her pack had suddenly increased by one.

Carl kept the speedometer at a steady seventy-five, rarely strayed from the middle lane, and arrived at their hotel just as the disk of the sun was touching the horizon. "Why were you watching the side-view mirror so much?" he asked Melody.

"Making sure someone wasn't going to run us over," she said.

They garaged the car in the basement, and took the keyed elevator up. Ebony headed straight for the bedroom and her exalted place on the bed until food was served. Sheila was impressed by the space they had rented. "You could fit three of my units in here," she said.

"We're here for at least three more months," said Melody. "The gate and the wall are up, but the interior work is only half finished. We'll have over seven thousand square feet there."

"We'll have a bigger kitchen," added Carl.

"He is a wonderful cook," said Melody. "Tonight we're having his noodle-goop, and I will make a salad. You can have the south bedroom, so just relax tonight. Tomorrow we'll do your makeover, and have some real fun."

Sheila didn't ask what noodle-goop was. The south bedroom seemed huge to her, had a king-size bed and a walk-in closet. She unpacked her little bag. Ebony came in to see what she was doing, and walked out again. The mattress was wonderfully firm. Sheila climbed up onto it and lay down to test its comfort. She closed her eyes, just for an instant—and was awakened by Melody standing in the doorway.

"Dinner is ready, and we're eating in the kitchen. You must have been exhausted from the day."

Sheila got up quickly, still drowsy, and followed Melody into the kitchen. Carl put a big bowl of something on the table, joining dishes of green salad and string beans, and a platter of warm, buttered garlic bread. The odor of something meaty, cheesy and spicy was heavy in the air.

Carl introduced her to his noodle-goop, ladling out a huge portion onto her plate. It looked like too much, but she ate all of it, a delicious blend of ground beef, cheese, corn, olives and paprika mixed with wide, flat noodles. With that and the salad, beans and incredible bread, she was stuffed at the end of the meal, but unable to turn down the little ball of ice cream Carl offered her for desert.

"He spoils me at the table," said Melody, "but works me hard in our gymnasium. Without the exercise, I would blow up like a balloon."

After dinner, they relaxed in the living room and watched a recording of Melody's favorite scenes from her shows. This included some hilarious out-takes of times when everything seemed to go wrong: flubbed lines, hysterical reactions gone wild and ending in giggling fits, a carpenter opening a door to the set and entering in the middle of a scene. Even Carl laughed at some of them. He sat shoulder to shoulder with Melody on a couch, two special people, as real as any humans could be, and Sheila thought it looked romantic. They were a couple, a blessing that Sheila wondered if she would ever experience. She also wondered if two synths could actually be in love. If Melody and Carl were putting on an act for her, they were doing it well.

The mood of the evening was light, but there were brief moments when Melody seemed to be nervous about something. She made several trips to the kitchen, returning with plates and bowls filled with crackers and cheese, sesame sticks and little chocolate balls for snacking. Each trip to and from she paused at a window and looked down at the street. Carl noticed it. "See something interesting down there?" he finally asked.

"No, just staying alert. That was your advice, dear."

"You were using the side view mirror a lot on the way home. Did you see something?"

"Just a feeling, and a grey car I first saw when Sheila and I were shopping. I thought I saw it again when we were half-way home, but then it disappeared. I guess I'm feeling uneasy with Max on the loose."

"Okay," said Carl. "A lot of people are looking for him now, not just us, and he's going to have to be careful about being seen."

"Maybe," said Melody, and she offered Sheila another chocolate ball, with a smile to brighten the mood again.

* * * *

Normal movement in public had become complicated for Max Schuler. He'd been observing the routine of the Davidson woman for less than a day when he found a sketch of his face being circulated online by a crime club calling him a suspect in the murder of Donovan Lane. Few people knew him from his association with Jacob Cross, or had seen his face. The list was short: all the AAAH board members, and the scientist Darin Post, who now lived because Max had been overly cautious in not finishing him off in the hospital. That was turning out to be a costly oversight on his part. No more mistakes for Max Schuler, not even one, he thought.

He was certain the police were looking for him, and suddenly they were everywhere. The Davidson woman lived alone in a complex he'd first thought easy to penetrate, but he'd watched the guards in the kiosk at the garage entrance turn back several visitors, and even chase a transient away at the point of a baton. They were professionals, those two men who guarded the garage day and night in alternating shifts. It was a good neighborhood on a one-way street along the beach, and police patrols were frequent. There were only a few turnouts for parking, all of them usually taken up by the cars of locals, and when he made moving observations it took him ten minutes to make a single loop. Twice he could not slow down in front of Davidson's building because there was a police car right behind him, and he worried about his rented vehicle being noticed multiple times.

He abandoned his watch over the Davidson home, and found a good place to watch her arrive for work in the morning and then follow her anywhere she went, always alert for an opportunity to dispose of her. His trunk was filled with weapons ranging from clubs and tasers to handguns and a heavy caliber rifle for precision shooting. And there were two compact explosive devices remaining in his inventory.

There was a three day period that exhausted him, for Davidson came to work one day and did not leave the plant until the evening of the third day later. He got only four hours of fitful sleep that night, but was rewarded in the morning when his second target, Melody Lane, arrived at the gate with her bodyguard and wolf, and reappeared hours later with Davidson added to her entourage for an afternoon of shopping. Max followed them on their rounds, parking a block down the street from where they shopped, and then back to Schutz Fabrik to wait again.

In late afternoon he was astonished when the red Mercedes appeared again, now filled with wolf, bodyguard, and both of his targets. He followed them back to the Davidson condo, and minutes later they were all in the same car, turning onto the freeway and heading north. The bodyguard was driving at a moderate speed, and Max stayed well behind them. His gas tank was nearly empty when they reached a residential hotel outside central Hollywood, and the Mercedes disappeared beneath the building. Minutes later, the lights went on along the entire top floor of the building. It seemed a likely place for a holo-star to live. Davidson was her guest, but how long would they be there?

Sitting in his car down the street from the hotel, he had a sudden idea and called Jacob Cross for the first time in weeks.

Cross answered immediately.

"It's Max."

"I've been trying to reach you."

"I've had my cell turned off during surveillance. Davidson is with Melody Lane in a hotel suite, and I have a chance to take them both out with one strike."

"So why are you calling me? Just do it."

"I want to discuss finances."

"Oh, dear, I didn't expect this of you, Max."

"There are no guarantees about your settlement with the board. I've done all your dirty work, and I have my own future to consider. This opportunity might not last a day. We both have accounts at First National. How long would it take to transfer funds?"

"If I call now, it can be done by late morning tomorrow."

"I want a hundred thousand. No discussion. If the money is there in the morning, I'll have the job done within twenty-four hours."

"And if the money isn't there?"

"I do nothing. There won't be another attempt, or any other work for me to do for you."

There was a long pause. Max held his breath.

"All right, but keep checking your account until noon. Transfers take time."

"Okay, until noon."

"And I want your promise to attend the final board meeting. I'll have one final need for your services."

Max thought for only a second, and then said, "The entire board?"

"They want their money back, and I've decided not to give it. They'll be very unhappy, and make trouble. Loose ends, Max, loose ends that have to be tied up. Do that for me, and I'll tack on a lot more than a hundred thousand extra dollars."

"Sounds like a deal. You can seal it in the morning."

"I've just sent in the transfer, marked urgent. Good hunting, Max."

"Good night, sir," said Max, and he broke the connection.

He watched the building until late the next morning, and his quarry did not reappear. At eleven, he made a call to his bank.

The transfer had been made.

CHAPTER 27

When he entered the room, Jacob Cross saw seven men there to meet him, and it was one more than he'd expected. Mister M was sitting on the edge of the conference table to talk to them, but the conversation ended abruptly when Cross arrived. Mister M went to one end of the table, and sat down. All the men looked grim and apprehensive, their hands folded tightly in front of them.

"Good afternoon, gentlemen," said Cross, and sat down at the other end of the table. "It's nice to see so many of you here, since we have some difficult issues to deal with."

"That is an understatement," said one man who had never spoken aloud at a board meeting. "We're here to dissolve the organization and the board, and to arrange a refund of the money you've taken from us."

"I didn't see that on the circulated agenda. I thought we were here to review progress and assess the impact of our efforts," said Mister M.

"It amounts to the same thing. There has been no progress, and the impact, if any, has been minimal. At best, we're nothing more than a minor irritant to the government."

"I disagree," said Cross. "Don't you keep up with media news, the union interviews, and the testimony on prosthetics gone badly?"

"We've seen all of it," said another man who had never said anything at a meeting, and contributed nothing. At the moment, Cross couldn't even remember his identity letter. "All of it is drama, entertainment, and nothing the news analysts take seriously. Every report is forgotten in a day. The only thing I've seen that could have the effect we want is the finger pointing that happened after the murder of Donovan Lane. The possibility he'd been murdered by the government to cover up illegal and offensive science was a widely accepted myth until our organization was publicly revealed. How did that happen, Mister Cross? Who is our traitor?"

"You underestimate government intelligence capabilities," said Cross. "They can get access to everything. Our accounts, cell messaging, contacts with newspapers, magazines, whatever, is all available to them. They are not stupid people."

Mister E interrupted by waving a hand. "None of this is relevant, Mister Cross. Our agenda has not been yours from the very start. Your focus has been on ISC and Donovan Lane when it could have been on other government laboratories and the companies that service them. I don't know why you made that choice, but you did, and there have been few positive results from it. In the meantime, we have contributed significant funds, and received no accounting summaries, and we wonder where our money has gone to. We suspect it has gone into your own private accounts, Mister Cross. We have done our own accounting. At present, you owe us a combined total of just over four million dollars, and we're willing to negotiate a partial refund. If you don't agree to this, our vote is for the immediate dissolution of AAAH, and the cancellation of all our activities.

"None of this has been discussed with me," said Cross.

"We've had our own meetings by cell, sir. There was no need for your presence."

"And are you responsible for this uprising, Mister E?" said Cross, with as much menace in his voice as he could bring to bear.

"We have worked as a group, and we do not react well to intimidation. We do not fear you, Mister Cross, and the man you call your associate is not here. He is likely responsible for the death of one of our colleagues who was vocal about our concerns in the past. You need to understand that we have our own resources for information and security, and we have made arrangements to safeguard our futures. Records and files can disappear, and if anything tragic happens to even one of us, your life expectancy, and that of your associate, will be measured in hours."

"Are you threatening me?" asked Cross indignantly.

"Yes, sir, I am," said Mister E. "You are responsible for several deaths that were not a part of our agenda, and this has placed us in a delicate legal situation. This will not happen again. None of us are willing to spend a lifetime in prison because you resort to murder to solve your problems and have a colleague to do that work for you. In short, we are finished with you, Mister Cross. Return our money to us, and we will go our separate ways. You can be sure that the crimes committed on our behalf assure our silence about everything."

"I'm not sure we have given Jacob an honest chance for his ideas to work," said Mister M. "I personally want more time for public opinion to develop, but I find myself alone with this opinion. I have no hard feelings against you, Jacob, and I respect what you have tried to do. I believe that violence can be appropriate, and was justified in the death of Donovan Lane. The head of a snake was cut off in his case, I think, because it was his mind behind the despicable science we know about, and more that is worse."

One supporter is not enough, thought Cross. We are finished here. "Thank you, Mister M. I wish other board members shared your insights, but they do not. I cannot continue to function without the full support of the board. Let us move to dissolve AAAH as a tax shelter for you, and return what monies remain after all expenses have been paid. I will have my accounting agency perform an audit, and prepare a formal summary, and then write checks for all of you and even your colleagues who are not here. As I announced before, we will complete our business at a final meeting in the Cook Islands. Please remember that meeting attendance will be required to receive a refund. Is this acceptable to all of you?"

Heads nodded. Mister M smiled.

"I'm sorry I haven't satisfied your desires. I have done what I can, and it wasn't enough. Our business is concluded."

Everyone except Mister M stood up and exited the room without saying another word to him. M paused, and put a hand on Cross's shoulder. His voice shook with emotion. "I'm so sorry, Jacob. I'm sure you did the best you could, but we didn't have the right board to make things happen. Maybe you and I can do business again someday. In the meantime, take care of yourself, and I'll look forward to seeing you soon on your beautiful island."

M left the room, and Cross sat for a while, thinking. He would make a plan with Max, and the board would be truly dissolved. Mister M was a possible exception.

Perhaps he could be spared.

* * * *

Max had no intention of remaining as an associate of Jacob Cross, but in a strange way he did have a professional obligation to the man. Circumstances had not allowed him much time for preparation, and luck was involved. If his targets left the hotel, he would have to make new plans on the fly. Late morning, they were still there. Maybe twelve hours is all I need, he thought.

Security was simple, but good, as far as it went. There was open entry to the basement garage, but once there he'd seen security cameras everywhere. These were monitored by the receptionist near the front doors on the main floor, but the guard there was absent from ten in the evening until six in the morning. An elevator from the garage to the residential floors was operated by key only, and the stairwell ended on the ground floor. His targets were on the top floor, and from the number of lights at night they were in a complex of suites taking up the entire floor. Why not? One of them was a holostar, with more money than God. It was nothing but the best for her.

There were occasional police patrols, and he moved his car twice, hunkering down when he saw a patrol car coming. He parked well down the street from the hotel, and at an intersection out of sight from the big windows on the street side of the top floor. Occasionally he used a monocular to observe the front entrance when people arrived or left the building, or when a car came up the steep driveway of the basement garage. Each time a car appeared, he held his breath.

The intercom box by the front door was his only entrance to the building. He had studied it, and knew how simply one could get buzzed in by punching multiple apartment buttons, but there was another problem he had to solve. The thick, muscled body of the man who accompanied his targets everywhere suggested a function as a bodyguard, and that man would have to be taken out first. It would have to be done silently, or other residents would be alerted and call the police. Max had a variety of weapons that would satisfy that requirement, and his firearms could be left in the car.

The plan was a simple one. After ten, when the receptionist was gone, and there was no traffic in the building, he would use the intercom box to lure the bodyguard to the front door, and then penetrate the building to do his job. He knew there was risk, but it was the best he could do.

And at eleven that evening, Max Schuler made his move.

CHAPTER 28

For Sheila, it was a wonderful, relaxing day, one of the happiest she'd ever experienced. She slept in until nine, was awakened by Carl clattering around in the kitchen. Ebony sensed she was awake, and came into thc room to jump up on the bed and nuzzle her in greeting. She showered, and dressed in her usual white blouse and black skirt, leaving the jacket off.

Melody was in the front room, talking on her cell and waving a script in the air to emphasize a point. She smiled, and waved the thing at Sheila when she saw her. Melody was still in a bathrobe, and Sheila suddenly felt overdressed. She felt better when she saw Carl in his muscle shirt and black slacks. He was actually a good looking man, she thought, but in a rugged sort of way. She wondered again what their private life was like without the cameras and guests like her.

Carl was making pancakes for them, and a plate stacked with pear slices was on the table. Sheila poured a cup of coffee for herself, and sat down as Melody arrived to plant a kiss on Carl's cheek and sit down with her. She tapped the script with a finger.

"This is wonderful. I can be a Russian princess from the twelfth century if I take this. How would you like to be the captain of my royal guard?"

"I don't think so," said Carl.

"Oh, but the princess and the captain are lovers."

Melody whispered to Sheila. "I've been trying to get him to take a small part in a project. It would be fun."

Carl put a plate stacked with pancakes on the table.

"Blueberry," he said. "Enjoy."

Carl sat down with them, and there was silence for a while as they ate.

"Do you enjoy the tastes of food?" asked Sheila.

"Mostly," said Melody, "but we could use some upgrading there. You could suggest it as a new project."

"We do well with individual flavors, but mixtures are confusing and bland. You see an example here." Carl pointed to his plate. "I don't put butter or syrup on these pancakes. The taste could be something like a salt-free cracker, not very good at all. There are many improvements to be made for us, but Doctor Post has his priorities."

"Something to look forward to," said Sheila.

Melody ate quickly. "Give me another hour with this script, and we'll get to your makeover. It's going to take time."

"Okay," said Sheila, a bit apprehensive, and Melody sensed it.

"You won't know yourself when I'm finished."

After breakfast, Melody went back to her reading in the living room. Carl excused himself, and went to his office. "John has returned from the meeting, and I have to catch up on his debriefing. Everything is going as planned," he explained.

If he meant to reassure her, he didn't. Sheila knew her separation from Jacob Cross had not been friendly, and Max Schuler was still on the loose. This did not make her feel safe.

She went back to her room, and changed into a more casual skirt and sleeveless blouse. Ebony came in, and lay on the bed to watch her. She didn't budge when Sheila sat down and began petting her. "You have such beautiful eyes," said Sheila, and a tail thumped the bed covers. The steady gaze of a wolf held her, reflecting intelligence, a dedication, and just a hint of menace.

Melody came in a few minutes later, still in her bathrobe. "Well, let's get at it," she said. "It's time to create the new you."

They went to the bathroom off of the bedroom shared by Melody and Carl. Melody draped a towel around her, and washed her hair with a pine-scented shampoo, her fingers kneading softly until Sheila was nearly dozing. Melody toweled her dry and did some clipping. "Your style might work in board rooms, but we can do much better with a swept up look. We'll leave the glasses, and work for the sexy librarian look. A lot of guys go for that."

She clipped and nipped and combed and teased and installed curlers in strategic positions, and then went over her work with a hairdryer. Sheila looked in the mirror, and saw a new person there, hair piled high, forehead bare, a sophisticated look.

"And now for makeup," said Melody. "You have lovely eyes, and you've hidden them with glasses. Your cheekbones are now invisible. We're going to change that."

For well over an hour, Melody worked on her with pen and brush, and Sheila watched the process in a mirror. A new face gradually emerged, and Sheila was astonished by the sight of it. "Wow," she finally said.

"See? I told you so," said Melody. "You're lovely, and shame on you if you ever hide it again."

"Thank you. I don't know what else to say."

"Say nothing, then. I'll put all this stuff in a bag for you to take home. Experiment, and try different looks. It's fun."

"This has been fun, Melody. You and Carl have been so nice to me."

"It's our pleasure. Relax a while, and then the curlers come out and we'll finish up. It's nearly time for lunch."

Carl joined them again, and smiled when he saw Sheila. "My, my, look at you. Quite a change."

Sheila blushed at the compliment. Even with her outstanding performances in school and work, she had never had such a day of praise as she'd had from these two—uh—people.

After lunch, Carl left them again. Melody knew that Sheila was a fan of the show, and offered to show her director cuts of three upcoming episodes in the new season. Sheila was thrilled by the shows, and by the fact that Melody actually solicited her comments and took notes on them. They finished the afternoon and early evening with curler removal and more teasing and quality time in front of a mirror, and then Carl called them to dinner and there were more compliments. She was astonished when Carl served them pizza, and ice cream for dessert. Surely a lot of research had gone into the creation of a synth's stomach and waste removal system. It seemed to digest anything.

Sheila helped Carl clean up the kitchen, and then they retired to the living room for a simple night at home, all three of them nestled together on a couch to watch holovision, and listen to Melody's comments about each show.

Sheila had never felt such belonging, so much at home as she did with these people.

She thought it was probably the most wonderful day in her life.

And then, at exactly eleven, the intercom buzzed loudly, and Carl got up to answer it.

"Somebody forgot their key," said Melody.

Carl pushed the button on the intercom panel. "Who is it, please?"

It was a male voice, deep, hysterical, babbling words none of them could understand. The man went on and on until Carl shouted, "I think you have the wrong suite," and clicked the intercom off.

"Is that Russian?" asked Melody.

"Some kind of Slavic," said Sheila.

The intercom buzzed again.

"What?" said Carl impatiently.

Again there was a man shouting hysterically in a strange tongue, his voice raspy and shaking, rising in tone like a whine.

"I think he's drunk," said Sheila.

"Go away!" shouted Carl. "I'll call the police!"

Carl clicked the intercom off, but immediately it was buzzing again.

"This isn't going to stop," said Melody.

"Yes it is," said Carl, and he bolted for the door in anger. He closed the door behind him, and used his key to take the elevator down to the ground floor. He could still hear the intercom buzzing just after he'd left the suite, and the elevator descended quickly, so there was a chance he would catch whoever was at the hotel entrance.

The lobby was empty, the attendant gone for the night, but it was brightly lit, and he thought he saw movement by the front doors as he came out of the elevator. But when he walked quickly to the doors and looked outside, nobody was there.

Carl opened the door, and stepped outside, holding the door open with one hand and stretching to peer around the right side of the building by the intercom panel.

The attack came from his left

He heard the crackle of an electric arc, and then every muscle in his body contracted spasmodically as something hard was rammed into his back once, then twice. Suddenly his legs wouldn't hold him up and he fell to his knees, saw the blurred image of a man towering over him and holding something that hissed and spit fire. The thing came towards him, and struck him in the forehead, and there was an explosion of light in many colors, fading to blackness as he slumped to the ground. His arms and legs seemed paralyzed, but jerked and twitched wildly. He was vaguely aware of being dragged across concrete, of fingers fumbling at his body, and then the crackling of electricity was again in his ears, and there was a terrible shock at the back of his neck that tumbled him into nothingness.

* * * *

Melody called down twice on the intercom. "Carl, are you still there? What's going on?"

The second time there was a muffled voice, almost a whisper. "Coming up."

She called again, but there was no answer. Melody was worried. She stood near the door after locking it. Ebony had come into the room to sit beside her, and Sheila was walking towards the kitchen, looking concerned.

Melody heard the elevator arrive, the doors open and close, and then soft footsteps along the hall.

There were three soft knocks on the door, and a muffled voice. "Carl. Forgot key."

Melody unlocked the door, and opened it.

A tall, dark and swarthy man stood there, grinning. She recognized his face immediately. He held an electric stunner in one hand, pressed a button, and the hallway glowed in blue light.

Melody moved to slam the door shut. Ebony growled low, and crouched. Behind them, Sheila cried out in dismay.

The man's right arm shot out and struck her in the chest near the big blood pump her father had built for her. For a normal human, it could have been a killing strike, but her heart did not react to it. The rest of her went into shutdown mode. Her legs collapsed, and she could not feel her arms or turn her head. She was still aware as she crashed to the floor.

She heard Sheila's terrified screams.

She heard Ebony growl and snarl, and then shriek with pain.

There was another shock to the back of her neck, and then there were no sensations at all.

* * * *

Melody awoke in terrible pain. Every muscle in her body was on fire, and there was a squeezing pressure on her upper arms. Sound and sight came last. She heard muffled sobs and moaning, and a man chuckled.

She opened her eyes, and found herself lying on the floor by the couch. Her ankles were bound with duct tape, and her arms were restrained tightly behind her with tape around her wrists and upper body. Sheila lay on the floor near her, and was bound in the same way. A cloth had been stuffed into her mouth, and was secured there with tape wrapped several times around her head. The gag was so tight her eyes bulged from their sockets. The makeup and mascara so lovingly applied in the afternoon had mixed with her tears, and was running in colorful rivulets across her face. She moaned and cried when she saw Melody open her eyes, and thrashed her body around in helpless frustration.

A man came out of the kitchen, closed the door there, and stepped between the two women. He looked down at Melody.

"I think you'll have to get a new dog," he said, and smiled nastily, "but I'm not going to let you live long enough to do it."

Melody worked herself up into a sitting position, her back against the couch. Her entire body was now tingling as feeling returned.

"You must be the infamous Max we've been hearing about," she said.

"That's me. You move pretty well after that zapping I gave you. Maybe you need another one."

"What for? You've got me where you want me, big man. What kind of game are we going to play? Something kinky?"

Max snorted."Don't you wish? I'm here to kill you, bitch, you and your little friend here. Nothing personal, just a job, like the job I did on your father."

"Oh, so you're the one after all. We suspected it," said Melody. The rage within her began as a small, hot ball in the pit of her stomach, and expanded rapidly into her chest. Her heart beat quickened, her legs and arms suddenly warm, and the tingling went away. She spread her knees apart briefly, and felt the tape around her ankles stretch.

"That's not to say we can't have a little fun. Can't stay for long. I'm not sure if your bodyguard is dead or crippled, but I'd just as soon not mess with him again. I've watched your little friend here for some time, and I have never seen her looking so good."

Max went over to Sheila, knelt beside her, and pulled out a knife with a six inch blade. "Want to play, little girl?" he asked.

Sheila's eyes went wide with terror. She screamed into her gag, and wiggled hard in her bonds.

"Oh, I like that," said Max. He brought the knife close, and snipped off the top button of Sheila's blouse.

Melody felt white heat throughout her body, and her heart was pounding. She wrenched her knees apart once, twice, and felt the tape tear apart at her ankles. She took a deep breath, and raised her elbows behind her, felt the tape stretching and overlapping ends shearing apart under the inhuman force she was applying.

"Get away from her, you filthy creep. Is this the only way you can get a woman, by tying her up?"

Max carefully snipped the second button from Sheila's blouse while she cried pitifully. He did not look at Melody.

"Shut up, bitch, or I'll kill you right now. Wait your turn."

Melody pulled apart the tape at her ankles and lurched to her feet. She flexed her upper body as she took a huge breath, felt and heard tape pop at her back. Her wrists were now bound loosely, but not free as she raised and twisted them behind her.

"A little dick, that's what you are. You like to prey on helpless women. I think you're pathetic."

Max jumped to his feet, face red with rage. "You just couldn't wait your turn, so I'll have to finish you first, and then have my fun."

He stepped towards her, holding the knife out waist high.

Melody screamed, and pulled her arms and hands from her back, tape flapping. She ripped the tape from her hands, hunched her shoulders, and glared at him. Max had stopped after a second step, frozen in surprise, but now he raised the knife again and his grin was a horrible thing.

"Come and get me, you bastard," she said softly.

Max lunged.

Melody's left arm shot forward, her fingers together and rigid as steel. Her fingers struck him in the throat and penetrated, snapping his head back and stopping his lunge in mid-stride. Max's eyes went wide with shock and surprise. He groped at his bleeding throat with one hand, and made a gurgling sound. The knife slipped from his other hand, and fell to the floor. He took a half step backwards, knees shaking as Melody stepped up in front of him and crouched, holding her fists at chest level.

"This is for my father," she said.

Her scream was primal as her right arm came forward like a piston to strike him in the heart with the heel of her hand, and she relished the feelings of breaking bones and an exploding organ as she penetrated his flesh. His body flew backwards before he tripped over Sheila and fell to the floor, gushing blood from nose and mouth.

Sheila stared at her in horror.

Melody knelt down, carefully unwrapped the tape holding Sheila's gag in place, and pulled the rag out of her mouth. Sheila just stared at her, making little hiccup sounds.

"The bastard ruined everything we worked on all afternoon," said Melody. "Now we'll have to do it again."

"What?" said Sheila.

Melody untied her ankles, arms, hands, but Sheila just sat here, shivering. Melody hugged her. "It's okay, now. The man is dead."

Sheila looked over at Max's body, the rivulets of blood running down his sides to the carpet, and her eyes again filled with tears.

Melody heard a new sound, a whine, and familiar. She rushed to the kitchen, and pushed the door open. Ebony lay on the floor, her legs moving wildly, her head raised, and she was struggling to get up. Melody knelt to hold her, and Ebony gave out an agonized howl before whining softly as she was petted and caressed. A few minutes later she was standing on wobbly legs. Melody led her carefully to the bedroom, and got her up onto the bed to rest, then returned to the front room to find Sheila still sitting on the floor and staring at the entrance doors.

"I hear something," said Sheila.

Melody heard it, too, a loud clang outside in the hall. She stepped close to the door to listen, heard the thud of footsteps approaching rapidly, and stepped back.

The door knob rattled once, and then the doors crashed open as Carl Hobbs hurtled through them into the room. His eyes were blazing, and there was a large, blackened area on his forehead. He took in the scene in one glance, and saw Max Schuler's body in a widening pool of blood on the floor.

"Are you okay?" he asked Melody.

"I am now. I think the doors were unlocked, hon."

"They weren't, and I was in a hurry again," said Carl.

Melody threw herself into his arms.

* * * *

Melody looked down at Max's body on the floor. "What do we do now? His blood is ruining our carpet," she said coldly. Even after killing the man, something dark remained inside her.

"I have to make some calls," said Carl. "What happened tonight can't be made public. It would interfere with the rest of our operation against Cross. I'll call Doctor Post first, then the FBI. Sheila, are you all right?"

“Better,” said Sheila, “but my heart is still pounding so hard I can hardly breathe.”

“I’ll brew some tea,” said Melody, “and make some treats for Ebony. She’s feeling poorly, but lucky to be alive. We’re all lucky to be alive. I’m still tingling from that shocker-thing Max used.”

Carl was already on his cell as she put water on the stove to boil, and then hung six tea bags in a pot for steeping. The native-American brew was said to be effective for relaxation and meditation.

Minutes later, Carl joined them at the table for tea. “Darin was up, and he’s called people at ISC. They’ll be here in an hour to take Max’s body away and clean up the mess. The door repair for our suite and the stairwell is our problem, and I’ll make calls in the morning.”

“Stairwell?” asked Melody.

“Max took the elevator key, and I had to use the stairwell. The lobby door is left unlocked by law, but I had to damage the locked door on our floor, and I suppose it’ll be considered a total loss.”

“Are we safe, now?” asked Sheila, sipping her tea. Color was returning to her cheeks, and her tears had dried.

“Probably,” said Carl. “As far as we know, Max was Cross’s only enforcer. Cross is likely out of the country by now, but very soon it’ll be time to cut off the head of the snake.”

“I’m sure you have a plan for that,” said Melody.

“I do, but it’s a secret for now. Sorry.”

Melody wiggled an eyebrow at him, and whispered to Sheila, “Need to know, you know.”

They had just finished their tea when the intercom began buzzing again, and Carl buzzed in two groups of men who came up the stairwell. He met them with a loaded shotgun and a dangerously short reaction time stemming from the events of the evening. Identities were established, and the crews entered the suite while Melody and Sheila remained in the kitchen. Ebony was sound asleep in the bedroom, and did not respond.

Max was taken away in a body bag, and equipment was brought in to clean up the bloody mess on the carpet. The man had bled out completely after lying on the carpet for over two hours. His heart had been pulped by the impact of Melody’s hand.

One small bonus was a carpenter who had come along with the ISC crew. He managed to cobble together a repair of the lock on their suite doors so they could lock it for the night, but the doors themselves were badly cracked and would have to be replaced.

By three in the morning, everyone had left. Melody helped Sheila get her face and hair in order again, and Sheila managed to doze for a couple of hours. For Carl and Melody, there was no rest. They packed small bags for the drive to San Diego. It was necessary to cut Sheila’s visit short by a day.

For Sheila, it would be another day of rest to recover from her ordeal. For Melody, it would be a day to shop, and care for her injured Ebony. With the killing of Max, she was already feeling a kind of closure in the death of her father, and was dreaming about what might happen next with him.

For Carl Hobbs it was the beginning of the final phase of a plan to remove the head of a snake named Jacob Cross. It was a plan he had formulated on his own, a plan approved by Darin and his contacts at the FBI, and two participants from the CIA. There would be total secrecy, and no records would be kept. Government involvement was logistical, and would be denied if necessary. Darin and ISC Industries were bound to total secrecy forever. Carl himself would make the final preparations as soon as they reached San Diego. Melody would not be told details of the plan, only that it existed.

Carl Hobbs loved Melody Lane with his entire being, both synthetic and human, and he knew she loved him, too. He worried that her knowledge of his plan might change that. He hoped it would not. She had dealt with Max Schuler in a very direct and violent way, despite her empathy and love for human beings. She had avenged her father, and that was another issue, one involving Darin's new project, which would soon be completed.

Carl worried about that, too.

CHAPTER 29

Carl met with Darin before a final briefing of the new John Modrin. Melody had taken still wobbly Ebony with her to go shopping, and their plan was to drive back to Hollywood late that evening.

"So what happened to Max?" asked Carl.

"We dissolved the body in a vat, and burned up the bones in our furnace. The ashes were put out with the rest of our trash," said Darin. "The government knows nothing about him or the attack on you."

Carl raised an eyebrow, and Darin winked at him. "Everything I tell them is unofficial," said Carl. "No records are being kept."

"I hope they keep honoring that."

"Is John ready?"

"He is. Are you?"

"Yes. It'll be our last briefing. He's done well, so far," said Carl.

"It's a new application, but I'm not crazy about it," said Darin. "I still want to keep the government in the dark about the synth program, even though they're funding a part of it indirectly. What do you think?"

"I think it's wise, at least for now. The first thing they'd want to do is use it to build a new army."

"Good for business," said Darin, smiling.

Carl was not amused. "But bad for the world," he said, then, "How is the new project going?"

"Nearing the finish, and I'm nervous as hell about it. There's no way to do it perfectly, and it's less than I owe her for my stupidity."

"Cross declared war against us on his own. It wasn't because of some angry thing you said to him on the cell. We all understand that," said Carl.

"I don't," said Darin.

Carl shrugged his shoulders. "Okay."

Darin escorted Carl to the printing lab where John Modrin's synth had been patiently waiting for them. Darin waved to John, and left them there.

"Nice to see you, Carl," said John.

"Good to see you. Let's get you wired up. If it works out, this will be your final field operation for us, at least for now. You've done very well."

John sat up on the edge of a table so Carl could work on him. The munitions pack was an inch thick, and went around the circumference of his upper body. Carl laced it up like a corset, and pressed the initiator into the pack just above John's left breast.

"I've enjoyed working with you and Doctor Post. I would like to do more," said John softly.

"We'll update your scan right after we finish here, John," said Carl. The tone of John's voice was disturbing, and gave him a bad feeling.

"Synths and humans both have such interesting qualities and similarities. This world has been stimulating for me. I have really enjoyed it," said John.

"I hear you, John. Just remember that nothing is truly lost, no ending defined for us. I'm finished here. Let's get that scan done."

They went to the scanning lab, and Darin did the scan, John all hooked up and with an expression that looked pleading, an expression that made Carl feel miserable inside.

John was dressed in his usual business suit, a very snug fit this time. Carl and Darin both accompanied him in a company limo to the airport, and walked with him as far as the security gate where they were met by two grim-faced men in black suits. Carl and Darin shook hands with John.

"Good hunting," said Carl, and John nodded, and the two men led him to a door near the security gate. Near the door, John looked over his shoulder, smiled faintly and waved to them as the door closed behind him.

They went back to the limo awaiting them in the taxi area, and pulled out onto the freeway in time to see the khaki colored cargo plane climb into the sky over the ocean.

Carl turned to Darin. "I'm hurting inside," he said.

"My heart hurts, too," said Darin, and they sat in silence the rest of the way back to Schutz Fabrik.

Melody and Ebony were waiting for them in the reception area.

"He's on his way," said Carl.

"And someday you'll tell me about what's going on," said Melody.

"Someday soon."

"Let's go home. We can have a bite on the way. I'm all shopped out. Ebony is pooped, but her limp is better."

Ebony heard her name, and her tail thumped the floor as Carl rubbed her head.

"Okay, let's go," said Carl.

"Let me know when you hear something," said Darin.

"As soon as they call me," said Carl.

Melody drove, and they stopped in Carlsbad for dinner, sitting in a dark corner, but were still discovered by two female fans who found paper for Melody to sign.

They arrived home after dark, and carefully opened the damaged doors to their suites. It would be three more days before repairmen replaced both their doors and the door leading to the stairwell.

Once in their suite, Melody dumped her bags and packages on the bed while Carl fixed Ebony some dinner and took it to her station in one corner of their bedroom.

Melody spread her day's shopping treasures on the bed. There were the usual clothes and underthings, a colorful bracelet, and two mysterious packages which Melody unwrapped in front of Carl. As she did so, she gave him what he thought was an alluring and provocative smile.

"After Max zapped me, I was all tingly for a day after, and some of it was nice. It reminded me of some human toys I've heard about, and I found this wonderful little store in old town. It's called Fetish Lane, and oh, my, they have some fun things there. They make me feel naughty, and very human. Let's see what you think."

She held up a simple, black cylinder and pressed the end of it. There was a soft buzzing sound, and she ran the cylinder softly across his cheek. For one moment, it seemed his entire head was vibrating. His eyes widened.

"Like it? It's even more fun in other places," she said, excited. "Now let me show you my favorite."

She showed him a thin, transparent rod with a heavy, black handle and a long electrical cable, which she plugged into the wall. She pressed a switch, and the rod glowed red, and when she brought it close to his arm little sparks danced along his skin and there was a light tingling sensation. This time he smiled at her.

"You like?" she asked, and smiled wickedly.

That night, they went to bed and played for two hours with Melody's new toys. All of it was wonderful, and for two hours Carl Hobbs forgot about John Modrin's mission.

In the morning, he remembered it again.

* * * *

The day was sunny with a few scattered clouds in the Rarotonga sky when John's plane landed. The plane taxied into a hanger away from the main terminal. His escorts followed him off the plane to an awaiting golf cart, and drove him to a tunnel used by the military to bypass civilian security checks. He was taken up by elevator to the main terminal ticketing area where he left his escorts behind and walked to the taxi area. He saw the vehicle with the AAAH sign in the front windshield, got into the back seat, showed his I.D. to the driver, a local boy just out of his teens.

"You're the last one," said the driver. "Everyone else came in this morning."

"Better hurry, then," said John. "I wouldn't want to miss the party."

The driver smiled.

* * * *

The board members all arrived grim-faced, but Jacob played the good host, and after a nice lunch and several drinks they were all relaxing nicely. Mister M was the last to arrive in early afternoon. He ate a light lunch, but only drank coffee. It was said he'd developed an allergy to anything alcoholic. He smiled when Jacob greeted him, and warmly shook his hand.

"It is a difficult day," said Mister M. "All one can do is experience it. Please remember to keep in touch with me after this is over."

"I will," said Jacob, and meant it, but at the moment he could think of nothing they might do together in the future.

Jacob was in the meeting room half an hour before the others. He set up his screen and digital projectors, and distributed packets with enclosed bank checks, all based on his presentation. It had taken him a week to cobble together the fabled audit, and he had no illusions about fooling anyone for long. The house had been sold, and his bags were awaiting him in two lockers at the airport. He would be gone by evening, most of the AAAH funds preceding him by two days.

Any plans to eliminate board members had disappeared with Max, who had taken the money to do a job and then run. He'd been trying to get hold of the man for two days, but there had been no answer, his line disconnected. Jacob's enemies were still alive. It wasn't entirely a surprise that Max would run off and leave him. There had been warning signs.

The material in the packets was deliberately made to be complex and convoluted. It would take a good accountant at least a day to tie together the spider web of errors and inconsistencies Jacob had devised. This meant the meeting would likely be short, with board members anxious to get their checks deposited before nightfall.

His first graph was on the screen when eight core members of AAAH filed into the room and took seats at their designated places around the table.

Mister M was the last to arrive. He went to his place, and stood there instead of sitting down. Someone outside the room closed the door, and it was suddenly very quiet. Everyone was looking curiously at Mister M, including Jacob Cross. The man remained standing,

"Before we begin, is there something you would like to say, Mister M?" said Jacob.

"Indeed there is," said Mister M, and he smiled. "Mister Cross, honored board members, it is my pleasure to bring you greetings from Doctor Donovan Lane and his family."

With his right fist, M struck himself hard just below his left breast.

There was a beep, and a buzzing sound coming from Mister M's chest area as he looked at Jacob. His smile disappeared.

"Executing," he said softly.

There was a sound perceived for a millisecond, and the light of a thousand suns, and then there was only flame and hot gas where a room had once existed.

* * * *

Production had started again for the new season, and Melody was not yet up to speed on the routine. The week she'd had for herself had been both terrifying and fun, and she was having trouble concentrating. For the first couple of days it had been four takes instead of one or two. Dennis was patient, and didn't yell at her, but a ten hour day on set turned into twelve, and she was exhausted.

The studio limo took her back to the hotel at eight. Carl had dinner for both of them warming in the oven, and met her at the door.

"My man," she said, and kissed him firmly on the mouth. "I'm so tired tonight I don't know if I can eat, but I'll try a small plate."

"Hard day?" said Carl.

"Not the studio, just me. I think I'm still hung over from my tussle with Max. I'm reliving it every night when I try to sleep."

Melody flopped down on the couch. Carl brought her a fork and a small plate of food. It was some kind of rice, cheesy thing, and the odor was enticing. She began to eat.

The cell buzzed in the kitchen, and Carl went to answer it. The conversation was short and muffled. When he returned to the living room, Melody had cleaned her plate and held it up for a refill. "This is wonderful, hon. I can eat another one."

Carl smiled, took her plate and put it on a table. "In a minute," he said, then looked very serious and knelt on the floor in front of her, taking her hands in his in her lap.

"Yes," she said.

"What?"

"Yes I'll marry you, if you're proposing."

Carl blinked and chuckled, and then he was serious again. "I just got a call from John Harper."

"The FBI guy?"

"There was an explosion at an estate the CIA has been watching in the Cook Islands. A small group of corporate executives were blown to vapor in it. The names are familiar."

Melody swallowed hard, and suddenly she was not so tired. "The Jacob Cross place?"

"He was with them. They're all gone. Two members didn't show, and had bailed out of AAAH weeks ago. The government is still watching them.

It's over, Melody. Cross, Max, the hard core of the organization, they're all dead."

She was thinking, and there was silence for seconds that seemed like minutes. She reached out a hand, and touched his cheek.

"This has something to do with the synth you and Darin were working on, the synth of that defector from the board."

"It was John Modrin's synth, yes. The bomb was strapped to him, and he set it off during their meeting. Investigators might wonder about traces of titanium in the debris, but I think the synth program is safe."

"You programmed him to do it," said Melody, and she took her hand away from his cheek.

"Yes, we did."

"I think it's cold, Carl. You made him into a suicide bomber. He died for you and Darin."

"He died for all of us. He didn't really die, anyway. We have his scan. A new body, neural matrix, he'll be back again."

"God, that's even colder. You're spending too much time with Darin, hon."

"You wanted them all dead, Melody."

"I know. I'm glad they're gone, Carl. I'm not objecting to what you did. I wanted revenge, and now I have it."

Melody put her arm around his neck. "It's the use of a synth to kill humans that bothers me. The precedent is dangerous."

Carl looked at her sadly. "It was worse than that for me. John knew he would die on his mission. He didn't want to die, but he was loyal to his program. The look on his face when he left will haunt me forever."

"So bring him back," said Melody.

"I'll talk to Darin about it."

"While you're at it, ask him again about my father. I keep asking, and he keeps putting me off. It's not just for me. Daddy was the real brains for the company."

"I've used that argument, but Darin is closed-mouthed on the subject. He feels responsible for your father's death. I know he's considering a synth for him."

Melody grasped his face with both hands. "I'm trying to be patient. We're safe, now, because of what you and Darin have done. Thank you for that. You are my man, my protector, my lover, all wrapped up in a big bundle of muscle, and I love you very much."

Carl had never looked more serious, and he brushed her lips with his. "I love you, too. No matter how long our lifetimes are, I want to spend all of it with you."

Melody though it was the nicest thing he had ever said to her, and she certainly felt the same way about him.

CHAPTER 30

It was her first open house, and intimate, since only those closest to her and the synth program were invited. For Melody, this mix of synthetics and humans was her inner circle, her tribe, her family, all the important influences in her life.

Only one person was absent.

The compound had been finished at last. What had once been a complex of condominiums was now a single estate with eight foot walls surrounding manicured lawns and boulder gardens, and a pool half inside and outside of the sprawling three-story structure. Cars and limos were parked in the circular driveway at the front of the complex, and guests were congregated in the entrance gallery for drinks and hors d'oeuvres provided by a catering service.

Food had been provided by Leon's Grill down the hill from the estate. Everything arrived by truck, and was kept warmed in the kitchen. Melody and Carl arranged a buffet line in the dining room, and their guests sat at designated places at a long table there. The empty chair at one end of the table was reserved for Donovan Lane.

Carl was kept busy in the kitchen while Melody welcomed their guests and mixed with them during the reception. Nathan was the first to arrive, and Melody hugged him.

"I hope Maurice wasn't offended by not being invited," she said.

Nathan smiled weakly. "He doesn't even know about it. Maurice moved out three days ago."

"Oh, Nathan, I'm so sorry," said Melody.

"Don't be. We're still friends. Maurice wanted things I couldn't give him, not in this lifetime. I guess I'm looking for something else."

"Let me know if I can help," said Melody, and hugged him again.

The Harpers arrived a few minutes later, and Melody shook their hands. "John, Jilian, so nice to see you again. Carl is anxious to talk to John, and I want to find out from Jilian how your new life is going."

"She's called Audrey, now," John reminded her.

"Yes, but today, in this small group, we can all be ourselves, and to me she is still Jilian."

John nodded, his eyes moist, and the couple smiled in agreement.

Sheila arrived later, after Carl had served snacks and punch for the synths, and added some wine for the three humans to be included among the guests. Melody opened the door, and gasped. "You are gorgeous," she said, and hugged the girl. "I couldn't have done better."

Sheila smiled brightly. "You've done so much. The rest is up to me."

"Nathan is here," said Melody, "and he's alone. I told you things might change. Check him out, girl."

Sheila laughed, and hugged her. Ebony suddenly appeared at Melody's side, looking up at Sheila and wagging her tail. Sheila cupped the dog's chin in her hand and then rubbed her head. "I'd like to have a nice dog like you," she said.

"I know just the place to find one," said Melody.

Darin was the last to arrive. The reception was already in full swing, and Melody was mixing with her guests. Carl was setting up warming trays for the buffet after a brief conversation with John Harper, and he gave her a thumbs up to indicate everything was on schedule.

Melody had left the front door unlocked, and Darin let himself in, and suddenly he was coming down the two steps to the foyer and smiling at her.

"Finally," she said, and gave him a hug. "We're almost ready for dinner. Everyone else is here."

"Sorry I was delayed."

"Marylyn?"

"No. Marylyn is visiting her parents in San Francisco. I'm going up there in two days to meet them."

"Uh, oh," said Melody, and smiled. "That sounds like things are getting serious."

"They are. We've been engaged since this morning."

"Well, congratulations, I think, but you look nervous about something," said Melody.

"I am, but it's not about Marylyn. I have an announcement to make. Could you gather people together for it? This will only take a minute."

"Oh, dear, I hope this isn't bad news about something."

Darin gave her a look of exasperation, so she left him there and went back to her guests.

It would be terrible if he left the company now. Sheila can't handle everything alone, she thought.

She gathered everyone together by the punch bowl. "Darin is here, and he wants to make an announcement," she said.

"Where is he?" asked Sheila.

Melody turned around, but Darin wasn't where he'd been standing by the steps. He'd gone to the front door, and opened it, and another man was standing there. Darin let him in, and escorted him back to the top of the stairs where they stood to look down on Melody and her guests. Carl came out of the kitchen with another warming tray, put it down and looked expectantly at Darin.

The man with Darin was tall and slender, dark haired, and a face with high cheekbones and a prominent nose. He was dressed casually in black slacks and a sport shirt, and had the bearing of someone important.

Ebony walked up to the man, sniffed at him, wagged her tail, then raised her head for attention and the man gently rubbed her forehead with a large hand. He smiled.

Melody's heart skipped a beat.

Darin took a deep breath, and said, "I wanted you folks to be the first to meet Edward Holmstrom, the new CEO of ISC and Schutz Fabrik. He's going to be the new brain for our company, beginning today."

"Hi everyone," said Edward. "It feels good to be here. It feels good to be, period."

He looked at Melody, raised one eyebrow, and wiggled it. "Hi, sweetie," he said.

Melody's eyes filled with tears, and her heart was pounding. "Hi, Daddy," she said, and rushed to him, threw her arms around his tall, strange body, and smelled the odors of musk and new polymer. "I missed you so much," she murmured.

"Me, too, once I was back. Hi, Carl."

Carl was suddenly there, shaking the man's hand. "Good to have you back, sir. You missed some excitement here."

"So I hear," said Edward, and smiled broadly as Melody gave him a squeeze. "I also know about you and my very physical daughter here, but I did see that coming."

There was vigorous applause from the others. Edward Holmstrom walked around and shook their hands.

"Wow, look at you," he said to Sheila. "What happened?"

"Melody," said Sheila.

Melody turned to Darin, who still looked nervous. She reached out and gave his arm a firm squeeze. "Thank you," she said.

"You're okay with it?" he asked.

"Nothing has changed except the body, Darin. You've given my father back to me, and I owe you big time for that."

Darin visibly relaxed.

Edward was now the old Donovan Lane, gesturing with his hands. "So now I have the synth perspective on life, and it is exciting. God, we have so many things to do, and some big challenges to face in the social and political areas as well."

Nathan raised his glass of punch. "You could start by giving us an upgrade for alcohol consumption."

Everyone laughed, except Edward. "Oh, that's just a materials issue, as long as the stuff can't get to your brain," he said.

"Well, there's no fun in that," said Nathan.

More chuckling, and then Edward raised his hand. "I'm not taking time from this party for a long-winded lecture, but here's a micro-version of it. On the technical side, we have lots of sensory work to do. The first social issue I have to face is how to reveal the success of the synth program."

There was a sudden and ominous silence in the room.

"Our contractors have to be told that synths are no longer a goal or a hope, but a reality, and that they have been successfully field tested in a variety of ways."

People were frowning, without exception.

"The first thing they'll do is declare the entire project top secret," said Carl. "They might put us under military control."

"National security agencies already suspect a synth exists, and was used in a targeted assassination," said John Harper. "I have no idea who else they've talked to about it, but it won't be a secret forever."

"Do they know about me?" asked Carl.

"No, but they're very pleased with the research and analysis work you did for them. They have a job for you if you want it," said John.

"Oh, my, Carl Hobbs the spy," said Melody, and Carl rolled his eyes at her.

"It might be good politics," said Edward. "We can discuss this later. I'm just saying our immediate problems are going to be social and political. We've seen how easy it was for Cross to stir up negative sentiment about artificial human beings. It might be years away, but eventually the public will know it's all true, and we'll have to have a good track record to justify their acceptance. And that, people, involves ethical issues."

"Like assassination," said Carl.

"Maybe immortality," said Nathan.

"Bringing back someone you love," said Melody. "Having said all that, we exist as functional human beings, and we live useful lives, and we are here to stay."

"I'll drink to that," said Nathan, and raised his glass.

"And to the adventure we'll have in doing it," said Edward.

"That's my dad," said Melody, and raised her glass.

They all drank to the toast, and then to several others before Carl finally called them to the table for the buffet dinner. Little cards marked their places. Melody led Edward to the head of the table where the card for the absent Donovan Lane had been placed. Melody and Carl sat to his immediate right, Darin and Sheila to his left, then Nathan and the Harpers. Carl had fed Ebony in the kitchen, and now she came out to circle the table and greet everyone fondly before retiring to her pillow in one corner of the room, and there she went soundly to sleep.

Carl announced dinner, and starting with Edward Holmstrom they all went through the buffet line, serving themselves from trays of chicken and barbecued beef, corn and beans and mashed potatoes with chicken gravy, and a spinach salad. Later, there were tubs of ice cream and goblets for self service to finish the meal.

Conversations were light and varied, constantly shifting between guests. Melody had strategically placed Nathan next to Sheila, even before she'd known he was available, and now she watched them with occasional glances. Nathan had his finger firmly on the charm button, leaning close to talk softly, Sheila listening attentively and flashing the occasional lovely smile.

Melody and Nathan both shared stories about mishaps on the set. The Harpers talked about the simple joys of their new life together. For Melody, that story alone was enough to justify the synth program, but she had no illusions about the general public seeing it that way.

Darin announced his engagement, and everyone applauded the news, but he also pointed out that Marylyn would have to be told about the synth program. She was, after all, an ISC marketing and publicity executive.

Carl had a compliment for everyone at the table, praising their work, their contributions to his own development, and then he took hold of Melody's hand and put it against his cheek as he gave her a look that made her heart flutter.

"As for this lady sitting next to me, my Melody, she has become the center of my life."

"My man," said Melody, and kissed Carl firmly on the mouth in front of everyone.

"Wow," said Edward, "you just never know what's going to happen in this world of ours."

Everyone finished their ice cream, and pots and pitchers of coffee and water were passed around.

"Please stay for a tour of our home," said Melody. Any of you are welcome to stay overnight, and if you'd like to swim we have towels and a variety of swimsuits in the pool area."

"I think I'll take you up on that, sweetie," said Edward. "We have a lot of catching up to do."

"Indeed we do," said Carl.

Edward stood up, and picked up his coffee cup. "Before we tour this wonderful house, this home that Carl and Melody have built, I want to make a final toast for the evening. It's a toast to something I know is dear to my daughter, and it's something that's also dear to me."

Edward raised his cup, Melody and Carl stood up, and the others followed.

"To family," said Edward.
Melody's face glowed with the joy she felt.
Around the table, cups and glasses clinked together.

Made in the USA
Middletown, DE
04 May 2019